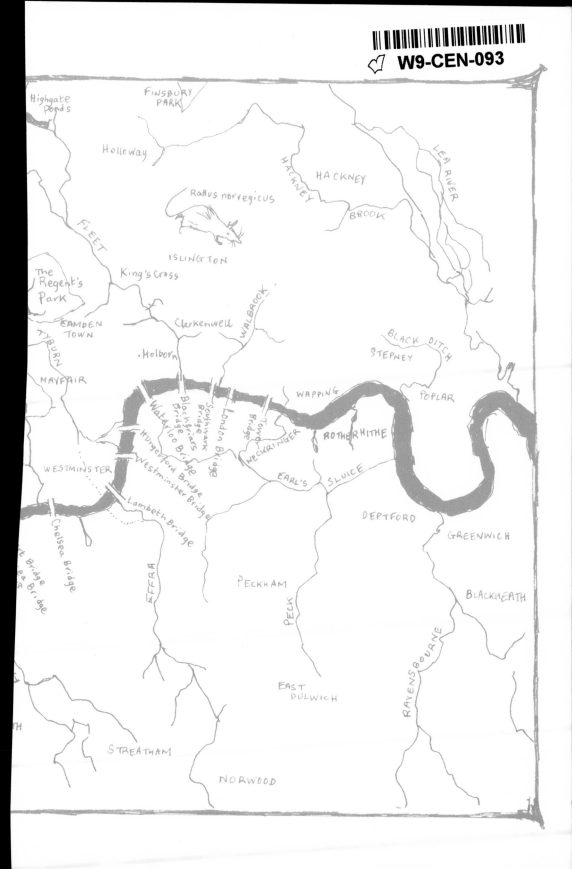

ALSO BY EMMA RICHLER

Feed My Dear Dogs

Sister Crazy

Be My Wolff

Be My Wolff

EMMA RICHLER

ALFRED A. KNOPF
NEW YORK | TORONTO
2017

Grateful acknowledgement is made to Boosey & Hawkes Music Publishers Ltd. for permission
to reprint an excerpt of "Peter and the Wolf, Op. 67" (Serge Prokofieff), copyright © 1937
by Hawkes & Son (London) Ltd., and Veronica Zolina for permission to reprint a translation
of an excerpt of "Borodino" by Mikhail Lermontov, copyright © Veronica Zolina.

Library of Congress Cataloging-in-Publication Data
Names: Richler, Emma, 1961– author.
Title: Be my Wolff : a novel / Emma Richler.
Description: First edition. | New York : Alfred A. Knopf, 2017.
Identifiers: LCCN 2016019130 (print) | LCCN 2016027815 (ebook) |
ISBN 9781101946527 (hardcover) | ISBN 9781101946534 (ebook)
Subjects: LCSH: Man-woman relationships—Fiction. | Brothers and
sisters—Fiction. | Orphans—Fiction. | BISAC: FICTION / Literary. |
FICTION / Sagas. | FICTION / Romance / Contemporary. | GSAFD: Romantic
suspense fiction.
Classification: LCC PR6068.I249 B4 2017 (print) | LCC PR6068.I249 (ebook) |
DDC 823/.914—dc23
LC record available at https://lccn.loc.gov/2016019130

Library and Archives Canada Cataloguing in Publication
Richler, Emma, 1961–, author   Be my wolff / Emma Richler.
Issued in print and electronic formats.
ISBN 978-0-345-81072-4
eBook ISBN 978-0-345-81074-8

I. Title.
PS8585.I3673B4 2017   C813'.6   C2016-904554-4

Illustrations and endpapers by the author
Jacket image: (upper right) Thomas Spring, 19th c. © Mary Evans Picture Library /
The Image Works
Jacket design by Janet Hansen

For Florence my mother,
and in memory of Mordecai my father,
and for Bob Gottlieb, my troika,
with love and gratitude

That the art of pugilism is founded in nature, is so obvious a truth, that it scarcely requires illustration.

—DANIEL MENDOZA, *The Memoirs of the Life of Daniel Mendoza*, 1816

Notwithstanding the Innocence of the Children, yet as they are exposed and abandoned by their Parents, they ought to submit to the lowest stations and should not be educated in such a manner as may put them upon a level with the Children of Parents who have the Humanity and Virtue to preserve them, and the Industry to Support them.

—Foundling Hospital sub-committee minutes, 12 April 1749

CONTENTS

Be My Wolff

{ ONE }

A WOLF PACK *may vary in number from two to fifty or so, typically amounting to three or four in Europe where the lone wolf is also preeminent, because prey, here, is less imposing in stature, consisting largely of hare and rodent. Bonds between wolves are uncommonly close, yet social structure is neither so rigidly hierarchical nor so immutable as man supposes, nor as man's own, indeed. The pack is a family, and wolf society, a dynamical system; sensitive to initial conditions, changing in time. Chaotic.*

"Zach? Are you awake? Wake up."

"I'm up, I'm up," he murmurs, his head rising and falling gently to the swell and ebb of Rachel's lungs, her heart bleating in his ear, a sound so naked, so virgin, he squeezes her ribs, presses and releases, pulsing his fingertips there for the queer delight of it, the sensation of her fine bones yielding like greenwood, like willow, *Salix caerulea*—cricket bat willow—the ribs yielding and springing free at his touch. He fans out his fives to encompass her, the right wall of her cage in the singular grasp of his throbbing left hand, injured in sparring. Zachariah Wolff's hands are bruised, but he possesses superior reach! Here, he thinks, here and in the ring, these are the highest places in all the hemispheres.

"Zachariah, Zachariah," whispers Rachel, casting a practised eye over the back of his head and down the length of him, from the shoulder blades where his wings once grew, epochs ago, in some other guise:

angel—guardian, avenging—or great vagrant bird—Daurian Jackdaw, Chimney Swift, Pacific Loon! Rachel explores his haunches and onwards, noting the marks she knows by heart, the old wounds, the stripes and lesions, and reading the new—left hand and eye—being well acquainted with all the stages of healing and finding patterns in his body, in the scoring and fretwork of the epidermis, in the eddies of hair. Rachel believes in it, the laws of pattern formation and how they are universal: whatever she sees, crystallising, a landscape of fractals, of emergence and symmetry, her world falling happily into shape where he must forge it, a pioneer of industry, sooty and scarred. For Rachel Wolff, quite simply, there are patterns everywhere, she can't help it; she is an illustrator, naturalist, cartographer—and her eye, a kaleidoscope.

She cups his occiput, slipping through the curls, marvelling, as per usual, at the weight and grace of them, and she feels the warmth and the moisture there, the heat of sleep and dreams that has condensed and evaporated now, matting the hair at his temples, falling like dew at the roots. She marvels at his head and his hands also, his pair of *fives* as he calls them, according to boxiana, hands she has seen in all conditions, ruddy and swollen and blistered and broken, but still beautiful, to her, moving her always because she cannot fathom it, how a man with such curls and hands can have so much fight in him. Nothing she can do.

The morning light is breaking in, muscling in, as Zach would say, and Rachel watches it slant through the sheets of lace billowing gracefully at the open window to lash the room with brightness in a filigree design of tendrils and leaves and something like raindrops, falling across the walls in a pattern of snowflakes tumbling, and she wants to jog Zach awake so he can see it too: Look what you're missing! Instead, she decides to do it for him, I'll look at what you're missing, I'll do it for you. I'll take the day shift, you take the night shift. Let me watch the day shift.

Rachel strokes the hair back from his ear so she can watch it a moment, another morning sight she loves, of light shining through the cartilage of his ear and exposing the skeleton of vessels there and the brilliant corpuscular flow, like the last hurrah of an autumn leaf. The ear, of course, like the leaf, comes in only a few shapes, a shape not determined only by its function, by purpose and design, but by physical causes also, this she knows, how the laws of growth and rhythm account for a strange universality of forms, sensitive and shifting and responsive to the invisible, a template, a pattern, the ghost of all things. There is a template for all things. *The laws of pattern formation are universal.* Leaf, snowflake, ear, she sees right through him, in a blood-red glow. Zachariah, Zachariah, my fighting man.

Wolves in a pack form the tightest of bonds, and are rarely combative, often playful.

"Zach, please please PLEASE wake up now please."

"All right," he says, not moving.

"I've been thinking," she begins, tugging at his hair.

"Rachel, Rachel, I've been thinking—"

"Oh yes," she says, smiling. "Sing that, Zach. Sing it."

"Rachel, Rachel, I've been think-ing WHAT a strange world—"

"No. Not strange," corrects Rachel. "Queer."

"WHAT a queer world THIS would be . . . IF the boys were all trans-por-ted far a-cross the Irish Sea."

"Such a funny song for her to sing, our Russian mama, don't you think about that? How strange, how queer! Every bedtime. Every bedtime she was *there* . . ."

"And bath time," adds Zachariah. "Long as we shared!"

"*That* didn't last long, did it, Zach?"

"No," Zach groans, shutting his eyes again.

Rachel sings. "Zach-ariah, I've been think-ing—WHAT a queer world this would be IF the girls were all trans-por-ted—But *how* Mama sang it, remember, Zach? A plaintive Katya. So unlike her. Plaintive and tender and teasing. All at once."

"Not always unlike. With Aunt Tasha, she was often like that with *Tyotya.*"

"Yes, that's true of course. Oh Zach, *Tyotya* must miss her so much!"

"Katya!" Zach exclaims, "Katya! Can you hear us? Do you hear us? In the end, you know, I don't think—that is—that she hated me quite so much."

"Don't, Zach."

"The fact of us, then," he persists. "Had she known."

"She knew," says Rachel.

"We weren't living together! She didn't know!"

"Zach, how many times do I—she *always* knew. I keep telling you. Why do you insist on—"

"All right then!" snaps Zach. "Proves my point though, doesn't it? If she always knew. That she didn't hate me quite so much. As Lev does. Or the fact of us," he adds. "In the end. And she forgave you, I believe. But Lev—"

"Please?" asks Rachel. "Stop now. Don't say 'Lev.' No Lev this morning."

"OK. Wait though! Something else. Yesterday, I was drinking straight from the carton. Of juice. Bloody thirsty. And I suddenly saw him—Lev—catching me one afternoon when just home from school, all sweaty from school and swigging straight from a carton—juice, milk—doesn't matter—and he said, "What if someone else wants to drink from that?" As if I had poisoned the milk. I was unclean!" he laughs. "I was fifteen, Rach. A boy. But it started early, didn't it? Before even the bath decree—his first *ukaz*. Making me feel dirty. Unclean. And finally the changing of the locks, remember that one? When I ran away for good. He changed the locks."

"Sorry," Rachel says softly. "It was so wretched. I'm so sorry."

"Why are *you* sorry? Silly bloody Billy! I don't care anyway," he adds brightly. "So yeah. I remember. The singing and all that. Course I do. Go on, then. What were you thinking? That you wanted to tell me."

"About loins."

"I can hear all your innards, you know," says Zach, smiling and pressing his ear closer to her, deeper. "All your innards, doing their innardly things. Fetching and carrying, setting up for the day, all the joe jobs. It's like Smithfield at dawn in there, Rach. All bustle and holler! You know. Smithfield Market."

"That's what I've been thinking about. Sort of. Meat—"

"Meat, ma'am, meat!" exclaims Zach, rearing up and stretching, but mindful of his body, listening to his bones and muscles and recording what he feels there, totting up the trouble spots. "You've overfed him, ma'am! If you kept the boy on gruel—"

"Stop it, Zach. Just for a minute."

"Sorry," he says, sitting back on his heels and sliding his knees apart for balance, and raising his fists to his nose—*snuff-box, smeller*—to paw the air until Rachel makes two fists also to tap knuckles with him. Let the day begin.

"I love that bit," adds Zach, boxing in air. "Oliver Twist v. Noah Claypole! Only time in the whole story Oliver sees red. Only bloody time! Noah insults his dead mother and BANG! Oliver knocks him flat. Punched above his weight, too. A single knockdown blow. Fantastic. And everything changes. Think about it! If he hadn't bashed Noah—"

"Zach!"

"Sorry! Carry on."

"Loins, then," Rachel states with a frown. "Well. You know how there are words that never really—they are never really quite right. You can't quite trust them. Use them. You know. Without pause."

"There are words I stare at," Zach says. "Strange. Every time. *Misled*, that's one. I see mizzled. And *unshed*. I read unched."

"Me too! But that's a different thing—except, now you mention it, it's odd about unshed, that it's only for tears. Mostly. Hardly ever blood, for instance, you don't see *unshed blood*. Unched. Not really."

"Not in my case anyway. Mine sheds all over the joint! I'm a bleeder all right."

"Don't fight today!" begs Rachel, impulsive, and apologising just as quickly, reaching out for his mouth to stop the age-old defense there, the rebuke on his lips. I know, Zach, I know, she thinks. *Nothing you can do. Nothing I can do.* "Loins, then," she resumes. "When we were—when I was small—"

"You're small now, Rach."

"Yes, yes. I mean, when I was a girl, I thought *loins* meant 'belt,' that it was a kind of belt, or an old word for it. In books, people girding their loins and so on. And then there was 'loincloth' and I asked you about it and you said it was that flap of cloth cricketers use, bowlers, some bowlers, tucked into their waistband, for wiping their fingers—is that it? But never mind, that's what you said and then, Ha ha! you went. Joke! So I thought it must be genitals. Loins is genitals, I decided. And then—then there was Mr. Harris the butcher."

"In Mount Street. Where Mum took us," states Zach.

"Yes. Wellington boots and boomy voices and white aprons—"

"For all the unched blood to come," says Zach. "I liked Mr. Harris."

"Exactly. I liked him too. And the great hooks, remember? And that row of carcasses and the sawdust and marble and shiny cleavers, and Mr. Harris saying that day, 'Lovely tenderloin, Mrs. Wolff, I have a lovely bit of tenderloin'—"

"You felt sick. Was it that day? Yeah yeah. We waited for Mum in the square, near the church. The Farm Street Church," Zach says with a grave expression, protective even now.

"Yes. That day. And she was cross. The *display*. *'Quelle cérémonie!'* she said. What a fuss! Funny how she often spoke in French when cross."

"I fanned you with leaves," Zach adds, brightening. "Remember?"

"I do. She told you to stop, I remember that too. But the thing is, that day, I saw I had to be wrong, you see, about loins—"

"Can't leave little kids in a park nowadays," says Zach. "While you shop. They'd be abducted, abused, chopped in small pieces. Freeze on day of purchase!"

"Frozen when caught, you mean."

"Fresh out of water, out of the forest, free-range, oh yes. Fee-fi-fo-fum! But we were safe then, weren't we, Rach? In the heydays, hey, Rach?"

"We were," she agrees, touching his lips, stopping his mouth again—*oration trap, kisser*. "But *loins*," she insists.

"She *pursued* his lips," Zach laughs. "Another one I misread! *Pursued* for 'pursed.' You know, She *pursed* her lips. So whenever you do that now, reach out and touch my lips to shut me up? I think, she *pursued his lips*."

"That's so silly," smiles Rachel.

"I know that. Now I'm pursuing your lips," he adds.

When Zach kisses her, Rachel is often aware of the pulse in his lower labial, a small heartbeat there. She is aware of a pulsing and a slight thickening of tissue. How many times has this boy bled from the mouth? How many times.

"Go on, then," Zach urges. "About loins."

"Yes," she continues. "Loins. It's that suddenly it meant more than genitals, more than naked. I saw something raw, you see, to be *severed*," Rachel says. "And that day at the butcher's, the lovely bit of tenderloin, once I had that vision in my head, everything struck me as, I don't know, terribly *grievous* and . . . perishing. I *do* mean perishing. Passing. Reduced, anatomical. And Mount Street was so pretty! For a butcher's. The grille work, the bright glass front, the calligraphy in sepia, and the lattice beds for the meats, the beautiful feathers, partridge, pheasant—"

"And RUDDY ducks!" exclaims Zach.

"Yes. And the elegant street. It was a special journey for us, wasn't it? An outing with Mama. Mayfair. I let her down that day, didn't I? Did I? Zach? And the thing is, it's not as if it smelled nasty, it didn't smell nasty, I would remember that, if it had smelled—butchery, cloying and rotten . . . Oh! *I* know! I know now. How could I not see—not make the association? I don't believe it! After a childhood of Russian fairy-tale-telling. It's Baba Yaga's hut, isn't it? Her hut on chicken legs . . . with children, perhaps, in her pot. Baba Yaga sniffing the air . . . *I smell the smell of a Russian soul!* And flying through the air in her mortar, driving it with a pestle. Zach, is there a more fearsome woman in folklore? Is there? Remember *Little Bear Cub*? Of all the horrid tales!"

"Uh . . . Is Baba Yaga in that one?"

"Yes!" says Rachel. "Come on. You know the story. Tasha read it often. Baby found, brought up by bears, adopted by old peasant and wife, grows very strong . . . meets the giants, then—"

"He gets the beautiful girl, doesn't he?"

"In the end. Yes. But first, there's Baba Yaga. She keeps tearing strips of flesh off the giants, beats them to jelly with her pestle. Hates Little Bear Cub for eluding her. Strips of flesh, Zach! Beats them to *jelly!*"

"Rachel."

"Sorry. It's just—Baba Yaga. She's so awful. Odious. So very awful. And since Mount Street, when loin became tenderloin and there was Baba Yaga, and so on, I have to hold my breath if I pass a butcher's, even a posh one, clean-smelling. I hold my breath for four or five paces before it and beyond it. Silly."

"How did you manage in life class?" Zach laughs. "Don't they use those words in art? *Torso, loins.* And didn't you have to do still lifes—dead game, slabs of meat, etc.? Whoopsy-daisy, there goes Miss Wolff! Felled again. Quick! Smelling salts, someone!"

"Loins. That reminds me. Zach, do you wear a box in the gym? I mean, even if you're just hitting the heavy bag. And speed bag. Or skipping."

"Not yesterday . . . it was all a bit—impromptu. I mean, the sparring. With All Souls, Thomas, I mean. Aubry. I'm an idiot! Never mind. But yeah. Normally. Yeah. You have to. In case you jump in the ring. And it's best to get used to wearing it. And ah, we don't say 'box' though."

"Oh. Really? So many terms in sports! And words for everything in boxing. Especially *then*. I love the old words. From—"

"*Boxiana!*" Zach declaims. "Pierce Egan. Bloody hell, I love that book. First of the great sportswriters, I daresay. Pierce 'Pip' Egan."

"*Boxiana*—yes. I love it too," says Rachel, thinking how the title alone evokes so very much for her, so quickly, how she sees all the pictures in her mind's eye, the fold-out portraits of prize-fighters, the jacket illustration of Tom Cribb and Tom Molineaux in attitude. She knows the weight of the pages, their faint odour of sun and smoke and dust, and she recalls the painstaking glossary they made as children, a precious lexicon of pugilism inked in plain and italic fonts on pages bound with thread. The words became a game, one of many, a childhood code that was increasingly irksome to a watchful Lev—excluding—and crude to his ears from his daughter's mouth. Base.

"Well? What is a box called, then? In boxing?" asks Rachel, anticipating a joke. "Nowadays."

"We call it . . . *tenderloinplate.*"

"Ha ha," says Rachel, rolling her eyes skywards.

"Or *loinplate* for short. Sometimes—*tenderbox.*"

"*En cocotte!*" declares Rachel. "So to speak."

"What? Yes! No. The foil thing."

"Ah! *En papillote.*"

"Yeah. A slow roast. In the heat of battle. *I have a lovely bit of tenderloin!* Ah, the loin, Miss Wolff! Just falling off the bone."

"Oh don't! Don't say that! *Falling off the bone*—it's—"

"Sorry, Rach. Rachel?"

"It's all right, I'm all right," she says, frowning and tapping at her forehead with the heels of her hands. "So I'm just going to finish, then. About *loins*. I mean to say—"

"I meantersay, old chap!"

"Yes. I mean to say, that from today, I embrace the word. *Loins.*"

"Hurrah!" exclaims Zach.

"I hear it now and it's all fine, you see. From gazing at you this morning. And drawing you in my head, and how you're always in what I draw, even the map of the Caucasus, the Baltic Sea, the shapes of you and the lines of you are in the figures and the animals and the maps too, do you understand?" asks Rachel. "So the word is you, also, and not sad anymore, or terrible," she adds, suddenly drained, folding at the waist and resting her face in the crook of him, of his loins, brushing her cheek to and fro against the soft skin there, and running her hand the length of his thigh, his *ham*, as he calls it in the Regency manner he favours, and she favours, for so long now, a second language. And she marvels again at the paradox of Zach the fighter, the pelt of his forearms and pectorals fine as silk, and the skin of his crotch—*gracilis, inguinal, linea alba*—soft as belly of dove.

"I love your loins, that's all," Rachel says quietly. "And now I love the word itself, and how words change, I love that too. And all the parts of you, I love them. That's all. And I'm not sad," she whispers, gasping a little at the shock of her own tears, hot and extravagant, tears that catch the light in her lashes before they drop and roll across Zach's thighs, sparkling capsules, kaleidoscopic, the flow dynamic.

"Marry me, Rachel."

"Not yet."

"Tomorrow, Rachel. Marry me."

"Maybe tomorrow."

"There is no common blood between us. Say it," pleads Zachariah.

"There is no common blood between us," murmurs Rachel.

"I am *not* your brother."

"I know."

He traces her face with his swollen fingers, across the brow bones and down the zygomatics, and along the jaw from earlobe to chin, sweeping away the brine as he goes.

"I am your Wolff," he says.

"And I am your Wolff," she replies.

Let the day begin.

Rachel slips out of bed and downstairs as Zach splashes in the bathroom, his ablutions remarkable always for vigour. His ins and outs of breath, accompanied in winter by howls of shock, amuse her without fail and she listens to him all the way to the kitchen where she follows the same quotidian route to the coffee machine, treading the same plank of pine she prefers for its singular rectitude of grain and absence of knot, and for the sensation on her bare soles of patination and shape and silkiness, stepping the well-worn hollows of generations of feet.

"I walk the plank," she muses, sweeping away the uncombed locks of auburn hair from her face and raising her arms aloft in a morning stretch. "I walk the plank of ages!"

Rachel recalls the tempest of dust she and Zach raised here in their Camden Town home, their dacha, they call it, before moving their scant belongings from rented rooms above a framer's in a nearby North London mews. Here in the close, they peeled back the corners of mouse-brown carpeting and tiles of tawdry linoleum, pitted as it were from smallpox. She remembers the dust.

They lift gingerly, at first, and then with abandon, marvelling at the great clouds of soot that rise and seem to fall, thereafter, for days and days.

"I just can't believe it," Rachel exclaims. "When will it stop? We cleaned and cleaned yesterday and there's a whole new layer of silt!"

"Some of this dust," Zach states, pulling his jumper and T-shirt off and stashing them in a plastic carrier, "is two hundred years old."

"Not quite," corrects Rachel. "Hundred and sixty, I believe."

"Rachel. The Gardens behind are well over two hundred. 1803, right? Let's say there's dust that's migrated from there too. Agreed?"

"Fine. But I'm off to buy face-masks. We can't keep inhaling this! Couldn't stop coughing last night. I'm going to Boots. Do we need anything else?"

"I'll go, Rach."

"You're half naked, silly."

"Bloody hell, though!" goes Zach, tying a bandana round his brows. "It's kind of fantastic. Dead follicles, most of this. Just think!"

"It's faintly cannibalistic. I don't want to think. Back soon. I'll buy more water too. And sweets or something."

The dirt fell and fell while they cleaned, every swipe of cloth and brush and aspiration of vacuum propelling as much dust into the air, so it seemed, as they could gather in sacks. The dirt was black as iron filings, as soot, black as the earth Aunt Tasha describes in Central Russia, of virgin land and forest steppe.

"I have a trick," says Rachel later that day, squatting on her haunches to survey the landscape. She slips her face-mask down and raises a shoulder to her chin to wipe the trickle of moisture there.

"What then?" asks Zach, leaning on his broom, his face and torso sticky and streaked with sweat and grime.

"You look like a Victorian crossing sweeper!" notes Rachel. "Why aren't you wearing your mask?"

"Driving me crazy. Feel bloody smothered. Hey, now what?" demands Zach, flipping the broom upside down and pumping the air. "Now what do I look like?"

"Chimney boy! No, no, no—the name? Damn!"

"Flue-faker!" he declares.

"Flue-faker!" echoes Rachel. "Yes."

"And how about you?" Zach demands. "What do you think *you* look like, sitting in the dirt? On your heels like that. Mudlark!"

"Sewer rat! Cinder-sifter!"

"Bone-grubber! OK, OK. So what's your trick?"

"Well," begins Rachel. "You have to sweep and PAUSE. Sweep and pause. Wait for the dust to settle, then sort of trap it gently with a damp cloth. If you keep sweeping without pause, the backwards stroke of the broom in air raises the dust again. See?"

"That's ridiculous. Take forever. And tomorrow I've got the sander, so what's the point in being that meticulous? We need to get the worst of it up. We're nearly there, looking good, Rach!"

"But I thought—I thought we were going to discuss the sander. The man said—the conservation man . . ."

"I already rented it. From tomorrow."

"But he said . . . about the patination . . . on the old pine. Better to wash with turps, he said. Wash and scrape. And also, I'm beginning to hate the dirt, Zach! It's everywhere, in everything. What if it just stays and stays and the floors never brighten and we're just adding to it all, the mess, the smut . . . this awful . . . slough!"

"You're tired."

"Don't! If ever I say something like that, you say I'm tired. It's so fucking patronising!"

"Whoa," goes Zach. "You swore. You never bloody swear. You must be tired. JOKE, JOKE!"

"Very funny. Pass me the water, please," says Rachel.

"Listen," he soothes. "It's going to be clean, super fucking clean! And I'm using the sander. This is our den, right? Our new den. Not a museum. I'm not spending months on my knees with a bloody bottle of turps and a cabinet scraper just because this pine is one hundred and sixty years old. That's fucking crazy. It's going to be old but new, right?

We are going to *live* here! We're gonna dance!" Zach exclaims, dropping the broom to do an Ali shuffle. "Hey," he adds, "think Tasha might move in? She can have a whole floor! Get her money's worth. Till we can pay her back. Man, that was close! We were almost outbid! Thanks, Tasha! Come on," he urges, seizing his broom again. "Get up! Let's go. We're nearly there."

"It wasn't Tasha," says Rachel, lowering her gaze.

"What wasn't?"

"Wasn't her. Who bailed us out. Topped us up, for the deposit. It was Papa, Zach. It was Lev."

Zachariah swings the broom like a great axe, hitting the wall so hard the handle cracks in two places, one part flying free and so close to Rachel's head he dives to shield her, skidding to a stop where she still sits in a squat, though she is coiled tightly now, knees together, eyes squeezed shut and covered by her pair of sooty hands.

"Rach? Sorry. Are you OK?"

"No."

Zach kneels. He tries to pry her fingers from her eyes.

"Sorry."

"Go away," she cries.

"It's . . ." He falters. "I thought the money was from *Tyotya,* that's all. And Lev wants to . . . humiliate. He hates me. Why would he help us? I'll pay it all fucking back, Rach. Why did he have to do that?"

"For me," she replies, avoiding his gaze. "He did it for me. Because he had no choice. There's a limit, you see, to just how much he hates you for loving me, can you understand that? And don't you think that makes it just a tiny bit harder?" she presses, staring fiercely at his breast. "Just a tiny bit harder to keep hating him straight back?"

"OK," he murmurs. "Can we go for a beer? Please? Aren't you tired? No no!" he adds quickly, seizing her shoulders for emphasis. "Not that way! Not *you're tired,* patronising, that way—I mean, *plain* tired. You know. I'm tired, for one."

Rachel looks hard into Zachariah's grimy face, his complexion flushed with helplessness and a simmering frustration. There are bright streaks in the murk where his laughter and frown lines are, and across the bridge of his nose and high cheekbones where the safety mask pinched him so uncomfortably, and the effect is of war paint.

"When you were a fighter," Rachel proposes, "and when you talk about fighters, you always insist that *rage* has no place in the ring. Breakneck, uncontrolled. Is that correct? How the best fighters use their aggression, don't go about their life in a rage? In or out of the ring?"

Zach nods.

"When you get angry like that, when I see you lash out, scream, smash things, it frightens me. I find it really frightening. I want it to stop. It hardly happens anymore and that's good. But I want it to stop. As much as possible. Are you listening?"

Zach reaches for her and she pushes him back, palm flat to his chest.

"Wait. I haven't finished. Papa. Lev. What he did."

"Rachel!" Zach shouts, leaping to a stand. "I don't want to fucking hear it!"

"Zach!" commands Rachel. "You let me speak! I did not expect it either, his help. But I shan't fight it. I can't tell why he gave us the money, maybe some strange patriarchal dutiful Russian sense of things, I don't know. And of course he's different since Mama died, but he did not do it to humiliate you, for pity's sake! He's not daring us to fail. Or putting a curse on our house. That's almost stupid! He did it for me, because he can't shut me out, no matter what. So this is not permission or absolution and it is very, very far from acceptance, but it is all we've got and this is our family, our pack, our small pack. Katya is gone and Nicky is gone and now we are four, only four. Things may well grow worse between us—Papa and the two of us—and they also may never be any better, but this will do for now and I don't want to destroy it and I need your help, I am asking for your help. I chose you, Zach. I choose you, but I love Papa. So there. I've finished now. That's my speech."

Zach jabs the air in front of him, throws a left-right combination, and Rachel watches the dense cloud of sparkling motes dance wildly in the shaft of light cast by the tall ground-floor windows in the lateness of the day.

"I just want to say, Mrs. Speaker, that you don't have a whole hell of a lot of authority sitting there in the dirt looking like a mole on a dig. Know what I mean?"

"Ha ha," she replies.

"Come on," he says, stretching out a hand. "Up you get. Up, up, up!"

Rachel and Zach draw the pine shutters closed across the windows and Zach runs his fingers along the blistered paint of the panels and mouldings.

"They painted over and over!" he scoffs. "Look at all these layers! I can strip and paint them properly, don't worry. And I had a squint at those box shutters upstairs. I'll make it all good, I can fix all of it. Original features! Very cool. It's going to look great, Rach, but I'm exiling you for a week. Maybe two. A lot of noise and dust and I want you to stay away."

"Can you take the time? Don't you have shifts at the gym? Can Isaac do without you? And what about your idea—your boxing book? I think it's a great idea! I can help you, but you need to start. I don't see how . . ."

"Already told Aubry and Iz I'm taking off till next month. He doesn't mind, said I'm owed holiday time, said I overwork there anyway. And Aubry's with us long term; plus he's not in serious training for two or three weeks from now. I can put my thing on hold a bit. It'll be fine."

"Did Aubry agree? To the biography?"

"It's not a biography."

"Sorry. But he's the subject, no?"

"Yeah yeah. It'll be fine, Rach. It's cool. Come on. Stop worrying."

"A book proposal takes time, that's all," says Rachel, struggling with the fastener on the meeting rail of a sash, ancient paint flickering free like sparks. "You've never done one."

"Hey! Let me do that," Zach commands, prising her away from the window. "It's splintering. Might get in your eyes."

"We've collaborated before, Zach. On a book. Remember *Sam the Russian?*"

"Course I bloody do!" he grins. "*Sam the Russian, His Strange Surprizing Adventures.* Where the hell are those books? Haven't seen them in ages! How many did we make? We were bloody hooked—fanatical!"

Rachel remembers the tiny volumes, the stitches she sewed to bind the pages, the jackets she decorated in coloured inks, the reviews and synopsis on the back. She recalls the measurements, a precise eighteen centimetres by eleven, and illustrations on every page. Above all, she summons their childish fervour, the fastidious research into times and places and words, and how whim turned to compulsion and competition, each infecting the other with a desire for perfection of detail and learning, Rachel startling Zachariah with her mounting enthusiasm, her knowledge of his subject waxing daily, his private passion for boxiana digested and reflected as he could never have foretold. Where his boyhood retreat had been a cave hewn for one, it now accommodated two. He was suddenly two and it amazed and delighted, causing a stir in the pit of him, a kind of fibrillation.

When he produced a glossary and chronology for transcription, and a cast of characters for her to complete, she was careful to praise him for their scope and quality and he cheerfully deferred to her superior skills in composition and in penmanship, his own script curiously deficient, inhibited and crabbed. They began to import the lingo into their childhood exchanges, even at table, the vocabulary infusing their speech quite naturally, habitually, drawing vague quizzical stares from their mother Katya and dark reproach from Lev.

Upon displaying their first completed volume, entitled *Sam the Russian, Lost Tsar of the Prize Ring, His Strange Surprizing Adventures, Part One, His Beginnings,* Katya perused all the pages, turning them slowly with long graceful fingers and glancing from page to child, and child back to page, saying nothing, now raising an eyebrow, now frowning, then smiling before closing the slim book on her lap and reaching over to ruffle Zach's tousled head. This is the best they could wish from her.

"The cast of characters," remarked Katya, "I find particularly amusing. Who is responsible?" she asked and the two children replied in one voice.

"Rachel!" said Zach. "I mean, both of us," he revised hurriedly, worried that *particularly amusing* might not be altogether a good thing.

"Zachariah!" said Rachel. "Mostly."

And she recalls it keenly now, the surge of blood and oxygen in her slight frame as she searched her father's face, feeling it still, even today, the heat of hurt and humiliation suffusing her own as he waved away the proffered book.

"Not now," he had said. "Busy." *Not now. Later.*

Out of his daughter's mouth, the lexicon offended him, strapping, ribald, base; words made flesh. The interest in boxing that he initially perceived as courtesy, little but an overture to her strange new brother, yet became obsession so quickly, Lev prayed it would fade just as fast. He studied the small tome in the privacy of his office, reading every word, bristling with trepidation and fierce dismay. What is happening under my roof? What change is occurring here? Summoning Rachel to his rooms at the top of the house, he questioned and listened, gathering clues. There must be a pattern.

"If Sam the Russian is invented, why is Charles Dickens in the story?" Lev demanded. "I don't understand. Explain."

"Because Zach loves him so," Rachel said. "It's fun."

"Fun? That is not rigorous. There must be rigour, or I can't trust. Do you see? You have a marvellous brain, little paws. Don't lose it. I trust you. Now go on, please. I want to learn. Why Alexander I? And . . . why Mendelssohn? Where does it all come from? I don't understand."

Lev and Rachel deliberated for some time, because they always talked things over, talked so much, the master and his pupil, his brilliant, luminous daughter, though she remembers faltering badly, increasingly faint and uncertain, waves of nausea rising. She babbled a litany of names of fighters, all, so it seemed to an imperious Lev, called Tom or Sam. Butchers by trade, coal heavers, watermen; illiterates. He listened to the litany of deaths and diseases and to digressions on rookeries and cholera, sewers and railways, ratting pits and boxing rings and hoped that, by hearing her out, by exposing the flaws in her thinking, the obsession would pass and his daughter would come up from beneath. He hoped that his daughter would exit the underworld. Rachel, come back to me! Come back.

"Rach?" asks Zach. "We still have the books, right? Somewhere?"

"Yes, yes," she replies with a touch of irritation, "I don't lose things."

"Hey, what's up? Rachel?"

"Nothing," she replies, taking his hands. "Tired and flustered and dirty!"

"OK. We'll be off in a minute. But you know what? Let's dig out the books and you rewrite them. New drawings, the lot. Make a great kids' book! Do a whole slew of them, a sequel. Series. We'll be rich, I tell you! Rolling!"

"Zachariah. Nobody wants to read to their kids about sweaty boxers."

"But what about all those history bits?" Zach insists. "Remember? That's super-educational! Parents love that."

"Boxing puts people off from the start. They'll never get that far."

"I don't know, Rach. Orphan stories. Top trumps!"

"It's still about boxers. Hopeless drunks and illiterates."

"You sound like Papa," Zach complains. "You sound like Lev!"

"Do I?" she asks idly, stroking his fingers and glancing fretfully about the rooms, unable to see, in her fatigue, past the dust and shambles to the home that might emerge.

"Yeah," he says. "You really do."

"Zachariah, Zachariah," smiles Rachel. "Our foundling boy! Now listen; about this house. It's a lot of work. If you won't let me help, why don't you get one of the boys at the gym, perhaps? If you won't let me. And why not me?"

"Noise, dust, I said no. And I want to do it by myself. You know I can. How do you think I lived before? When I ran away. And before you came?"

"Your exile," says Rachel, releasing his hands. "Your Siberia."

"It was OK," he says, jabbing the air once more. "Restoration work all day, training at night. Learned so much. And I was so bloody fit!"

Rachel shakes the worst of the muck from her jacket before slipping it on and swabs an area free of smut in the window seat where she perches, waiting for Zach to secure the latches and pull on his clothes. She loves his purpose, the muscularity in every task.

"Why do you say 'Isaac the cutman,' when he's a trainer?" she asks.

"Because he was a cutman. Still is. But mainly a trainer now, since he bought the gym in Whitechapel. Oh hey! When you were cussing me out about being in a huff—"

"First of all, I don't cuss anyone out ever. Secondly, I would not call that a huff! You bloody smashed a broom in three pieces and nearly blinded me!"

"Right," says Zach, grinning. "So, when you were going on about *rage*, I remembered an Izzyism. That's what we call it, All Souls and I, Izzyism. Anyway, Izzy comes bursting out of the office, he's hopping mad from some phone call with a promoter or agent or someone, and he goes, 'I could spit! I could spit! I'm apops—aplops—apocalyptic!'"

"He didn't."

"He really did!"

"You didn't laugh at him, did you?"

"Apocalyptic with rage! I bloody love it! Come on, Rach! Beer time.

Let's hit the road. Hey, ever wondered why this house went up for auction?"

"Haunted, of course," replies Rachel, as Zach pockets the keys on the doorstep and steps back a pace or two to observe their new façade. She slips her hand in his and they both gaze upwards at the old stock bricks and bold windows and Welsh slate tiles, at the pleasing austerity of the whole.

"Definitely," he nods. "And maybe some of this dust is Dickens! His first London abode, right round the corner. Fantastic!"

"The close wasn't built till the 1850s. He lived here in the twenties."

"Well, the gardens are 1803, so maybe some of him sloughed off there and wafted in under our foundations, how about that?"

"Perfectly plausible," Rachel agrees. "Here lies the slough of ages! Under our very feet. In our very foundations. All hail the old stones!"

"Will he come," asks Zach quietly as they exit the street and round the corner, heading north. "To the house? Lev?"

"No, I don't think so," she replies, eyes cast down.

"When I'm out, of course. By arrangement. He'll need to see you in your new den. He'll want to, no?"

"No, Zach," she says, squeezing him tight as they walk. "He shan't come."

"Well!" he declares, swinging arms with her jauntily, "we'll bloody have to get a samovar in, then. Stick up some pictures of dead Russians. Gogol, Prokofiev, Pushkin, the pack of them! And you can wear a whatsit—*sarafan*. Do the bread and salt thing."

"*Khleb da sol!*" exclaims Rachel.

"*Khleb da sol,*" repeats Zach. *Bread and salt.* "Exactly! So that'll do it. He'll have to come! For you in a *sarafan*."

Rachel leans into Zach's shoulder, aspirating happily.

"You know what, Rach? When I first saw those portraits in your house, when I first arrived and I was—was I seven, eight?"

"Eight."

"Eight. Right. I thought they were your ancestors. Especially the great bloody painting of Alexander I on the landing. Hell's bells, I thought. Very spruce! Must be her great grandfather. I didn't say anything when you explained them to me. All the portraits. Afraid you'd laugh. Did I never tell you that?"

"Our icons, family icons. God, how funny! No, you did not," she replies, pulling him back from the busy corner of Camden Road and Camden Street, "tell me. You never did. And I hate when you want to cross here! It's not a proper crossing! You have to cross at the lights."

"These are lights!" he protests.

"Not for people! Direction lights for cars! You know perfectly well. Why don't you just hurl yourself into the traffic and be done with it? Honestly! Come on," she commands, tugging him along. "This way."

"Just imagine, though," Zach sputters. "If I had said in front of Lev, at the time, about the Tsar: 'Um, excuse me, sir, *is that your grandfather?*'"

"Your Imperial Highness!" exclaims Rachel, dipping into a curtsey.

"We need wine," Zach states. "Let's nip in to Sainsbury's."

"Tsar Alexander I," recites Rachel. "Born 1777, died 1825. Reign: 1801 unto death. Married Louisa of Baden (Elisabeth Alexeyevna). He had very lovely curly hair and was a very good dancer. He held liberal views in his youth and was keen on reform and was deaf in one ear and was not a good sailor, as the saying goes, suffering from the *mal de mer*. His famous battles against Napoleon need no exposition here. He loved to speed along in horse-drawn vehicles, often at the most inconvenient times. Later in life he became thwarted and mystical and exceedingly sick from erysipelas of the leg. He was very close to his favourite sister Ekaterina Pavlovna, called Katya. She was ten years younger and very vivacious and imperious, but I am afraid to say she died before him, of erysipelas plus pneumonia. Alexander died of a very very bad cold five years later. Because his tomb was found to be empty of bones when opened over a hundred years after his demise, it is rumoured he did not die at all, but lived on as a *starets,* which is a Russian word for 'holy man,' doing good deeds far and wide in his native place. The authors of *Sam the Russian, His Strange Surprizing Adventures,* however, doubt this very much."

"From our little books?" asks Zach. "You've been looking!"

"Not really. Just a memory. The biographies definitely went something like that," replies Rachel. "We were VERY emphatic," she laughs, stopping at the entrance to Sainsbury's. "And presently, we're so VERY grotty! Filthy in fact."

"It's Camden Town, Rach! We'll fit right in."

"Uncle Nicky loved our Cast of Characters! Do you remember? He used to greet us at the door, when we came calling, with little biographical speeches! Slightly different each time."

"I remember now," nods Zach.

"We failed, quite, to see the humour, didn't we, Zach? Because I am sure we wrote them in all earnestness, those biographical summaries, and there was *Dyadya*, opening the front door to us and piping: 'Zachariah Wolff is a foundling boy. He is a VERY avid reader, which does not seem to improve his orthography. He wears his hair long and is a VERY keen sportsman and very good at singing. He is sometimes VERY clumsy and is happy to wear the same jeans every day for a year and eat potatoes three times a day. Which is a very good thing as there are *draniki* for lunch! Come in, come in, what are you standing there for?'"

"I miss him," says Zach.

"And it wouldn't have been so stupid," says Rachel, following Zach into the shop, running the gauntlet of sanctioned beggars listlessly touting their charity magazines, and of bruising security men strolling the portals, broad-chested and stoney-faced as nightclub bouncers.

"What wouldn't?" he asks, scanning the shelves in the wine section. "Hey, I remember this one. We've had this one," he says, holding up a bottle of red for her approbation. "Is it good enough?"

"Boris GOODENOUGH!" she replies. "Yes. It's fine. Anyway, I meant what you thought as a child about Alexander I being our ancestor. It wasn't so far-fetched. The Tsar is the *Little Father*, isn't he? To all his people."

"Well. It's hardly what was on my mind at the time! When I nearly asked my very first stupid question in your household."

"I know. I'm thinking it now, though. And I still have a soft spot for Tsar Alexander. A thwarted man, he was thwarted. Too sensitive, too romantic."

"For what?" asks Zach. "Leadership? Success? That's a crap argument. Let's make pizza tonight. What do we need?"

"What's a crap argument?"

"That sensitive and romantic types can't be leaders. I mean, look at you. You're too sensitive and too romantic and you never mess up. You've never messed anything up. Mozzarella, mozzarella . . . ah. Here."

"But Zach," Rachel protests quietly, "I'm not a tsarina. An empress. I don't lead a vast country. There's just you. You and me. Not a vast country."

"Tsarina Rachel!" he says, grabbing her wrist. "Tsarina Rachel is not a foundling. She is a very keen reader and is very good at drawing. Her eyes are blue as the Blue Bridge on the Moika! She is an exceedingly keen walker and cartographer. The older she grows, the farther she walks. It is a good thing the world is round and she is fond of walking in circles or else she might disappear across three times nine countries in the thirtieth tsardom! Didn't get it as a kid, by the way, that line in fairy tales," Zach adds. "'The thirtieth tsardom.' Then Tasha explained—took me aside one day and explained about Old Russia, all the principalities. All that. Damn, that's one big country! One wide expanse. As in the song. That song! Katya and Tasha sang it all the time—'You are my field, my wide expanse!'"

"'O My Field,'" nods Rachel. "It's beautiful, they sang it beautifully," she adds, sadness rising. She places onions in their basket, and herbs; basil, thyme, parsley and rosemary. Mama, she thinks. There's rosemary. *There's rosemary, that's for remembrance. Pray you, love, remember.*

On the evening Zachariah finishes his fevered work of restoration, after days of toil that grow longer and longer as the project nears its end and he staggers home later and later, giddy with endeavour and stumbling with fatigue, when he has finished sanding and oiling and waxing and painting, he purchases a bottle of wine and a bag of ice from the Turkish off licence in Pratt Street and leaves it to chill in the cleanest of his builder's buckets while he races the several blocks home on his bike to fetch Rachel. When they enter the house in the close, he takes off her shoes and socks and leads her by the hand to skate with her across the burnished floors warm with the glow of time and the flickering light of the candle Zach carries from room to room, his face ruddy with pride and excitement as they climb to the first floor and he urges her to raise and lower the Victorian box shutters that now glide gracefully on their stays with no hint of the rumble and shudder and cascade of cobweb and creaking of sash cords so very lately furred and blackened with grease. He has painted the walls a pale and greyish green in a colour named "stone white," which Rachel favoured, and drops of pigment still daub his face and anoint his dark brown waves of hair.

"I wanted to show you by candlelight, because—"

"It's beautiful, you've made it so beautiful, Zach."

"Not quite done, but we can move in," he says.

"It's like a forest, a forest and a vessel all at once. A palace!"

"It can't be all those things," laughs Zach.

"It is, though! A great woods! And a palace. A beautiful ship!"

"Champagne," says Zach. "I should have bought fizz. To break against the bows. For good luck and so on."

"Nonsense!" scoffs Rachel, twirling about the room, touching the walls and window seats. "The finish you achieved! It's amazing. And the smell in here! All resin and beeswax and dried flowers and darkened pine. And sandalwood soap. Like a gentleman's outfitter, shoemaker. Crockett & Jones, John Lobb. It smells handsome and private; I love it! And we don't need champagne. Or good luck. The wine will do fine. Anyway, in the Royal Navy, I believe, they christen submarines in beer. So there. We'll go through the house and anoint. We'll raise a glass in each room."

"Bloody hell, Rach. Glasses! I fucking forgot glasses. Got paper cups though. Have to rinse them out. Damn!"

"But it doesn't matter," soothes Rachel, tugging at his sleeves and coaxing him to the floor. "Sit with me a moment! Let's sit right here in the middle of the floor. It doesn't matter about proper glasses or champagne; none of that matters. Remember how you told me you'd make it all good? It's an expression in the trade, isn't it? To repair and make good. When we were helping Tasha with the insurance—that awful leak from above—I was struck by it, these words, 'to repair and make good.' Ominous, don't you think? Fabular."

"Fabulous?" says Zach.

"No. Fabular. A long long time ago there lived a tsar with three sons. One day he told them it was time to build palaces of their own. He commanded them to take a bow and shoot an arrow and wherever the arrow lands, there they must make good. The first son's arrow landed in a rich valley with sumptuous woods and gardens as far as the eye could see. The second son's arrow landed in limestone cliffs in a coastline of epic grandeur. But the youngest son's arrow landed in the splintered door of a broken-down house in an early Victorian street in Camden. What was he to do? He never flinched from his task. He repaired and made good!"

"Wait a minute!" breathes Zach, swallowing hard. "You think I did all this," he asks, seizing her shoulders, "for *him*? To appease Lev? Out of—because of—the money?"

"No! Oh my goodness, no! Oh what have I done? What a ninny I am. I didn't mean that at all!"

"It's for you, Rach. For you. Because of you," Zach says, speaking low. "And Tasha. I want her to come."

"I know. And that's all I wanted to say. That you have made good. You have made it beautiful and good and it's ours and I think that nothing can hurt us here."

"Better not open the hall cupboard then," smiles Zach.

"Oh?"

"Crammed my gear in there before coming to get you. Running late. Wanted everything clean, all the surfaces. You open that door, there'll be a cascade of hurt—blades, hammers, nails, caustic, the lot. A torture chamber."

"Well, thanks for the warning."

Zach grips her softly above her crossed knees, and stands. "I'm going down for the wine. Hell of a thirst!"

"And dirty cups. Don't forget the dirty cups," says Rachel.

"Hey!" Zach calls out from halfway up the stairs. "Look what I found! Two wine glasses. Did you bring them? I didn't. Or did I? Weird."

"Maybe it was Katya," suggests Rachel.

"Don't," he says. "It was you, right?"

"It'll be one year this winter, Zach. Since she died."

"One. Man," he says, opening wine. "I wish . . . I think that . . . I mean, she was hard, difficult, a piece of work! But I miss her so much. If she were—"

"If all the world were paper," chants Rachel, "and all the sea were ink, and all the trees were bread and cheese, what should we have to drink?"

"Start on this," he laughs, handing Rachel a glass. "Still. Things would be different, no? If she were still here. Lev—"

"None of it matters, I told you," Rachel swears. "*If* this, *if* that. It doesn't signify. We make our own stories. So let's play," she whispers. "In fact, I am sure I see Mama now, wandering the rooms, assessing. She stops in a corner and folds her arms in that way—see her! Do you? Balletic, poised. Never a wasted move, never a step without intent. Can you see her, Zach?"

"I look for her, you know. I don't see her. Not like you do. You see the dead! Even as kids, when we were doing the little books, they were your friends almost, our fave rave characters. Dickens, Tsar Alexander . . ."

"John Clare!" exclaims Rachel. "I loved him. The walking poet."

"Clare, yeah. Dreamed he was Tom Spring. In the loony bin. You had a craze for Clare," Zach teases.

"'Into the nothingness of scorn and noise,'" Rachel recites. "'Into the living sea of waking dreams—'"

"What the blue blazes does that mean?" complains Zach. "The 'nothingness of scorn and noise'? Maybe he was going to fill it in later on. Just wrote 'nothingness' until he could think of something right. And forgot."

"You've made *me* forget the next lines! Two lines . . . something something then, 'Even the dearest that I loved the best, Are strange, nay—stranger than the rest.' It's so poignant!" says Rachel.

"And all my fighters," Zach continues. "I taught you all the boxers, they were my guys, that was *my* craze, but—"

"I stole them?"

"In a way," he concedes, leaning over to butt her gently in the chest with the top of his head. "Not quite stole. I didn't mind. You just made them—different—alive again. Anyway, when you said this house is ours, it's good and it's ours," he frowns. "I thought how when I was working on it these last weeks, through the night lately, I forgot. I forgot about Lev and the money and wondering why he did it, why he helped us. Helped you. The place *did* feel ours. But now I don't know. I don't know anymore."

"Katya's pleased," Rachel persists. "Head to one side, that amused tilt, a slight smile. She touches the windowsill, turns to face you. And she speaks."

"Stop it," murmurs Zach, disconsolate.

"Remember that box you made as a boy? A wooden case for her new baton."

"Thing it came in was crap! Couldn't bloody believe it," he pipes, brightening. "Antique ivory baton and it comes in a crap case. Cheap little hinges, rubbish wood. I had to do it. First proper thing I made."

"She loved it, Zach."

"She never really said anything."

"That's how she was. She did, though."

"What?" he asks.

"Say something. At the time. *'Khoroshiy mal'chik.'* Good boy. She said, *'Khoroshiy mal'chik.'*"

"Yeah. I remember now."

"And it *is* ours," Rachel assures him. "We'll make our own stories here."

"Once upon a time!" Zach proclaims.

"Far away," says Rachel, "over the steppes and rivers and forests . . ."

Can it be nearly a year ago? One year in this house.

"O my field," sings Rachel in Russian, "my open field, you are my wide expanse."

Rachel stretches at her desk before the tall windows of the first floor, the tallest windows in the house. There is so much light this morning, her artist papers glow bright and she blinks to adjust her vision. She smooths the page of A3 with a gentle sweep of the forearm in a gesture of long standing. This too is my field, she muses. My wide expanse. Rachel sketches loosely, easily; warm-up exercises. She thinks of Zach at the gym, warming up, because though he retired some two years ago, he still trains, and even more regularly now that he is not only Izzy's new assistant, but wants to cover the story of Thomas "All Souls" Aubry's pursuit of the title and rise from the amateurs. "The Last Gentleman," Zach calls him.

"He's not technically a *gentleman* if he's professional," Rachel argued when Zach proposed the title.

"Yes, he is," Zach replied. "It's kind of a—philosophical thing."

"Oh," she had said, doubtfully. "Know something extraordinary, Zach?"

"Lots of things!" he replied. "You put physalis in my lunch box the other day. Thanks very much. Entertainment for the whole fucking gym!"

"Something about Thomas, I wanted to tell you. His *name*. I'm reading about 1812, Borodino, the fire of Moscow, the retreat. So much has burned, but the Foundling Home is spared. Everything around it was destroyed yet the Foundling Home did not burn. It's full of children and wounded soldiers from both armies, French and Russian, and one of the officers covers himself in glory there, a wounded Captain of Chasseurs. He organises the defence of the Hospital alongside three Russian generals. Napoleon has entered the city and some French have run amok. And criminals, a local rabble, though most Russians have left. The city is burning! Guess the Captain's name."

"Tell me, Rachel."

"Captain Thomas Aubry."

"Really?" Zach asked. "Odd's teeth!"

"Everything is connected," stated Rachel. "Patterns everywhere."

"Yeah yeah," said Zach. "You're so scientific."

"So are you. So *were* you. The scientific boxer."

Zach still trains, but he no longer fights and is not meant to spar, though he does, of course. Now and again, he tells her, only now and again, sparring just to stay quick on his feet, quick in himself. *I'm careful,* he assures her when she reminds him how he told her himself that most accidents happen in sparring, in mismatches in the gym. She thinks about the words "careful" and "fighting." She wonders how caution and fighting go together. Nothing she can do.

Rachel scrawled an encomium one day on her desk pad alongside a sketch of a pugilist in attitude, an encomium to Zach's career. She used the Regency style they both enjoy so much and read it to Zach when he was home.

"Listen!" she commanded, reciting in exuberant tones. "If the single-most opinion ever noised of him were that he handled his fives well and had a fine sportsmanlike demeanour, then Zachariah Wolff might hang up his mufflers with pride, for he is a fighting man in a long line of fighting men and shall be true to this until the end of days, let the world know it. Let All England know it."

"That's me all right!" Zach laughed. "Cue hurrahs from the crowd!"

"So," she said, "you write Aubry's tale and I'll write yours. Well, I'll draw it, I mean."

"You'll do the *Sam the Russian* books, then? Revive them? Is that what you mean?" he asked excitedly. "Do it, Rach! Do it!"

"We shall see . . . We shall see."

And this morning Rachel draws another pugilist in attitude, after the figure that keeps appearing to her in dreams of late, sometimes at three o'clock in the morning, sometimes at four. Night after night, he comes, ever since she recalled their early endeavours, the tiny books written and bound by hand from stories imagined deep into the small hours, Rachel and Zachariah sitting up in the casement window of his bedroom, chattering in fevered childhood tones. Here he comes now, her dream bare-knuckle boy, so many years dormant, here he comes to Rachel, toeing the line. Is it he? Who are you? What is your name? What can I do for you? Is it you, Sam?

Rachel gets out of her chair. She takes up the stance classical. She laughs.

"A diller, a dollar, a ten o'clock boxer!" she chants. "What makes you come so soon? You used to come at ten o'clock, but now you come at noon."

Rachel sits. She draws the squared circle, called a ring, to place her boxer in. That is *his* field. It's you, Zach, isn't it? My fighting man. Where does it all begin, though, she asks herself, filling in the spaces on her sheet of Bristol smooth 270 g/m². Tell me please. The fight in you. Where does it all begin?

Rachel draws him again and again, her dream bare-knuckle boy, every time in finer detail, the shape emerging. Her lines grow quick and confident; she knows this boy, she feels him. She gives the head definition and lustrous curls and a boxer's proud mien, the boy's skin yet unmarked. He has not a mark on his face! Zachariah once had not a mark on his face. Rachel thinks how she often roams Zach's skull, threading her fingers through his hair, instinctively seeking that hair-less place, a silken scar maybe eight centimetres long behind his left ear, her touchstone, like a favourite path in a forest, her *tropa,* she names it, because all Russian words between them are endearments and because by calling it wolf track, path, it becomes, thereby, a place of cultiva-tion, of contemplation and homeliness and fair weather. Travelling this path where there will be no more growth, the follicles dead, the place barren, Rachel wills it away, the power of the scar to alarm and evoke fearful memories and dread of the future. *Tropa,* she intones. *Tropa!* Yet the outrage endures, of the rude operation on his head—his *knowledge-box*—that rendered her apoplectic at the time, wild with fury and help-lessness for being so quickly reduced to this in a technological age, the desperate techniques of lancing and sawing and bloodletting, basic and ancient, while Zach lay unconscious, in paradoxical sleep, she hoped, in some dream of intactness, she prayed, and not on the verge of nev-ermore, a tumult of blood and bone and bare protesting organs. This cannot be right, she recalls thinking, feeling betrayed by the fallibility of science. Are we truly still this vulnerable, this fragile, no better? And don't they know whose knowledge-box that is? You *medulla* and *pons*, *corpus callosum*, grey matter, white—come to scratch! Toe the line! You belong to Zachariah Wolff and must rally! The man is a prize-fighter, fight for him.

Zachariah Wolff, British, Commonwealth, and European welter-weight champion, is prematurely retired. As a lad, an emerging bruiser, he is in detention one dark autumn afternoon for fighting on school grounds and, determined not to be late for his sister whom he promised to collect from piano lessons, he wraps a canvas satchel strap round his right fist and excuses himself from detention by punching a hole through the first-floor window of the classroom and shinning down the wall. He remembers to tuck his thumb under his fingers and hit straight. When he is not only persistently late for his own music lessons, but begins to miss them entirely, staying on and on at the gym, Katya frees him from choir practice without a word or smile, whereupon he proceeds to win regional and national schoolboy boxing titles.

When Zach told Rachel of the impromptu sparring with All Souls, he talked with increasing fervour and expressive articulations, illuminated by his love of the game, and of gameness itself. She wanted to know how he got hurt. She wanted to ask him outright and could not think how without dispelling his mood, so she listened quietly, biding her time, watching his hands in air. *The hands, the beauty of his hands.*

"Tell me, then," she said finally, with deliberate insouciance. "About the eye, your stitches. And your hands. What happened?" she asked, noting him wince as he hoisted himself up on to the worktop and twisted the cap from a bottle of beer.

"Camden Town Brewery. *Camden Hells lager!* Oh yeah," he said, kicking his heels against the kitchen cabinets, his feet dangling like a child's. "Oh YEAH."

Rachel smiled then, noticing the bare threads at the toes of his socks, resisting the urge to drop the question entirely—*How did it happen?*—and move between his knees, and kiss his swollen orbital, and palpate the lengths of his thighs, enjoying the density of tissue there, the mar-vellous tautness of quadriceps, abductor. Instead, she turned her back to him to stand at the sink and scrub the shells of mussels.

"I can do that," he offered. "Let me do that."

"I don't think so," she replied. "Not with those hands."

"It's not so bad," Zach protested. "Bit of bruising, that's all."

"Tell me," repeated Rachel. "What did you do? What happened?"

"Sparred with Aubry!" he exclaimed. "A *barney*, Rach! Great fun!"

Izzy's gym, Whitechapel. Thomas "All Souls" Aubry, welterweight champion of Great Britain, and his camp. In which there is occasioned a bout of sparring.

"Well, Mr. Wolff?" invites Thomas.

"Coming up!" says Zach, flexing his fives, rolling his shoulders, tugging at his civvies, summoning his science.

"I'll keep clear of your head, man," promises Aubry, dancing, dancing. "Your nut, your nob! Knowledge-box! Whatever you call it! Your head."

Damn his nob, everyone in the game knows about it, the hit to the head that meant the end for Zach the welterweight and the indefinite suspension of his licence, consequence of a clot that nearly killed him, nearly blinded him, and which can flare up again, a possibility Rachel declares a blessing in NO disguise, an injunction against a life in the Prize Ring she can no longer countenance for him, though it was always his calling, Zach always destined for the ring, thanks to his speed and agility in the squared circle, and the Zachariah two-step as it is still known in some parts, and for his gameness, the well-timed violence, and reach, of course, his superior reach.

"Coming!" he tells Aubry, stripping off and pulling on a leather helmet, tapping and bouncing his feet off the floor from where he sits while All Souls Aubry's very own cutman, cornerman, wraps his hands for him, Isaac "Izzy" Sawyer being most adept at this operation, his wraps a work of art. Izzy well knows that Zach's head is not the only trouble, there are his hands, the fists prone to swelling and the knuckles to breaking, and he has forever been a bleeder also, his eyebrows splitting and puffing and forcing his eyes shut, leaking red. Zach's a bleeder all right.

Aubry forgets himself, throws a hook to Zach's head.

One clip is all it takes for the singing in Zach's ears to start, on the beat of his eardrum and the patter of three bones and the rush and spiral of notes in the labyrinth, and then the fiery toot on his Eustachian tube that causes his jaw to drop, perhaps for the release of it all, the chorus of voices piping, the familiar motet of his mighty fathers, his bold heredity of fighting men. Zach gapes for wind, seeing double now, and his jaw drops, and his hands too, opening him up to the blow on the button he never catches in time, because there is Aubry, there he is in duplicate, greater and greater, blue shifting Zach's way like Stephenson's Rocket, and when the machinery is so grand, so looming, how do you parry, how can you block?

"Sorry, man. You OK? You can fight! Damn, I was carried away, good fight! You're still a star, Zach! Need a hand, can you get up?"

"Not a problem!" says Zach, flat in the dust, arms akimbo, but grinning up at his new friend All Souls Aubry and at Isaac the cutman, Izzy all-knowing, with his ready sponge and permanent frown of long-seeing, tenacious custodian of boxing morality. Boxing *is* the noble art, and Izzy never diminished, never despairing, though he notes it wryly, the daily erosion of his sport by the crude machinations of the industry and the proliferation of organisations and titles, and fighters with skills inconspicuous in the extreme. No move surprises Isaac, and no man either, not even All Souls with his First in Natural Sciences to go with his welterweight crown, presently raining drops of perspiration upon Zachariah's stomach to splash and leap there, drops of glee and exertion and sheer supremacy in the ring. Flat on his back, Zach has a powerful awareness of his own scent, intense and private, a swirl of sweat and scalp and body oil he inhales, the vapours dissolving in his throat and mouth along with the trickle of blood, a dusky flavour of salt and metal from the split in his lip he probes with his tongue, sampling the *claret,* so to speak, the haemoglobin now spilling forth. Zach samples the claret, tasting the genes contained therein, of that great long line of fighting men.

"Not a problem!" Zach swears. "Good fight!" he agrees, exultant, merrily winking away the blood flowing from the cut in his brow while Izzy applies the sponge to his eyes and surmises on stitches, two or three neat ones, he adjudges, will do. Or maybe a butterfly; this boy's brows can't take much more. Wolff, he reflects, was always a natural. Shame about the injury. Crying shame. Now swab the decks and sew up that shiner, old man! Izzy be nimble, Izzy be quick.

"Yes, lad," nods Isaac. "Good fight!"

.　　.　　.

But not *today,* don't fight today, please, thinks Rachel, recalling the sight of Zach's fingers the morning after, wrapped round his bowl of coffee, the rawness of the knuckles and the bruises shining blue. Making the bed later, she brushed flecks of scarlet from the sheets, dust from the seam of tissue above his left eye, tight with neat stitches encrusted with blood. "Not today," she says aloud, glancing at the clock. *Please.* She gathers her things, mindful to pack her precious volume of Hogarth facsimiles she had promised to show her class, surprised to find a marker in the book at *The Four Stages of Cruelty.*

"There it is!" she exclaims, turning it over in her hands, the invitation to St. Petersburg for Mama's memorial with Lev's imperious note attached by golden paper clip, the words brisk: *You must make a decision. The flights must be booked. Come and see me.* Rachel marvels that she has mislaid the card surely three times so far yet she is not forgetful, never forgetful. She touches the embossed and elaborate lettering, reading the time and place and Katya's name and then her own beneath, in a fine handwritten script, out of time, elegance of an epoch past. And Zachariah's name is not there. Zachariah has no invitation.

Rachel feels a fluttering in her stomach and a ringing in her ears as she searches the room for a suitable spot, finally slipping the card and Lev's note under the blotter on her desk, wondering will she forget this hiding place too? She shuts her eyes a moment and summons imperatives of her own. Yes, you must make a decision. You must go and see Papa. And you must talk to Zach, you have to tell Zach. But first you must hurry. It is time for your boys.

TWO

RACHEL WALKS NORTH, negotiating the doldrums of a midweek Camden Market into Chalk Farm and beyond to Belsize Park and the school where she teaches a weekly class in art. Rachel instructs a group of waggish floppy-haired boys most of whom are so naturally skilled at cricket, they speak of *flight* and *direction, loft, swing* and *spin,* and perform mysteries of deception with a ball by a mere flick of the wrist, a touch of the fingertips, yet manipulation of a pencil will often defeat them. The pencil in hand is unwieldy as a tree trunk. Rachel is amused to note that deftness is rarely transcendent. It was so for Zach as a boy, is so for Zach as a man. Largely. *It all begins with the boy.* Everything begins with the boy. Rachel is very fond of her pupils. She loves to see this, the man emerging.

Rachel remembers the first time she saw him. She remembers the coming of Zachariah. It started out like a tale, another Russian tale.

In a certain land, in a certain kingdom, there lived a king and a queen and they had an only daughter who was only seven years of age, and such a beauty she was, no tongue can tell of nor pen describe.

When Aunt Natasha and Uncle Nikolai arrive in Chelsea to mind little Rachel, Lev hurries away to bring Katya home from hospital. The boy is lost, explains Nicky.

"Your mama has lost the baby."

l. And shall continue to do so. If the rest of the world wants to
nes together to make fire and speak in sign language, let them.
a adds. "The fish."

they are all seated again, over pike and pickled cabbage and
tato salad, Katya tells her husband she has changed her mind
see Tasha's boy again, and though Lev understands her very
he news is far from unexpected, he asks her pointedly, glancing
, "What boy?"

now which boy, the one at the home, Tasha's children's home."

he Coram Family. That home."

es," asserts Katya. "You are being silly. This is the family discus-
one you wanted. Stop it, Lev."

!" Lev persists. "I thought you had no time to give music les-
e charity homes. I'm sure Nicky told me so."

s not the point!" laughs Nicky. "She loves the children, can't
. It's quite the passion with her. Now listen to your wife. She
s to say."

ands, he circles the table pouring wine, touching Katya's neck
ses, clasping her there.

he says. "Is it the boy who was so good at the piano? Sad face."

," whispers Tasha. Melancholy.

now perfectly well not. The singer. Hands in pockets. Had a fit
r. Made me laugh. Him."

Hands-in-pockets. I remember."

he hair, lots of hair."

as the bones," adds Tasha.

s!" exclaims Nicky the osteopath. "That is my department."

ellous cheekbones," says Tasha. "Isn't that true, Katyenka?"

ow Lev remembers his name."

Lev nods. "Zygomatics. Zachariah."

t a name. He must be *foreign*!" laughs Nicky, squeezing Rachel's

Mama," she pipes. "I don't understand. Is he for the choir? I
your choir was just men. Men only. Not boys."

her," urges Lev softly. "Katya. It's time."

for the choir," explains Katya. "For the family. A brother for you.
r after all."

"Lost?" pipes Rachel, much distressed. "How lost? *Dyadya!*" Uncle! "It can't be lost!"

"No, no, little paws!" says Nicky. "A miscarriage. Spontaneous abortion."

"Nicky," says Tasha, in mild reproach.

"Oh, it's all right!" he exclaims. "Rachel understands. Miscarriage. It happens all the time. Nothing to worry about. Nothing at all."

"Yes," soothes Tasha. "It's true. *Ne boysya*, Rachel." Don't be afraid. "Come," she adds. "Let's sit and tell stories. Let's read. Sit," invites Tasha, stroking the seat of the deep feather pad of the sofa, a place Rachel loves to nestle, the silken cotton cooling in summer, forbidding in winter, a repeating pattern known to her in every detail, a scene of men and hounds with birds and deer amongst the trees against a coloured field of hunter green, and of gold and hues of darkest red. All forests, Rachel learns, are dark and full of creatures, full of animals and men.

"One day," announces Rachel, "I shall have a pair of trousers coloured exactly this very shade of hunter green. I cannot say why, but I know it."

Nicky says, "It is quite right to respect the things one is absolutely sure of. This is fate. So much else is mystery, little red cheeks. Good girl!"

"In a certain land," begins Tasha, "in a certain kingdom . . ."

A year later, there is another miscarriage, another lost boy, and then an operation and Rachel is in a muddle. Another *missed carriage,* she hears, conjuring a vision of Mama in a typical dash from the house, hurrying for trains to other cities where she will conduct music and choirs. Rachel sees Katya on a railway platform, suitcase and baton box in hand, but Mama is too late, the train hurtles by, screaming through the arches, a great train of missed carriages. Rachel's night-time wish is granted then, that though Katya has left her once again, she must return home as quickly. She has missed her carriage.

"Mama," Rachel whispers into the night bedroom air, "Mama, hurry home!"

Ekaterina Wolff, née Byelova, has two miscarriages, both boys. She loses two babies and then, as a precaution, her womb—to science, Lev cajoles cheerfully, to science! Science is projection and precaution, cause and conjecture!

"Birth," he remarks sometime later over a family dinner, "is a game of chance."

"I see," responds Katya archly. "So is it fate, then, barrenness? First Tasha, then myself? Though Tasha has never been . . ." Katya adds hesitantly, pausing to glance at her young daughter.

"Fertile," says Aunt Tasha, smiling.

"It's all right," insists Lev. "Rachel is very sophisticated, Katyenka. A woman of science. We talk it all over, don't we, little red cheeks? And *Dyadya* too. Uncle Nicky too. He has taught you all the terms of gross anatomy, hasn't he? Remarkable!"

"And microscopic anatomy," says Rachel. "He teaches me musculature. And tissues and organs and vessels! Blood!"

"Indeed!" smiles Lev.

"I do, I do. *Eto pravda!*" It's the truth. "A toast!" exclaims Nicky. "To fate and science and anatomy and—I don't know—vodka and herrings."

"And music?" suggests Tasha.

"Of course music! My goodness. And to all five of us. All five! *Vashe zdorov'ye!*" Cheers! "To the five of us."

"Six of us. Soon we'll be six," notes Katya. "Very soon. Six."

"Dendritic," says Lev with pleasure. "A tree, frost, Rachel. Sixfold symmetry! *On the Six-Cornered Snowflake.* Kepler, 1611."

"Enough now, Lev," scolds Katya.

"Rachel is my little pupil," Lev continues. "Aren't you?" he asks.

"Yes, Papa. I really am," confirms Rachel, frowning slightly over soup, momentarily unsure of sixfold symmetry. Rachel battles with soup, endeavouring to eat it as Mama and Tasha do, tipping the platter deftly away from the body instead of towards it, a perilous task. Soup in lap, it seems, would be so much less awful than soup across mahogany table, rushing forth like a wave. A wave, which is a . . . Papa says a wave is a . . . *dynamical system.* Is that right? But sixfold symmetry . . .

"And it is fateful, my love," resumes Lev. "I think so. Why not? Fateful and absolutely all right," he adds with a smile.

"*Why not?*" Katya echoes. "Why not? That's hardly scientific."

"Why six?" queries Rachel, tucking her dark hair behind an ear.

"It is perfectly scientific," Lev protests, rising to draw the heavy dining room curtains against the streetlamp light, reducing it to a glow that bleeds amber round the edges and between the panels of plum brocade.

Lev turns back into the room but stays
observe the new play of light, the chan
upon mahogany and bold shadows acros
planes of Katya's timeless face. *Oh my wi*

Rachel struggles with the last of her b
soup spoon too wide and deep, quite lik
the waves.

"Leave it," commands Katya, touchi
"Don't play with food."

"Mama! I wasn't . . ."

"Just leave it," she repeats. "You've fin
Rachel looks for her father at the win
distance between them, nervous of her

"What are you doing, Lev?" deman
down."

"Katyusha," Nicky scoffs. "Always so

"I'm not cross. All this fidgeting and
hate it. And I'm trying to talk to you, Le

"I'll just bring the fish, my dove, and t

"I don't think 'dove' is quite so apt an
Tasha, disarming her sister who turns sl
mouth to speak, stopping short. Katya d
with mirth. She extends a hand for Nata
of alchemy, Nicky calls it. *You should le*
tells her. *There would be no wars, no strife!*

"Let me help, Papa!" says Rachel, leap
then Tasha's. "I want to."

"Careful," warns Katya. "You'll drop

"Katyenka!" Tasha scolds.

"I won't, Mama! I'm very careful."

"Shan't. I think 'shan't' is better."

Nicky laughs, taking the bowls from

"But, Mama. That sounds funny. I say
funny. Foreign. They say so. It's old-fashi

"That's ridiculous," scoffs Lev. "It's
is . . ."

"Well, we are a little foreign," says K

"What do you think, little paws?" asks Uncle Nicky.

"What do you think?" mimics Katya. "I am sorry, but this is not a committee! Lev! I want this to stop! Let me handle it. Nicky! *Ostanovis'!* Stop! You'll turn her into a monster, a little tsarina. She's a child."

"You stop, Katya," commands her sister, rising from the table. "Enough."

Rachel's eyes sting. She pictures favourite things to quell the tears. Sharpened pencils, she thinks. Fresh sheets of paper. Uncle Nicky's apple cake and Aunt Tasha's stories, and blackbirds and trees and dried apricots dipped in chocolate. New shoes! Yes, and walks with Papa in Richmond Park and how he warms her hands on his beard which is like fur, animal. She thinks of colours, of forest green and dark red and how well they go together and how *krasniy* is Russian for 'red' and for 'beautiful,' too. It means red and beautiful, it means both things.

"I'm nine, Mama," she says in a small, strangled voice. "Quite quite grown up."

"Come here, little one," says Katya. "Aren't I the monster tonight? A Baba Yaga! Oh dear. Very tired today. You will like this boy. A brother for you, a brother after all. They call him Zachariah," she laughs. "Which is really rather odd. Really rather un-English. So there. We'll be happy."

"Will *Tyotya* have a boy, too? Shouldn't she adopt a boy, too?"

Natasha smiles.

"What," asks Katya, "does Papa always say? About what people should or should not do?"

"I don't know," replies Rachel. "I can't remember everything. There is so much! I can't remember."

"Of course you can," prompts her father. "About fate. The game of chance."

"This is too hard, Papa!"

"*Bozhe moy!*" snaps Nicky. My god! "Help her. And let's go into the other room for a drink."

"Everyone," recites Tasha. "Everyone has—"

"Oh, I know it now," exclaims Rachel. "Everyone has a part and a destiny!"

"Yes," says Aunt Tasha. "And I am an aunt, your *tyotya*. And your mother is a mother, that's how it is," she concludes.

"It's quite true." Katya nods, pinching the napkin from her lap between fingers and thumb and shaking it thrice to the right before laying it in a neat cone shape of folds by the side of her plate. "I am a mother and I want this boy. Nothing I can do," she adds, rising from her place, pushing her chair in at the table.

"Mama, where are you going?"

"To the living room, silly," Nicky pronounces. "The pack of us! Come, little red cheeks. Come," he says, a bottle in one hand and Rachel's paw in the other.

In the living room, Katya announces that she expects to be home for the best part of a year, that she is refusing all outside engagements and has accepted the offer of *Eugene Onegin*. A whole new production, she says. In London. She will be home for a year, she repeats, giggling suddenly.

"What is it?" asks Tasha.

"A meeting with the board," her sister explains. "Yesterday. And one of the trustees wished us every success and there was a small toast, you know, and he said—I told Lev about it," she says, spluttering. "I can't even . . ."

Lev raises his own glass and stands up from the sofa, "To Eugene ON-e-gin!" he exclaims, pronouncing the "g" in Onegin with a "j" sound.

"I don't see what's so funny," protests Nicky.

"It sounded like 'on the gin,' Nicky! That's all. And they want to cast that pest Meinhardt and, apart from everything else, he drinks like a fish! And I looked at Anders—sets and costume, Nicky; we've worked together many times—Anders made his eyes wide and we were off. Hysteria! It was silly," says Katya. "Never mind. But really! On the gin!"

"Oh my goodness," says Tasha. "*Boris Godunov.* Remember?"

"Oh Lord, I do!" says Nicky. "You two were terrible. Lev? Were you there? No. I think not."

"No, thank the stars, I was not! But I heard about it all right."

"The pair of them!" Nicky bellows. "Doubling over and squeaking. We were in house seats!"

"It was Tasha's fault," says Katya.

"Well, he was poor, wasn't he? That Godunov."

"Boris isn't really *gud enuff. You* whispered it, Tasha! It was awful!"

Rachel watches them, her family. She sits cross-legged on the Sarouk rug, tracing the pattern of tendrils and leaves and smiling wide. The laughter makes her smile, it makes her innards flutter. And Mama will be home for a year, she tells herself. The best part of a year! We'll be happy, she said. We'll be so happy when that boy comes.

There are times today when Rachel looks at Zach and sees an effusion, she sees him in colours of yellow and blue, sun and sky. She sees the yellow crew-neck jumper and blue jeans the boy of eight years old appeared in the day he came to Chelsea from the Coram Family via the two or three previous fosterers who returned him there, defeated, pronouncing him uncommunicative and maladroit in the extreme, *animal*, said one; unruly. So why *this* boy? For Katya the fractious? Of all orphan boys in the world, why him? Of all potential mothers, why Katya? What did she see? *Everyone has a part and a destiny.* Rachel remembers the yellow jumper the boy rarely removed, even after the family shopping spree for a new wardrobe at Harrods followed by lunch in a restaurant with napkins large as small tablecloths, and heavy cutlery and wine for Katya and Lev and a pervasive daunting hush. Zach had never been to a restaurant before and chose spaghetti, because he knew what it was. He ate it with knife and fork.

On the day he arrived in Chelsea, he stopped in the vestibule to slip his feet from lace-ups without undoing the bows, removing his shoes with institutional efficiency, left hand still held in Katya's right. Rachel sees that boy still, blue and yellow. Sky and sun.

There are brief formalities in the entrance after which Katya asks Rachel to show the boy his room, and Rachel hesitates a moment before setting off and turns on the fourth step to face her parents quizzically, because neither Lev nor Katya is following.

"We'll be up in a minute," states Katya, speaking from a particular stillness, in sudden recognition of a dream made real, a dream annulled, so she had thought, by long words of the womb—"endometriosis," "hyperplasia"—and now made true, this vision of a boy on a staircase answering to his name, coming to her call. *My son.* She raises one arm slightly in front of Lev at her side, in gentle impediment. Not yet. Wait here. Let me *see*. This was always preordained.

Katya and Lev watch with interest from the foot of the stairwell as

Rachel leads the way past the gallery of Russian eminences, a wall of poets and composers, Pushkin, Lermontov and Gogol, Cui, Prokofiev and Taneyev, and, on the first landing, commanding the ascent, a large canvas of Alexander I, Tsar of All the Russias, in a reproduction of the portrait by François Pascal Simon that Lev hauled home from an antiquarian's in Kensington one high-spirited afternoon after too many drinks with Uncle Nicky.

"Your Imperial Majesty!" chants Rachel in Russian, bobbing briefly in front of the portrait, according to family custom.

Katya smiles. What must the boy be thinking? she wonders. What a queer world this must be! Our Little Russia. Forbidding, perhaps. Family customs are so very excluding. But he shall be all right; he is strong. *He has the cheekbones,* said Tasha. Yes, he does.

"Go," orders Katya. "Show him the way."

"Come!" invites Rachel, motioning to the boy encouragingly, aware of the darkness in his face.

Zachariah follows in silence. He stands in the doorway, appraising the room like a well-versed traveller, rucksack over one shoulder. These are the first moments they ever spend alone.

"Who else is in here?" he asks.

"What do you mean? It's your room," answers Rachel. "For you. Plus there's only one bed, silly."

Whereupon the boy empties his rucksack onto the duvet, spilling his scanty kit: two pairs of pants, two pairs of socks, pyjamas, a second pair of jeans, cheap school flannels and two once-white shirts, a laminated sponge-bag, a pencil case, two red tennis balls and three paperback Puffins. He piles the books on the bedside table.

"Is that your only pully? The one you're wearing?" Rachel wonders aloud. "That is," she adds, embarrassed, "are these all your things? All?"

"I might have left some stuff behind," he mutters. "I'm not sure. By accident maybe. I don't need them. It's all right, isn't it?"

"Oh yes!" she says, with enthusiasm. "Of course it is. And I also have that book. *Robinson Crusoe.*"

"The full title is better. You have to say the full title, *The Life and Strange Surprizing Adventures of Robinson Crusoe of York, Mariner.* Well, that's not exactly the whole title, but the most important part."

"I see," she says. "I didn't know. I suppose everyone uses the short version. The long one is better. I agree," she nods. "And *The Eagle of the*

Ninth. Rosemary Sutcliff. I like her very much. That book, especially. It's very good."

"It's not for girls," he bristles, clearly expecting a fight.

"I didn't know that," says Rachel quite simply. "Well. I liked it anyway. You can come and see my books if you like, do you want to? *Smith*. By Leon Garfield. Now I really don't know *that* one! Is it good?"

"It's not . . ." begins the boy, hesitant now. "Here," he says, plucking it from the pile and thrusting the book her way. "Borrow it."

"Oh thank you," Rachel says merrily. "I'll read it next."

Zachariah frowns, the heavy dark curls partially masking his gaze.

"You don't have to," he argues. "Read it next."

"I want to, though," she smiles. "I will. Shall, I mean," she adds, examining the jacket with keen anticipation.

The boy stares at her, perplexed and suspicious. Though he is only eight, two faint creases mark his forehead between the brows, running upwards from the bridge of his Roman nose.

"Shall I show you the rest? We can see the other rooms, all my places, the whole house and the garden."

"Now?" he asks, shuffling his feet. "I'll need my shoes."

"I think now would be good, yes. We can start outdoors, go round the garden then come in and do all of down below and work our way up, right to the attic. I love the attic. It's dusty, but great fun, and there's a window in the roof! I'll show you everything, then you won't get lost."

"Won't," he asserts gruffly.

"Won't what?" says Rachel in worried tones. "Come with me?"

"Get lost," he explains. "Won't get lost."

"Oh I see!" she says, noting how he stuffs his hands into pockets and locks his elbows, so that shoulders almost meet his flame-red ears.

"Because I'm not—stupid," he adds, scowling.

"No," whispers Rachel, alarmed. "I never . . . Oh dear!"

"It's all right now," the boy announces. "We can be friends now."

"Yes," agrees Rachel, after brief consideration. "I think so too," she says, marvelling at him, wondering just how it must feel to be such a boy and so full of decision and hands-in-pockets and grown-up frowns on the face. To have a thatch of wavy hair and sport a rough yellow jumper—a veritable seaman's guernsey—and carry all one's things in a sack. How fierce he is! How free, she supposes, to be such a boy!

.　　　.　　　.

In Zachariah's third week, Rachel passes the door of his room and watches him mend a seam of the yellow guernsey, stapling the frayed edges and loosened seams with the stapler from Papa's desk.

"Hallo!" she calls. "What are you doing?"

"I asked first," he replies, clutching the stapler like a thief. "Before I took it."

"To your jumper, I mean. It's all torn. Why don't you wear one of the new ones? You have new clothes now. Don't you like them?"

"Yes. They're good. It's just . . . I'm messy and dirty. They'll get dirty. I'll be in trouble."

"No, Zachariah," says Rachel, kneeling on the floor. "You won't! You really won't," she insists, reaching for the old rocking horse, nudging it into rhythm. "I love this horse," she says. "It's very old, you know."

"I like it, too," he says. "I like the wood. Oak."

"Nearly a hundred years old, I believe. Most of the paint has come off, just worn away. How can you tell?"

"What?" he asks distractedly, searching under the bed for his well-travelled rucksack. "Tell what?"

"Oak," she states, watching him spread the raggedy yellow jumper on the floor and lay the sleeves across the chest, as if in penitence for itself. He folds the sorry garment in two, horizontally, waist to neck, before rolling it into a ball from the side seam, frowning as he goes. He has clearly done this before.

"You said 'oak.' How can you tell?"

"Saw a book," he replies tersely, packing the jumper away. "About wood."

"Oh. You must be quite interested in wood to read a whole book about it!"

"What's wrong with that?" he demands, a stone in his throat.

"Nothing!" she exclaims. "I'm interested in lots of things. History, for instance. Oh. And science, of course. Science is terribly important. But just think!" she pipes, touching the withers of the old rocking horse. "How many children sat up here! When I was very small, about four, and rode the horse every day, I used to imagine I was a child in history. I wondered—"

"History is battles," he scolds. "Battles and wars. Not old toys and children. It's battles and wars. And kings and dates. And inventions. The steam engine! Things like that," he insists, flushing crimson at his unaccustomed volubility.

"Stephenson's Rocket," Rachel offers gamely. "But you don't have to be so cross," she adds. "You sound so cross."

The boy hangs his head, pulls angrily on his burning left ear, and reaches out for the horse. He strokes a foreleg and picks absently at ageing paint, stopping short with alarm at the sight of falling flakes, a small shower of enamel and gesso.

"Hell," he breathes, swiping the rug, dispersing ancient flecks.

"It happens all the time," Rachel says.

"I barely touched it," pleads the boy.

"It doesn't matter," she confirms.

"Are you sure?"

"*Dyadya*—Uncle Nicky—says that usually the only thing wrong with old things is that they're old! That's funny, isn't it? I had homework on aqueducts, you see, because we were on Ancient Rome at school, and Nicky said aqueducts are a great wonder and worked brilliantly for centuries and centuries and the only thing wrong with them is age! Even very great things, he meant, can't last forever. Or beautiful things, I suppose. Those too. Things that don't really need replacing except because they fall apart. It was the way he put it, though. *Dyadya* is funny!"

"*Dyadya*," he echoes.

"Yes," she says encouragingly. "*Dyadya*—uncle."

"Your house is full of old things."

"Is it?" muses Rachel. "Perhaps it is. The pictures and furniture and—"

"That big silver thing," he adds. "With the tap."

"Samovar," she states. "Yes. That *is* old!"

"When's it for? Does it work?"

"Well," she explains, "it's for people dropping in, you know, lots of friends. And family. You have to have tea always ready. It's traditional."

"Are there any more?"

"More what?" asks Rachel.

"People," the boy murmurs. "In your family."

"Oh no!" she replies gaily. "There's only us, really. Mama and Papa, *Tyotya* and *Dyadya*. And me, of course. And now you. You're in our family now."

"OK," he nods.

The boy stares at the rug, his mouth tight and twitching. He picks up the most salient of the fallen paint chips and crushes it between finger and thumb.

"Don't be afraid, Zachariah. *Ne boysya.*"

"I'm Zach. I'm not afraid. Call me Zach. For short. Say that again."

"Zach."

"No. The other thing."

"*Ne boysya*," says Rachel. "It means don't be afraid."

"*Ne boysya*," he repeats, pitch-perfect.

Zach takes to Russian like a true-born.

The Hall, Belsize Park, North London. Senior School Art Room.

"See you next week, boys!" says Rachel, sweeping her things from the desk into a satchel, brushing words from the board—*perspective, foreshortening, chiaroscuro*—replacing the eraser with a smile, enjoying its timelessness, the wooden back and felt bottom, striped skunk white, just as it ever was, just as she remembers. There is a high sheer light this late spring day, a London spectacular! Rachel will walk on, she decides. To Covent Garden, yes. She will buy cheese for the weekend, and Covent Garden things. Zachariah likes cheese very much. Zach is partial to the fermented, to cheese and bread and pickles, yoghourt, beer, wine and vodka, his appetite decidedly zymological. And Russian.

"Miss Wolff?"

"James."

"Well . . . I hate to remind you, Miss Wolff," begins the boy, his tone ironic, "but, ah, homework?" he asks, exciting jeers and a light rain of projectiles upon his head, of kneadable art rubbers and crimps of paper, friendly fire.

"Thank you, James," replies Rachel. "We ALL thank you."

"Oh yes!" says Reed with relish. "We'll be sure to thank him heartily after class. One by one," he adds menacingly, inciting a round of gentlemanly desk-thumping, laughter and hear-hears.

Rachel smiles, enjoying the merriment. Girls never really do this, she thinks. Never so plainly. Joshing, chaff and banter. She touches an index to her lips and the din abates very quickly, the boys attentive. Her boys.

"So let's see," she continues. "Draw for me—a London scene. Try to draw from life, not photographs. If possible. Work with the chalks and pastels, and the graphite pencils. Draw anything you fancy, a façade, a bridge, the river. A tree, the London plane. A window, a balcony, wall. I don't know. Railings, gates, a paving stone, cobbles."

"A *paving* stone, Miss Wolff?" exclaims Burgess-Webb to ironic titters and murmuring. *A murmuration of starlings.*

"Yes!" replies Rachel. "Why not? A paving stone. Not easy to draw. Draw with imagination! Picture all the feet that walked those stones . . ."

London stock, she recites to herself. Yellows. York and Portland stone. All the old stones, how she loves the old stones!

"Or a bird," she says. "A bird in the city. Gull, pigeon, blackbird, robin, crow. On a rooftop, an aerial, draw that for me."

Whenever home and awaiting Zach, Rachel will listen for her evening blackbird, her Camden Town rooftop bird across the close, always perched on the same aerial, that urban weathervane, his body outlined sharply, stark against the dusk. Against the *darky*. Her nerve cells vibrate to the clarion sound, blackbird piping the hour, calling the streets. Zachariah is coming, Zachariah is coming!

"Urban fox?" queries Clayton. "How's that?"

"HOWZAT?" cries Reed, leaping out of his seat, tossing up an imaginary ball. "Apologies, Miss Wolff. Cricket fever. It's the season, you know."

"I quite understand," says Rachel, nodding gravely, before turning to Clayton. "Of course a fox. Absolutely," says Rachel. "We have so many in town."

"Rat, then," suggests another. "Many of those about too."

"Bit of a *pest* problem at home, Baines?" chides Farquhar.

"Ha ha, hilarious," drawls Baines.

"Any idea," Rachel interposes, "how many rats there are in London? How many per head?"

"It depends," mumbles François, averting his eyes the moment Rachel's meet his. François is half French. He is dashing and terse.

"Indeed, it does. On many things: rubbish, building works, weather. And I doubt they're all living at Baines's house."

"They're super-smart, you know, FARQUHAR," says Baines with a leer. "Plus, as it *happens*," he adds, "my brother has one for a pet. They make excellent pets!" he insists over the instant thunder of cheerful desk-banging.

"Boys!" calls Rachel, slinging her satchel over a shoulder. "Surprise me, then. And see you next week!"

Rachel walks.

Rachel has always been a walker, the child lighting out, at first, for the far reaches of the Chelsea garden, seeing the world as a round already, a wheel indeed, the family home its hub and every line of sight, a spoke. I spy with my little eye! Little Rachel walked her world and mapped it also, skirting the perimeter of the garden, beating the bounds. She took to carrying a notebook for the recording of features of scale, topography and landmark, and seasonal variations. A landscape, she observed, changes in time. She drew trees in all the stages of growth, dormant, burgeoning, full-blown, and marvelled at the great copper beech, deciduous, though it will not let go of its leaves. Searching Papa's encyclopaedia, she discovered there is a name for such tenacity in the *Fagus sylvatica purpurea*. It is marcescence. Although the tree is deciduous, the leaves are likely to stay on throughout the winter. This is known as marcescence. Rachel watched the tree from her bedroom window, listened to its angry rustling on windy nights.

"O copper beech," she wondered, "why must you hang on quite so tightly? You'll have new leaves next year! Do you feel the cold? Is that why?"

Rachel filled her map with drawings and icons, here the copper beech, there the cherry; here a blackbird nest, a tree stump, rose bed, declivity, incline. She touched the old stones of the high-walled garden and imagined a time when there were few such walls and England was all open field.

In her teenaged years, Rachel began to map the city, her world expanding. She walked alone, occasionally with Zach. True walking, she explained, is a solitary pursuit. On certain holiday mornings in summer, she would light out for the horizon, intent on walking there, to the place where sky meets ground. She noted how weather clothed and unclothed the city, how the streets were altered by the days and months.

A landscape changes in time.

. . .

Rachel walks.

At the convergence in Covent Garden they call Seven Dials, a Catherine-wheel-shaped spray of triangular plots bound by seven streets with a monument for a pin, Rachel smiles. The Sundial Pillar has six faces, the style of which acts as seventh, a gnomon. The spot has a playground feel. Here is a child's cartography, visionary, as was its planner in 1690, Thomas Neale, yet his dream of form and grace, urbanity and wealth, was so very quickly perverted, Seven Dials within St. Giles, soon a byword for criminality and destitution, the Sundial Pillar, its meeting point. Hopes are so well constructed, so monstrously dashed! See it now, though, Mr. Neale! See it now in its modish glory, your earthly dream come true at last.

Rachel steps in to Shorts Gardens and on to the Dairy in Neal's Yard with its ramparts of cheese wheels and cheerful aproned and caparisoned staff proffering tasters on the ends of knives and listing the names of cheeses, a roll call. Shropshire Blue! Lincolnshire Poacher! Stinking Bishop, Waterloo. The cheese names of England have a pugnacious sound, ringing, to Rachel, like the nicknames of Regency boxers, the great bruisers of England. Here they all come, the "Tipton Slasher," "Bath Butcher," "Lancashire Giant" and "Brighton Bill," from Bristol and Thorpe, Derby and York, Baunton, Redditch, Hinckley and Thame! Here they all *broom*, to London, where purses are raised and enthusiasts gather. The *Fancy*. The cheese names and place names of England have a pugilistic sound!

A Correct Statement, muses Rachel, *of the Famous Battle between Lincolnshire Poacher and Shropshire Blue! For One Hundred Guineas a side, at Seven Dials, Covent Garden, London.*

Rachel laughs.

Heading north with her bag of cheese, Rachel skirts St. Giles where the most infamous of rookeries once stood—the *back slums,* she hears Zach say, the *stews*! Here it stood, she reminds herself, with a tingling in her feet, the Rookery itself. How many rats ran here? How many per head? Rachel stands still a moment, feeling the old stones through her soles. She presses on, veering right at the top of Endell Street just as a crusty rattles by, huge in his greatcoat and unseasonal layers, a glaring presence against such a backdrop. The man gnaws a little wildly at a piece of fried chicken and Rachel notes the trail of rubbish in his wake, freshly disturbed, with a carton of takeaway chicken in prominence, a box of gristle and bone.

Bone-grubber, cinder-sifter.

In High Holborn, Rachel bears left, up Museum Street to Great Russell and pauses at the gates of the British Museum, the passage masked by the billows of a frankfurter van, its theatrical plumes of grease, seductive and repelling, a conjuror's smokescreen, a London particular! She reads her watch. Two hours or so until Zach is due home. So into the yard she goes.

This is Rachel's fourth visit to the exhibition, *"London 1753."* She returns and returns, entranced by the vision of Hogarth in his scenes of St. Giles, teeming pictures he calls *Gin Lane* and *The First Stage of Cruelty.*

Gin Lane. In the parish of St. Giles, not counting the twopenny houses where the destitute lodge, and the footpads and whores, gin is sold from one in four dwellings. One in four. Staring into the picture, Rachel is dizzied by crazy drunks and pestiferous infants, by leering pawnbroker, undertaker and distiller, by the hanging corpse and crumbling edifice, the gin-swilling mother and charity girls, and, in the lower right corner, a cadaverous figure she can barely countenance—a starving man and his dog, a blind balladeer with his dog. *Gin Lane* bursts into life, the figures articulated for Rachel, before her very eyes, a penny in the slot automata. A museum amusement.

Papa! Is this not a dynamic system? Chaotic?

Rachel thinks so. And the blind singer and dog, balladeer and dog, this hurts Rachel the most, somehow the most! Why? She cannot think why.

Rachel looks around for a seat; she must sit. There is a paucity of seating, as if the expectation of visitors to the exhibition were rather humble. This is no place to linger. St. Giles, Gin Lane . . . Oh! Rachel stops. *Tyotya!* Tasha, Aunt Natasha. Is it you? It's you I see. The blind balladeer with dog. Oh *Tyotya.* It's you.

Rachel dips her head, stares at the floor.

·　　·　　·

Tasha's blindness.

Nearly a year to the day after Uncle Nicky dies, Katya receives an apologetic summons from Natasha, who, she learns, has spent an inordinate amount of time fumbling with the digits on the telephone handset before ringing her younger sister successfully. And she knows the Chelsea number by heart. Tasha summons her sister because she needs to see a specialist and is unable to read her address book or search the directory, or ring enquiries and write down the instructions. Tasha's world has dimmed very suddenly.

Rachel recalls the subsequent hurtling in taxis to and from Tasha's home and on to Harley Street and back to the Wolffs' in Chelsea where they hope Tasha will rest after the brutish injections to her eyes, and other such terrible intrusions. Tasha does not respond well to the treatments intended to halt the strong probability of total occlusion, and a teenaged Rachel is shocked to the core one afternoon by the apprehension of blood-red tears flowing from her aunt's luminous eyes, flowing from behind what *Tyotya* calls her "smoked glasses." *Lunettes fumées.*

Lev takes Tasha's arm one late afternoon, strolling her up and down the garden with the children in tow, distracting her with spoffish chatter in the greenhouse and guiding her along the borders to scent his prized Old Garden roses: Damask, Bourbon and Musk. Zach is taciturn and conflicted, kicking at stones. He is much attached to Natasha, his music teacher at the Coram Family and the kindest person he had ever encountered and now, magically, his aunt.

"I cannot quite see them," remarks Tasha gamely, "but I can smell!"

Passing an open doorway that evening, Rachel and Zachariah observe her listening like a bird to the room tone to ascertain she is alone before approaching the Blüthner grand piano and sounding the keys with unnatural trepidation and strangeness. This time she drops regular tears, tears of profound despair, and Zach's ensuing rage knows no bounds.

Only Rachel can stop him from attacking the Blüthner with hammer and chisel, wrestling him ineffectually, pleading with him to down tools and surrender, which he does, not before swiping at her accidentally with one wild arm and bruising her nasal bone so that it throbs for days thereafter with a persistent ache.

Zach is abject and Lev's fury awful and quiet.

"*Ty golovorez i vandal,*" he begins. You are a thug and a vandal. "If you do anything like this ever again, you will leave and not come back. I will stop your school fees. You will go into trade. I don't understand you. There are disconnections in your brain and it disturbs me infinitely. Now please get out while we dine. This is a civilised house. A civilised family. *Tsivilizovannyi.*" Civilised.

"Thank you, Lev," snaps Katya. "That's enough."

"*Ubiraytes,*" Lev commands the boy. Go now. "And *you* stay," he adds, as a stricken Rachel rises from her seat. "Rachel. Stay."

Before Zach can exit, Tasha stops his way, reaching for his fists and uncurling his fingers, clasping them in her own.

"*Sladkiy mal'chik,*" she says. Sweet boy. "Feel here. Here," she insists, pressing his hands to her temples. "There is music in *here*. Music and singing. Nothing can change this. *Ne boysya, Zachashka.*" Don't be afraid.

Lev arranges for Zach to spend the rest of that summer in Germany working the family vineyard of a colleague at the University. There is a terrible summer storm the evening before he is due to depart and Rachel knows just where to find him as the thunder grows louder and the peals more frequent. London storms are peculiar in their brevity and intensity, descending the atmosphere to catch in the Georgian and early Victorian squares of Chelsea and knock against the Yellow Stocks and Staffordshire Blues, and batter the rooftops, sounding a different tune on Welsh clay, on lead and slate, and rattling the windows in their sashes before sweeping the river and the bridges across it, the Chelsea, Albert and Battersea, in search of open space.

"Zach?" calls Rachel from beneath the attic door. "Are you there?"

Zach lifts the hatch by way of response, lowers the attic stairs.

"Remember," begins Rachel, settling in the dust amongst the handsome steamer trunks and worn leather suitcases, the empty picture frames and wooden packing crates and sagging cardboard boxes filled with sheet music and scientific papers and mouse droppings. "Remember the first time I found you here?"

Zach frowns.

"There was a storm and I looked and looked for you all over the house and garden and then I heard the hatch shift in the hall ceiling and you calling my name and when I asked if we were allowed up there, did we need permission—"

"I said 'We don't need permission for everything.'"

"You do remember," says Rachel, brushing cobweb from her face.

"Spider webs give me the chills," she adds. "It's ghostly. A ghost touching my face. Ghostly-ghastly. I hate it."

Zach reaches across very suddenly to touch her face with both hands, running his thumbs across her fine dark eyebrows and his palms down her cheeks, surprising them both.

"Cobweb," he says, retracting his hands and folding his arms, clamping his fingers tight against his ribs. "There were strands floating," he mumbles.

"Oh," says Rachel, colouring slightly and rubbing her face vigorously to disguise it. "Is it all gone now?" she demands matter-of-factly. "Quite gone?"

"Yeah," he replies, staring.

When the rain begins to clatter the tiles above their heads, she remarks, "I always felt the rain sounded like horses' hooves, the pitch of battle, hooves thundering and musket and rifle shot. Apparently the din of small arms was tremendous, even louder than cannon. I always thought, here I am, fallen from my horse in the Battle of Borodino, and gunshot and canisters exploding all round me!"

"It does sound a bit like that," Zach allows. "You used to shiver. You were a bit scared. You sat super-close to me. Because you were scared."

"It was the sound, you see," explains Rachel. "It's very—oh, I wish you weren't going!" blurts Rachel. "I hate that too! Cobwebs and Germany and you not coming to France—we always have the sea and France for our holidays. And Tasha says she's not coming now, because you're not coming. And *Dyadya* is dead and *Tyotya* is blind and Mama's so cross and Papa is horrid and I hate all of it! Everything's ruined!"

"Only for August. Maybe September," he says with boyish decision. "Might stay on for some of the harvest. Start school a bit late. Don't cry. I'll write letters."

"You won't!"

"I will. Shall. Which is it, Rach? Fuck. Stop crying."

"What if *I* had tried to wreck the piano? Would he have sent me to Germany?"

"You don't wreck things. You're good. And no, he wouldn't. He'd never send you away for anything," Zach replies without rancour.

"Why didn't Mama stop him? Sending you away. I don't understand!"

"Oh wow! Listen to that! Storm right above our house now. Right above our heads. Come on!" he urges, sliding closer to her, the rivets of his jeans scraping against the old boards. He raises an arm to shoulder height, according to custom, the arm crooked softly at the elbow, a spreading wing.

Rachel takes her place there, sharply aware of change in him, a thickening of tissue and muscle, a new weight and density to the lattice of tissue across his chest and flanks, to his triceps and biceps, even to the scent he emits. When did this happen? How could she not see? Seemingly sudden change!

—*Rachel, what is seemingly sudden change?*

—*Catastrophe, Papa. Bifurcation, catastrophe.*

Rachel's eyelids flicker. The side of her face closest to Zachariah and the place where his fingers clasp her elbow tingle with a rare sensitivity.

"You're all stiff!" he protests. "Don't think about battles! Borodino, Waterloo. Don't."

"What should I think then? I don't know what to think," she complains.

"Just think about *rain*, Rach. Sometimes you just have to think about rain."

Rachel lifts her head. She looks at the drawing again, at *Gin Lane* and the blind balladeer, recalling how Tasha was too stoic and gay in the aftermath of loss, of Nicky and sightedness. What Natasha gained in fortitude, overtly at least, her younger sister lost. To begin with, Nikolai's death unseated them all. He was their little father, a *bogatyr*—man of power! And when Tasha was struck blind, Katya assumed it as an infirmity of her own. She never knew how far she depended on Nicky, how far she needed Tasha to see. Why does knowledge come so late, so uselessly? The summer of Tasha's blindness changed her sister forever, Katya increasingly brittle, increasingly stark of mood, attenuated in elegant shape. She fell ill, succumbing to infection that first autumn, a bronchitis that quickly turned to pneumonia in the face of her intransigence. Katya would not rest; she must work, she must work without pause. When finally bedridden, she was visited by Lev's friend Dr. Tombs, a cheerful pulmonologist with a name that sent Rachel and Zach into fits of nervous mirth, Zach appearing in Rachel's doorway one night, holding a curved paring knife taped to a broomstick.

"Who am I?" he asked in lugubrious tones.

"I haven't the slightest idea!" cried Rachel, collapsing in giggles.

"I am Dr. Tombs!" moaned Zach, eyes wide.

In truth, they were all frightened that summer, frightened and restive, Zach in particular, bringing Russian tisanes to Katya's bedside to gabble about his German exile or his classes at school, Zach uncharacteristically voluble, and sitting stubbornly outside her door when she refused to let anyone in. He visited Tasha almost daily, cycling at speed between Chelsea and Richmond, often returning quite late to creep into Rachel's room and tell his tale of the day. *Which way did you go?* Rachel would ask, the better to hear his story, first mapping his route in her mind. Rachel loved the streets of the city and the course of the river and taught them to Zach. She walked the London streets and criss-crossed the parks and river in wonder, like so many before her, learning the stones, carving a path. *Tropa.*

William Hogarth knew the stones and walked his city, and to escape it, this London he could never truly elude, not at heart, thinks Rachel, he bought a house in Chiswick for himself and his wife Jane. And his dogs and birds. Rachel has seen them there, the graves he marked for their poignant deaths, the deaths of his dogs and birds. He produced *The Four Stages of Cruelty,* as he explained, "in hopes of preventing in some degree that cruel treatment of poor Animals which makes the streets of London more disagreeable to the human mind, than anything what ever, the very describing of which gives pain." Hogarth's St. Giles, in sum, is a battlefield. In *The First Stage of Cruelty,* boys of the parish go about the gleeful business of torturing animals, boys who will grow into men and perform man-sized cruelties. *How it all begins with the boy,* Rachel frowns. See how it always begins with the boy!

Rachel delights in the singular fascination this exhibition holds for her, in the special unknowingness of immediate fascination, an absorption unfettered by analysis. *The First Stage of Fascination!* laughs Rachel. She feels a strange attraction to the views and artefacts relating to the *Hospital for the Maintenance and Education of exposed and deserted Young Children,* and peers with intent and ever-mounting fondness at the portrait of its founder, Captain Thomas Coram, in the mezzotint after William Hogarth's great painting. There is something of Papa here, she thinks. Something . . . She loves the folds and rumples in the Captain's greatcoat and breeches, the ruddy knuckles of his weathered hands, the rosy cheeks and perturbation in his face, and tentative shadow of a smile. And oh, look here! Here is the ticket Hogarth etched for George Handel's *Messiah,* bearing the coat of arms he designed for the Hospital, of naked baby under two stars and half moon, flanked by Artemis and Britannia, symbols of nature and liberty, with the Hospital logo at the crest, a lamb with a sprig of thyme in its mouth. Thyme, not rosemary, though rosemary goes very well with lamb, thinks Rachel. But what a Baba Yaga thought that is! Baba Yaga roasts the innocent with rosemary and thyme! The lamb is innocence, of course, but what is thyme? Rachel asks herself. She cannot remember.

Beneath the coat of arms, she reads the bare word in bold lettering: "HELP." Handel's oratorio, she learns, is performed yearly between 1750 and 1754 in the Chapel of the Hospital, for the raising of funds, and is so very well attended, Hogarth engraves a plea at the foot of the ticket that *Gentlemen are desired to come without Swords, and the Ladies without Hoops.* Coram, Hogarth and Handel are principal benefactors, all three. Handel writes the Foundling Hospital anthem, inspired by Psalm 41. *Blessed are They that Considereth the Poor.* Coram, Hogarth and Handel are, all three, middle-aged and childless. And Handel is blind. Another blind balladeer. I know rosemary, frowns Rachel: *Here's rosemary,* says Ophelia to her brother, *that's for remembrance; pray, love, remember.* Now what is thyme?

Rachel pores over the cabinet of foundling tokens with particular wonderment. Oh Captain Thomas Coram! Look what you did, what you began! So many stories here, Rachel thinks, so much history in these oddments and shards. She sees them now in her sleep, a procession of foundlings, tatterdemalions, each with an item betokening their beginnings. She has memorised all the tokens: the child's necklace, the coin and key, the thimble and ring, the child's bracelet with padlock, the silver heart, school badge, infant's purse, and doll's arm, and hazelnut shell, and half of a silver shilling. There is a brass button of a Coldstream Guardsman, an enamelled bottle ticket marked "ale" and a gambling token, a fish carved from bone with a black etched eye and mouth slightly ajar, as if waiting to speak.

In Russian fairy tales, Rachel muses, fish do speak. And grant wishes, typically in exchange for mercy. Save a fish's life, throw him back to sea, and your wishes may be granted. Just don't push it, do not ask for too much.

> *Head in air and tail in sea,*
> *Fish, fish, listen to me.*

"O fish," whispers Rachel to the cabinet of foundling tokens, attracting the glance of a gentleman visitor to the exhibition, at whom she smiles slightly.

"O fish," she continues in her head.

What is it?

"I need to tell you a story."

What about?

Zachariah, Zachariah, my foundling boy. "A boy. A boxer, a fighting man. A brother. No. About brothers, sisters. Foundlings, laid-in-the-streets. Fights, fighting. A boy, it all begins with the boy. My love. A wolf. Peter and the Wolf! Oh dear! I am very crazy! Let me—I must tell you this story."

Why?

"I'm frightened."

Of?

"Fractals. Patterns."

Ah, says the fish, looking at Rachel with his wise eyes. Chaos!

"Yes," thinks Rachel. "Chaos. *Fearful symmetry.*"

Go home, says the fish, flipping over, flashing in light, and diving down into the great blue sea.

Rachel sits again, choosing a bench facing *A Perspective View of the Foundling Hospital with Emblematic Figures,* one of several, and her favourite. She shuts her eyes for a moment before taking it in. There is little competition for this seat. No one dreams here for very long; perhaps none but her. And the picture is so very prosy! Rachel rises, steps in close. Here in the foreground are effeminate French dandies, tourists, and the more pragmatically togged indigenous. True-born. Children with adult physiognomy dance round a statue of Venus and, in the background, behind iron railings, a boy pushes a hoop, and runs towards a porter at the open gates by a statue of Artemis. Before the gates is another foundling boy wielding a slender stick—as it were, a makeshift cricket bat. He eyes a ball at his feet, his stance elegant beyond his years. He is evidently of an athletic disposition. The foundling's superior concentration evokes Zachariah for Rachel, the boy ennobled by sport. Zach is ennobled by sport, enabled, the boy and the man, the noisome cranks and gears of his system instantly calibrated by the bat in his grip, the ball in hand, the gloves on his fists. And by her, perhaps, yes, by her, Rachel encompassed, within his uncommon reach. Uncommon, electric. For even in sleep, Zachariah is never quiet, never wholly quiet, the flutter of tissue and pulsing of veins, rampant as he falls into dreams, a tenebrous place!

—*Rachel.*

—*Papa?*

—*What is paradoxical sleep?*

—*Not sleep, nor waking. Paradoxical sleep is as different from sleeping as sleep is from wakefulness; it is a third state of the brain. Paradoxical sleep is a periodic cycle and proportional to mass, coming every seven minutes in a mouse and every ninety in a human. Normally. Safety is a requisite. A hunted animal sleeps light. The hunted dream not much more than fifteen minutes every day.*

—*Good, Rachel. Good.*

Rachel often watches Zach in his febrile sleep, how he plunges into dreams, no drifting, and she might gasp in the steeling of his arms, alive to his every contraction and tremor, murmuring the names of his parts for solace, his beloved parts, a litany all her own. Triceps, biceps, abductors! Ulnar vein, ulnar artery, radial, brachial. Zach's knee jerks upwards, his right thigh flung across her body, Rachel, a life raft. Great saphenous vein, femoral, popliteal. Semitendinous muscle, gracilis, inguinal. With his head beneath her chin and against her throat, she feels the pricking of his scalp, the shift and twitch of membrane and tissue, of eyelids and jaw—occipitals, orbicularis oculi, masseter! She feels the fearful thickening of carotid and jugular, the irregular thrum of his racing heart.

Wakeful, Zach and Rachel will whisper and smile, nuzzle and chide until sleep comes again, though some nights, some times, he must cajole a stricken Rachel who simply cannot explain her grief, or how it is she sees such terrible beauty in his workings, in the very lifeblood of him.

.   .   .

"Time, Miss!"

A museum guard pads across the floor, takes up a new position, displacing the air, the polite stillness of the room, and Rachel checks her
watch. Nearly six. Go home, Rachel. She so likes to be there for his
return. *Zachariah is coming, Zachariah is coming!* Rachel is all gravity now,
nudged from dreams, a swift transition. Rachel dreams much and often.
She is not hunted. She adjusts a satchel strap, tucks a stray lock of hair
behind an ear. She buttons her jacket, braces her grip on the bag of
cheese and steps back from *A Perspective View of the Foundling Hospital,
with Emblematic Figures.* What an unremarkable print it is! she decides.
Prosy indeed! Arid and functional, static, a solicitation, not so very far
removed from the plaster-cast charity statues that so irked her as a girl,
sentinels of gloom and misery at the entrances of shops; the yellow
guide dog with the awful gash in his head, the slot for coins! And the
seated boy in yellow jumper and blue trousers, a red book on his lap
with its more seemly slot for coins. *Please Give to the Blind.* And the child
with leg brace, charity box in hand. *Please Give Generously.* Once she had
seen this statue in the entrance of a newsagent's, she could no longer
countenance the braced boy in her very own school without colouring
deeply, yet he was cheerful and handsome and always so hale, thump-
thump-thumping down the corridors and across the playground green,
as it were in a world without impediments.

See the boy! Rachel casts a parting glance at *A Perspective View of the
Foundling Hospital, with Emblematic Figures,* at the child by the gates, his
eye on the ball, a veritable study in sporting concentration, and she
thinks again how he might so easily be Zach! No, Rachel. Don't be silly.
He is nothing like. Just a foundling boy with a stick and ball. And yet . . .
there is a template . . . a template for all things. She loves this boy now, the
boy in the picture, and she conjures a history for him, and an exotic
provenance, and assigns him a foundling token, the fish carved from
bone.

"O fish!"

What is it? What can I do for you?

"I need to tell you a story, a tale of fate and emergence."

But what is it you want?

"Take us with you. Please take us away with you. Beneath. Somewhere safe."

Here's thyme, says the fish, offering a posy. That's for courage and strength. Now go home, he adds, and turns over with a flap of his tail, head first into the blue sea waters.

And Captain Coram, thinks Rachel, hurrying out of the British Museum, is nothing like my father! Surely nothing like. Why ever did she think so? She sees Coram now in his rumpled red coat, the creases at his ankles, the gnarled veins in his seafaring hands. The forbearance.

An Infinite Scale, or, Captain Coram's Heart

Leicester Fields, London 1738.

Captain Thomas Coram is a fitful sleeper at best.

He slips free of the covers and fishes for slippers, ready to slide out of bed, from poop deck to lower deck, thundering off his poop—ha!—and onto his gouty toes, to land like a rusty anchor, reaching for his nightcap as he drops. Thar she blows! And is there anything more foolish than an old fellow in a nightshirt, that's what he wants to know, what with his knotted knees open to the night breezes and the beam of his pale shins and his mighty grizzled hams peeping out at every flap of linen, where's my gown? Or my red greatcoat—my trusty benjamin—or a blanket, any wrap will do! Ah, there. And a lamp, take a lamp and quiet as you go on your ageing sea-legs, creak, creak. Shhh! Sleep, Eunice, my dove, my dear. I am sorry for the roar and clatter! I am just an old sea captain, shipbuilder, fool, and I am all at sea some days, but though my limbs might be salty and barnacled, I am still sea-worthy! It will all come right, as you say. *A Hospital for the Maintenance and Education of exposed and deserted Young Children.*

My hospital, a home!

He recalls his walks through the city, from Rotherhithe, and the desperate sight of little corpses, babies cast aside like rotten meat, pitched onto dung heaps like night soil, but how long can a man petition? It's been nearly fifteen years. I am old and childless, but I have Eunice, my dearly beloved wife, and no end of hats, bless Eunice and bless the Hatters Company for keeping me in hats, though I would have nothing, I scolded, for the small kindness I did them. What a fuss, what a fuss!

Nearly fifteen years.

In the morning, he'll cross the Fields to Hogarth's, to William who will be a hospital governor, like himself, and then on to Brook Street for Handel, who might well be interested, says Hogarth, and join their cause, sooner or later, as it pleases him. And they will fashion such a collection of duchesses with whom to petition the King, it will not be long now for the Charter. What a gang he has pressed! Portly and rough, though not Handel, good George with his fine bearing and weak eyes— yet ailing, increasing poorly, Coram can tell—and all three—all three!— childless. What a *teazer*! What a triumvirate! Pity, pity! Blessed are they that considereth the aged and gouty, the balding and blind! Ha!

Nearly light, muses Thomas, raising the lamp a little at the window so that his shadow shifts on the wall behind him, restless, hulking, rumpled, frayed, shape of a coastline. There is a child in the Captain's eye. Everywhere he looks, from wherever he stands, a child discarded, dismayed. It all begins here. He breathes heavily. He has a dream of immanence.

How long is the coast of Britain? How great is the kindness of Coram?

{ THREE }

You'll do the Sam the Russian books, then? Revive them?"
"We shall see . . . We shall see."

Though she has never told him so, Rachel often peruses the little volumes she and Zach wrought with such intent and desire over twenty years ago, retrieving them from the unmarked box file she keeps in her studio amongst similar box files containing illustrations and studies, articles and oddments; her aides-mémoire. Home from the exhibition, she takes the books out again, turning the pages quite slowly. How pristine they still are!

The invention of Sam the Russian started out as a game, a question, a search for clues, for patterns. The more she learned about her new brother Zachariah, the more Sam sprang alive, a figure of Russian fairy tale, sprinkled with water of life! And the more alive Sam became, the quicker she forgot he was Zach. How innocent is the process of invention!

"Don't you want to know?" young Rachel had asked him one day. "Who your parents are? Where you come from?"

"No," he frowned. "I don't think so."

"We should make them up!" she said excitedly. "Make *you* up. A whole history! In history. Pick a time, pick your favourite time. We'll start there."

She remembers him staring, weighing it up.

"We can't do that," he protested. "What do you mean?"

"Of course we can, Zach. For fun. We can do anything."

"Will I be called Zach?"

"No. Another name. It will be you, but different. You, not you."

Zach scratched his head vigorously with both hands, tugged the hair at his crown.

"You look a bit feral now," Rachel observed. "Your hair's gone all wild."

"GRAAAH!" he growled.

"Well?" she asked.

"Well what?"

"Pick a time."

"I'll be a pugilist in the 1800s," he stated. "That would be tremendous."

"Tremendous," agreed Rachel.

—Rachel, in a dynamical system, what are patterns?

—Clues. Patterns are clues, Papa. Clues to the rules.

—And can the same set of rules have different effects, different patterns?

—Yes.

—Are there patterns in the breaking of symmetry?

—Yes!

—What is symmetry?

—A transformation. A shape is symmetric if it is unchanged when transformed in some way. If it looks the same.

Rachel turns the books over and over in her hands and looks at the clock. He'll be home soon. She thinks how much more she knows now. How different Sam's story might be, were she to bring him back to life today. Different and the same. Rachel replaces the books in the file and, before settling it back in its place on the shelf, sketches a fish in the blank white space on the spine. She draws a fish much akin to the token she saw at the British Museum.

"O fish!"

What is it? What can I do for you?

"I need to tell you a story, a tale of fate and emergence."

LAID-IN-THE-STREETS,
BEING THE ONLY AND ORIGINAL COMPLETE LIFE
OF SAMUEL ALEXANDER,
uncrowned bare-knuckle Champion of All England,
known to the Fancy as "Sam the Russian"
or the "Tsar of the Prize Ring."

The Castle Tavern, Holborn, 1832.

Samuel's eyes pain him, every blink pains him, worse than a blow to the kidneys, he thinks, and it's because of the wood smoke and the lamplight fumes, the daily fog of bishop and ale, of gin and tobacco, and this closeness of men he is not accustomed to, but Spring says he was a potboy once too, as were other fighters, it's nigh on traditional. Spring was once potboy for the great Champion of England Tom Cribb at his tavern, the Union Arms, and a butcher's boy before that, before he came to London to train in Cribb's rooms at the back and work as potboy in front, and everyone in the game went to the Arms, backers and fighters, everyone. Spring is bringing Sam up by hand like Cribb did for Spring, and Sam will endure, though he does muse on his old life and his outdoor days whenever he holds a candle to the glass for a good look at his sore optics, the whites puffed and creased as the skin on hot milk. Samuel muses on it, the partiality he harbours for the White Horse Inn and his days as waterboy, and for Old Abel the coachman, even for those times he had to hop from foot to foot so as not to perish from cold, times he had to punch bare-knuckled through ice to water the horses, ferrying shallow draughts one by one, warming them in his breath, because surely an ivory-freezing drink will shock a coach horse as it would a man. Blow on it, son! Warm it for him, Old Abel would say, shivering in fellow feeling, Old Abel with only a few ivories left of his own, chipped and browning, long steeped in tea and coffee, port and stew.

Times were fine, then, at the White Horse. Sam remembers it all, how he could read in the slow hours by the light of the coffee-house windows, and at no cost to anyone, reading *The Life and Strange Surprizing Adventures of Robinson Crusoe, of York, Mariner* and other titles. He remembers the hopping and running, the jumping at the sound of his name, Young Sam! And the bare-knuckle blows to solid ice and the scurrying on slick ground with buckets of water, look sharp! It was all learning as he sees it now, all science. Samuel is a prize-fighter in the works, which is why he is here at the Castle for Tom Spring to bring up by hand in the long-standing manner historical.

"Ready, Sam? Watch me, watch my moves in the air here. I'm going to demonstrate the cross-buttock and then we'll have a set-to! Just you picture some old file charging at you, some thunder-and-lightning fighter the likes of Peter Crawley, say, 'Young Rumpsteak' himself. If you throw him with a cross-buttock, he'll not come to scratch in a hurry! But what's that hanging there, if you please?" demands Spring, fingering Sam's necklace. "My eyes! Jewels, is it?" he teases.

The boy frowns, troubled by memory.

"So what is it, boy, round your squeezer?" Spring asks, lifting Sam's medallion from his chest, the painted likeness on its loop of silver.

Sam grasps it back, pulling so tight the links of chain crimp the young skin of his neck. *My token. Mine.*

Before Sam was placed out apprentice by the governors of the Foundling Hospital and separated from his bosom friend Jonah the Needle, Jonah unpicked the locked parlour where the foundling receipts and keepsakes were sealed. Against the date of Sam's arrival, *the 15th Day of March 1815,* he read a number and his new name, *Samuel Alexander,* and a description of the *writing and remarkable Things* deposited with his infant self. There were two tokens to his name: "*A Medallion of the reign of Tsar Alexander I, with chain, and a gambling token, that is, a fish carved from bone.*" There was also a note written in French: "*Je reviens, je reviens, je reviens, je reviens.*" Sam did not take the note with him. The bosom friends exchanged looks of profound solemnity as Jonah pocketed his own token, "a porcelain bottle ticket marked 'ale,'" and Sam his fish and medallion with chain, whereupon Jonah resealed the cabinet and drawers and parlour door behind them, with eminent dexterity. He is Jonah the Needle.

"Sam!" chides Spring. "I say! You can't fight with that on!"

"I must, I can't take it off. My father—"

"Your father?" says Tom, peering closer.

"I mean to say—" *I cannot, will not take it off,* Samuel recites to himself. He left it to me, to know me by. A medallion and a bone-fish, he left them for me. For when he returns. "It's mine!"

"No one's taking it off you, boy. Of course it's yours."

"It's my token. From Coram's. The Hospital. They gave it to me. This and another, I have two tokens. I'm sure I told you, sir. My mother is dead." *Never take it off.* "But I daresay my father, sir—"

"Pipe down. And I'm Spring to you. Spring, or Tom. Tom in private congress, Spring in a crowd. Lest there be any confusion, for, truly, we are many Toms."

Tom Spring, born Winter in 1795, is rechristened at twenty years of age on his own first outing at the Fives Court in St. Martin's Street, Leicester Fields, when Tom "Paddington" Jones, retired bruiser, now occasional second and master of ceremonies, bustles the novice into the ring with a bellow in the ear.

What's your name, boy, what's your name?

Winter, sir!

Well, let it be Spring! declared Jones.

And Spring it was, Spring it is.

"I mean to say," continues Sam, raising the miniature in his palm and holding it up to Spring's eyes, "it's the Tsar, you see. It's why they called me Alexander. The Tsar, like our William. King, that is. And my father . . ."

"I know what a tsar is, young Sam! I know Alexander! Your father, you say?"

"No, no. He's dead—"

"That's what I tell you, you'll have to trust to fortune now, I keep telling you."

"No! Tsar Alexander! *He's* dead!" shouts Sam, his blood in a ferment. "His brother is Tsar now—and father, he's with the Cossacks. Or Hussars. I believe so."

"Your father! I'm your father now, young Sam, tsar of the Prize Ring! And Tsar of All England, you'll be," Spring tells Sam, palpating the image of Alexander I, victor of Borodino.

"Come, Sam. Rest yourself. Retire for a wipe! Match stopped, ha! I have a tale for you about . . . your *father* . . . Tsar Alexander. Why, Cribb was there! *They were all there.* Ask Cribb. Ask him. Belcher—Tom, that is—and Bill Richmond and Ned Painter! 'Flatnose' Ned! And Jackson, yes, all of them were there, milling for your Alexander, Tsar of All the Russias. June 1814. And not just once, but twice. There were two exhibitions, young Sam. Marvellous bright occasions, not forgotten. What a crowd of upper customers! Let Cribb tell you. Even his dog was there— Billy, finest ratcatcher you ever saw. Your father, you say?"

"No! I mean—"

"Chaff, Sam! I'm a teazer. I know what you mean. But, who's to say? Eh? Who's to say! He might be your father! Tsar Alexander. Never mind. I'm your pater now. Your father and your mother, pater and mater! Like Cribb was to me. And just you ask him about it, ask Cribb about how he sparred for kings and generals. By invitation, Sam! *By invitation!*"

If he does not come, Sam swears, shrugging on his shirt that sticks to his back and tying on his neck-cloth, the colours sky blue, if he does not come for me, my father, I will find him, and by this token, this above all, he shall know me.

"It was before you were born, Sam, and before I came to London. Before the Arms, and Cribb, and all that I've told you about, do you remember? How Cribb spots me at Mordiford on his sparring tour, and such a crowd there was on the bridge that day and Tom Cribb himself watching and myself not yet twenty, toeing the line with 'The Hammer' Hollands, the Hammer resigning to me in one hour and twenty minutes, whereupon Cribb beholds me as a champion in the works, same as I beheld you at the White Horse this winter past, which is *your* beginning, and a story for you to tell on *your* retirement, you'll see.

"So that year Cribb spots me is the very year he spars at Lord Lowther's for Tsar Alexander, and such a success it was, there is a second show, the second finer than the first, with more kings and princes in attendance! Why, it was wild in London then, Cribb says, and there was never so great an exhibition, so great an assemblage of bruisers and royalty together, Sam, not until the Coronation—George's, that is—and upon which occasion, I was there in person, as I have related to you. I was engaged, Sam, on that famous day, along with Cribb and the Gentleman and fifteen other bruisers, as ushers. Royal ushers we were and royal thanks we had furthermore. And the spectators were IMMENSE! I've shown you the letter, haven't I?"

"You have," replies Sam, nodding vigorously.

"They gave us a medal and a great dinner. *For our services*. We held a raffle for that medal and Belcher won it, Tom, of course, Jem being long buried, and Jem was a great man though I never knew him, and a greater fighter than ever Tom was, they all say so, yet blinded in one eye playing fives—racquets, that is—and never the same thereafter, and dead aged but twenty-nine, much lamented. So many stories, young Sam, some to make a fellow weep," observes Tom, bowing his head briefly, pausing for remembrance. "But do not we wear the spotted kerchief in his name?" resumes Tom brightly. "The *belcher* coloured bird's-eye blue; blue-and-white, blue-and-yellow? Indeed we do! For Jem was unrivalled in elegance, young Sam, within and without the ring. A beacon for you. Mark him and mark the times, though you are but a boy, and not even born when the Russians were at Lord Lowther's, June 1814."

"I was born the year after," states Sam Alexander.

"So you were," Tom agrees. "Quite so. And you were maybe only so high the day I stood at the very doors of Westminster Hall. Only so high," muses Spring, his large raw hand hovering at table height, brows tensed in conjecture. "Yes, you and I were as nothing to each other yet and, truly, though our acquaintance feels long-standing, it is not until so very lately that I beheld you battling like a hero outside the White Horse Inn. How you handled your fives well, Sam, as I remarked! It was a capital day all round, no? We might drink to that, I daresay, Samuel—though just one pot, a peg or two of Danzig spruce, I think. Just the one pot! You're in training, don't forget it."

"I don't," says Sam. "I don't forget it."

"Well then," says Spring, waxing paternal. "Well then."

My father, thinks Sam, was a soldier. Is a soldier, a fighting man. I have a true father and I will find him. And by this token, he shall know me.

THE BOY HUSSAR

The Pulteney Hotel, Piccadilly. London, 1814. After an exhibition of sparring for Alexander I, Tsar of All the Russias.

When the Hussar has seen to General Platov the hetman, all is quiet at the Pulteney Hotel, Piccadilly, and though the gaslight burns, it is still too dark to draw, and he snuffs out the candle that is casting impossible shadows across the rippling pages of his old notebook, Borodino-worn, sun-scorched and winter-brittle, that he leaves open, however, as he lays his head on one hand, restlessly fingering pages with the other, so few of them filled, so few for so many thoughts and visions! But there is never enough time, or never the right time, perhaps, for drawings, for all the stories and sights that make his blood rush to think about, in his loins, that make his heart drum and his digits and eyelids flutter with the strain of remembering everything and putting it all in order, in sketches and in poems—or the beginnings of poems—for his sister who loves his drawings and laughs at his words, at his beginnings of poems. Ekaterina. So much has happened in so short a time, his head might explode—like a cannon shell! And he is not yet eighteen.

The Hussar waits for daylight to brighten the blank page under his pen for the sketch he dreams of the Englishwoman's face, a drawing he must accomplish because he might never meet her again, she may not be there at His Lordship's on Friday for the second exhibition as she was tonight, smiling bravely at English champions with bare white chests and muscles like horses, and coloured sashes tied at the waist, he must draw them too. On Friday, the Prussians are invited, their king and Blücher, of course. He will never trust the Prussians; turncoats, who can trust them? With their voices like gloves slapping the ground, speaking both Russian and French as if there were dust in their mouths. Their voices grate in the Hussar's ears, a clash of sabres. Davydov says that the Tsar, may God bless him, has bad eyes and worse hearing. Good. The Hussar hopes he did not hear it, then, nor see it, how the Prussians sneered on the crossing to Dover when Tsar Alexander was seasick. Davydov is a poet. He can write poems from beginning to end. He is a poet and a hero.

The officer's eyelids droop and he wonders what English ladies are like, and what they desire, knowing if Davydov had seen this one tonight, he would start *and* finish a poem about her, fast as horses, light or no light to write by. The Hussar thanks God for Davydov and also, ha! for his absence tonight, forgive me! And then, as he shall every day until death, he thanks God for sparing the Kremlin and the Foundling Hospital from the great fire of Moscow. He gives thanks above all for saving the Foundling Hospital where his sister minds orphans not much older than herself. And he blesses the wounds of Captain Thomas-Joseph Aubry, Chasseur, who held off the murderous remnants of the evacuated city alongside three wounded Russian generals in a ward full of the helplessly injured, defending the Hospital until Russian troops arrived. What a strange war it is. The French he thought were his cousins, the Prussians not his cousins. Captain Aubry, a blessing upon him . . . many blessings! Ekaterina, he says, murmuring. *Ekaterina* . . . and when the pen drops to the page, jolting him awake, the soldier reaches for the chain around his neck with the portrait of his Tsar hanging there, and grips it firmly as he falls into deeper sleep at the window in the feeble English light, calling out Prussians by name as he goes, to stand at six paces, full on, arm extended, and he charges on Frenchmen in huddles, quite frozen, and flies at the looters and rapists of Moscow, on horseback, sword raised, piercing and slicing and shooting for Alexander and God, for the hetman and Ekaterina and Davydov, for *Rus* and cherry dumplings and Kakhetian wine, amen, and what reach he has! What superior reach!

In his tiny room at the top of the Castle Tavern in Holborn, all is quiet and Sam dances in his nightshirt, backwards and forwards and from side to side, dropping now one shoulder, now the other, skipping across those protesting, creaking boards he has committed to memory, that one loose, this one cracked, but he is so light on his feet, a slip would hardly signify. He pads about like a wolf, and he braves the cold like a wolf. Sam dances in the grimy winter beam of moon he loves for the free night light it brings to read by, and for the great hush it brings also, his ears singing with the quiet and with the strange expectation someone might call for him at any moment. In the quietest quiet, he can sometimes hear voices calling. He's not tired, he's spry.

Sam toes the line written in moonlight and takes the stance classical, just as Spring taught him, left hand extended, chin protected, left foot forward, weight even, perfectly balanced, and he recites the words Spring taught him, of Mendoza's first principle. Daniel Mendoza, the scientific and champion!

The first principle in boxing is to be perfectly master of the equilibrium of the body, so as to be able to change from a right to a left handed position, to

*advance or retreat, striking or parrying; and to throw the body either backward
or forward, without difficulty or embarrassment.*

Sam drops his fives and bounds into bed, thinking about embarrassment and how it might possibly figure in the life of a fighter. He fumbles
for the book he left under the covers somewhere in this icy plain—here
it is!—and then he makes a cave of his covers, pulling them high beyond
the tips of his frozen ringing ears, breathing in the vigorous warmth
of his own body and the aromas of Spring's famous rub, Spring's own
father's recipe, as he told Sam, his father the butcher who trained him
before Cribb, rubbing his body as Spring now rubs Sam's with a paste
of crushed herbs, of comfrey and madder and mint oil, and feverfew for
vigour.

Sam's medallion is the coldest thing now, as it were a frozen sixpence
on his breast—a *bender*—burning a hole there, so he grabs it in his left
fist—*mauley*—to draw out the cold, clasping it so hard to his body he
can feel his heart thundering against the tautness of his forearm, his
leading arm.

You can't fight with that on!

But I must!

Spring is his father now, that's what he says, and Sam recalls the day
they met outside the White Horse early this year, when Young Sam (as
was his epithet) leaped out of the darky to fight for Old Abel the coachman sitting hunched in his rumpled jemmy, peepers squeezed shut
against the wind, surprised by two swells in tall shiny hats who prodded
the old man as if he were a dead dog, a lazy tyke. Sam has bottom and
quickness, and hit with both hands, but he had no science yet and the
ground was slick and his temper high, and he was no match for two full-
grown swells with sticks.

How Tom Spring Meets Sam the Russian

Tom Spring, Champion of All England of 1824 and present landlord of
the Castle Tavern, also trainer and second and, not to forget, first trea-
surer and chairman of the Fair Play Club, enters the slippery ring, a
sheet of black ice, and, stepping neatly between the floored boy and his
antagonists, tips his hat the sooner to be recognized, his prepossessing

appearance being well known from the pages of such keenly devoured publications as *Bell's Life, Pugilistica* and *Boxiana,* and from engraved cups and glazed plaques and painted portraits. And then, with these preliminaries acquitted, Tom swiftly puts in two tremendous blows on the throat—one, two—to send the swells staggering.

"Begging your pardon, sirs! My name is Tom Spring and I cry foul! A man on his knees," he adds, indicating young Sam on the ground, his toplights already swollen and the claret dripping from his smeller, "a man on his knees to be reckoned down. Broughton's Rules. I declare my man beaten! Enough!"

And off they stump it, the two lushy blades, with Tom calling "Shame, shame!" at their backs. And off they go, he shouldn't wonder, to recount some starch of how they shook hands with the retired great champion Tom Spring, now landlord of the Castle, second and trainer and consort of princes.

"You handled your fives well!" Tom tells Sam, pulling him to his wobbly understandings before inviting him to the Castle, Holborn, when it might please him, to meet some fellows there. "Whereupon we shall see what we shall see!" he adds, while Old Abel the coachman flings his greatcoated arms around his waterboy, soon to be Tom Spring's potboy, the tears falling from his bloodshot shutters to tumble over his jaws and freeze in the folds of his face ridged and furrowed as tree bark.

"Young Sam," he pipes. "My friend! Young Sam! I was in bodily fear, you know. Bodily fear!"

And there, too, is Sam's friend Dickens, fellow pedestrian and scholar, with the long flow of hair and the proud collar and bright ogles, a reporter, presently, at the Houses of Parliament, recording what he hears there from the far-flung benches of the Stranger's Gallery, as it is called, taking it all down at speed, in shorthand, a turn of phrase, to Sam, that calls to mind his great friend Jonah from Coram's Foundling Hospital. Jonah the Needle is apprenticed to a tailor now, Jonah with his creaky leather brace and heavy shoe and one arm shorter than the other, and fingers so fine and deft he could mend anything in no time, toys and book bindings, sleeves and shoe straps, his fives artful as wands, slight as needles, instruments that will surely make his fortune, as Sam wished him the day they were both sent out apprenticed. When Jonah left the Hospital, and bade his friend Sam farewell, he shook him deftly by the short hand.

"Well done, Sam!" says Dickens. "And you sprang like a wolf!" he adds, dancing around on the ice, muttering and exclaiming to himself about what he has seen as Old Abel shuffles inside for a brandy, leaving behind the rumpus of Sam playing out his moves and blows, and Dickens repeating in snatches what he heard Spring tell Samuel on the matter of his fives, how he handled them well, and that the coachman exclaimed how he had been in bodily fear. Charles rehearses the words in the champion's voice and then in the coachman's voice and, later, he takes it all down in shorthand.

Yes it *was* a capital day. It was. Capital!

Sam Alexander reaches for *Robinson Crusoe, The Life and Strange Surprizing Adventures,* settling the book in the crook of his neck, collaring the light there, the waves and particles finding their way through the sooty mullioned panes to glance off the page and shine in his phiz and sparklers, a promise of things to come, of more capital days, and of greatness for Jonah the Needle, Tailor of London, and for Dickens also, a scribe now, one of the black-letter gentry. What a rum fellow! And game! Sam's eyelids flicker, fall and rise, heavier each time . . . Cannibals . . . there are cannibals on Crusoe's island.

> *I liv'd uncomfortably, by reason of the constant apprehension I was in of their coming upon me by surprise; from whence I observe that the expectation of evil is more bitter than the suffering . . . During all this time, I was in the murthering humour and took up most of my hours . . . in contriving how to circumvent and fall upon them . . .*

As Sam drifts into paradoxical sleep, as different from sleep as sleep is from wakefulness, he sees cannibals dancing and coming his way, raising fine polished sticks in a rude manner, wearing tall shiny hats akin to stove-pipes, and thunder-and-lightning waistcoats and high white collars and flowing spotted neckerchiefs after the style of Jem Belcher, the extraordinary champion, the perfect phenomenon. The belchers are yellow-spotted ones, very spruce. Sam the Russian assumes the stance classical and hollers into the clear air.

"*My name is Sam Alexander! My name is Sam the Russian!*" he calls, and his voice flies at the enemy, a voice with uncommon reach.

No more noises from above, notes Spring. All is quiet. No more pitter-patter of pedestals, that boy's asleep. Good. He will soon be ready. Every-one gets the fidgets before a battle, Spring knows, everyone, trainer, backers, seconds and bottle-holders, and the Fancy, and the fighter most of all, but then, Tom reminds himself, when the time comes, though the belly quivers involuntarily, there is no greater readiness, nor grandeur, neither more exultant feeling in human nature.

When I threw my hat into the ring and saw my colours tied to the stakes, it seemed like taking a ton weight off my mind, and I would not have changed places with the King of England.

Sleep, Tom Spring, you king of All England.

Rachel draws a sleeping boy in gabled attic rooms. The left arm dangles by the side of his bed, fingertips brushing the pages of a book he has dropped. Rachel makes the right elbow and forearm prominent under the bedclothes, conveying the tension still there in the boy's fist as he clutches a foundling token to his chest, a medallion of Tsar Alexander I. He holds tight, though he is nearly asleep.

Sleep now, Sam. Sleep.

{ FOUR }

RACHEL SITS AT HER DESK where she will continue to illustrate the new translation of Russian folk tales and she tries to empty her mind before resuming, feeling the handmade paper she uses, her fingers sensitive to all the knots and striations, the familiar imperfections. She leaves Sam the Russian asleep in the attic and takes a walk in the taiga. She shuts her eyes a moment to see them all; Koschei the Deathless and Baba Yaga and Father Frost and the Golden Fish and the Pike with the Long Teeth and the Firebird and . . . *Little Bear Cub, Little Bear Cub* . . . Yes, that's where we are. Ready now. Rachel flexes her spine, looks up and around, listening to her house, aware of the simmering quiet Zach leaves in his wake, something tremulous to it always, the very mortar and caulking alive with change in this aftermath of turbulence, the tectonic shift from departure to waiting.

"All is QUI-et!" she sings, calling out to Zach in his absence in that other shorthand of theirs, a second language, musical, familial and Russian, of course. Russia, Russia, motherland, fatherland, *Rus*. Rachel and Zachariah know every lyric and nigh on every note from *Peter and the Wolf*. The whole twenty-seven minutes.

Begin. A tree, she thinks. A tree is a good place to start, because there are always dark woods in Russian folk tales. Otherwise, steppe, endless steppe, winter-swept, wind-striped by air-flow, the snow heaped into sickle-shapes and star-shapes, barchanoid, dome. Winter steppe geometry is a *multi-phase flow problem*—am I right, Papa? A multi-phase flow problem involving air and snow. And in a storm the shapes are ever-changing, sometimes impossible, because there is just no separating them, air and snow.

A tree, then. There are always dark woods in Russian folk tales, this realm of no-comfort certitudes, of see-sawing fortunes and comeuppance, and carnivorous appetites with nothing off the menu, certainly not children. A child is a comestible of choice, especially the innocent, the kindly, the fetching, the seeming ninny. The outsider, the exile. They are eaten roasted or boiled, or simply hacked to pieces, though resuscitation is not out of the question. In the Russian tale, nothing is inanimate, or quite what it should be, what with menacing trees—spruce, fir, pine and larch, birch and ash, walnut and elm—and imperious fish, voluble dolls and irascible bears and always a figure of wisdom, some regal soul in scruffy togs, tatterdemalion. With much to impart. And who might shape-shift, appearing as bird or wolf.

Raven and wolf follow each other for food, wolf watching the skies for where the ravens circle and raven waiting upon wolf for scraps he might leave. Raven and wolf enjoy each other's company, often playing together.

Zach lies in, a half day at the gym ahead. He is only roused from sleep by the scent of warm toast and cheese and rich coffee. He finds Rachel at the kitchen table, the surface piled with books.

"Hallo, sleepyhead!" she says. "Your eye looks worse. Should be better by now."

"It's fine, it's fine!" Zach replies, perusing the books. "Hey! You've got all my boxing tomes out!"

"I have not. Just a few. And some of them are mine."

"What you up to?" he laughs, kneeling on the floor and bopping her gently on the head with a book.

Rachel touches his brow, gingerly running a finger across the swelling there and across the stitches Izzy applied early this week. "Zachariah, Zachariah," she begins.

"I know, I know!" he protests. "No fighting! But what can I say?" he adds. "I boast a science sprung from manly pride! Linked . . ."

"Oh my goodness," exclaims Rachel. "That silly verse! I was reading it just yesterday! Pass me . . . oh where was it? I know. The yellow hardcover."

"*Bucks and Bruisers*? This one?" asks Zach.

"No, no. I'll find it. Here!" she says, opening the volume and turning the pages at speed. "Listen!" says Rachel. " 'Scorning all treacherous feud and deadly strife / The dark stiletto and the murderous knife / We boast a science sprung from manly pride / Linked with true courage and to health allied—A noble pastime, void of vain pretence—The fine old English art of self-defence.' Isn't that great? Isn't it crap?! I love it!"

"I love . . . when you say 'crap'!" notes Zach, taking the book from her. "Let's see that fine bit of doggerel—of *crambonian*! Used to know it by heart."

"Why? Why do you love it?"

"Love what? Oh. Dunno. It has a special quality. Your *crap*."

"Very funny."

"Oh man, yeah! I remember," says Zach, flipping the pages of Rachel's book. "Jem Burn's snuggery in Windmill Street. Verses over the mantel. The Queen's Head. Better publican than fighter, I reckon. Never the same after losing to Ned Neale! At Moulsey Hurst, 1824."

"Zachariah."

"Rachel."

"You are truly a phenomenon of boxiana!"

"I am, yes I am!"

"I thought I might well do that book one day—about pugilism," Rachel muses. "Boximania for kids, 'young adults' or whatever they call it. Well, I mean—about our bare-knuckle fighter. And foundling boy. What larks! What do you think?"

"I say, old chap," replies Zach, laying the book back onto the table. "What larks indeed! Hmm," he adds. "Seriously, though. Now I'm Mr. Doubtful. Think parents will really buy a boxing book for their kids? The *IG*-noble Art!"

"Why not? I had a think on it. The pugilism isn't the main thing. And after all, *Mother Goose* is pretty gruesome. And fairy tales are full of blood. Anyway, Papa bought us a boxing book. When we were little."

"*Prize-fighting, the Age of Regency Boximania*. John Ford."

"Yes."

"Wasn't a kids' book. And it was appeasement, a peace offering. Plus he thought—hoped—it was a craze with us, boxing. Me, he wasn't so worried about. Just a young gentleman thing, he thought. Young blade, sprog. Just a rite of passage."

"He was misled," says Rachel brightly.

"Mizzled, yeah. You know, of course, he'd never have bought us that book had it been only my thing. But I infected you. So it vexed the hell out of him."

"I don't agree," states Rachel. "And you're eating all my toast."

"I'm bloody right, though. What did he care when it became a big big thing with me? He cut me off, that's all. I fulfilled his expectations of mindless thuggery and he closed his mind."

"He never said 'thug' or 'thuggery.' Or 'mindless'!"

"Didn't bloody have to. And it doesn't matter anymore. Signify. I'm a boxer, a fighter. Was, that is. And a gym hand—"

"Assistant coach," corrects Rachel. "With plans for a book! And you've done some sports writing."

"Rachel?" Zach asks, affliction in his voice. "Does that make me better?"

"No! No, Zach! Oh I'm sorry," she exclaims, reaching out for his face, cupping his jaw in her hands, pressing her forehead to his. "That sounded so wrong. I was thinking of Papa, I suppose. Forgive me, please. Please."

"Sports writing ain't proper writing anyway, is it, like?" says Zach in mock vernacular. "Know what I mean, mate?" he adds, smiling weakly.

"Papa worried about you," Rachel insists, rising to put more bread in the toaster. "This Hoxton rye is very good, isn't it?"

"He worried about me? Rot, Rach! I offend him. Always did. And he never bloody worried about me. I disgusted him, them. Lev mostly. Pug, hack, chippie, *muzhik*! Peasant. Offensive. On every count. There's an art to it and I've got it down. The Sweet Science, the Noble Art of Offence! The Art of Zach's Offence. Fuck!"

"Stop it. You're in a huff now. I'm making you sandwiches for later. We have run out of almond butter, but this peanut one is very nice."

"'Let no one sneer at the bruisers of England'!" Zach declares, raising his fists in attitude before clasping her between his elbows.

"I'm ignoring you, Zach," says Rachel, struggling to finish her sandwiches.

"They're in a clinch!" he says in urgent commentating tones as he forces her round to face him. "She's up against the ropes!" he continues as he locks her willowy arms and butts her gently under the ear. "Did you SEE that? Wolff's done it again! Used his head! Made a fist of it, ha ha! Foul! Foul! Lord, I think he just *bit* her! God's teeth! Would you Adam and Eve it?"

"I'm still ignoring you," whispers Rachel, kissing his brows, *frontalis, galea, orbicularis oculi*. "Now go away. I have to work. Go now. Go to the gym."

"Hoxton rye," he reads from the packet on the counter. "Flour Power City. What a name for a baker. And so many boxers were bakers . . . Jack Martin, Master of the Rolls! But do you see, Rach? You just made me a sandwich of power. Means I must be a *bogatyr*. Man of power, that's me!"

"On the branch of a big tree," Rachel recites, "sat a little bird, Peter's friend. Chirped the bird gaily, 'All is QUI-et!'"

At her desk, Rachel looks to the windows and the dance of dust in the rays of London light. It is a myth, she knows, that most of this dirt is sloughed human skin, yet a small proportion surely . . . Yes, in the feverish dance of dust, she thinks, there is surely a peck of Zachariah. Even in his absence, in so many ways, he is so very much here. Rachel pictures him as a boy, very young, all limbs and fidgets and rushing blood, heedless of Lev's reproving eye, Zach who so quickly became a beggar for Mama, slinking round the dinner table like Peter's wolf and winning a peal of laughter from her, laughter so rare they all stop to take it in, the boy amazed that an act so simple, so physical, can afford him so much joy. Rachel remembers how Papa flushed in the reflected light of Mama's smile, despite his increasing unease. *The house is not a gym,* he scolds Zachariah. *Why must you touch everything, everyone? Leave things alone!* See the boy in the man, thinks Rachel, recalling Zach at the gate this morning, on his way to the gym, swinging it shut with a mighty sweep as always, the ensuing clang echoing through the close, bruising the auriculars.

"Close the gate, Peter!" Rachel called from the doorway of their dacha in Camden Town this morning, leaning against the jamb as Zach paused to face her a moment, his eyes bright as flame.

"It's a dangerous place!" he intoned. "If a WOLF should come out of the forest, THEN what would you do!"

Rachel watched him walk, the sway of his shoulders, the scrape of his heels, the twist in his collar, the contraction of muscle under denim and wool. *Gluteus medius, gluteus maximus,* observed Rachel and, from across the close, two ladies staring. The stark cold gaze, the meeting of heads, and murmuring! A *murmuration,* she thought. Murmuration of crones. Camden is such a sharp-eyed place.

Camden Town!

Rachel and Zach walk the streets and surely know every stone by now, every tree, all the players, their perambulations rarely passing without event. Rachel will be greeted by name in many quarters, despite her poise and quiet, and where Zach earns a scowl she leaves smiling faces in her wake. What starts out as a stroll might become a parade, a processional.

A Royal Mail van slows in its hurried path and the postman bibs his horn, calls out to Rachel, beams at her, waves.

"Man oh man! Do ALL the posties know your name?"

"My name's on the parcels, silly."

"My name's on stuff. None of them say my name or grin like that!"

"I get lots of parcels. And I'm nicer than you. Oh look!" she whispers, nudging Zach. "There's 'I-don't-drink.'"

"Who?"

"There! On the bench outside the restaurant. In the High Street. See him? That's his corner," she explains. "He's new round here. He selects the right passer-by and asks for money, shakes his head sadly and goes *I don't drink, I don't smoke, all I want is some food.* It really works! Then he spends the rest of the day in Pratt Street with a fifth of gin, a bag of beer cans and a roll-up fag between his fingers. So I call him 'I-don't-drink.'"

"Right," says Zach. "So what's the story? Does he bother you?"

"No. But he's a bit irascible. I shouldn't look at him if I were you."

Walk on.

The Indian newsagent slaps his copy of *Boxing Monthly* atop a neatly folded *Times* even before Zach steps over the threshold.

"Good morning, Miss Rachel. Hello, sir!" he says with cheery officiousness, a bright expression on his face.

"Thank you, Ravi," smiles Rachel.

And there they are at work in Bayham Street, the elegant trio of Cypriot street cleaners, beards trim, who will settle their carts at the end of the close on a roll-up and tea break to hold their daily moot and salute Rachel at her window, disappointed when she is not home, reticent when they spot only Zach. They will pause with their brooms, bow their heads as Rachel passes.

"Fuck-hell," Zach laughs. "Walking out with you, Rach, it's like the Happy Valley here!"

"Do you know who I haven't seen in ages?" Rachel asks.

"No," says Zach.

"Jesus," she answers.

Oh where has he gone, Jesus of Camden Town, the shirtless black fellow in overcoat and jeans wont to stalk the borders of Kentish Town, dragging a crucifix? Jesus makes his way up and down streets, ignoring the languorous stares of Somali minicab drivers reclining against street railings in their double-breasted jackets and shiny shoes, oblivious to the glances of lean Turkish shopkeepers, joshing smiles on their shadowy chins. Jesus is passing! He is not judged.

But there is Camden Kitchen, bent deep as a croquet hoop, the better to commune with pigeons, perhaps, the better to spread her wares. Surely this is how it began. The deeper she crooked, the closer she came to the earth and the scavenging birds in the city. So now there she stands, always at the busiest thoroughfares, a fag end glued to her lip, scattering seed like a farmer, in generous arcs. She has an escort wherever she goes, a flock of raucous gulls and feral pigeons flying low, flapping wildly, waiting for the crookback to set her pitch.

Hello! Here's Dan Donnelly, bestriding the High Street to shake a fist in air and hurl imprecations at the chosen few in his fighting Irish tones, typically collaring Zach—on one occasion, between hearty bites of a raw chicken leg. What the bloody hell are you doing, man? Zach wants to say, but Dan is wild with defiance, shaking his fives tremendously. Zach clenches his own, tight in his pocket, knowing he could floor the old soak with a single straight right. Rachel slips her hand in Zach's pocket and leans into his body, feeling his tension escape.

"Bloody Mr. Fisticuffs," he mutters. "Bloody Dan Donnelly!" he says, recalling the day he and Rach ennobled him thus, looking up the boxing ditty and intoning it together.

Epitaph for Sir Daniel Donnelly
Underneath this pillar high
Lies Sir Daniel Donnelly.

He was a stout and handy man
And people called him "Buffing Dan,"
Knighthood he took from George's sword
And well he wore it, by my word!
He died at last from forty-seven
Tumblers of punch he drank one even;
Overthrown by punch, unharmed by fist,
He dies unbeaten pugilist!
Such a buffer as Donnelly
Ireland never again will see.

At the very edge of Bayham Street, they cross the well-worn path the boy Dickens once walked on his troubled way to the blacking factory by the Strand, and stumble into a gaggle of *aliks*, spilling out of an offy with their bottles and tinnies. The off-licence is their assembly point, their lost and found; they find each other here. The lushies are primed, curiously, to holler at Zachariah on sight, even in the company of Rachel, his presence somehow incendiary. They are headed for their haunt by Camden Town Tube station to nurse their complaints in bellicose tones, touched, Rachel fancies, by spirits of the condemned. Here, where the Mother Red Cap coaching inn once stood, a gibbet was erected close by, purposefully far from the more populated quarters of a radical London. She shuts her eyes to see it, this once-remote crossroads, this mortiferous place.

Rachel and Zach run the gauntlet, and on past the slap-bang diners towards the *lido*, as they coin it, the proud row of Portuguese and Greek establishments of Pratt Street with their draped fish nets and gay decorations and sandwich blackboards with coloured chalk offerings. Their favourite café is run by a Greek who can be seen in almost all weathers seated on his cramped patio, feet planted firmly apart to accommodate his imposing paunch as he gazes wilfully into the distance so that his eyes, Rachel swears, reflect not car park and council estate but sparkling blue waters and merry bobbing boats.

Skirting the red pillar-box at the end of the close, vintage Elizabeth II, Rachel notes the familiar shadow cast by the corner signpost in end-of-day sunlight, slanting across the cream washed wall of the Gardens, a shadow remarkably akin to a graveyard marker, baleful. She takes

Zach's arm as they approach their front door, heads down to avoid the evil squint of that odious aged, their next-door neighbour, out for an airing. Alla, once a patient of Nicky's, was introduced to Camden thanks to a lingering and irregular association with his wife, Tasha apprising her of the availability of the flat in Rachel and Zach's Victorian row, which she buys instantly despite perpetual claims to poverty, filling it, furthermore, with several antique birch fretwork chairs, Biedermeier mahogany pieces, rare icons and porcelain knick-knacks. She has a small Repin, a reproduction, keeping the original at her bank.

"She's mafia," Zach is fond of announcing. "*Russkaya Mafiya!* Definitely."

And here she comes, grasping her stick with imperious menace. In her waning days, increasingly arched since the death of Nicky, her saviour, Alla commands an army of souls on her dwindling estate. She is catered to by social workers, home help, nurses, doctors and therapists, by dial-a-ride cabbies, librarians and cooks-on-wheels, benevolent high street pharmacists and newsagents, and brow-beaten neighbours, all of whom she cajoles and abuses by turn, her serfs.

"Your SISTER is at home," Alla will inform Zach if she crosses him alone, her emphasis inflammatory, though today she is somewhat pacific. Rachel is useful to her and so she offers the weakest of smiles in greeting.

"Now there's *one* Russian," Zach declares with a slam of their door, "they might have bloody purged!"

"Alla is old," offers Rachel, smiling.

"That's not it, Rach. Tasha will never be like that! Alla's mean. *Leary, scaley!*"

"Nicky used to say she was—what was it? *Unfailingly civil*. Charming, even."

"Because she's a *mace!* Swindler! He never charged her for treatments. She only ever grunted at Tasha. If she had wanted free piano lessons from the famous composer, she would have charmed her too! She's right out of one of your folk tales, isn't she? The evil something. Not Baba Yaga, but—you know."

"Sorceress, miser? Pike with the long teeth! *Tasha's* folk tales, you mean. She started it. When we were small."

"I clap eyes on Alla," Zach says, "my hackles rise!"

"She's frightened of dying."

"Ready for the long room, you reckon?" Zach says. "Needs a nudge, perhaps? A drop of the shoulder is all it would take," he adds, sparring in air. "A little feint, a jab, a push—one, two, it's all over. Into the long room!"

"That's cruel, Zach," smiles Rachel.

"Put her to bed with a shovel! Dust to bloody dust!"

From dust to dust, Rachel will intone, *full circle!*

Moscow, after the great fire of 1812, was partially rebuilt from London's old stones. From the dust-heaps of King's Cross—Battle Bridge, as it was known—to the houses and squares of Moscow and back again, fly London stock yellows. Bricks and brick dust. Every bone-grubber has a dream of place. What's in a bone, a stone? Life is infinitely patterned, Rachel always tells him, its morphology—spectacular!

And so she traverses the city and hangs her hat in Camden, her lungs expanding upon the approach. This is air she knows. And it is home for Zachariah, his patch for being hers, and so here he protects his own and has marked the territory. Though it is she who has padded every stone and mapped the landmarks, human, natural, man-made, Zach it is who cocks a leg, Rachel teases, over the wide expanse. This is his field. A hound marks throughout a territory, not merely the perimeter. Rachel's Camden is less fractious, more fanciful, perhaps, than his, being also a place of grassland, stream and tree, habitat of fox and bird, passerine and wader, seabird and vagrant. In Camden Town, Rachel listens to gulls in the Gardens, wailing, swooping, calling the streets, just another London cry, territorial, vagabond, savage. The seabirds divine that the water-table is high and skim the ground, nosing the Westbourne, Tyburn, Fleet, roving north to Highgate Ponds. Gull trawls the city, alighting on rubbish tips, outfalls, docks, tracing the waters from west to east, from Wormwood Scrubs to the Lea, and westwards again, from Deptford to Barnes. Caw! Caw! As the myth goes, gulls are dead souls and the Kittiwake, the most sea-faring of them all, is the dead soul of a child. The London gull has not been a true seabird for ages. Gull is a citizen now, like her rooftop blackbird, a herald, singing out the song of Zach's return.

Spruce, pine, birch and fir. A fish, a bird, a wolf, Rachel hardly leaves her desk this day. She draws and draws.

He is surely halfway home by now, halfway home from the City, Izzy's Whitechapel gym. Stumping it in his Loake "Kempton," classic chukka, Goodyear welted. Zach walks in his Loakes. He lopes. *Patterns of locomotion in animals are known as gaits. When the ground is level and the animal moves at constant speed, he repeats the same leg movements again and again. Gaits are periodic cycles.*

Rachel draws a spruce, because there are always trees in Russian folk tales, forests of trees with wanderers abroad, wandering purposefully, it's a special gait. She will do the maps last, as endpapers, and where there are seas—Black, Caspian, Baltic, Barents, Kara—she will draw ships and fish, perhaps a pike bobbing in the water, head in air, and when she reaches the Caucasus, Rachel will draw Cossacks, and where the forests are, she will make wolves. A wolf is her signature.

Don't fight today! Rachel incanted this morning, in her head, at his retreating shape, certain he would hear her, willing the message on towards his hyperacusive ears as he travelled at walking pace and into a trot, both of which gaits are symmetric in periodic cycles. Zach walks and moulds his boots into familiar creases, little dune shapes and barchans forming across the smooth calf uppers. Rachel sometimes prances in his shoes at home, clowning for Zach, and sometimes she plays alone, slipping into them very slowly, just to sense him from the inside out.

Where are you now? How long is it from there to here? Are you nearly home? Rachel is certain he hears her, because wolves, she knows, have such mobile ears they can move them almost 180 degrees to tell where a sound is coming from. It's coming from here, Zach. It's me. And all the old voices calling, they come from here too. Zachariah, Zachariah, my fighting man.

Zachariah, Zachariah, our foundling boy.

[FIVE]

Z ACHARIAH WALKS.

It's been a two-bone, one turn-up, no-*alik* day. So far.

Nearly home, Rachel! And I have wine and flowers. And the fish, hey!
Zach laughs and hums the Russian song he and Rach revelled in the very
first time they heard it, as children.

> *Oh, baby mine, oh you dearest one,*
> *Yes, a stew with parsley.*
> *Cook this fish, so we'll have a stew,*
> *Come and kiss me, my darling.*

Zach summons up an old memory, of fidgets in the stalls of the Wigmore Hall after school, attending rehearsals for another of Mama's song
cycles. They were so young, he and Rachel; perhaps twelve and thirteen. They listened to a song of old *Rus* and collapsed in giggles, earning
Katya's ire and a cool eviction from the auditorium. They were so rarely
admitted to rehearsals. This was Katya's realm.

Wigmore Hall, London, 1980s.

Song Recital Series. Byelova Male Choir, conductor Ekaterina
Byelova-Wolff. *Songs of Old Rus,* Rehearsal.

Along Peterskaya Yamskaya Street, with my little bell,
Hey!
Here comes my beloved, driving all alone,
All alone in a troika,
Down the little side streets, hey!

I was at a feast, at a merry party,
I did not drink mead,
I drank sweet vodka, hey!
I drank sweet vodka from a half-pail.
It's not ice cracking,
It's not a mosquito singing,
That's a boy to his girl,
Bringing a fish.

Oh, baby mine—

The eruption of snorts and gaiety from the stalls prompts Katya to raise one hand to stop the singing. She lowers her baton, looks over her shoulder at Zachariah and Rachel.

"Out," she states. *"Pozhaluysta."* Please.

"But it's so *silly,* Mama!" pipes Zach, protesting with all the might of his twelve-year-old bellows and leaping to his feet, chest puffed, to fling a proprietary arm around his sister who fits so neatly in the crook of him, as if wrought for this place. He speaks for them both, though Rachel is some months his elder.

Katya is silent, showing them the door with a glance, not a shadow of a smile on her face. What a fighter that boy is, she thinks, observing the fierceness of his hold on Rachel, the tension in his grip, in the muscles of his neck, observing it not without a flicker of disquiet. How he has grown. And what a sound he makes. Clarion. And what pitch, for a boy. If only he were truly musical. If only he were not so—rough. She turns back to her male choir as they wait out the exit of her children to the sound of slapping seats and gathering of satchels, the hurried bash up the aisle.

"Bye, Mama! Bye!" they call, before Zach slams the hall door, wincing as he goes, having misjudged it all yet again: weight of the door, strength of his body, timing and distance.

Katya's choristers shuffle uncertainly on the stage above, wrong-footed by the family scene they have witnessed, unable to read her for once, oppressed by intimacy. They know her every gesture, she knows their every note, but the men with their rough-hewn frames and tomb-deep voices are bashful now and yearn for cues, feeling strangely blunt and outranked in the light of Katya's gaze, which is full of age-old divides, and withering. *Noble and serf, kulak and muzhik, White and Red; Your Honour, Your Worship, Your Radiance.* Close the gap, clear the air, pray the men. Hurry. Let us sing!

My children, thinks Katya, watching her men. *My boys.*

"'Along Peterskaya Street,' please," she commands. "Again."

And so the men sing, with impossible grace.

At St. Sepulchre-without-Newgate, Zach enters the yard, seeks out a bench. Corner time, pit stop. He laughs at the memory of his child-ish wilfulness and Katya's infinite aplomb. Katya! Hear me now! If you could hear me now! Singing your song of old *Rus*!

Zach decides to cab it home the rest of the way, fagged after his day at the gym and this morning's walk, stumping it, as he did, from Camden to Clerkenwell, and on to Whitechapel, doing a bone count as always, not a day without bones afoot! Chicken, mostly, and sometimes lamb— legs, wings, whole carcasses. Nearly home now, and he is showered, scrubbed up and spruce, but in need of a half minute before his ride, to gather himself. Gather yourself, Zach! Take half a minute. Retire for a wipe. He sits in the squat churchyard of St. Sepulchre-without-Newgate, combing his still-damp wavy hair with his fingers.

Half a minute! Zach knows all the rules by heart, all seven of the first written rules of the Prize Ring.

Rules to be Observed in All Battles on the Stage
II. That, in order to prevent any Disputes, the time a Man lies after a fall, if the Second does not bring his Man to the side of the square, within the space of half a minute, he shall be deemed a beaten Man.

Cabbing it home means Zach stays cleaner, less creased and sweaty. Hell! His beard grows fast as blazes, like a damp wicket in springtime sun, green, and Rachel's skin is so fine, his bristles can score her red the way a new ball marks a bat, English alum on English unbleached willow, finest quality, special selection, Rachel-grade. Zach, my man, you have cricket on the brain! Thomas has asked him to play on Sunday. *Bring Rachel*, he said. Thomas "All Souls" Aubry, gentleman, corinthian at heart, and half French yet more English than a true-born.

But can I bowl, can I bat by Sunday? Zach wonders, slowly flexing his brittle fists inside his coat pockets, slowly, slowly. Half a minute! He needs this respite, he needs to find the words to explain today's turn-up to his girl, how he hit out at Sandbag Shaw, nothing he could do. It just bloody happens! Another fight. *Turn-up, barney, battle.* There Zach was, minding his own business, ringside at the time, in his civvies, eyes on All Souls when along comes Sandbag, stirring it up as per usual. The thing is, Rach, a man must take a stand, he must ply it, the art of self-defence.

Will he be fit for cricket on Sunday? And what should he tell his girl about the new welts on his hands? Only days after his sparring with Thomas and the cut above the eye that Shaw worked over today. What shall he say? This is one story he cannot tell her. Not in all its particulars . . . Zach hangs his head a moment, recalling the fool he was today. How he took the bait, fell into a trap. Sucker-punched.

Zach rests his elbows on the ring apron, standing with a tilt of the hips, legs crossed jauntily at the ankles. He watches Aubry with a bruiser of some power and an ability both to leap into a well-disguised blow off the balls of his feet, and to switch from a right to southpaw stance in a flash. To sharpen his instincts, Aubry opts for the occasional sparring session in which he is almost dangerously overmatched. He will sometimes spar without a headguard, believing the guard is an invitation to a headshot and can lead to a cavalier attitude in the wearer. Devil-may-care. A fighter in a helmet might forget to move his head.

"Move yer 'ead!" implores Izzy.

When Sandbag Shaw sidles up like a sad dog at the bar, a cowboy villain, he is breathing hard from a workout and sweating through his favourite vest, a cast-off Marvin Hagler once gave him with the famously awkward slogan emblazoned upon it, "Destruction and Destroy." Shaw's a middleweight now and more comfortable at nearly a stone heavier, with a couple of good wins in the bag. He is looking thicker, but cut, and it suits him, thinks Zach. He has a naturally low centre of gravity, a classic puncher's anatomy.

"Hiya," he says.

"Marvellous Marvin, eh?" goes Zachariah. "That's some top."

"A gift. I was a kid, Dad got me into the gym to see Marvin. He was here for the Alan Minter fight. I was just a kid."

"*Marvin*. Right. Nice one," says Zach, trying to stay cool, having heard the yarn at least eight times before.

"How's the head?"

The head, thinks Zach, suddenly recalling a thing he read about Hagler. Hagler's temporal muscles. Yes! A doctor doing some routine examination finds that Marvin's temporal muscles are four times the normal thickness. Four times. Hit him right there on the temporalis, he feels it four times less! Marvellous Marvin!

"What about my head? Oh *this*?" asks Wolff indicating his eyebrow wound. "It's nothing. Was messing around with Aubry."

"Not that! I mean, you know, the brain damage."

"I don't have fucking brain damage, Shaw. Subdural haematoma. Happens all the time. I retired, that's all."

"They took your licence away, mate."

"Old news, old news. A precaution. I'm fucking fine."

"So," Shaw resumes, looking up at the action and unable to keep the sneer out of his voice. "I hear you're gonna try and write a whole book about him? Aubry? You're a writer now?"

"Ever read a book, Shaw?" asks Zach, bumping shoulders with the big man, jovial as he can muster. "You know. Start to finish? Just joking. Don't worry."

Shaw shuffles his feet, rolls his shoulders; biding time.

"Might do that meself. When I retire. Write a book. I've got ideas. I wrote a poem once."

"Hell's bells," exclaims Zach none too enthusiastically, fearing a flourish of turgid misspelled poetry from Shaw's kitbag. "A poem."

"With rhymes. None of that modern shit."

"Well, well. Thought you were taking up training. When you retire, that is. Start a stable. Train, manage."

"Nah. Too many fights left in me. I'm not thinking retirement. And anyways, there's no one out there to train but roof racks and rag heads—

macaroons! Drive me fucking crazy, all that rap and bling and Jesus and Allah, time out for prayers and whatnot, family members in the gym busy-bodying around. Can't be arsed. And the fucking promoters and managers—always skinny! Like money from a stone! I mean blood from a stone. Fucking four-be-twos! Sorry, mate."

"Four-be-two?"

"Jew. Four by two, you know. Plank of wood."

"Thick, you mean?"

"Never heard that before?" asks Shaw, incredulous. "Just rhyming slang, me old china plate!" he adds, cuffing Zach in the arm.

"WELL then," says Zach, laughing. "In THAT case. As it's just SLANG. Who could possibly be offended? So why 'sorry, mate'?"

"Jewish, aren't you? *Zachariah* and all that."

"You're a quiz, Shaw. A right quiz."

"What?"

"Nothing. And why are we even talking, man? I don't like you."

"I'm extending the hand of friendship, Wolff."

"Shake hands and come out fighting?"

"Hey! I'm doing my best here."

"OK. Anything else on your mind?"

"Yeah, mate. Is it true Jewish wives get their teeth knocked out and wear wooden ones? I saw this documentary."

"Fuck! UKIP make documentaries now? I mean, do half Jews lose only their lower teeth? Are you crazy, Shaw?"

"Well, that's what I heard. And Jews get buried standing up."

"You're lucky I'm not touchy, man. Say any of this around Izzy, he'll bloody bury *you* standing up. Wooden teeth. Izzy, you know. He's an all-out Jew."

"You met his wife?"

"Why? You want me to check her chops? Idiot."

"What?" asks Shaw. "I'm an idiot?"

"Just drop it! Hell, man. Change the subject."

"Sorry, mate. Anyway. Point is: I've better things to do than train a bunch of Somali pirates, know what I mean? That's it. And I'm going for a belt. You listening? I apologise. Didn't mean to be derogatory to you."

"What? You didn't mean . . . Ah, forget it. No worries," mumbles Zach, surprised by Shaw's sudden primness.

"One more thing. I don't mean to be funny, but—what's the pong?

Excuse me. Meaty smell. Stinks round here, if you don't mind my saying. Not sweat and all that. Something else. Don't want to offend."

"You mean this?" asks Zach slowly, pulling the remnants of a peanut butter sandwich from the pocket of his sweats. "My sarnie? This? It's peanut butter," he explains, wondering at Sandbag's strange new litany. *Don't want to offend; excuse me; if you don't mind; sorry, mate; sorry.*

"Smells like shit, if you'll pardon my French! That's Yank food, am I right? Girly grub. Vegetarian."

"Jewish?" goes Zach.

"You having a laugh?"

"Mmm," he says, trying to focus on All Souls and blank out Shaw's coiled presence. "It's protein, man. Unsaturated fat. Know what I'm saying? Good fat. Rachel made it, slips it in with my gear, different thing every day. And here's something else. Ever heard of Joseph Mitchell? Never mind. Listen to this. Man wrote a story about a ratcatcher on the waterfront. In New York, 1940s, right? So the guy discovers how rats zero in on his sarnie, bold as brass. Useful knowledge, I reckon, Shaw. Keep a peanut butter sandwich in your pocket, see who comes sniffing by. Like bait. I smell a rat. See? Call it pest control."

Sandbag narrows his eyes, uncertain, suspicious, the rat story ringing in his ears like a storm brewing. He spits on the sprung floor of the gym, a gesture of self-assertion. "I'll make a note of that," he says darkly.

"Write a poem about it, why don't you?" Zach suggests.

"You don't write poems about rats, Wolff. Or fucking peanut butter rolls. You write poems about pretty things, girls, flowers and things. Come on!"

"When your career's over, Shaw, you should open a pub. Write poems, frame them, hang 'em over the mantelpiece. Up there with your trophies, right? Your belts. It's a fine tradition! Ah yes, I can see it! Know this old one? Golden oldie, man. Listen! '*We boast a science sprung from manly pride. A noble pastime void of vain pretence, the fine old English art of self-defence . . .*'"

Zach finishes the chaunt and slaps the ring apron, laughing into his chest.

"You've gone doolally, mate. You're a nut-nut."

"Peanut butter nut-nut, that's me! How about this? "And a boxing we will go, will go, will go—" SING WITH ME, SHAW! "And a boxing we will go!"

"You're doing my head in, Wolff."

"Just saying, man. Getting you inspired, know what I mean? You can write poems about boxing. Boxing's a *pretty* thing. Sweet. Just watch Aubry!"

"Speaking of pretty things, then. How's your sister? She's pretty."

"Yeah," says Zach absently, distracted by All Souls who dances his way and hangs on the ropes overhead, calling Zach's name. And just as Zach looks up, Aubry shakes his head over him, shivering like a wet dog, letting the sweat fly.

Wolff shakes a fist in mock fury, wipes his face on his sleeve.

"Well?" Shaw insists, pressing, grinding. "Well?"

"Well what? What do you want, Sandbag?" snaps Zachariah.

"Your sis?"

"She's fine, mate, she's fine."

"Still shagging her, then?"

BANG!

Zach is sure he has broken Sandbag's nose, though the man takes the hit so gamely, Wolff wonders did he hit straight enough, did he use enough force, has he lost his touch? Or perhaps in that empty sphere behind Shaw's eyes, between the auriculars, there are simply no pain receptors, nothing but a great urge to oppugn, because without blinking, Sandbag hits out at Zach's brow and works at the wound All Souls inflicted upon him last week, the injury Shaw clocked at first sight of his old enemy, a raw wound in the early stages of healing, red rag to a bull. So he bided his time in idle chaff before reopening it with one savage twist of the knuckles and Zach is sandbagged again, falling for *courtesy* this time, falling like a tree.

The gym is a hive of noise now, of noise and sudden activity, and there they are a second time in not so many more days looming in Zach's hazy vision, the troubled faces of Izzy the cutman and All Souls Aubry, troubled but chipper.

"You smashed his nose, Wolff!" Aubry whispers, having jumped out of the ring to his side.

All Souls is an *out-and-outer* if he ever knew one, a splendid fellow and a gentleman. *My friend,* Zach thinks, before spurting a jet of bloody froth and sitting up to hurl at Shaw's retreating shape with such fury Shaw lurches in the restraining arms of two trainers, a convict rattling his chains.

"Sandbag!" Zach shouts. "Hey, Lord bloody Byron! Arsehole! Shag? Did you say 'shag'? Fuck off with that word! If you mean *fuck*, fucking say so! Idiot! Her name is Rachel, you fucking ape, now fuck off! Go home and write some poems!"

"Bring it on, Wolff! Get up, you bum!" snarls Shaw.

"Get him out of here!" snarls Izzy.

"Fucking FUCK OFF!" Zach yells.

"Wow. That was eloquent, old chap," says All Souls, smiling. "Now cool it. He's gone. Ah . . . I mean, fucking cool it."

"OK, fuck," goes Zach, grinning, a film of pink saliva staining his teeth. "I've got to get home, need to buy fish, supposed to buy fish. Wine merchant, fishmonger, I promised. I'm bringing a fish to my girl, hey!"

"Hey—what?"

"It's a song, a fucking song!"

"Ah. I fucking see. Right then," says Aubry, mopping at Zach's bleeding physiognomy with a sweat-damp towel. "We'll shop together. Know just the place. Let's clean you up first. For your girl! For Rachel. Yes?"

"Yeah," Zach says. "OK."

"Oh. And while you're down there—captive audience, old chap—you will remember to tell her about my lunch on Sunday? The cricket?"

"Yeah, man," goes Zach, smiling through blood-stained teeth.

"Fuck me, Wolff!" scolds Izzy, tearing up swabs of cotton. "Don't know why you rise to the geezer. Waste of ruddy time! Bloke's on a roll, thinks he's a bit special. But know what? He's not a *fighter*. A fighter don't scrap, he's cool, keeps it in the ring. Get me? This boy, he'll be working the door at some fancy boozer two years from now, I'm telling you. And you? Want to end up punchy? I thought you were a smart feller. Stay smart. No more rucks! Right? Right!"

"Sorry, Iz."

"Just grow up, lad! Sorry ain't good enough! Act your ruddy age! And now," Izzy adds with a wink, fishing in his box of tricks. "Better fucking stay still. If you want to stay pretty. I'm just about to STITCH YOU UP!"

St. Sepulchre-without-Newgate.

It's been a two-bone, one turn-up, no-*alik* day so far.

Sorry, Rach.

Zachariah leans back against the churchyard bench, extends his legs, raising his heels off the ground, contracting the great femoral muscles and *sartorius,* aware of the strain there, the feeling not unpleasant. He recalls the verses from "The Fine Old English Art of Self-Defence!" The verses, more akin to a song, a ditty—*chaunt, crambonian*—were framed to hang above the mantel at Jem Burn's pub in Piccadilly, in the Dilly, haunt of flower-sellers and other ladies, too, of the night, with keys around the necks betokening their profession—*Cyprians, strums.* Jem Burn had milling in the blood, what with two prize-fighting uncles and his wife a pugilist's daughter. Burn was once an animal skinner and apprenticed to a *skiver,* and therefore a fellow well acquainted with the flaying of skin and the tapping of claret and all the shades of oxidised blood, of lesions and bruises, port, ruby, scarlet, navy and maroon. It would be no surprise to him, when he took up the art of self-defence, the palette of colours staining his skin, nor the scars criss-crossing. Jem "Young Skiver" Burn never made champion, but became a fine publican, respected and hearty, no lush. Upon his retirement from the P.R.—the Prize Ring—he stayed afloat, no *castaway.*

Sometimes it ends well for a bruiser, reflects Zach, patting the parcel of halibut and wine that wants chilling, excited by the two bottles so proudly wrapped in tissue coloured Bristolian blue and chosen by Aubry who is well versed in oenology, his old man a winemaker. No. *Viticulteur.* Thomas Aubry is the last gentleman boxer in all the wide world, decides Zach, Thomas the viticulturist and ichthyologist. Ichthyology. Who in blazes makes a life study of fish? laughs Zach. Most peculiar. A man of science all round then. Thomas "All Souls" Aubry, man of sciences!

Fish, fish.

Rachel, Zach knows, is very partial to fish and crustaceans. She has particular faith in the properties of seafood, dishing it up for them both with zeal; cod and whitebait, monkfish and snapper, trout and sardine, salmon, pilchard, sole, mussel and oyster, crab. She pounds fine bones for the purveying of calcium, feeding bones to their bones. *For your joints, Zach! And your knowledge-box!* There is more. She slips him capsules of fish oil, tablets of seaweed. She swims almost daily at the local baths, she lines the stairs with sea grass. She sports a yellow oilskin in the rains and her eyes are Bristolian blue, Avon and Severn blue. And Rachel dreams of Lake Vostok, a five-hundred-metre depth of water buried deep beneath Antarctic ice.

"Is there anything in it?" Zach will ask.

"*Bezmolviye!*" Isolation, quiet.

"Not in the lake! In your craze for fish! *Bezmolviye, Bezmolviye!* It's kind of fishy, you know. Your craze."

"Amazing, though. A whole ancient *atmosphere*, Zachashka. Lake Vostok. With fungi, algae."

"We'll make old bones, won't we?" he always adds, swallowing tablets, scoffing fish. "Make old bones with me, Rachel!"

"I want to swim with you, Wolff. In Lake Vostok. Four kilometres beneath. One day."

"One day then. And Rach? I just want you to know. Anytime you have a craving and are lost for bones? You can chew on me. Feel free."

"Why, thank you."

"You're just a bone yard."

"And you're a graveyard charley."

Go home, Wolff, thinks Zach. Grab a cab. Into a *boneshaker* with you. You graveyard charley.

Highgate, Norwood, Whitechapel, St. Marylebone, St. James at St. Pancras, St. Sepulchre-without-Newgate, she's right, Zach, it's you, the graveyard charley, the rambler and recorder of old sites and boxers' headstones, warden of monuments and epitaphs. All you need is a lamp, man, and a nightshift. But here at St. Sepulchre's, where is he? Where are the bones of Big Ben Brain?

Big Ben the Bristolian once beat the great Tom Johnson. Ben the collier turned London coal porter, was a prize-fighter for half his short life, yet taken up to the gods on the eve of a glorious comeback, perishing in small rooms in Gray's Inn Road and put to bed with a shovel right here at St. Sepulchre's. Somewhere here. His marker is lost, explains the vicar's wife to Zach one afternoon in the kindly back-room shambles amidst the leisurely rumble and holler of builders in the forecourts.

"There is simply no record of your bare-knuckle boxer," she informed him. "And you are not the first to look."

"Not the first?"

"No," she smiled. "There has been one before you, quite recently. Asking for Ben Brain."

"A historian?"

"An artist, I believe. She had a sketchbook."

"She?"

An angelic, Zach thought. Rachel? Was it Rachel?

The vicar's wife told Zachariah of World War Two bomb damage and the sorry displacement of headstones and destruction of others, and of how a school once stood in the north yard where there is now an osteopathic surgery, and it is only later that Zach hears the joke in this, about a fellow plying his trade of skeletal realignment right here above the forever disjointed, an underground of odds and ends and smashed eternity boxes, of car-boot-sale bones. Laugh, man. It's a lark.

Zach makes a fist. There is soft-tissue damage but, despite the swelling, Izzy dismissed the possibility of a scaphoid fracture. Good. There are twenty-seven bones in the human hand, Rachel likes to remind him, all of them breakable. Zach tots it up, his history of fractures from early youth, counting the bones he broke—his own, and other boys'. The cracked mandibles in boxing, the carpals in cricket. Wolff threw a fast brutal hook as a schoolboy, bowled a mean bouncer. Bone-shaking.

Zach was ever so keen a cricketer as a boy. Imperious with the bat, intimidating with the ball. Turning out for the school's First Eleven, he would scan the crowd in a studiously offhand manner, searching the proud smattering of parents and friends and family for Lev, for Katya. Are they here? For once? They never came, Zach recalls. Well, Katya once or twice, Lev good as never. He cannot remember a single Sports Day, a single match they ever attended together. He does, however, remember a day it riled him very much, that they rarely ever came. He remembers how the hurt flickered and flared in his guts.

Wolves are the most socially equable of all mammals. Females have identical status to males.

"Papa never comes. They never come," says Zach, cap tipped back and bat over the shoulder, his birthday gift Newbery with the massive sweet spot and slightly bowed blade, lovingly oiled and knocked-in under the watchful eyes of his sister. Rachel is in thrall to the gravity of it, this preparation of willow, the caressing with cloth and bat oil, and bashing with mallet. And the practice hits ensuing, Zach swinging and scything in air, effecting classic cuts and drives and pulls of imaginary balls, each stroke set to accompanying steps. Move the feet. Don't get stuck in the crease. Stroke-play, he says to Rachel, by way of explanation. This is stroke-play. Zach learns the feel of his bat, the weight and pick-up, the length of its grip; he is both stroke-player and hard-hitter, not above the occasional agricultural slog.

Zach's eyes flash with light, caught by the peculiar greenness of early summer grass and the strobe effect of sun through wrought-iron fencing and trees. He kicks at dust and gravel with his unlaced desert boots, cricket spikes slung around his neck by the laces, his tread lazy and ostentatious, full of close-of-play sensuality. The shapes of things are crisp and stand-out in the coming dusk, all the shapes and voices, of stragglers in the field and the dwindling gaggle of parents and kids at fête tables, and of Rachel several steps ahead of him, jauntily clad in his batting gloves and slipover with the sky-blue stripes at collar and waist-band. The band of his jumper skirts her knees, the shoulders fall clean to her elbows. *He has grown so fast.*

"You look bloody ridiculous," he says.

"Oh goody," replies Rachel. "Papa's not sporty, you know. That's all it is. You don't really expect him to come, do you? You don't grouse about Mama not coming."

"She's never bloody home. Anyway, she came once. At least once."

"She would have come today, Zach. But she's away. I was there. I'm here. I watched you! You were great!" she says, turning back to him and throwing her hands high in the end-of-day air. "HOWZAT!"

"I don't need anyone to bloody watch me! And she wouldn't have come. Too bloody busy for bloody *Games.*"

"Well, bloody everything, then," says Rachel as Zach plumps onto a bench to prod at the ground with the toe of his bat.

"When a player does this at the wicket," he asks absently, "between balls, know what they call it?"

"Gardening," she replies.

"Right."

"You're in such a huff, Zach. Stop it."

"She wouldn't have come. She says Games—sports—bring out the *muzhik* in people. It brings out the *muzhik*. She said that."

"It's not a bad word. Papa calls you *muzhik*."

"Exactly. And you think it's affectionate."

"Yes."

"Hardly. Peasant? Fuck! There's more than just music and science in the world. There's sport and, I don't know, farming! And firefighters and cobblers."

"You want to make shoes, Zach?"

"Of course bloody not! I'm just saying. Maybe I'll join the Royal Navy, who knows? But I *am* going to box. Be a fighter."

"She would have been proud today."

"Missed a catch."

"You made so many runs!"

"Forty-seven. No great shakes."

"FORTY-SEVEN NOT OUT, Zach. Not out!"

"Mmm. You can tell her, if you like. You don't have to," he adds, tossing his head, his hair shaped by damp and the helmet, flattened at the crown, corkscrewed at the nape and temples.

"I definitely am going to," Rachel replies, turning his gloves over and over, marvelling at the stitching and architecture of batting gloves, the padding and articulation and little diamonds of checkerboard material at the knuckles coloured black and gold, the pattern repeated at the elasticated wrist that feels loose on her, tenuous, indeed, as Zach's own new grasp when they cross a busy road, thumb and index circling her radius and ulna with but the merest of holds, gruff and reluctant. Where they once sat huddled, on benches and sofas, he now leaves space between. And he stares these days, straight at her across rooms. She can sense it without looking. What have I done? she thinks. I've done something wrong. Perhaps we are no longer friends. *He is growing so fast.*

Rachel attempts to undo a glove with her teeth, as she has seen Zach do at the batting crease, ripping it open and jamming it under an arm to liberate his hand at the end of a testing over. He will adjust the helmet, flick sweat away with a swipe of the fingertip, shift a slipping box, and stride down the wicket to tamp at earth and blades of grass, at cracks and declivities—doing a spot of gardening, as it is known—and

all these manoeuvres, to Rachel, are marvellous, replete with authority and secret sporting knowledge, and otherness. Maleness. Mimicking him now, she shudders at the contact of teeth and PVC, hating the
sound, furthermore, of Velcro, that awful scream of separation, and so
she slips the gloves between her knees, freeing herself in a trice.

"Remember the Velcro story? Invention of Velcro?" asks Rachel.

"No."

"Papa told us. You know, the scientist and his dog."

"Don't remember. And not bloody bothered."

"Oh. I see. All the same," suggests Rachel, "one day, someone might
invent *quiet* Velcro."

"Well it won't be me," says Zach. "I'm no scientist."

"Oh yes you are," she counters, prompting him.

"Of the Noble Art!" he declaims.

"Of SELF-DEFENCE!" says she.

In Camden Town, Rachel glances at her watch—he'll be home soon—
and notices the plaster she applied to a silly kitchen wound incurred this
morning after Zach had left for the day. *Fee-fi-fo-fum.* Whenever she cuts
herself, whenever she bleeds, Rachel recites it. She looks over her shoulder and smiles wryly. Is he coming? The giant, the ogre. Giant, ogre,
Baba Yaga—they all look for a weakness, they can smell blood.

> *Fee-fi-fo-fum,*
> *I smell the blood of an Englishman,*
> *Be he alive or be he dead,*
> *I'll grind his bones to make my bread.*

Rachel smiles and rips off the plaster, wincing slightly. *Velcro,* she
thinks, and pictures Zach at the gym. When his duties are done, he
makes time to work out. He strokes closed the ankle straps of his boxing boots, straps that fasten neatly and swiftly thanks to Velcro, a tenacious communion of opposing surfaces made from minute and velvety
nylon loops and hooks.

—*Rachel? The invention of Velcro.*

—*Georges de Mestral, Papa! Cockleburs. The fruiting head of the Xanthium strumarium is covered in hooked spines. He saw how they stuck to his dog's coat. Velours, crochet! Velcro.*

—*Good, Rachel.*

Rachel shuts her eyes, seeing Zach. He throws a left hook at the heavy bag, rips the straps from his boots. He always had a super left hook. If he is in luck and Izzy has time, Zach may get a rub-down. His skin, thinks Rachel, is velvet. On the way home, he might sing a tune, some Russian music, with crotchets.

She steps to the windows of the first floor and looks down into the close and there, loitering, is one of Zach's favourite drunks. *Alkash, alik.* Lush, soak, *castaway.* Zach, she knows, does a head count as he walks the city, of *aliks* and other crusting souls. It's tribal, he says. It's London. This fellow, the one he names Lucifer, found body parts in a bin liner last year, only a few streets away. And he is short on marbles, says Zach. Not much left in the *idea-pot.* Empty garret.

"Is that what tipped him over the edge?" she asked. "Finding the body?"

"He had already tipped, I think. Not a lot farther to go."

Rachel watches him now, the poor jingle brains, rocking to and fro on his feet, shod in sandals as always, the flesh bare until the bitterest days, his toenails barnacled and tinged with verdigris, a patina of old rooftops.

"Got a lucifer—got a lucifer—got a lucifer?" Rachel hears him recite, waving the choicest of his collection of fag ends. "Got a lucifer?" he asks, though he is alone in the close.

If Zach were here, he'd go outdoors with a box of safety matches—what does Lucifer *do* with all those matches? Yes, Zach would bring him the lucifers and a beer, perhaps. Pair of socks, a few quid. They might chaff a while, the exchange irregular.

"Ta, mate. Off to Epsom," Lucifer announced one day, nodding vigorously. "Must dash."

"Races?"

"Forest."

"You don't mean Epping?"

"I say what I mean."

"Right."

"I had a dog," said Lucifer.

"Today? Is he lost?" asked Zach, perplexed.

"Gypsies. Threw him in the canal. I found that dog, fished him out. And you should have seen him, made me spew my guts, he was *so* emancipated!"

"Ah. You mean—"

"I mean what I say. What's wrong with you? Ta for the gear and all that."

Zach will chaff with these fellows, see them right. Yet commands Rachel never to go outdoors herself.

"Not for any of them," he insists. "Even if I'm home."

"Don't worry. I shan't."

"Can't tell how they'll react. In the streets."

It's a dangerous place! If a wolf should come out of the forest, THEN what would you do?

Rachel thinks how he always had an eye for these fellows, even as a boy, and that some were quite young themselves. She asked him once, on the way home from piano lessons, from which Zach always took it upon himself to fetch her, how does he suppose it happens to a boy? How is it he turns lushy—lushy and homeless? Cracked, perhaps. Where does it all begin? When Zach answered that it can happen to anyone, to a *laid-in-the-streets*, to a posh boy, to anyone, she wondered aloud how he knew, is it because he has special knowledge, regretting her surmise as soon as uttered. The memory returns to her now, clarion.

"You must have special knowledge, I suppose. I mean. Because you're—"

"It's all right," says Zach, staring at her. "And I said," he adds absently, "it can happen to anyone. Becoming lushy, homeless. I think so. You don't have to be rough or stupid or anything. A foundling or orphan or whatever. Reject. It can happen to anyone."

"But that's special knowledge, isn't it? That's what I meant. Because you're—oh, I'm stupid, what a booby. I'm sorry, I'm sorry."

"I don't get it," says Zach as if he hadn't heard her. "Why can't you take piano from Aunt Tasha? It's great there, at Tasha and Nicky's."

"Do you mind picking me up here?"

"Why should I?" he asks, frowning. "Not my point. Just don't understand it. When you could learn from *Tyotya.*"

Whereupon Rachel describes a scene she witnessed lately between

Mama and *Tyotya,* happy for the change of subject, a passing reprieve, telling Zach how she asked Mama the very same question one day, to which Katya replied sharply that Natasha is a composer, not a piano teacher, and that one would not consult a specialist before a general practitioner, or play Stravinsky before Brahms, a response that raised a gentle laugh in Tasha.

"Don't you think," she smiled, "Rachel would enjoy it more? And learn faster? I would teach her happily."

"It's not important," Katya quipped, "that she enjoy it. Not yet."

"Oh my sister," Tasha exclaimed in Russian, embracing her. "My darling little sister. How thin you are growing!"

"Then what?" asks Zach. "What happened?"

"They just laughed and danced around the kitchen."

"Right. Well. I still don't get it. And I don't like nasty guts, your teacher. Hatchet-face, old dry boots. Looks like bloody Frankenstein. Frankenstein's monster, I mean. Bloody whosit. Boris Karloff."

"Zach! His name *is* Karloff. Karlov!"

"Joking?"

"Serious," Rachel swears. "Karlov."

"Wow," says Zachariah, clapping his hands. "Amazing. Amazed of Chelsea, that's me!"

"Sorry about before, Zach. You know. The street thing. The roughs. Foundlings, strays. How you know about them. I didn't mean—sorry."

"I don't care," he insists, stark-eyed.

"What I was really thinking," resumes Rachel, "is—well, that there's fate, you see. I don't dismiss it, I don't think it's idiotic. It's quite scientific, actually. What we become. Who we—meet, end up with," she continues, flames in her cheeks.

"You think we would have met, no matter what? Even if I were some lushy? Some loon? Street kid?"

"You're laughing at me."

"Just asking," he says.

"Everyone has one person, I think. For life. That's all."

"Will we have children, then?" he asks, grinning, eyes bright.

"Ha ha, very funny," says Rachel.

Zach watches her closely then drops his gaze, assuming a cricketer's stance, left side on, buttocks out, spine straight and upright, toes aligned, knees slightly bent and eyes over the forward shoulder, steady and level, facing imaginary bowler. He slaps the ground behind his feet astride the popping crease with imaginary bat, reciting silently from an old cricket manual, "Imagine you are a boxer ready to move forward or back." He slides the left foot forward, his leading leg, and drops right knee to ground as he swings the bat in a scything motion, sweeping to deep square on the on side with a sweet roll of the wrists. These are all steps in a dance.

"Four," he says. "That's the fifty partnership," he adds, raising his right fist to present knuckles, an inviting look on his face. Rachel pauses a moment before raising her own in response and they tap imaginary gloves, batsmen celebrating a milestone, a boundary, a good call, a brave stand, the fifty partnership. It's a gavotte. Runs are accumulating, luck is with them; it's a capital innings. There is footwork and timing, and hope. Hopes are so very well constructed.

Rachel steps back from the windows, returns to her desk, checks her watch again. Her cut finger has begun to bleed slightly and she licks the blood away. Salt, metal, black earth. Blood has such a tenebrous taste.

Zach flicks his cuff, reads the time on his watch, the face scratched as ice.

Go home, Wolff!

Along Holborn with my little bell, hey! Up Tottenham Court Road, from south to north, all alone in a troika, down the little side streets, hey! To my beloved, bringing a fish. Zach gazes into falling shadows, at the trap-door shapes in the lee of gravestones, dark oblongs where moments ago there was racing-green grass and old paving, pummelled by footsteps and weather. The change in the light nudges his idling brain into the reality of the yawning pits once dug here, at least six feet deep. It is proclaimed since days of plague, that *all graves shall be at least six feet deep*. This is the three-centuries-old ordinance designed to prevent pestilence from creeping up from beneath and over ground to poison the quick and lively. Fellows such as I, Zach smiles. Such as me.

Zach sings.

Oh, baby mine, oh, you dearest one,
Cook this fish, so we'll have a stew,
Yes, a stew with parsley.
Come and kiss me, my darling.

Zach hugs the packages to his flank and fingers the fresh dressing Izzy applied to his brow for the cut Sandbag Shaw reopened, Sandbag who'd raise his fists to a slight breeze if it ruffled his mouse-brown rug, bloody blazes. Sandbag Shaw! You *Rattus rattus,* you mar-all, paper skull, rusty guts, why cross my path today? I made a promise to my girl, hey! Or did I? Ah, but nobody dies from boxing, Rach, not really, not anymore!

Seven years before the publication of Jack Broughton's Rules, the *Northampton Mercury* records 420 deaths in London during one summer week of 1736, out of which are numbered "2 killed by boxing." Two only, hardly an epidemic! Yet Zach and Rachel took note, as children, of the times and places, causes and consequences of the deaths of millers, later perambulating the graveyards to search their eroding epitaphs, these monuments to the bruisers of England. What a pastime! And how it endures, another game they play, roaming the yards and vaults of Highgate, Brompton and Kensal Green, Marylebone and Whitechapel, St. James at St. Pancras, Woolwich and St. Sepulchre! Rachel enters the particulars in her little book and Zach celebrates his own vigour amongst the headstones, throwing combinations in air, a jab and fast right, ducking and slipping and covering on his merry dancing feet. *You came here alone, didn't you, Rach? With your sketchbook.*

Zach sits up on the bench, arches his back and stamps his feet, looking to earth. Here, somewhere beneath, here at St. Sepulchre-without-Newgate, lies Big Ben Brain, who beat Tom Johnson for the Championship only to retire thereafter, lingering painfully from the kidney blows incurred in the mill, a title fight he would never defend because his days were numbered now, amounting to not quite thirty-eight ailing months' worth of days. And yet. A fellow is less likely to perish from boxing than from festering halibut! Go home, Wolff!

It's been a two-bone, one turn-up, no-*alik* day. So far.

But what's this? An *alik, alkash,* ogling me and my bench, my corner. Here we go. Oh yes! Here he comes with his wandering eye and stone-coloured skin, and trudge of centuries, wobbly on his legs—his *under-*

standings—choosing each step with care, his world a minefield. And he is dressed, typically, for the duration, in all-weather togs, a cloth cap and ear-flaps on his head, scarf wound tightly round his neck—his *squeezer*—and an extraordinary greatcoat envelops his body, caparisoned to the waist. This *alik* is dressed for the duration of everything, every cursed eventuality. Armageddon, revolution, plague, Siberian exile.

If he talks to me, Zach reminds himself, I chalk him up. Otherwise it's still a no-*alik* day. Ah, but just look at him with his lordly prance and fish-eye squint! Marvel at the great stink of his mouldering garments, dense and weighty, heavy, perhaps, with the reek of executions here by Snow Hill and old Newgate, reek of ghosts-without-Newgate, trawling the air with their rope-burned necks, outraged for eternity. This old soul is on watch for them, perhaps, Lord of St. Sepulchre!

Zach rises at the call of time, off the knee of his imaginary second.

"I'm off home!" he protests, as the red-nosed man halts him officiously, a graveyard charley on the beat, prodding the air under Zach's offended senses with two stiffened digits, an imperious gesture of faded authority.

"Ho there, young man!"

Here we go.

The hours stretch out in summer, the evenings go on and on; has he lost track of hours? Where are you, Zachariah? Come home! Rachel stands by the windows again, listening to the thrum in Camden Road and the Gardens behind, everything noisier on long summer afternoons, streets and voices, people speaking louder even face-to-face as if fighting to be heard over the seasonal rush of blood, over the bright light and heightened smells and unusual clamour of days. The city transfigured this year almost overnight and it has not rained in weeks. How the sun shines, how the rains fall, the qualities of light and precipitation, London has a microclimate all its own. London weather has powers of change, change and conjuration.

Rachel washes a page in heavy lines of grey and blue, leaving a white gleam high in one corner, the rheumy eye of the sun peering though layers of altostratus. The London summer of 1814 was cold, with but a few days set fair in June in a month of cloud and rain.

. . .

Pulteney Hotel, Piccadilly, 1814.

My dearest own sister,

Ekaterina, Ekaterina, I am sick! Here is a drawing of myself
in Piccadilly, sick. If you look carefully and apply imagination,
you can see my pale face and staring eyes! Please do not marry a
Cossack. He will talk of *volya, volya* and Fatherland and drink like
a fish. I don't know if there is such a thing as freedom. Do not
marry a Cossack, except perhaps Davydov, who is a poet and a
hero and a man of his word.

Platov lets us drink and drink. For now. Because soon we
return to Paris and I will serve him and stay sober and rejoin
the Hussars, and count the days until home. Please go back to
Petersburg where I will come for you. Moscow is so sad now. You
know you can stay with the Danilovs and then I will find rooms
for us and you can teach, remember how we talked about this.

London is noisy and you must be careful in the streets or foul
water will fall on your head, people throw water from windows,
they throw all kinds of dirt, even bones! They have all kinds of
names for collectors of dirt and I wrote the names down. There
are old bones in the gutters, game and mutton, and men drive
carts at night, carts for night soil, and there are boys with brooms
in the day, crossing-sweepers, and women and children on dust
heaps, or by the river, *cinder-sifters, bone-grubbers.* I never thought
so much about dirt, Katyenka! Or noise!

I have seen a lady who looks so like you, my heart nearly burst.
You will not believe me but her name is Katherine. I cannot draw
ladies very well, as you know—as you tell me! So I have made
some flowers as well. Look at the flowers instead! Women sell
flowers near the hotel, young and old women, like peasants, but
noisy. All varieties of flowers. I have drawn lavender for you and
a fox also, because I saw one in the street late at night. He did not
run away, he stopped to look at me with his yellow flashing eyes,
straight into mine! The London fox is a *bone-grubber* too.

We drink *genièvre* here—gin—herbal and sweet and pale as
vodka, but not so good. There are many different names for it in

taverns, and the men we met at Lord Lowther's—where I saw
the lady—try to teach us these words. I remember *daffy* and *blue
ruin*. Tom Cribb taught me. Cribb took the hetman and myself
and others to a tavern which is famous. Cribb is famous also, a
famous champion. At Bob's Chop House, the landlord is an old
fighter. He was in prison for debt and a great poet helped him out
of there, Lord Byron the famous poet who takes boxing lessons
from the old champions, although he has an infirmity. Were it
not for his infirmity, he might be a soldier, a hero, because they
say there is art and science in boxing and they call a fight a *battle*.
One of our men stripped to the waist and had a lesson in how to
face the enemy, in how to stand in the Ring! I am afraid I drank
too much of a strange mixture of beer, warm, with gin and spices
for which there is also a special name. I was too sick for a lesson.
I don't recall the name of this terrible drink. Here is my sketch of
a man stripped to the waist and performing the classical stance
according to art and science. Everything must be placed just so,
the distance between the feet and their position back and front,
each pointing in especial directions, and then the arms—raised to
a certain height with one more forward than the other, depending
on your disposition, right- or left-handed. The elbows and knees
are bent, the head high, everything calculated for readiness of
the body to spring and retreat, attack and defend! This is the first
lesson only!

I have drawn a fox and lavender—is it blue? Green? Blue-green.
And a tree, I drew a tree called a London plane, because trees and
flowers are beautiful things and I am so sad and sick for you and
for home.

Bearish bear hugs from your useless *alik* brother who is sick
sick sick and may be with you before you hold this letter in your
hands.

Aleksei

Before Aleksei takes leave of General Matvei Ivanovich Platov, the hetman remarks that London is a city of stone, built in stone, on stone.
The journey from south to north, from quay to metropolis, he says, was

all stone where Russia is all wood and there is a lesson in this, he adds, but hetman and Hussar-Cossack are too drunk to think what that lesson might be, and too melancholic, clasping each other briefly with furious frowns on their faces, concerted frowns of nostalgia and experience infusing their hold on each other with more purpose than power, physical strength being quite beyond them now, at this hour, in this state, *castaway*. Nostalgia is catching, not fatal. Not so far. Surely not.

Hetman and Cossack are too lushy to think about stone and wood, immanence and neglect, fire. There is a lesson in this! exclaims Platov, having no idea what he means, what it means, though there is certainly poetry within. Where is Davydov? Find Davydov! Davydov is a poet. He will find the poetry within.

"When we leave this country of stone," declares Matvei Ivanovich, "I will shave off my moustache!"

"So shall I!" swears the Hussar, fingering his slender adornment, and the two men clasp one another again.

In his room by the flickering light of a greasy candle, the Hussar hunts down his razor, still razor sharp because his beard is so fine, and a subject of mirth. *Ahh*, his comrades will warble, *such skin! Just like a girl's! Come to me, Aleksei!* The men are always teasing. Aleksei clips the drawings from the letter he will not, cannot, send to his sister, the words too sad and foolish. He folds the clippings into a page from his notebook, and tucks the fold into his sabretache. He looks at all his things, these are all his things, there is nothing else, he has become so self-contained. I am sick, he thinks, ailing, ailing!

He feels certain he will never know it again, the throwing open of windows, and happy gulping of air. If he ever knows it again, he will be unable to rest for the newfound freedom! Here he is in London and all he can do is drink and dream of Petersburg and Caucasian summers, and his sister in both places. Still, he can find it in him to kneel in front of an English lady called Katherine and press his stupid head against her waist for her to touch the curls his comrades find so very amusing. *Come to me, Aleksei*, she said. Aleksei wants to press his head against her again, an ear, and listen to that place from whence new life might spring, though he knows women can die from it, his own mother died when he was born. He asks God not to let it happen, he prays that his love will not kill her.

The Hussar is still a little drunk. He recalls the japes and chaunts of the evening at Bob's Chop House, the tales. The men laughed tremendously, jumping to their feet every so often to raise glasses of wine and pots of ale and call out names of departed fighters, killed in the ring and outside the ring, killed by boxing. Boxing bare-knuckled for a purse is illegal, a crime. Like duelling, declared the hetman, though the Englishmen did not agree. Like war, then! Platov conceded, whereupon all the soldiers stood and more names were named, of mortally wounded, from General Bagration to company dog, and Aleksei thought how sad it is that most heroes are dead men, departed.

When pots were refilled, the fighter Tom Belcher stood in memory of his brother Jem and up went the Englishmen, some slipping white-spotted scarves from their necks, dark blue or deep yellow, while somebody wept, and Aleksei saw how fine it is to be so famous for fighting that men wear scarves in your honour, and in your name. How much better to be Belcher than Bagration. He rubbed his sore eyes, smoke- and gas-lamp-swollen—damn his eyes, always stinging and leaking, worse and worse—and he asked God for one more thing, that his child, if he is to have one, be a girl, and no fighting man. Oh Lord, what is this affliction he feels, a draining sorrow! More wine! Claret, please!

Platov said that the burning of Moscow has changed the world forever, it has changed Russians forever, landowner and serf, officer and peasant, all souls, nobody will ever think the same again, and Aleksei tried to fathom it, irreversible change, but it was raining in his head, as that Prussian fellow at the next table kept moaning. *I am Prussian and it rains in my head!* Rain, rain! he complained in French. Not too bad a fellow for a Prussian. Markus somebody-or-other. Name of a colour. Von Blau, von Gruen? Not too bad a fellow, thought the Hussar, yet still the hackles rose. *It rains in my head!* bemoaned the stiff-backed Prussian, as if melancholy were a preserve of Teutons. But you know nothing, reflected Aleksei, truly you know nothing of rain in the head.

In his rooms, the Hussar watches the guttering candle, the flame leaping crazily. Moscow will be rebuilt and even more glorious! See London! The great metropolis, he has learned, is built on the ashes of plague and fire, and more glorious than ever, as if some kinds of destruction were timely, fated. Upon the old stones, Platov said, new beginnings.

A fox! There's my fox! Aleksei snuffs the candle and skips to the window, intent on the dark street below. Fox meets him eye to eye.

Fox, fox, thinks the Hussar, speak to me.

"Would you like me to marry you to the English Katherine?"

"What's that you said, little fox?" asks Aleksei, but Fox is gone.

I am truly sick now! he tells himself, alarmed. Oh yes! I am changed forever. Ekaterina, my sister! Help me! I have never known sickness like this! There must be a poet for such feelings, where is the poet for such feelings?

Aleksei's tears are hot against his skin, and he shivers in his *surtout* though it is nearly high summer in this phoenix of a city, this country of stone. He wipes his face roughly, disgusted, and yanks his collar up, leaning back in the hard chair and sliding his heels straight out before him with a scrape of Borodino-worn bluchers. He thrusts both hands deep into his *surtout* pockets, stiffening the arms, shoulders high about the ears, and he fingers the oddments in his coat, finding the new gloves he purchased in the left pocket—a pair of fine wool berlins—and coins in the right, coins and something small and sharp he does not recognise until bringing it up to his eyes to turn this way and that in the gauzy streams of breaking day. Ah yes. The gambling token he took to tonight with such drunken intensity, they let him keep it for remembrance, this ghost-like sliver of a fish with a hole for an eye, carved out of bone. The Hussar turns it this way and that to catch the light, then shuts his eyes to see a Caucasian spring and teeming blue waters with carp beneath, carp and pike in blue waters dotted with dancing shards of cold spring sun, the wavelets speckled white and yellow, flashing Belcher blue. Nearly home, I am so very nearly home! But when he is home, he knows, it too will be changed forever, because he once missed it so much.

The Hussar turns his gambling token this way and that, over and over, watching the play of light on a sliver of bone in the shape of a fish with a hole for an eye. He hurries out of his rooms at the Pulteney Hotel and hails a hansom, still a bit drunk—*foxed,* as the Englishmen say—and the coachman drives down the little side streets, hey! Aleksei was at a merry party, he drank vodka from a half-pail. That's a boy to his girl, bringing a fish. Oh where is the poet for all this!

Where are you, Zach?

You're late. Ring his mobile? No. Let him be, he will come. For Zachariah, Rachel knows, the streets have always been full of attractions, distractions. She smiles wryly at her own impatience, fidgets, anticipation.

Where are you? She remembers explaining his absences, once upon a time, covering for his schoolboy meanderings.

"Sometimes, he stops for a kickabout. On the way home," she would tell Lev and Katya. "Or he goes to the library. Often, the library."

"He's a vagrant," says Papa.

"Mama, what is the difference? Between volya and svoboda?"

"What? Rachel, Rachel, so many questions. Ask your aunt. Tasha can explain so much better. But both mean 'freedom.' Of a kind. And there is 'Cossack' also. Free man. Cossack means 'free man.' Tyotya can tell you the differences. Where is your brother?"

"Still at school, Mama. Oh! He has Games. Yes, I forgot."

"Ah," says Katya. "Games."

"Games," scoffs Lev. "Why can't he just tell us? In the morning. Somehow tell us. It's not difficult."

"He doesn't always remember. And I'm telling you. I'm telling you now."

Rachel listens for Zachariah.

A wolf's sense of hearing is remarkably acute. A wolf can detect another's howl from as far as nineteen kilometres away.

Zach. He's here. Rachel can tell, no matter how he travels, hansom, troika, foot. In his absence, she is aware of all comings and goings in their little side street, and can always discern his, even in a crowd. Rachel raises her chin, tilts the head slightly, holds still. No. Not Zach, not yet. Wait. Yes! *That's* him.

Rachel knows him by the very weight of the cab in the street, the particular trudge of Dunlop on tarmac, the slight gasp of growling diesel as Zach's mass shifts from seat to exit with a certain momentum, body in a crouch. She knows the singular smack of handle unlatching, the heavy thrust of door and squeak of hinge. Zachariah alights. She knows that leap to ground, his body lithe, and the mighty report of door—slam!— Zach still unapprised of his own strength, reluctant to own it, perhaps, his power and reach. Slam!

"Sorry, mate!"

His footfall, of course she knows this, she would know it anywhere. Here he comes, loping to the gate, clang! And at the threshold, a gear change as he polishes the toes of his Loakes against the back of his trousers, then knocks them against the wall one by one to release excess dirt from the sole, the dust of his day. Leave your muck outdoors, be clean! Do not fall short of her. Like Byron's right foot! Often, he will hit the bell three times before rattling the key in the lock and flinging it open, a horse at the starting gate. Rachel finds scuff marks on the bottom rail of their front door, and his paw prints on the panels and muntin, and smears on the glass, signs of Zachariah she allows to linger, endearing dust.

"Rachel!" Zach calls. "I'm home! And I'm bringing a fish, hey!"

"Hello," smiles Rachel.

"Look! Wine, two bottles, the good stuff. And flowers!" he adds, handing over the lavender, lavender and willow and privet with dark berries, a marvellous grin creasing his face. "Aubry helped. Helped me choose!"

"Lavender's blue, diddle, diddle," Rachel begins. "Sing, Zach."

"Lavender's green. When I am king, diddle, diddle, you shall be queen!"

"You boxed, didn't you?"

"It was nothing. A barney. I had to, anyway. It was Shaw. Always picking fights. Pain in the arse. Don't worry."

"What was he doing there? Sandbags," asks Rachel, slipping bottles to ice.

"*Sandbag*. Sandbag Shaw. Trains there sometimes—plus he's eyeing up Aubry. Sandbag wants his belt. He'll never make the weight for a start, Shaw. Unless Aubry moves up a class. I think he should. He'll always be too quick for Shaw, even at a bigger weight . . . Only thing with All Souls is—he doesn't fight enough. Too much time between bouts!" Zach complains, peeling his jumper off inside out, revealing a T-shirt with fraying neckline and split in one seam. "He's got to fight, Rach! A fighter fights! But Shaw's weird. Some fighters look bad in the gym, good fighters, I'm talking about. With Shaw it's a con, a tease, sandbagging. But he can't sucker All Souls, can't rattle him. Shaw's been lucky in the ring, he has a good chin and he'll prey on a guy's weak point, lives for it. And he's white! A rarity, and a pull, that is. Puts bums on seats, I mean. Like it or not. The white guy. But, man! He's a dirty infighter, I hate that. Thinks he's a name, too! A name fighter, marquee fighter. Crazy. I try to like him, but hell . . ."

"You *had* to hit him, yes?"

"He can jab," Zach continues. "I'll give him that. And he has a good straight right when he needs it. 'All credit to him,' as the sports saying goes. But he irks me. He's deep. You know. *Sly.*"

"Zachariah?"

"Self-defence, Rach! It was self-defence," he replies, nuzzling her nape.

"Ah," says Rachel, unwrapping fish. "Halibut."

"We'll make old bones, won't we? Make old bones with me, Rach!"

When Zach envelops her, turning her round to face him, she smells the gym in his clothing, an odour of leather and hemp, sweat and speed. She smells the streets of the city, and breathes in at his neck, feeling the veins and arteries pulsing there against her lips, *subclavian, internal jugular, common carotid.* She holds her arms out straight to the sides to stop from touching him.

"I'm fishy," she explains. "Fish fingers!"

"Don't fly away," he says. "You're like a bird."

"What species?"

"Hmm. Seabird. Must be. Loon!"

"Diver! Great Northern Diver."

"Peter—AND—the WOLF!" Zach intones. "What kind of bird are YOU, if you can't FLY?"

"What kind of bird are YOU," Rachel counters, "if you can't SWIM?"

"Cold enough, do you think?" asks Zach. "The wine?"

"I don't care," she says. "Open it."

Rachel watches him for a moment, with cloth and corkscrew, a grimace of endeavour on his shining face, the arm muscles flickering— *radialis, brachialis, biceps, extensor.* She watches the decision in motion.

"You're coming to Aubry's party, right?" asks Zach, drawing the cork with a flourish.

"When? What party?"

"Summer party! With the cricket and the marquee lunch and all that. Does it every year, apparently. I told you. I'm playing in the match."

"Oh yes, I remember."

"Aubry really wants you there. Me too. Obviously."

"Why wouldn't I come?"

"All this work you're doing, I don't know. Sometimes you . . ."

"I like Thomas," says Rachel, chopping and stirring. "Don't understand why he boxes though."

"Well, that's what I want to write about, I guess," notes Zach. "Gentleman Tom."

"Zach the Russian," smiles Rachel.

"What?"

"They should have called you that when you boxed. I'm working on it, you know. The pugilism book. So I'm on two at once, the fairy tales and you. Well. Sam. At least it's nearly end of term. All my boys will be swanning about on their hols soon. In France and Italy, no doubt. Perhaps one or two slumming it in Cornwall."

"Zach the Russian, eh?" muses Zachariah, propping himself up on the worktop and twisting round to search the cabinets. "No crisps!"

"Better than 'Wolfman,' for heaven's sake," scoffs Rachel. "Can't believe they called you that."

"Yes, well . . . Hardly paragons of originality in the nickname game! What's my name! What's my name! Remember that?"

"Ali?" says Rachel.

"Yep. Just changed his name from Cassius Clay and Ernie Terrell refused to use his Muslim name."

"I know the story, Zach. I don't like it."

"I think of it lots, don't know why. *What's my name! What's my name!* Not a question at all. Brutal fight, that was. Savage. Terrell was cowering by the end. Had a fucked-up retina, broken bone under the eye. Said Ali thumbed him, dragged his eye across the ropes. It was ugly. So! Your boxing story. It is about me!"

"Always was. And there are crisps, by the way. Top of the fridge."

"Do I get the girl? Is there a girl in it? Youse gotta have a girl!"

"It's a kids' book, Zach."

"So what? Those Russian fairy tales are full of girls! Boys getting girls!"

"This wine is delicious," Rachel pronounces.

"Aubry's choice. Fucking expensive!" laughs Zach.

"As I said," Rachel teases. "I like Thomas. More wine, please."

"Man, I love those trousers on you," says Zachariah, pouring wine. "Your green fanteegs with braces. Button braces, no messing around!"

"Albert Thurston braces, I've had them ages. I love the shade of burgundy. And the tiny polka dots—more like stars. Tasha gave them to me, remember? They were Nicky's. A birthday present from Katya one year, I think. Yes I'm sure that's right. I love that you don't mind. That she gave them to me."

Zach shrugs; he smiles. "She might have given them to Lev."

"Papa's not really a braces man, is he?" says Rachel, remembering Nicky's birthday party.

"We Russians in the West!" Katya laughs as Nikolai unwraps her gift of button braces. "In Paris we dressed so very comme il faut, no? But France was home in so many ways. Now in London you gentlemen must have your English shirts, the English shoes, yet you are unmistakably Russian. You buy an English foulard, écharpe—and wear it like a Frenchman. Always Russian!"

"They're best on you," Zach nods. "You look great. You always look great. And it's hell's bells sexy, too!"

Rachel returns to the fish. She cooks a stew with parsley. And has a dream of immanence.

{ SIX }

London, 1832.

A Miller wears forest-green trousers. She is dark-haired and willowy and has a quality of stillness, an enviable quality in an observer of men. Were she to walk in a forest, she might not be seen for the trees. She might be mistaken for a moss-covered tree. Moss and lichen colonise on the side of a tree facing the prevailing wind.

A Miller writes:

A Fair Wind Blows in Holborn! Cries of Foul at Seven Dials! Sam the Russian reckoned down, not beaten.

As at Borodino, so at Covent Garden. Where there is a Man, a Battle! Where once, perhaps, his fathers fell, only to come to the scratch once more and bring Boney to his knees, young Sam the Russian, yet to formally grace the Prize Ring with his elegant form and noble upperworks, has suffered an untimely rattler on the cobbles of Seven Dials, floored by three dirty hooks on the prowl from St. Giles whither they were seen hopping the twig by Sam's lame companion, Jonah the Needle, hotfooting it directly back to the suck-cribs where they abide, leaving Sam Alexander quite unable to preserve the perpendicular, and spilling the crimson. The boy was thereafter unlawfully abstracted of his personals, namely: one keepsake, his flash, a volume by the recently departed RL Stevenson, and a fine new pair of berlins.

The flight of the scoundrels, files, every one, and fated for the stone-jug to be sure, was observed from a window by one Jonah the Needle, Sam's friend from Foundling Hospital days and presently apprentice tailor of Monmouth Street, Covent Garden, who reported on the crime in an extreme state of abjection and nervous disorder, modestly omitting his own heroic part in the battle. According to his master, Jonah, having merrily seen off his old friend some moments earlier, was subsequently alerted by a commotion and gave chase to the criminals in the darkling light with a show of enormous bottle, notwithstanding his impediments, the boy being unfortunately disadvantaged by one abbreviated arm and one short leg, an affliction he bears with utmost coolness and modesty. Fear is not within the range of his ideas and the apprentice tailor was observed to hurtle out of the shop and shout loudly for the blues in a passing watch-box whilst sawing at the air with a stick of blackthorn, wielding it with tremendous vigour and a fearsomeness worthy of Genghis Khan.

"No gamer fellow," declared his master, "ever waved a walking stick! No gamer fellow ever came to the defence of a friend!"

'No, no!" protested Jonah blushingly from the confines of an apothecary's whence he helped convey his injured friend. "I am quite helpless, as you see. It was all Sam," he said, fretful, nevertheless embarking upon a shadow play of the barney involving hearty blows and excitable commentary, which, since he lacks the appropriate sporting vernacular, I shall interpret for the reader:

Sam the Russian, unwary opponent in a most vexing and irregular turn-up and in an intimation, surely, of things to come, acquitted himself thus in the siege of Seven Dials, by way of a flurry of counter-hits, fibs and dabs, boxing low, the right mauley across the bread-box, the left snaking out at will after the modern manner scientific, and so lively was he in his tout ensemble, now breaking away and sparring for wind, now effecting a lodgement, holding his own against manifold might, not to mention the brutishness of sticks, it is fair to assume a sensation was seen in Monmouth Street, a young master of the noble art of self-defence, dodging and charging in his invisible Ring on merry dancing feet.

Do you hear it, England, the call to arms? High above the lonely field of battle, above the cries of "foul!" at Seven Dials, hear the cry of ancient Rus, of the Cossack and Hussar, Borodino-brave, and of the Mosaic likewise! Behold a fighter born and bred, for freedom and country, never shall he be a slave! What is a son of the Fatherland? Why, Sam the Russian.

Spring! It is time. Throw in the hat, Tom Spring, born Winter, set the challenge for your boy, name the particulars! All England awaits.

A Miller

Between insensibility on the cobbles of Monmouth Street and ministrations at the back of the apothecary's, involving bleeding and poulticing and doses of salts, etc., Sam the Russian swoons. Just as the constable stumps it to the Castle for Spring, and Sam fingers his frame for wounds, and his pockets for abstracted personals, he watches Jonah the Needle from where he lies prone, Jonah with stick in air, bold as Robinson Crusoe after cannibals, and only then does he plummet deep into some cavernous place, light-filled, and charged with voices and changing shapes and jewel-bright patterns, causing him to gasp for wind before passing out cold and into a dream wherein he is changed forever.

And in this dream, young Sam sees eternity, or things to come, things he dreams might come. He sees Old Abel the coachman, an ostler as a boy, with a feeling for speed. Sam sees Abel driving Stephenson's Rocket, and it flies along the rails, and his hair flies too, a lustrous mop, because Old Abel is young again. In Sam's dream, he is a passenger on the train as it races across the downs and through valleys, over bridges and aqueducts. His country flies past the window. He wears a medallion and a fine pair of berlins. Fly, Abel! Fly!

Upon waking, Sam is aware of busy fives patting and prodding his person, and the kind face of a spoffish apothecary, with furrowed frontispiece and greasy rimless barnacles riding low on his smeller. And there is Spring peering at Sam and totting up the damage done to his ward and apprentice champion, while Jonah murmurs in his ear. Samuel Alexander tries to speak, he tries to smile, but is not yet in command of his senses. He turns his head on the pillow to catch sight of some exquisite in a pale frockcoat and wintergreen—nay, forest-green—indescribables, writing spiritedly into a black leather notebook, his stance unusually effeminate, and Sam remembers the dandy now, appearing on the scene in the company of the constabulary—the blues, the peelers—and gazing feelingly into Sam's phiz as he lay upon the stones. The scribe's name is A Miller, said he, in a girlish voice. *Can you hear me, Sam?*

Now the young fighter appraises the loss of his personals; the fine present his friend made him of a pair of berlins, the gloves sprinkled with lavender, the stitching nigh invisible in the uncommon style of Jonah the Needle. Gone too is the book lent by Dickens whose presence is fleeting of late, Charles fevered by work and, furthermore, the heady pursuit of a lady. An *angelic*. Maria. Her name is Maria. And Sam's medallion is gone, distressing him deeply, leaving only the gambling token for his father to know him by, the fish made from bone with a hole for an eye. Sam has a fish, and friends, and attempts to say so, but the words die in his maw, the lips crusted with claret and conspicuously swollen.

Sam's eyelids fall. He rues the day, how he gave in to surprise, dropped his guard. He reviews the battle in his mind, seeking the flaw in his science, his tell-tale symptom of weakness.

Sam's Flaw

Sam walks, swinging his parcel from Jonah the Needle, merrily kicking a bone in his path. Bones, dust. It's been a two-bone, no turn-up, no lushy day. So far!

"Got a lucifer?"

Lucifer.

Though matches were invented only five years ago, the Fancy always carry lucifers and Sam the potboy clears them away, saving the unspent he finds amongst the pots and glasses, oyster shells and ashes. I do have a lucifer.

"Yes, I do!"

What a *deep*-looking cove, Sam notes, searching his pockets for a match. *Sly.* Bit of a dry boots, perhaps. Whereupon Sam is bonneted from behind, his adversary joined swiftly out of the shadows by two other files—*hooks,* as they are known—and while Sam squares up to them with hooks of his own; right, left, he is nevertheless struck from all sides as his fathers were at Borodino, and when he is floored and Jonah is giving chase, he feels the pitter-patter of rat paws across his grubbery and down along his hams, *Rattus norvegicus* pausing momentarily to sniff the air with superior poise, taking advantage of Sam's weakness. *Look for a weakness!* Tom Spring will say. *Especially when overmatched.*

"Please don't bite me, Rat," whispers Sam. "I'm down. Man down."

And Sam the Russian faints, as if dead.

Rules to be Observed in All Battles on the Stage
VII. That no person is to hit his Adversary when he is down, or seize him by the ham, the breeches, or any part below the waist: a man on his knees to be reckoned down.

Rat does not bite Sam the Russian. He watches the three sneaks who kye-bosked the boy hotfoot it towards the back slums of St. Giles, though his eyesight is very poor. Rat's optics are tiny, his view panoramic and blurry at best, but he is a good detector of movement and peculiarly sensitive to brightness. And his hearing is fine. He perceives one of the criminals drop, unwittingly in all the noise of shouts and hasty padding feet, a shiny round disc that slips from the stolen necklace in his hand, pinging to the paving beneath. Rat follows the roll of the disc with his ogles and auriculars as well as his twitching whiskers, long and short hairs that vibrate like the strings of a harp. Rat's whiskers sing the world to him.

SEVEN

Hoxton, London.

"Tasha! Auntie? It's me! Zachariah!"

Though he is expected on Friday afternoons, his day of early finish at Izzy's, Zach smacks the doorbell once, twice, three times before plunging into a pocket for his set of keys and scraping at the lock, sparing Natasha the fumble with entry phone, or any uncertainty regarding unwanted guests. This can only be Zach.

"Auntie? Tasha! Hey, Volya! Hello there, my friend!" goes Zach, dumping his kit to the floor, thump, and freeing himself to slap at the dog's rich golden flanks and ruffle him vigorously behind the ears. "Volya, Volya!" Zach says, muzzle to muzzle with the dog, eliciting a low hum of pleasure. "*Tyotya,* I'm here!" he adds, kicking the door shut behind him, slam! He stamps and swipes his feet on the mat as if putting out fire and slides the cone of flowers from the bat pouch of his kitbag. A cricket bat pouch is excellent for the safekeeping of posies. "Tasha!"

"I'm going to compose a piece, you know—"

"There you are!"

"I'll call it *Enter Zachariah!*"

"Lots of percussion?" asks Zach, striding into the kitchen and crouching before his aunt, encompassing her and chair with his superior reach. "Lots of boom-boom?"

"Full orchestra, Zachashka. For a boy with hyperacusis, and whatever else—"

"Tinnitus! In both ears."

"Yes. That. Considering all that, you make such an extraordinary rumpus! Not unpleasant somehow. But then, of course, I am love-struck."

"My auntie!" exclaims Zach, resting his head on Tasha's lap. *"Moya tyotya!"*

"Your face," says Tasha, running her hand across his brows.

"It's nothing," he murmurs. "Stitched up twice this week. Sparred with All Souls—man, that was fun! Then there was a bit of a barney. Guy hit the same eye. That idiot Sandbag. Told you about him. I'm fine, though. Stitches out Monday. Doesn't hurt, *Tyotya.* It's all fine!" Zach closes his eyes a moment, revels in the familiar surge of feeling for Natasha and for the forest-like scents in her domain, of wood and herbs and undergrowth, and the smell of Russian tea and music and long hours of thinking in chairs, and of Golden Retriever.

"Volya?" Zach and Rachel once queried of their aunt Natasha when she introduced them to her new guide dog and divulged his name.

"Greater than freedom," she explained. "That's svoboda. Volya *means 'the right to gallop into open steppe,' 'the right to life, to a life of one's choosing.' Freedom to hunt and fish and ride. If one so chooses. A Cossack life. This is* volya.*"*

Zach inhales it here, an odour of Cossack freedom and steppe, endless steppe, with taiga beyond! May Natasha, not yet old, not truly old, may she never smell of age, of sour moods and bewilderment, of thrice-used tea bags, mouldering newspapers, and of waiting. Not while I'm around, Zach declares. No.

Zach scouts the flat. Ines has been here. He notes the monogrammed linen towels by the sink, threadbare yet ironed with military correctness, washed scrupulously clean, these hand towels and their special laundering appealing to Ines's image of Tasha the grand lady, and artist, while dignifying Ines in her present occupation of housekeeper. Once a young teacher in Warsaw, Ines now attends to fine ladies with whom she assumes a common language of exile and past privilege. Ines cleans selectively, polishing Tasha's piano and portraits and books and few items of French furniture with zealous application, while leaving a veil of cobweb in kitchen and bedroom, the stray filigrees rising and falling at Zach's approach and in the waves of lamplight, and now and again he will find a fossilized insect hanging in the threads, and mouse droppings in the lee of the fridge and cooker—where do they come from? There is a special microclimate here in Aunt Natasha's flat, earthy, faintly wild, a landscape of strangely epic dimensions.

Zach removes the trapped fly, spider, wasp, in a huff, irked that this department of husbandry should be quite beyond her province, Ines confining herself as she does to dusting objects of distinction only, and without ever displacing them, sidestepping areas of no importance where she will merely move dirt around with impatient strokes of a toothless broom or limp rag, or mop dipped in brackish waters, describing furious grey whorls of diluted soil on tile and wood to mark her passage, working with grave silence under the virtually sightless gaze of an amused and immaculate Tasha. Wherever Zach shifts a chair, tower of books, issue of *Rossica,* hatbox, artefact, samovar, silver-backed brush, mysterious bevelled glass receptacle or pointless vanity mirror, vase, CD rack, telephone, wherever Zach dislodges an item, he sees its spectral shape, a pure clean space bordered by dust, marking its position in Tasha's landscape, its history, and progress through it.

"I brought flowers," Zach says.

"Freesias. Are they white?"

Zach raises the flowers to her eyes and watches her scan them slowly, the way a bird listens for a fellow bird, angling the ears to equalise the volume and calculate distance. Tasha turns her head this way and that, elegant and animal-like, catching the whiteness of freesia in what peripheral vision is left to her, causing an involuntary flutter in Zach's diaphragm, of grief and rage. Tasha's grace in blindness amazes him. Tasha is blind, not beat! Like the great Broughton before her, Jack Broughton, great champion of the Prize Ring and father of the Rules.

Zach beams at his aunt Tasha as she holds the flowers to her eyes.

"I told you," says Zach, "the story of Jack Broughton and Jack Slack?"

"White," says Tasha. "Lovely."

"Have I? Told you the story?"

"*I am blind, but not beat,*" she recites.

"Yes! You remember! Blind, but not beat!"

.　　.　　.

London, April 1750. Jack Broughton v. Jack Slack. The Duke of Cumberland, Broughton's patron, has wagered thousands on his man, but the ageing fighter is cavalier in the ring and takes a sucker punch between the eyes.

"What are you about, Broughton?" shouts the Duke. "You can't fight! You're beat!"

"I can't see my man, Your Highness; I am blind, but not beat; only let me be placed before my antagonist and he shall not gain the day yet."

"The flowers are truly perfect. I thank you, Zasha."

"I bring flowers to all my girls."

"How is she?"

"Beautiful. A loon! She's on two books at once, folk tales—Russian, of course—and one on rats and things. And other animals. Crows, wolves, I don't know. *The Natural History of London,* she calls it. Secret book; she won't show me. Not yet. She also calls it a boxing book. About a boy pugilist called Sam the Russian. Remember the little books we made as kids? She's reviving the story. Sprucing it up! Making it a proper book. She says it has battles and everything. Napoleonic Wars! Crazy. We'll see. Boxing! Bloody hell. Pugilism, to be precise. For kids! Lev will hate it! Anyway, would you Adam and Eve it? *The Natural History of London.*"

"It's about you, don't you think? Like my concerto. *Enter Zachariah!*"

"Fee-fi-fo-fum," Zach says, rummaging in the kitchen. "I smell the grub of Ines, by gum! She came today, didn't she? Cooked for you?"

"So kind."

"Debatable," Zach smirks. "I have Polish friends who can actually cook, you know. No bone-and-slops stew. Tasha! I've never seen cuts like this. What did she ask for at the butcher's? A half kilo of best guts? For twenty quid, no change? You collude, you know! It's a conspiracy. Landowner and serf! She's not family, you *hire* her. Strewth! Why don't you set the table for two, ask her to stay?"

"Now that *would* be patronising."

"Yeah, but maybe she'd dish up something edible! Ha! I'm chucking this."

"Not here. She'll notice. She takes the rubbish on Thursday. Just take it with you when you go, find a street bin. Please."

"Tasha! I'll cook for you. Might need to shop, though. Or you could come to us. But tell me," he adds, peering into the fridge. "I don't get it. What privileges are you apologising for exactly? Bloody hell, *Tyotya!* You're not rich or—"

"Rich enough. And fortunate."

"Hounded out of Russia, your family! And how about Lev's lot? Fortunate? That you made it out, you mean? Never the right kind of Russian, none of you. Too White, too liberal, Jewish, Bolshevik, imperialist, subversive—Masonic, Decembrist, forget it. Musicians and scientists! Fucking disaster! Sorry, Tasha! And you pine for the place. But you won't go. Mama went back, again and again. Not you."

"Zachashka, Zasha . . . I'm English now."

"Not true-born!"

"Ahh. That. Shall we have a drink, do you think? Do you have time? I don't need you to cook. I'm not even hungry. Please put the flowers in water."

"Live with us, Tasha!"

"I'm quite happy right here."

"Happy of Hoxton!" Zach exclaims.

Hoxton. Tasha and Nicky were always migratory creatures, with Cossack blood, says Rachel. Finsbury Park, Stoke Newington, Victoria Park, where once they travelled the Hackney Brook, pausing each time, no doubt, to perch upon their suitcases a while before dropping the keys through the letterbox, they soon swept north again, describing a restless arc north, north-west to Nicky's last surgery in Highgate from where Tasha has since fled downriver, bypassing Chelsea to Richmond and Battersea, then back east and north of the river again, to Clerkenwell and Hoxton, following the Fleet. Where will it end?

Live with us, Tasha!

Hoxton. So close to Camden, a few kilometres away—a few *verst,* indeed—but so far. A shadowy place, Zach feels, though Camden has its own dark vicissitudes and Rachel notes them all, every malingerer there, every footpad, laid-in-the-streets, monologist, hawker, crack-brain and lush, all elbows and cursing, she records them, every one, reporting to Zach, couching her warnings in merry detail. Hers are cautionary tales. Zach is a tinder-box and she cannot have him inflamed. *Do you know what I saw today?* she might begin. *Picture this!* Then Rachel tells him her tales of Camden, but the alerts are implicit. Beware this corner, that alley. Do not eyeball this fellow, that hag. Do not engage! It's a dangerous place! Camden has muscle and shape and occasional grace, it is full of history and signs. It is their country, for now, their Wolff den. Their field.

In Natasha's kitchen, Zachariah takes in his aunt's face, enjoying every plane and contour, line and feature, and the eyes, oh her eyes, Rachel-blue, colour of speed and sparkling waters! Rachel says how interesting it is that Tasha should select a borough with, officially, the highest count of aliens in London, a borough of polyphony. Hoxton, they decide, with its steady stream of Russians, is as close to home as she can find, yet still they wonder at it, how a woman with such a long history of exile and ten years of widowhood can choose to live so estranged.

"Live with us, Tasha!"

"What about your father? That would leave him alone."

"Why's there an upside-down pot on the table?"

"Don't move it!"

"And *Tyotya?*" says Zach, noting the salt bowl. "Sorry, but—I think you've got weevils. In the salt."

Tasha laughs. "Ines puts grains of rice in salt. Absorbs moisture, apparently. Weevils indeed!"

"It looks a bit nasty, *Tyotya.*"

"Well, I can't see it."

"That's true," Zach concedes cheerfully, opening the fridge. "So! Burgundy for Tasha and—hey! Camden Pale Ale, Camden Hell's unfiltered! Wow! Where did you go? Were you in Camden? When? You went by yourself?"

"Stop it. I ring up. Waitrose and that place in Gray's Inn Road where you took me once. You've not seen them all. Look at the back of the top shelf."

"Brewdog! Punk IPA. Hey, you got Russian Doll! That's funny!"

"I thought so. I wanted several of each, you see. And the man read all the names on the phone. Russian Doll is new, he said. Each one is different. You see? There should be four Russian Doll ones. He sent them by cab for me. For you."

"You don't have to do that."

"I choose to."

"You're my bottle-holder, Tasha! My second! My dove! I'll ring Rachel, tell her we're having a peg or two. Of *bub*! Then you can explain the upside-down pot."

"A *peg*?" queries Tasha as Zachariah pours wine and beer, hangs up the phone.

"Measure," he replies. "And bub . . ."

"I know *bub*! Drink."

"Yes! Now, this upside-down pot situation . . ."

"It's a trap," states Tasha. "I saw something move and I trapped it. It's under there. And rather big."

"Spider?"

"No, no. Mouse, I think. Or—"

"Quick hands you've got, then. Fighter's hands! Right, I'll settle you in the other room and then I'll go a-hunting! We can always save the meat for Ines. She can make a stew."

"Very amusing," says Tasha, and as Zach follows her into the living room, he is amazed, as usual, by her sure and graceful gait. *I am blind, but not beat!* He feels the involuntary tremble again, in his tripes, of anger and resentment: *Why her, why her? Why did it have to happen to her?* How his very veins fizz! How the follicles bristle at the nape of his neck! But *this* lady, he thinks, this *angelic*, can take a punch. She is blind, but not beat.

"I'll be right back," he tells her. "Need to have a word with a mouse."

"*Little Burrowing Mouse!*" says Tasha.

"What's that, *Tyotya*?"

"You remember. It was one of Rachel's favourite fairy tales. The Little Burrowing Mouse makes a home of a horse's skull and a procession of animals comes. One by one, the creatures call out, *Little house, little house! Who lives in the little house?* And Little Burrowing Mouse lets them all move in, Croaking Frog, Hare Hide-in-the-Hill, Fox Run-About-Everywhere, Wolf Leap-Out-of-the-Bushes until along comes—"

"Bear Squash-the-Lot!" exclaims Zach.

"Yes. You do remember!" smiles Tasha.

"That's me all right! Bear Squash-the-Lot! I'll be right back!"

In Tasha's kitchen, Zach quickly lifts the lid on *Tyotya*'s Little Burrowing Mouse and slams it back down just as fast. That's no mouse. Bloody hell, Tasha. You caught a rat. Zach slides the upturned pot to the edge of the table and drops into a Jack Dempsey crouch the better to spring at his opponent, hit him a floorer. Power and accuracy, he tells himself. Timing and footwork.

Wolff fells Rat in one and when Rat is kyeboshed, Zach feels strangely deflated. He returns Rat to the pot, crashes a lid on top and hurries into the street, calling out to Tasha as he goes.

"Back in a minute!"

Zach tips the body into the gutter and stares. Sorry, Rat.

In the kitchen again, Zach examines labels on cleaning fluids and selects the bottle of Domestos Lemon Fresh All Purpose Hygienic Cleaning plus Active Disinfection. Perfect, he thinks, scraping at his fingers with a Vileda scourer, Active Wave. *Removes difficult dirt but will not scratch non-stick and other delicate surfaces.* This is not quite true. *Before use on very delicate surfaces,* Zach reads too late, burying his blazing hands under the armpits for succour, *test an inconspicuous area first.*

"No such thing, there is no such area!" Zach says aloud, "Fuck!" he shouts, examining his fists now, turning them this way and that, the hands that love her. Rachel! He is afraid they will never be clean again.

"Zachashka! What are you doing?"

"Coming!"

Be clean! Zach laughs ruefully now at his burning fingers, at Domestos and scouring pad, and how he scrubbed with such furious intent, he never once made the association with yesterday's *alik*, the Lord of St. Sepulchre, the stinking *alik* with his bag of alarming personal grooming materials, the bottle of economy bleach and horse brush. Zach never stopped to think about bleach and abrasion, carried away, as he was, by sheer momentum and desire. Be clean! Zach's impulses of nature, as Papa always said, propel him forward like Stephenson's Rocket, the hemispheres of his brain disconnecting as in sleep and dreams, or neurasthenia.

"Creative man is an organiser, a pattern seeker!" Lev says when the boy Zach has done it again, toppled a tower of books, crashed into a room unannounced, struck a cricket ball into conservatory windows. "Use your head, Zachashka," Lev adds with a touch of resignation, planting a rare kiss on his skull. "Your brain, Zach, is wanted on the voyage."

I never told her, thinks Zach, searching the hall for Aunt Tasha's coat, I forgot to tell Rach about my Lord of St. Sepulchre!

"*Tyotya!*" he announces, holding her coat up by the shoulders. "I'm taking you home to Rachel! Get your overnight things. I'm not taking no for an answer!"

In Camden, Rachel hears them coming, Zach and *Tyotya,* and hurries for the door. She listens to them chaffing in the street, giddy as children and, in the doorway, Zach bursts into his story of his fight with a rat, the Battle of Hoxton, he calls it, the combatants Wolff and Rat, or Tasha's Little Burrowing Mouse.

"Are you going to floor every rat in town?" asks Rachel.

Zach grins and is all industry, settling Tasha in a chair in the kitchen, pouring her wine and filling a dish of water for Volya, finally shuffling off his own coat and opening a beer, the returning conqueror.

"It was a knockout," explains Tasha. "KO in one. Is that right, Zachashka?"

"You'll have to wear the colours," suggests Rachel. "Both of you," she adds, telling them how London's foundlings once wore blue coats and yellow stockings, both colours deemed effective in the repulsing of rats.

"Same as the belcher!" exclaims Zach. "Jem Belcher, his neckerchief—*fogles*! Bird's-eye blue and yellow!"

"Fighting colours indeed," smiles Rachel.

Foundling, pugilist, gull, rat, they converge on the city, tie their *fogles* to the Ring. London is a strange attractor.

—*Rachel? Explain "strange attractor."*

—*A strange attractor is fractal. Having intricate structure on the finest scale. An infinitely complex pattern of curves, surfaces, and manifolds with sensitive dependence on initial conditions.*

—*Why strange?*

—*Chaotic, Papa, that's all. A dynamical system changes in time, the trajectories—the flowlines—of that system home in on complex shapes. An attractor is a geometric expression of long-term behaviour.*

—*Such as?*

—*Turbulence. Population dynamics. The interactions of predator and prey.*

—*Good, Rachel. Good.*

Rachel lies awake, her head full of strange attractors, of rodent and boy, and the scent of calendula and vitamin oil with which she treated

Zach's poor hands, blotched and raw from Domestos, souvenir of his battle with Tasha's rat. Zachariah shifts, flings an arm across Rachel's breast. He is wakeful, too.

"How do I smell, Rach?"

"What do you mean?"

"I met this man the other day. When I was late and had the fish and everything—the fight with Sandbag—that day. I stopped in St. Sepulchre's. You know. Holborn, top of Snow Hill."

"I know it. I've been there."

"Well, I had this encounter with a crusty. Old guy. I forgot to tell you."

"Tell me now," she says.

"I was just leaving and saw him coming!" Zach laughs. "Here we go, I thought! Here comes my nut-of-the-day! My *alik*. I'm a crazy-boots magnet!"

Here we go, thinks Zach. Here we go.

Rosy was his nose, rheumy were his eyes, his voice like engine failure. Here he comes, the old peasant, with his poisonous breath and reek of ages, rotten enough to fell a man at eight paces.

"Ho there, young man! Halloa!"

So it's a one-*alik* day after all. So far.

"That's my bench!" he trumpets, the Lord of St. Sepulchre. "Who are *you*?"

"I'm just off, mate," says Zach. "It's all yours."

"NOT so fast! I'm just pointing it out, son. That's my bench. You with me? No need to take it personal."

"Thanks. Must be off, though."

"Do I pong? A bit whiffy, am I?"

Zach stops, hugs the parcels to his chest, cocks his head to one side. "Truth, man?"

"I know the truth. TO-be-honest! TO-be-honest! What do you think I've got here?" asks the Lord of St. Sepulchre, slapping his overcoat pockets. "Piss and vinegar?"

"I really have to go, mate. Sorry," mumbles Zach, fishing for coins.

"I didn't ask you for change. Did I? How does *she* smell?"

"Who?"

"Your girl. Where you're off to in such a blinking hurry. Go on, son. Tell me ALL your troubles! Good boots, you have, I see. The Loake 'Kempton'—premium chukka, Goodyear welted, tan grain burnished calf upper, 026 last. F fitting. Tell me I'm wrong! I had a girl once. And then we died. She died. Then I died."

"Sorry. You know shoes?"

"Loake Shoemakers, 1880. Kettering, Northants. Three founding brothers; Thomas, John and William Loake. Northamptonshire! The River Nene and the forests of oak! Northampton is sovereign for shoes!"

"Sovereign, eh?"

"Loake, Grenson, Crockett & Jones, Edward Green! Alfred Sargent, Joseph Cheaney, Sanders and Tricker's! You think I'm a know-nothing? A low-life? Because I pong? Because I'm homeless and squiffy?" *Rosy-nosey.*

"No, man. No. So you were a shoe—"

"Seller, you think? Wrong, son! Maker, shoeMAKER! Bespoke. Hundreds of quid a pair. Cobblers, you think? Ha ha. Tosh? God's truth. And my old man? Finest shoemaker IN THESE PARTS. Made boots for Tommy Burns when he were in London in 1907 to defend the title. And for Peerless himself."

"Jim Driscoll? Featherweight champ? Died of TB, forty-something."

"Where there's muck, there's brass. And who are you?"

Zach perches on the arm of the bench and smiles at the *alik*, piqued.

"Your old man made boots for fighters?"

"For gentlemen and sportsmen. Cricketers and boxers chiefly."

"What happened to you, mate?"

"Snakes and ladders, snakes and ladders. How does she smell?"

How does she smell, Zach? How does she smell? Like winning.

"Well, son?"

"What? I don't know. It's private. She smells great, all right?" Zach replies, gruff suddenly.

"I'll tell you a story," resumes the Lord of St. Sepulchre. "I was strolling the South Bank the other day—oh yes, I *do* get around—and see a couple coming out of Festival Hall. Ahoy there! I say. What did you hear? Schumann! they say, and dash off like rabbits—*everyone's* in a blinking hurry! And I says to myself, Schumann. *Or did they say,* Shoo, man? SHOO, man! Understand me? You wiv me?"

The Lord of St. Sepulchre splutters with delight, shoulders heaving, and Zach is momentarily ashamed of his gruffness, yet irritated that he should feel the need to appease this old fellow with the brackish stench who has stopped him on the way home to his girl, when he has wine and flowers and is bringing a fish. What does he want, the old boy? Money for jokes? My story?

"I boxed," Zach begins, reluctant. "Won the Gloves, went pro, record was seven and one, six by KO. I got hurt, head injury, had to stop. I coach now. Well. I assist. At Izzy's Gym."

"Did I *ask* you what you do? I'm not nosy!" says the man, staring at the ground. "Take care of your boots. A man must walk."

"Right," goes Zach, sheepish.

"My wife died and I drank like a fish. Now I walk and walk. I know a walker when I see one."

"I have a home, mister."

"For now," suggests the old *alik*.

"OK, sir. I've got to go," Zach says, feeling punchy.

"SCHU-mann!"

"OK."

"Wait, son! What do you call a dog who likes music?"

"I'm off, I said."

"BACH! *Bach*—BARK! See? You wiv me? Now, what's in my coat?"

"Is this a trick? I don't know, man. Pack of cards? Pet mouse?"

The Lord of St. Sepulchre flexes his gnarled digits in fingerless gloves and plunges them into the voluminous pockets of his greatcoat, spilling their contents on the bench for Zach's perusal: one bottle of economy bleach, a cake of carbolic soap, sandpaper and a wood-backed brush with bristles coarse as thatch.

"Be clean!" he says. "And take care of your boots!"

"You mean to wash your body with that? Are you crazy?"

But the red-nosed man discourseth no more. The red-nosed man is lord of all he surveys, and an amateur of boots. He is Lord of St. Sepulchre.

"Wow!" sighs Rachel. "He's the wise man, isn't he?"

"Who is?" asks Zach.

"Your Lord of St. Sepuchre-without-Newgate. And the churchyard, well, it's perfect! That's his forest."

And Rachel reminds him that in Russian folk tales, there is always dense forest, and often a wise man, and that the heart, as Tasha taught them, the soul, lives outside the body in some sacred place, a tree, a stone, or maybe an egg in a hollow at the base of an uprooted oak. A duck might collect it and drop it into the ocean to be swallowed by a fish. *Use your head.* If you catch this fish and do not fry him in a pan, Fish might grant you your dreams and wishes out of gratitude. If you crack the egg, you may lose out on dreams and wishes.

"If this, if that!" Zach exclaims. "Bloody hell, Rach. It's a lottery."

"It's true, Zach. You're right. Gambling tales. *Moralised* gambling!"

"Yeah, well. Not very wise, that old boy. My Lord of St. Sepulchre."

"Maybe he was a ghost. You're seeing ghosts now, my graveyard charley!"

"Bloody pong was real enough!" says Zach. "So! How do *I* smell, then?"

"With your nose, sir! Your *conk! Smeller, snuff-box, nozzle!*"

"*Scent-bottle!* You forgot *scent-bottle.*"

"Good, you smell good."

"But of what?" Zach insists.

"Many things. Bonfire night and—do you really want to know?"

Zach raises himself, rests on an elbow. He nods. *Yes, I do.*

"Well. Sometimes of books and stones—and earth. Strange! And you can smell of ships and boats, and of upholstery, leather, old train compartments—"

"Mouldy, in other words."

"No!"

"Hmm," Zach groans, dubious.

"And you smell of bat oil in summer, and . . . wet dog in autumn. And engines and engineering—Victorian, yes! Like bridges and embankments, railways and pumping stations and gas lamps—"

"Whoa there! And sewers?"

"And bricks! Staffordshire blues and Portland stone, London stock—yellows! And often," she adds, "of course, you are simply sweaty. Lovely, though—mineral and powdery and steamy. Sporting sweat."

"Golly, Rach. You're just a sewer rat."

"I'm *very* ratty right now. I've been drawing them for days! Rats and pugilists and soldiers. I'm really well up on rats! Making me late with the fairy tales, actually," adds Rachel. "Have a deadline for that one. Damn, I'm all awake now! What time is it? And now I have to pee."

"It's a rat race!"

Sewer rat, bone-grubber, mudlark, tosher. Yes, yes, Zach smells like engines and weather and fighting, and motion, Rachel decides, catching his essence in the air, breathing it off her own skin, in the bathroom towels. Scent is dynamic, she thinks, a strange attractor. The fine hairs of Rachel's nostrils tingle and vibrate like the strings of a harp, like the whiskers of *Rattus rattus*.

"Do you hear that?" Zach asks, when she returns from the bathroom, his voice thick with sleep.

"Foxes," replies Rachel. "They're in season."

"No, no. Not that! Listen. It's Tasha, isn't it? Singing?"

According to the laws of Russian Orthodoxy, the human voice, a gift of Nature and God's creation, is the only permissible musical instrument in the church service. This voice, until the early twentieth century, was strictly male.

Natasha sings.

"*Step da step krugom.*" Steppe, endless steppe.

In her song, a coachman lies dying.

"Bury me here," he asks his friend, "in this dense steppe."

> *Give to my wife*
> *A word of farewell*
> *And give back to her*
> *This wedding ring*
> *And tell her that I died here*
> *In the freezing steppe*
> *And that I have taken her love*
> *Away with me.*

Of all the coachman's requests, Tasha knows, burial in the freezing steppe is the most testing. The hardest task. She smiles, enjoying the joke.

"*Step da step krugom . . .*"

Tasha is not in Hoxton anymore. The swish of traffic is less charged here in Camden, and the Gardens behind Zach and Rachel's house are alive with animal and bird sounds. There is a smell of man in this house, of boy, godlike! Animal! Fee-fi-fo-fum! In Hoxton, Nicky's smell is long gone. Oh Nikolai.

Volya butts Tasha's hand, swipes his tongue across her fingers, asking permission to leap onto the bed and rest his handsome jaws on her chest. This is frowned upon in the guide dog manual, but Natasha is flexible. Nicky always said so. He said there is no anatomy so fine as hers, no vertebrae so beautifully aligned. Nicky took Tasha's love away with him. Nicky!

"Come," Tasha whispers.

Volya springs onto the bed from a standing start, alighting deftly, to settle in her lee. He rests his muzzle on Natasha's chest, one paw across her rib cage. The dog and the woman form a single shape, a fractal, with intricate structure on the finest scale.

You are blind, she hears the dog thinking, *but not beat.*

"Volya," she says. "You smell of steppe, endless steppe."

{ EIGHT }

The Natural History of London
or Laid-in-the-Streets,
Being the Only and Original Complete Life of Samuel Alexander,
uncrowned bare-knuckle champion of All England,
known to the Fancy as "Sam the Russian" or the "Tsar of the Prize Ring."
The Life and Strange Surprizing Adventures.
by RACHEL WOLFF.

NEITHER THE BLACK RAT (*Rattus rattus*) typically referred to as "roof rat" and "ship rat," nor the brown rat (*Rattus norvegicus*), typically referred to as "common rat," "Hanoverian rat" and "Russian rat," is a true-born English rat, both hailing from Asia. The rat is quite partial to waterways and is fond of travel. The brown rat, larger than *Rattus rattus,* and with a thicker, shorter tail and smaller ears, but likewise very dark and therefore often mistaken for the black rat by the untrained observer, is a fine swimmer and famous, for instance, for swimming the Volga in 1727 in hopeful hordes, on a bold foray westwards, a journey some consider rash and inexplicable, and others, fateful. There is still some debate.

Here is a drawing of a brown rat crossing the Volga, going west.

{Go west, young rat.}
Idi na zapad, molodaya krysa.

VOLGA {river}
reKa

The black rat is particularly drawn to ocean voyages, travelling the world by sea in a rather less sporting manner than his brown cousin, often as stowaway, crowding the rails with his fellows by night to sniff the sea breezes and observe the play of star and moonlight upon the waters, notwithstanding the fact some are poor sailors, bewildered, too far from their native place, and ill-equipped for long-haul sea-faring in unpredictable weather. On very rough crossings, black rat is all at sea, and may well jump ship. Rat overboard!

Rattus rattus is a very rare sight in Britain today.

Here is a drawing of a black rat travelling the world by ship.

Black rat (Rattus rattus)
travelling
the world by ship.

The brown rat is known as *Rattus norvegicus* due to a belief it came to England from Norway in the holds of timber ships. This is a myth. The brown rat was first sighted in Britain some thirty-four years before its first official appearance in Norway in 1762. The brown rat is much more likely a Russian émigré, casting off from that wide expanse in a spirit of adventure, or defence of the realm, or simply in search of more clement and peaceable pastures, ever travelling west.

The human ear is poorly attuned to the *Rattus* frequency. Were rats voluble, it would be the very devil to know, though the prevailing prejudice is that a rat's topic of choice is dinner: its prospects, ingredients and nutritional value. A rat's batterie de cuisine consists of claw and teeth. If a rat does not eat regularly his teeth will grow to uncomfortable lengths. This is another myth. The rat's incisors pare down quite normally and his teeth are harder than iron, closest to steel. He can exert up to 7,000 psi of biting pressure. He is very keen on pickled fish, due to his beginnings.

Here is a drawing of *Rattus norvegicus*, beneath an upside-down Le Creuset casserole, and calling for help.

Rattus norvegicus beneath an upside-down le creuset casserole, and calling for help.

HELP!

Rat's cries cannot be heard by humans. He assuages his fear by indulging in nostalgia, notably dreams of caviar—*ikra*—and vodka and sparkling blue waters. He tries to gnaw through enamel, because he does not want to die alone. Time is not of the essence to him; indeed, in no wise does he want to grow long in the tooth, but he cannot abide a lonely death.

Sam saw a rat in Seven Dials, felt it toddle across his anatomy, he is sure of that. He doesn't know what the weakness might be in a rat, how to look for it. He has heard they come by ship, as his father must have done. They come and go by ship, yet England's rats are not true-born, so Jonah tells him, Jonah the Needle who, very likely, is true-born, though no one can swear to it, no one can say quite where the Needle was born. Jonah and Sam are foundling boys, laid-in-the-streets.

On the eve of their placing out, Jonah the Needle dipped for the foundling tokens, desiring for Sam and himself what was rightly theirs to complement the rest of their scant personals, i.e., suit of togs, Bible, Book of Common Prayer and *Instructions to Apprentices* with the Hospital coat of arms printed upon it, featuring Hogarth's lamb with a sprig of thyme in its mouth, all of which said items comprised the sum total of their belongings and parting gifts.

With picks he had fashioned from scraps, and skeleton key from a spoon, Jonah did spring the lock to the parlour and cabinet within moments, bypassing wards and lifting levers in less time than it took to find the two tokens in Samuel's name and the one in his own. Jonah's is a white porcelain bottle-neck label with two pin-holes where a chain once looped, and the word "ale" emblazoned across it in proud black letters with fine cracks running into the ink. The flow of fine cracks put Jonah in mind of the river, he tells Sam later, of the river Thames, that is, and all its courses. In consequence thereafter, when Sam is potboy at Tom Spring's Castle and serves up pots of ale, gently overflowing, he is often put in mind of Jonah and his token, and of the river also, what with ale beginning as river and entering a man by the chaffer to emerge later by other parts into the sewers and back to the river. The river comes and goes and so do ships, and so do soldiers, and rats and adventurers, sailors and merchants and convicts; all sorts.

Rat! I see a rat, thinks Sam in his fevered state. I hear murmurings and I see a rat! Though suffering the hurt his frame has sustained with determined courage, the safety of his life, he hears Jones the apothecary whisper before leaving the room, is endangered without doubt. Sam strains to focus through his swollen toplights: *there*! A rat, yes, skimming the uppers of Spring's high-lows as he slumbers in an armchair, toes poking free of the rug Jones has thrown over the ex-champion's body. Tom keeps vigil for Sam the Russian, his wounded apprentice, adopted son, good as his own.

.   .   .

In Sam's attic rooms, Tom wears a nightcap against the November effect, pulled well down below his ears, though he listens out impatiently for Elizabeth—where is she with that bowl of caudle? Will she remember to warm beer, not wine? Ale is better for the boy. And plenty of spice, he insisted, to draw the fever out. Tom wears a muffler round his neck and fingerless gloves and his very warmest indescribables. He is much distressed. The boy's wounds will heal, but the fever worries him.

"Nothing but the November effect that's kye-bosked him," insists Mr. Jones the apothecary, with insufficient persuasion. "To use the sporting vernacular! If it were the cholera, I'd know it. No mistake!"

The air is clear in Tom's castle, no graveyard odours here, no pestilence nor gaol fever. Some establishments require a sprinkling of herbs and flowers to smother the stink, but not here. Tom keeps the place clean, forbidding the smoking of pipes and cigars in his private parlour, noting how Sam's optics swell upon exposure to smoke, and a fighter who cannot spot his mark in the ring is defenceless. There will be no enfeebling vapours in Tom's Castle if he can help it. Some say there's fever in the water. The Metropolitan Brewers tell him they have been drawing well-water instead of river-water for years now, and Tom is reassured. Fevers can come from any quarter, it seems, and a man might as well take precautions. Why, a person can drop dead from any number of unhappy events. A person might perish of spontaneous combustion!

Where is my wife? For a schoolmaster's daughter, she is not a very good timekeeper, not so very . . . fastidious. Spring leans forward in his seat to peer at Sam, never certain the boy's peepers are closed or open, the swellings being still so terrific. Jones showed great vexation when Tom called for a lancet previously, and firmly dissuaded him from applying himself to the patient, though Tom claims a lancing to be a most useful operation. In support of his claim, he recounted the battle some four years ago on Knowle Hill, Berkshire, between Young Dutch Sam and the ageing Jack Martin, known as Master of the Rolls (being a baker by trade), in which Tom acted as second. Tom recalls lancing Jack's ogles to release the gore and claret and return him to the fray in time and, though Martin soon fell to a tremendous facer, still Tom's confidence in the benefits of lancing cannot be shaken.

"If you please, Mr. Spring!" commands Mr. Jones, and how great is Tom's surprise when the apothecary snaps his instrument drawer shut on the ex-champion's fives as he searches for a knife. "Stand aside, sir!"

Messrs. Jones and Spring take leave of the patient and descend the stairs softly, retiring to Tom's parlour for brief respite. Jones might have been a physician, he confides to Spring that evening over a pot or two of finest, he might have been a swell with rooms in Broad Street or Finsbury Square instead of an overqualified apothecary in Covent Garden too hard by the stews of St. Giles. He might have been a surgeon, indeed, but for want of funds and the inheritance of his poor father's debts.

"In sum, those are the unfortunate particulars," says he to Tom while rising from his chair to straighten his habiliments in a spoffish manner, and brush the dust from his chimney pot before placing it back upon his nut where it sits low on his furrowed brow. "What a day, Mr. Spring! How very glad I am that boy ran into my shop! See how it ends well! I play my part! Everyone has a part and a destiny, that's my perspective. I shall call tomorrow and examine the boy."

Jones stops at the door of the Castle, Holborn, and, prodding at the barnacles forever slipping down his sneezer, praises Tom's establishment in forthright tones, deeming the tavern fine and salubrious, the decoration and company pleasing, and the bub excellent. He draws attention, lastly and curiously, to the lack of corruption in the air, clearly the mark, Jones suggests, to Tom's happy amazement, of as upright and gentlemanly a publican as Spring was once prize-fighter and champion!

"I speak as a student and amateur of the fistic art," Jones adds in bashful tones, "and not only as a man of science. I was there at your last fight! *The great battle between Spring and Langan.* Kindness, sir! I hold this quality in high estimation! And so," he concludes feelingly, "goodnight, sir!"

My last fight, thinks Tom Spring. I remember it, not forgotten.

Near Chichester it was. 8 June 1824 . . .

Jack Langan, glutton, staggered on his pedestals, refusing surrender, and when Spring might so easily hit him a floorer to end the match, he merely fibbed his opponent gently and lowered him to the ground. These seventy-six rounds prove to be Spring's last, and his opponent's likewise. Langan was so severely beaten he would not fight again. Towards the close, Tom pulled his punches and attempted to force a knockdown with a single hot one, his humanity ascendant in spite of Langan's foul blows and repeated practice of rushing head down to draw Tom's fives upon his nut in the hopes of breaking Tom's famously weak hands. Tom Cribb, Spring's mentor and second, feared that his humanity, for which Spring was renowned, might well lose him the title. Mercifully, the match was stopped by the umpire and to loud acclaim for both sides, most especially in praise of the Champion's manliness and propriety. His kindness.

How great is the kindness of Spring? How long is the coast of Britain? Think on it, Tom. The complexity of roughness!

Did not the very same Tom Spring only four years later, acting as second to Jack Martin, push his man off his knee when Jack wished to surrender, clearly a beaten man? In defeat, Jack would not shake Young Dutch by the hand, though he accepted the proffered ten pounds and broomed for the Castle without a word to soak himself in blue ruin, three-outs at a time, before moving on to goes of scotch with half and half on the side. Jack has since recovered, Tom knows, and is wed to a lady worth £25,000. It is noised, however, that she has been seduced, latterly, by none other than Young Dutch, Jack's victor within and without the P.R.

"Everyone has a part and a destiny," said Jones. That's his perspective.

Nearly dawn.

Tom stretches and returns to the attic. He palpates Sam's anatomy, running his hands gently upwards and downwards in an effort to enliven the boy by excitement of the circulation, and quite suddenly he weeps for Sam and his injuries, wishing the sharps who kye-bosked him so cruelly onto the hulks and even wishes the derrick on them! He wishes for the early morning bell to sound, that unholy toll of the bell at St. Sepulchre-without-Newgate with cruel death ensuing! Ah no, not that! Lord, forgive me. My name is Tom Spring, once champion, and renowned for humanity.

"I'm so sorry, young Sam," Tom murmurs, smoothing the rugs he disordered in his earnest examination of the boy. "I'm sorry for it all."

Sam the Russian feels the trickle of *Rattus* across his hams, fly as a pickpocket fingering a flat's jemmy, choosing easy prey, an aged, say, or a lushy—some swell all round his hat. Yes, rat is an area sneak working by the darky, hiding under wraps of a London particular. Sam's leg twitches as his rat dream retreats, and he wakes with an urge to impart that, notwithstanding his defeat at the Battle of Seven Dials, yet he floored one of the sharps with Broughton's mark, that hit to the short rib and onto the liver, just as Spring taught him. And how he danced! Sam danced out and in again, effecting a lodgement with no tell-tale pull of the elbow, putting in a left-hand jab his foe never saw coming. Surprise is key. Not all was lost! Not *all,* sir!

"Broughton's mark!" says Sam. "A floorer!" he shouts, sitting up so violently he spews the supper he shared with Jonah on the eve of the Battle, flashing the hash into Spring's lap, warming his indescribables, spattering his high-lows.

"Welcome back, son!" shouts Spring, unperturbed by blood-speckled pie and porter, short-crust and gravy. "Welcome home! Nothing like the vomits and sweats to purge a fighter! Go on, Sam, spew! Elizabeth! Elizabeth!" he calls, dashing to the door of Sam's room and back to the bedside, thumping Sam's body, kneading him in thew and sinew. "A little farrier's oil and opodeldoc, a few swipes of the flesh brush and you'll be right as rain! You're full of gross humours, that's all, young Sam, from swallowing the crimson and taking a chill and lying a-bed. Vomit, boy! Elizabeth, the caudle! And hot water—and linens! Ah, Sam," says Spring, "we'll have you fit in no time, bobbish even. But what a stink, eh? What a stink!"

Tom whips the dirty rugs from the bed and works at Sam's togs, beginning with the blue waistcoat lined in yellow silk, tailored by Jonah the Needle in Belcher blue and yellow, colours known also for their property of deterring rats and mice. Sam's *perpetual,* Tom calls it, because Sam is rarely seen without it. He strips the enfeebled boy right down to his elegant anatomy, exposing his mark of the Mosaic, peeling him of shirt and drabs, continuations and undergarments. Sam has spewed from every orifice.

"Well done, Sam! Welcome back!"

Anxiously awaiting his wife with caudle, hot water and rags, Spring casts a practised eye over Sam's noble frame, his fighter's build unfinished, still emerging, and wholly undebauched. The ex-champion rubs his hands to and fro to warm the boy, meanwhile muttering recipes for embrocations and liniments and vigorous infusions, pondering emetics of tartar and ipecacuanha, the blue pill of mercury and senna, purgatives of salts and aloes, and sudorific of Dover's powders, rubs of almond oil and camphor. So much to do, so much to do! But first, an application of opodeldoc as soon as the boy is washed. Tom swears by opodeldoc, this veterinary compound of camphor, soap and spirits of wine, to remedy the ligaments and restore the tendons. And then, Sam, you shall take small doses of ale and from a single brewer only so as not to confuse and derange the bowels.

"Hurry, Elizabeth! Hurry, hurry."

{ NINE }

THE CASTLE is filled to an overflow tonight, and Tom Spring is more than usually animated. He is, furthermore, in uncommonly fine voice. Mine host contributes readily to the chaunting and circulates happily among his visitors, quite often shaking them by the hand, acquaintances and strangers alike. The assemblage is promiscuous, comprising both fixtures and newcomers, and Tom smiles upon the motley crowd, upon lord and scribe, M.P. and surgeon, blade, boxer, artist, quiz and wag. Tom Spring is much esteemed and many persons are drawn by curiosity alone, keen to peep shyly at the ex-champion and observe the company of public characters and sporting heroes, both veteran and novice. All are present! All are welcome! Though rules are to be observed here, as in the Ring.

"You may talk about fighting as much as you please," Tom will say, "to promote milling, but not a blow shall pass in my presence."

Tom is more than usually animated, more than usually contented, for Sam is now back on his stampers and, if not yet in the highest state of condition, is ferrying three-outs and goes of scotch, pots of ale and jugs of claret with considerable vigour and gaiety, notwithstanding his recent afflictions. Sam the Russian and his bosom friend Jonah the Needle have excited much interest for the Battle of Seven Dials, the particulars of which have been recorded in the pages of *Bell's Life* by A Miller, a novice author who is in attendance this very evening and can be seen seated in a snuggery with Mr. Jones, an eminent apothecary of Covent Garden. The scribe, sipping at a glass of genuine stunning, resplendent in a pair of forest-green indescribables, is the very same A Miller, indeed, who witnessed Sam's unveiling at the Castle and wrote, famously, "A Fresh Wind Blows in Holborn!" in which article the author observed Sam to be "uncommonly well-proportioned" and noted that his "temperament and elegance of form recall the great and lamented Jem Belcher, that perfect phenomenon." A Miller presumed, furthermore, that "Sam will be much in demand amongst those sketchers of the Royal Academy who now frequent the Castle as they once did the hallowed places of blessed memory, the Fives Court in Little Saint Martin's and Jackson's Rooms, Piccadilly, where these artists could be seen busily perusing the finest and comeliest practitioners of the fistic art," ever in search of a muse. A Miller expressed the hope, in conclusion, that Sam might "equal, if not surpass his antecedents in both skill and mannerliness! A fresh wind blows in Holborn!"

As it does tonight, muses Tom, watching another pair of swells sweep through his portals in a flap of garments and a flurry of snow, rosy-cheeked and wind-blasted, leaving the ghost of their warm breath in the freezing doorway. What a night! He remembers a winter not so long ago, when two unfortunate coves travelling by coach paid the less considerable fares to ride on the outside and froze to death on the Bath to Chippenham! And Spring's old foe Jack Carter once fought Jack Power in conditions so intemperate, Power's mauleys froze stiff and, in sum, he died of cold. Perhaps the Thames will freeze this winter, as it did the year Jack Broughton felled George "The Coachman" Stevenson with a winder to the heart, the younger man tragically hopping the twig a month later, a fatal victim of Broughton's superior skills and his own foolish bottom. The Coachman should never have issued the challenge, being overweighted in both education and anatomy! Why, the man had apartments to let! His brain, an empty garret!

"Sam?" Tom asks. "Are you well? Are you feeling the cold?"

"No, sir!" Sam bellows, still deaf in one ear. "Feeling bobbish!"

"Well done, Sam! Remarkable boy!"

And here too comes Jonah himself, the hero of Seven Dials, in the finest of knee-smalls and continuations, his smile a leading feature in his composition, and his stride considerably spry for a fellow with such irregular undertakings he must support the unfortunate encumbrance of a leg brace.

"Jonah the Needle!" says Spring, "What'll it be? I have some lovely hock! To which you are partial as I recall. And who is the young buck with Sam there, fellow with the flash belcher and thunder-and-lightning waistcoat?"

"He's not a buck, sir, not exactly. And he's a reporter!"

"Ah. One of the black-letter gentry. On *Bell's*, is he? *Illustrated Sporting? Sporting Mag?*"

"No, sir. A parliamentary reporter!"

"Indeed. Well, well. Now, you take this jug to your friends and tell Sam to retire presently. John and Sarah can manage without him. We don't want him dished and falling from weakness! I'll have him training again in but a few days."

"Bless you, sir!" pipes Jonah. "Thank you!" he says, accepting the wine and bracing himself to negotiate a path to Sam, brushing past a well-proportioned swell on his way, a man proud of countenance and altogether elegant and striking. The fellow has a cheerful expression on his upperworks as he makes for mine host, Tom Spring, whose gaze is diverted by a tug at his stockings and light step on his toes.

"Thomas!" Spring exclaims, gathering the child in his arms. "Why aren't you a-bed? Sarah! Take the boy to Mrs. Spring. Thomas! I thought you were a rat."

"In need of a ratcatcher, Tom?" asks the prepossessing cove. "I know one or two as good as Cribb's famous old tyke. Billy, wasn't it?"

"Sam Elias," Tom declares. "Young Dutch. How do you do? Heavy whet? Or champagne?"

"What's my name?" demands Young Dutch Sam, bordering irritable. "Did you call me Elias? *What's* my name?"

"Your father," Tom says, "was a gin man, of course. Trained on three glasses of eye-water a day, God rest him. Though no fighter, I am told, had a more terrific punch. One hundred battles, two defeats and not a single cross. And your pater, as the story goes, once was offered £1,000 in flimsies to lose a match, but refused, exposing the sharps for good measure, so I hear. Firmness was his criterion! But a daffy man, he was. Gin was certainly his tipple. You, of course, are more refined. So what will it be?"

"My mother, you know, is not of the Mosaic. I call myself Evans. My name is Evans. Sam Evans. As you are well apprised, Spring."

Young Dutch Sam, born Elias, was eight years old when his father,

Dutch Sam, died dozzened and cut up, awash in blue ruin and without a penny to his name. Young Dutch entered the lists aged fifteen, trained by Gentleman Jackson himself, and in the seven years he has graced the P.R., Young Dutch has never been beat, dazzling the Fancy with the speed and accuracy of his blows, his fleetness of foot and manifest boxing ability. He is a dancing master, attracting the upper customer as patron and backer while making numerous enemies among Dutch Sam's old crowd for his irascible temper and conceited disposition. They search and hope for a fighter to level him, they seek the man still. Spring, ever a study in fairness and humanity, has no quarrel with Young Dutch. But he is up on the man. Well up.

"How old is your boy?" asks Young Dutch.

"I have two sons. Thomas is seven."

"A ball of fire, please, Tom. Your very best! And I didn't mean your son, but the Russian. Samuel Alexander, Sam the Russian, your kid, your study. Let me meet the novice! And do not call me Elias again! It vexes me exceedingly."

"Always on your high ropes, Sam Evans! You're a quiz and a tinder-box, but never mind. Come and meet my very own Sam," says Tom affably, pouring his best brandy. "Then we'll raise a purse so you can meet him next time in the Ring! How's that? If you are not too aged and debauched," he adds, casting a friendly arm around the bruiser's young shoulders. "He is seven years your junior, you know. Are you not afraid?"

"I'm unbeatable, Tom."

"So said the Gas! Remember the Gasman!"

Remember the Gasman, the Gas-light Man, the Gas!

Tom Hickman, Pet of the Fancy, the very model of physical beauty and a powerful hitter for a figure of such unimposing proportions. The Gas was of the opinion that he could conquer any man, no matter by how much he might be overweighted, and so in 1821, in the great fight for the Championship between Hickman and Neat on Hungerford Downs, he gave two stones to Neat the "Bristol Butcher." Spring recalls it now, how the Gas was on the totter and almost blind, the claret pouring from one ogle in torrents and the other being swelled to the point of dropping from his very phiz, and still the Gas would not surrender, notwithstanding shouts of "Take the brave fellow away!" In the final round, he was so very wild and pitiable, he appeared at the scratch fumbling confusedly with the undone flap of his breeches, and Neat, albeit waiting courteously for his opponent to recover, promptly hit a floorer from which the Gas could not arise in time.

"What about the Gas?" asks Young Dutch, enchafed.

"He was a fiery cove," Tom explains. "Hot! A fighter must preserve his cool! There you are, Evans, in your snow-white chimney pot and fine toggery and shiny pair of tops, boasting seven years in the ring and so far unbeaten, yet on your high ropes always. Impatient. Ready to throw your hat in the ring no matter what odds or conditions. Why, you are on such excellent terms with yourself, no man might have a higher opinion of Young Dutch than Young Dutch himself! You're endless sarsy and prefer to strut with the Diamond Squad and forget your beginnings. That's the buzz. You are a fiery cove, sir! Ever heard of spontaneous combustion?"

Young Dutch tips his ball of fire in a single swallow, eyeing Spring with displeasure. "Coming it a bit strong, Tom, aren't you? Spontaneous combustion! I daresay if I overturn in a trap one day and get my nut cracked, as did befall the Gas, or am killed by boxing or cholera or by some ramper with a knife, then that day has my name on it, nothing to be done. But presently, the only thing I foresee with my name on it is the Championship of All England! Now cut the chaff! Where's your boy?"

"Follow me," orders Spring, crossing the floor.

"Halloa, sir!" shouts Sam the Russian, who can hardly hear himself, his auscultatory faculties not yet recovered. "My name is Samuel Alexander!"

And so Spring performs the preliminaries before turning away to circulate amongst his guests, not without a flicker of trepidation for his apprentice, who rose so quickly to his stampers at the sight of Young Dutch, extending his fives and feeling by instinct for the medallion of Tsar Alexander I no longer round his neck, touchstone of his native place and prigged from his body in the Battle of Seven Dials. Jonah assures him they will recover his token if they have to knock up every pawn shop in the Holy Land, as St. Giles is often known. It's gone up the spout, says Jonah, and we shall search it out. A chill wind blows through Sam as he shakes Young Dutch by the hand and stands in admiration of his athletic form, fine features and flash apparel, a chill wind and a peculiar apprehension of strange and surprizing adventures. My Borodino, perhaps! My Waterloo!

"Halloa, sir!" bellows Sam once more. "My name is Samuel Alexander!"

"I know who you are. I've come to meet you," Young Dutch pronounces, extending a hand. "And I am Sam Evans, undefeated."

"I know who *you* are, sir. Seven years a professional, no losses so far!"

"Precisely. You need a haircut, I daresay," he adds, flicking at Sam's curls not much longer than his own. "And you likewise, sir!" he adds, glaring at Dickens. "But you are not a miller, I think," he continues, losing interest and glancing at Jonah, eyeing the Needle's leg brace and abbreviated arm with the lofty detachment and faint disgust of the physically pre-eminent. Sam Evans, at twenty-three years of his age and 5 feet 8 and ¾ inches in height since last measured, famous for speed and boxing ability, is possessed of perfect anatomy.

"Well," begins Dickens, stripped to the loins in his mind's eye, toeing the line before letting fly with his fives, his gameness manifest, "that is to say, I have been known to—"

"To be sure," goes Young Dutch, waving him off with a white kid leather glove. "Sam," he says in artful tones, "recall Mendoza v. Gentleman Jackson 1795, fifth round."

"He—"

"Precisely. The Gentleman grabbed Dan by the hair and locked him in chancery, fibbing the champion until he fell. The Gentleman won the title! And retired, offering no return, clever fellow!"

"Spring tells me Jackson was the stronger—in full bodily vigour, and Dan exhausted. He had the advantage, I mean to say. Notwithstanding."

"Perhaps, perhaps. I will not convince you otherwise," concedes Young Dutch, perching high in his seat as if accused, allowing Jonah the Needle to observe a flaw in Evans's tailoring, his benjamin—albeit a coat most assuredly purchased at great expense—constraining the wearer across the pectorals and cut too high under the arms, ill suiting a fellow so well proportioned. Ill befitting! "A haircut, a haircut," Young Dutch concludes, "is what I advise."

"Thank you, sir," replies Sam, somewhat dismayed.

·　　·　　·

The manual of instruction, it occurs to Sam, is never complete. Ever since his unveiling at the Castle and the Battle of Seven Dials, there have been so many persons with method to impart, professional and otherwise, even the well-breeched Mr. Jones the apothecary and amateur of the P.R. into whose rooms Sam happily repairs when work and training permit.

"I have been making a study of the properties of particles," offers Jones one evening. "Why, quite everything is formed of particles," he explains, reaching for his decanter.

Particles, articles, muses Sam. He is not in want of instruction! The manual is never complete. His existence is formed of articles, from foundling days to his imminent novitiate, his life, so far, is a book of rules! Instructions to apprentices, articles on self-defence, rules of boxing, articles of agreement. Yes! Spring has written the articles! Sam's first battle looms!

"Another glass of port, Sam?"

"No, sir. I'm in training, you see."

"Very good, Sam. Debauchery is a scourge of the Prize Ring. You are without corruption. It is laudable indeed. Beware debauchery!"

Instructions to Apprentices.

You may find temptations to do wickedly, when you are in the world; but by all means fly from them.

"These are the properties of particles, Samuel," resumes Jones the apothecary. "In sum: position and momentum! This is my understanding. Newton is surpassed! Newton believed in *forces,* but interactions are defined by changes in momentum, not forces! The momentum of a particle is the mass of that particle multiplied by its velocity. In the ring," Jones proposes, "you are the embodiment of particles. You take a stance: that's position. You make a tremendous hit: this is momentum. Leverage! Position and momentum. Do you see it now, Sam?"

"I think so, sir. Yes."

"Gain the momentum and you will rise and rise! Dear boy!"

The apothecary's rooms are full of tomes and dust, dust of merry occupation and considerable learning and perpetual flickering of the pages of books and journals—*The Lancet* and *Bell's Life* and *The Sporting Magazine* amongst them. When Sam sneezes, Jones explains how the heart stops momentarily upon a *sternutation,* and Sam pictures the heart and the blood coursing through his anatomy, and marvels at Jones's illustrations of the cardiovascular system, at the quantity and length of vein, capillary and artery. He marvels at how so much can be contained within the body. *How long is the bloodline of Sam the Russian?*

Rachel draws three squares across a page of A3 Bristol board Extra Smooth Surface. In the first she draws a boy in the yard of a coaching inn, punching a hole through the frozen surface of a pail of water. He wants to water his horse and it is winter and very cold. He has a good punch. In the second frame, Rachel draws the Emperor Napoleon standing in a window at the Kremlin by a guttering candle in a ruined city, a Moscow of embers. He peers out into the dark where he can see flakes of snow falling, catching the light. The Russians are coming. He can feel it. And amongst them will be a very young Hussar-Cossack with a fine complexion, fine as a girl's. He will have a love affair in London and his child will be born there in 1815, the year of the Battle of Waterloo, and well after the young soldier has left, never to return. The child will be a boy and they will never meet. In the third square, Rachel draws her father Lev at a desk covered in papers and books and glasses of Kusmi tea that have long since grown cold. He holds his head in his hands and might well be crying. He is a scientist of chaos and emergence. Lev Wolff's father died on the Eastern Front in another wintry field of battle. Lev's father was a meteorologist and they never met.

Operation Bagration, The Eastern Front, Spring 1944.
   Lev's father the meteorologist is stationed on the outskirts of Odessa a month or two before travelling north on the eve of Operation Bagration. He is called in to pronounce upon weather systems so that General Malinovsky can remain a step ahead of the 6th Army, the Red Army outweighing the Wehrmacht in three departments particular to Russia: in profligacy of souls, in stoicism, and in respect for meteorology, a legacy made famous at Borodino and in the crossing of the Berezina and enduring now, at Leningrad and Stalingrad and onwards to the liberation of the Ukraine and the crossing of the Dniepr. The Russian respects weather. Lev's father respects his science as well as the generals Zhukov,

Rodintsev, Rokossovsky and Malinovsky. He respects his pregnant wife and trusts to fate also. He trusts that fate will keep him alive.

Russians are music lovers, often heralding an offensive on the Eastern Front with a little chamber music, either on the day or eve of battle, placing their army musicians in advance of the regulars or in high-risk spots for the sake of inspiration. A musician is deployed as dangerously as a Molotov dog or punishment squad recruit, *shtrafnik*. The Red Army musician must be cavalier, and when Lev's father the meteorologist meets Katya's father the violinist, they strike up an acquaintance of instinctual empathy, dispensing with the measured conventions of appraisal and rapprochement most typical of peacetime, instead liking each other so very much straight away that the violinist's vulnerability in the prelude to combat causes the meteorologist a distracting, aching concern.

The violinist's wife has a baby girl named Natasha and is expecting another. The meteorologist's wife is pregnant also, and when the two new friends survive into the New Year to become attached to the 1st Belorussian Front in the march on Western Poland, they swear to mind each other's new family in the event of disaster, toasting the vows in vodka on the icy banks of the Pilica, a tributary of the Vistula they will cross in the next big push. When Gusakovsky's Tank Armies break up the frozen tributary, blasting it into makeshift bridgeheads, they blast the meteorologist's eardrum in the process as he stands watching the violent uproar of ice, the great boulders crashing back down like falling stars into ready-made building blocks.

In his increasing deafness and joy in friendship, the meteorologist is at a happier remove from reality and revels too in the happy sight of the Polikarpov I -16 swooping in amongst the clouds, a sight that cheers the men without fail though they know the tiny fighter is no match for the Messerschmitt 109. They call it "little seagull"—*chayka*—for its gull-shaped wings. In his deafness and joy, not to mention his professional guise as observer of the skies and the patterns he sees there, the meteorologist's gaze is cast upwards and as he spots the flight of the *chayka*, deaf to the hum of its engine, he imposes upon it a sound of his own, out of the past. The sound he hears is a seaside chant, of the Neva and the Baltic coast, a sound of glorious isolation—*bezmolviye*—music so sweet he feels it flower in his belly and bleed through his anatomy, a sudden savage pain of anti-tank grenade shot he mistakes momentarily for bliss. Lev's father is twenty-seven years old.

When the Tank Armies forge the Pilica and capture the German airfields by Warsaw, Katya's father the violinist plays "The Little Blue Shawl," a ditty much beloved of Russian fighting men, though written by a Russian Jew. This is a song about a soldier at the front, missing his girl, and one the violinist and meteorologist were wont to sing when drunk on sweet vodka by the half-pail, chanting away like a pair of *aliks* on a park bench, making a terrible happy sound.

The musician is not laughing now, nor crying, and he is suddenly grave beyond his years. He plays and plays.

{ TEN }

H EAR IT NOW, RACH?" asks Zach. "The singing?"
"I do now. I thought you meant the foxes. Or gulls."
"No. Tasha."

"Amazing, though, isn't it?" begins Rachel, rising to an elbow, draping her other arm across Zach's smooth chest, hairless as a dancer's but for a slight flourish on the left pectoral. "The seagulls in Camden."

"High water-table."

"I know. But how the sound enters your dreams—one's dreams. Well, my dreams—floods the brain, changes the scene, takes me straight to sea!"

"Lake Vostok?" asks Zach. "And am I there?"

"Always. I'd say, always. You're everywhere, in all the dreams. Sometimes it's your face I dream, but not you. Not your personality, not you at all except for the face. And sometimes I know it's you, definitely you, but your face is a blur—or you're not a person, but a dog or—"

"Fuck. I forgot to bring the dog food from Tasha's. Special stuff. Psycho-allergenic. Hypo. Hypo-allergenic. And or-bloody-ganic, of course. Feeds Volya better than herself! I'll pick it up when I let in Pest Control. Bloody hell, Rach. A rat! If there's one, there are more. Need to let the guy in for 10 a.m.—10 a.m. at Tasha's. Right. Hey. Rach? When I took Volya into the garden for a pee last thing, there was a fox on the wall. Eyeballing us. A bare metre away. Bold! There's probably fox shit out there now. Damn. Volya rolls in that . . . infernal stink. Would he? Guide dogs are too well trained to do stuff like that, no?"

"What I was saying before—that dream thing—Papa explained it to me—and there's a term for it, you know, the blurring of names and faces, the transposition—it's a phenomenon."

"*You're* a phenomenon. The *perfect phenomenon!*"

"Why, thank you, sir."

"Jem Belcher. The *perfect phenomenon*. They called him that."

"I know, Zach."

"Rach! Something else—completely forgot. Yesterday. Stopped the cab in the High Street—with Tasha and Volya, you know. For wine, to buy wine, and we walked home along Pratt and a gull—one of your bloody gulls—bloody dive-bombed us! Me, mostly. Three fucking times, screeching and diving at my head. *My* head! I mean it. We had to duck into the Turks. People came out of the shops to watch. Rat, fox, gull—it's a bloody hunting ground, North London. Bloody jungle!"

"Golly," says Rachel.

"*Golly?* Is that all you can say?" exclaims Zach, sitting up and astride her, pinning her wrists with his hands. "Man, it was wild! I might have been killed. Skewered by gull beak. Like—what's it called, therapy thing, stick a rod in your knowledge-box?"

"Lobotomy?"

"No, NO! The other thing, like bloodletting."

"Oh! Trepanation."

"Right. That. Could have been trepanned! Trepannatised. Whatever. Anyway, better get up."

"Zach, wait. I wanted to finish about the dream phenomenon. Papa. He was writing a paper on sleep and dreams. Quizzed us on sleep patterns."

"Quizzed you. Not me. Too stupid, me. *Muzhik.* Hey, know what I'll do later? Pee round the perimeter of the garden. Foxes won't cross a line of human pee. Male pee. Think it has to be male. Apparently. Where the hell did I read that? Or did Izzy tell me? Fuck. I'm losing my marbles. Maybe I was trepanned. Can't remember. I mean, who told me. Boy pee as fox deterrent. Worth a try, though. Though I think urban foxes are a bit of a PHENOMENON themselves. Doubt there's a line they won't cross . . ."

"Maybe," suggests Rachel excitedly, "we could get Emily to cast a spell. Anti-predator spell. Or strew some herbs and so on."

"Emily!" pipes Zach. "Emily. Think if she still lived in Ghana instead of a council house in our street, she'd be some village sage? Get loads of respect? She's in the wrong damn place."

"Zach! Seriously. She was reading on a bench in the Gardens the other day and I was passing and greeted her and she showed me her book. Huge tome on herbs. She was absolutely beaming. Said Jesus came to her in a dream and gave her the cure for cancer. Complete recipe and everything. A herbal concoction."

"Very useful," says Zach. "About time, Jesus! I mean, what's he bloody done since the loaves and fishes? Put his feet up, that's what. Cure for cancer. Now we're talking!"

"Yes, but the thing is . . . Emily *forgot what he said*. Forgot the recipe."

"Jesus better bloody make another house call then," Zach replies, rubbing his eyes with the heels of his hands. "Ouch! Fuck. Keep forgetting my cut."

Rachel gently pulls his hands free and kisses his eyes, the one still grossly puffed from his turn-up with Sandbag Shaw, swollen big as an egg.

"Are you tired?" she asks. "Does it hurt? Do you want us to move, shall we move out of Camden? Take Tasha?"

"I don't know, my dove. I just can't think this morning."

"You really did toss and turn last night. More than usual, I mean."

"Sorry," says Zach, lying down again, on to his back, bringing Rachel down with him. "I don't know why. Gimme five. Minutes, I mean. Five more."

"The hunted dream not much more than fifteen minutes every day."

"What?"

"That's true of animals in the wild."

"Right," says Zach. "I see."

"Well. There was Tasha's rat, then the gull and the fox. Maybe you're feeling a bit persecuted. Oh listen!" exclaims Rachel, pushing up on her elbows. "And look!"

"Bloody hell, Rach! Sharp bloody bones! I'm punctured."

"Gulls! A whole flight. What a sound! Where are they going?"

"Don't care. Long as they keep clear of my head, fuck. Bloody nightmare, that was."

"You're so FUCK and BLOODY this morning."

"Yeah," he concedes. "Sorry."

"But really. Where do you suppose they're off to?"

"Bering Strait," states Zach, shutting his eyes. "BLOODY Bering Strait."

"Why?"

"Something Tasha was telling me," he murmurs. "How a Cossack discovered the strait of Bering before Bering. A hundred or so years earlier. And the Cossack boats, well—glorified rafts really—were called *chayka*."

"Seagulls," says Rachel. "*Chayka*. Little seagulls."

"Yeah. Like the Red Army planes—"

"Polikarpov."

"You remember!"

"You must have made six or seven model kits of the *chayka*."

"I did, I did. Polikarpov I-16. You took over the painting of them, actually. I was too impatient. Messy. Anyway, the Cossack was a taxman, Tasha said. Collected tax in furs. So there he is, boating in a *chayka,* collecting furs, and he stumbles upon a passage between Siberia and Alaska. He realises Asia and America are separate. Asia and Arctic: separate!"

"So why Bering? Bering Strait."

"Hopeless Russian bureaucracy. They lost the Cossack's report."

"For a hundred years?" Rachel asks.

"For a hundred years."

"That's so Russian, Zach."

"Now," he says, sitting up, stretching. "I'm off to Hoxton. Shall I get eggs on the way back? And bacon? Let's do Tasha a great big breakfast."

"I smell the smell of a Russian soul!" Rachel intones, watching him slip into jeans, pull on his thick fisherman's jumper. "Hands up who knows that one?"

"I do, actually," Zach replies, swiping a hand through his hair, scooping coins and keys from the dresser. "Nicky brought gulls' eggs one Sunday lunch and Tasha told one of her tales. About the king and his kidnapped princesses and how they were rescued and rolled up their palaces into eggs with a wave of a magic hanky. Belcher. And there's a snake who goes 'I smell the smell of a Russian soul' anytime the hero comes along—the young peasant, strong man—"

"*Bogatyr,*" says Rachel.

"Right. *Bogatyr.* And you wouldn't eat your egg."

"My palace was inside."

Nikolai and Natasha have come to Chelsea with a treasure of six gulls'
eggs, one for each of them, and as they sit down to eat, Tasha holds her
egg to an ear, mesmerising young Rachel. She tells them how a king
loved his three daughters so much, he built a palace underground to
protect the princesses from weather, from wind and sunburn, but the
girls have a lively interest in the great world and learn much from books.
They must see the world. They beg the king their father to let them
dance in the garden and he relents.

"A whirlwind strikes," Tasha says, "uprooting trees and houses, coming down into the king's garden to carry off his three daughters, the
loveliest princesses in the world."

"Climate," Lev states, "is a strange attractor."

"Shhh," commands Katya.

The girls, Tasha continues, are imprisoned in the underworld, living apart in three palaces, one of copper, one of silver and one of gold.
Each palace is guarded, respectively, by a three-headed, six-headed and
twelve-headed dragon. The king calls for help amongst the rich and
powerful, promising his daughters and rich dowries in return, yet none
is willing. Then a poor village widow with three sons heeds the call. The
three brothers are commoners, but *men of power*, all born in one night.
They are named Evening, Midnight and Sunrise.

"*Bogatyrs!*" Nicky says. "Heroes, warriors. Men of power. And the
youngest," he adds, slapping Zach on the shoulders, "gets the loveliest!"

"Do you know," interjects Lev, "I used to find these tales insufferable.
So many of them arbitrary. Random. But it's all quite scientific. They're
seemingly random. Chaotic. Do you see?"

"Stop it, Lev," says Katya.

"Can women give birth to triplets like horses and cows then?" asks
Zach, recalling a half-term holiday spent on a farm. "Hours apart? Evening, midnight and sunrise. I thought babies came all in one go. More
or less."

"That's idiotic," Lev scolds. "Are you seriously asking that question?"

"I smell the smell of a Russian soul!" Tasha resumes, above the tension. "I smell the smell of a Russian soul, say the dragons! And one
by one, they threaten Sunrise the youngest son. He is the bravest and

smartest and has drunk the water of life and defeats the three dragons, cutting off all of their heads, twenty-one heads all told! When the three princesses are on their way back to the king, they pack up their homes with a wave of scarlet handkerchief," Tasha says, flapping her napkin dramatically in the air. "And miraculously reduce their palaces into eggs—of copper, silver and gold—though the king does not know this. How can he marry three girls to three *bogatyrs* with only his own palace to his name? So what do the princesses do, Rachel?"

"Break the eggs?"

"Yes. They break the eggs and roll out their palaces. And Sunrise marries the youngest and loveliest and they live in the palace of copper. And there is feasting and singing and the king makes Sunrise his heir."

"Because he's the smartest and bravest?" asks Lev in derisive tones.

"Yes," says Tasha.

"And since when was Russia ever a meritocracy?"

"In fairy tales."

"Precisely!"

"Lev," cajoles Nicky, throwing an arm round his shoulders. "He gets the worst dacha! No?"

"*Eto pravda,*" Lev concedes. True.

"Rachel?" says Katya. "You don't want your egg?"

"Yours is copper," Tasha whispers in Rachel's ear.

"I'm not sure, Mama."

"Well, don't let it go cold," warns Katya.

"And all because of a whirlwind," remarks Lev. "Everything begins with weather. A complex system. Do you see that, Rachel?"

"I do, Papa."

And no egg is ever simple again. No handkerchief—*belcher*—ever simple again. Nor wind nor rain.

Zachariah crams his pockets, straps on a watch, skips to the loo for a splash.

"Skip to the loo, my DAR-ling!" sings Rachel, stroking the bed where Zach lay, moving into that place. *I smell the smell of a Russian soul.* If she were a dog, she would see the shape of the smell he has left in this imprint on the sheets, she could make an olfactory portrait of the man in his absence, yes. If she were a dog with a twentyfold amount of primary receptors and an ability to detect an odour at concentrations one hundred times smaller than man's, she could see him in scent. A dog can distinguish between molecules of smell that have mirror symmetry, virtually identical, but drastically different, such as caraway and peppermint.

In Rachel's dreams, Zachariah is sometimes a dog. Papa says this confusion is a well-known feature of sleep and dreaming, because there is a disconnection of brain hemispheres in the dormant callosus, between the hemisphere for recognition of speech and the hemisphere for recognition of faces. Rachel dreams Zachariah in various shapes—dog, wolf, bird, boy—and then wakes to the man, seeing him always in infinite detail, taking note this morning, for instance, as he exits the bathroom, of the overnight change in hue round his swollen sparkler, the emergence into lighter shades of blue and yellow, Belcher blue and yellow.

Don't fight today.

"Whatever happened?" she asks. "The other day? You never said. Between you and Sandbags Shaw?"

"*Sandbag*, Rach. It's Sandbag."

"Sandbag, then."

"Got to fly, Rach! Tell you later."

"You won't."

"It was nothing," he tells her. "A barney, a mere scrap. Man's an idiot. Hit him in the head, there's an echo! Blow in one ear, snuff a candle out the other end! Empty garret. With breezes blowing through it."

Sandbag Shaw.

Rachel mistakes the name accidentally-on-purpose, because it irks her, hurts to utter. *Shaw is an ogre in the forest.*

Professionally, Wolff and Shaw fought twice and stand at 1–1, Zach losing the first, but winning the return, the title fight. It was Zach's Pyrrhic victory, Rachel decries, because of the damage done that freezing January night when the two men fought at light welter on the undercard of a name fighter who had drawn a big crowd. Theirs, however, was the battle of distinction and Zach became a name thereafter, for his fine win and gameness. Zach fought again too soon, defended his title too soon while still carrying the pain he would not own to of the orbital fracture Shaw inflicted in that famous return, a fracture entailing a legacy of recurring headache and double vision Zach cannot shake. Yet, in the usual hype of the pre-fight medical, Wolff was declared in prime condition for the bout that would prove to be his last, against a sharp Georgian bruiser named Kubriashvili.

The Georgian was a walk-in fighter who punched at crazy angles, had a thunderous left hook and a brazen right-hand lead and was known not to be above raking the eyes, and hitting on the break and other indelicacies. Moments before the bell to end the third round, Kubriashvili blindsided the ref to butt out of a clinch, using his head, or "third fist" as it is sometimes known, the hardest part of the body, to open a spectacular cut on Zach's cheekbone, those sculpted zygomatics leaving him more than usually prone to cuts. In the following round, as Zach gaped for air, pushing at his mouthpiece in a tell-tale sign of exhaustion, his antagonist pounced, breaking his jaw, gashing the tongue and catching Zach with an uppercut as he fell, adding a scything blow to the ear to help him on his way to the floor, where he landed with sickening finality, one leg twitching. Zach had a clot removed and his licence also. It was not safe for him to fight ever again.

The ring is not safe, it's a dangerous place! So what happens, Rachel wonders, when Zach sees Shaw? When the ogre comes at him out of the forest? What does he see that so unhinges him? What are the dynamics of rage, Papa? Tell me.

—*Rachel. Explain reflection.*

—*A reflection is a mathematical concept, not a formula, not a shape. It's a transformation.*

—*Expound.*

—*We are not bilaterally symmetric. Not invariant in reflection.*

—*Good, Rachel.*

Perhaps, thinks Rachel, when Wolff and Shaw exchange glances at Izzy's gym in Clerkenwell, they see into a glass, sharing a kind of mirror symmetry, each reflecting loss. Loss and fate. Sandbag feels a roiling fury because of that epic fight he lost in his prime, perhaps his one shot at the title, a bout after which he is not ever the same, eternally outclassed. And Zach sees in Shaw the bruiser he beat in such style he lost his head and gambled his title too soon, propelled like Stephenson's Rocket into the ring with Kubriashvili to contest a title fight he barely survives.

"*Muzhik!*" Zach had called himself as she sat in his hospital room in those long days of recovery. "Had they not passed me fit!" he mused. "If I had ducked, if I had danced, if I had hit through the target. If I had been fully fit. If I had not been so—"

"Bloody-minded?" she teased. "Hot? Impetuous?"

"All of that," he smiled. "All of that."

"Rubbish!" Rachel countered. "I mean, *walker*! As you love to say. Stuff and nonsense! You are a fighter," she added. "Were a fighter. Nothing you could do," she insisted, offering consolation now that she is certain he will not ever be allowed to fight again. One of Nicky's favourite sayings came to mind, though she did not voice it, words of the old soldier, his special wisdom.

"What is the point of ducking?" says the old soldier to the young soldier. "Each shot has a man's name on it anyway!" he laughs. "Nothing you can do."

Zach pats his pockets in the bedroom doorway: keys, cash, mobile, yes.

"Bashing off now, be right back," he says, frowning with decision. "And the Shaw thing—I'll tell you later, Rach. OK? Full particulars, no holds barred!"

"You're running away!" she accuses.

"I'm not! I'm late, that's all. I need you to call the rat man. Tell him I'll be a few minutes late. OK? Left the number on the kitchen table."

"Come here for a moment," says Rachel, and Zach kneels by the bed. "Does it hurt?" she asks, brushing his brow. "You don't answer me."

"It's all your fault," Zach smiles. "The scrap with Shaw. You and your rats. That essay you read to me. The ratcatcher in New York City."

"Joseph Mitchell? *The Rats on the Waterfront*."

"Yeah. The catcher and his peanut butter sarnie. What he discovered."

"The efficacy of peanut butter in attracting rats. But I don't—"

"I called Shaw a rat," Zach confesses, hangdog.

"That's all? You fought over *that*? Can it be so silly?"

"Stupid," he concedes.

"Didn't you tell me about a fighter who won a round without ever throwing a punch? In the forties?"

"Willie Pep! Willie Pep, Will o' the Wisp. Great featherweight. Yeah."

"He won on skill, yes? Not a single blow thrown. I like that story," insists Rachel. "Very much."

"Well, he's also famous for one of the dirtiest fights in history. OK?"

"I still like it," she says, and slips her hands up his sleeves, clasping him gently by the forearms—*brachioradialis*—forearms her fingers cannot quite encompass. "Makes one think, doesn't it? Winning a round without a blow. *Without a blow,* Wolff!"

"Marry me," Zach murmurs, dropping chin to chest.

"We are married. We've always been married. Every day, we marry," she says quietly. "Can't you see?"

In 1975, Benoit Mandelbrot invents the term "fractal" from the Latin *fractus,* a broken stone. A fractal is a geometric shape that is wholly irregular. Fractal roughness is a distinction of topographic complexity. A seascape, for instance, has complex roughness, irregular to the same degree on all scales. It looks the same, Mandelbrot explains, when examined from far away or nearby. It is self-similar.

A fighter, muses Rachel, is a fighter through and through, consistently irregular, a fighting man on every scale. Fractal, fractious, with a rough complexity! Nothing she can do. A fractal, Papa once told her, is a way of seeing infinity.

In Zachariah, she sees infinity.

Mandelbrot famously wrote a paper called "How Long Is the Coast of Britain?," the answer to which, of course, is that it depends how you look at it. The closer one looks, the larger it is. And more and more intricate, on an infinite scale.

There is a template for all things.

At his most fanciful, Lev Wolff will say he was born with a belief in templates, in flow and emergence and inherent patterns in the seemingly random. He will point out that he was born the son of a meteorologist who sought patterns in weather and applied them to military strategic effect on the Eastern Front. Lev is a scientist of chaos and emergence who never met his father the meteorologist. His father was killed before they could meet.

Lev will insist he was born with a legacy, a scientific birthright involving a belief in symmetry and determinism—which is not the same as predictability, of course—and that these beliefs have made him what he is, a scientist of chaos and emergence. This is a fallacy, he knows, because man is not born with beliefs, he is merely a template. Lev's fanciful side is rarely on show. Katya saw it, and Katya has died and taken his love away with her. Rachel sees it, now and then, and Rachel is alive but living an untenable offence with his adopted son Zachariah, whom he can no longer countenance, not only because a boy brought up as one's own son should not be one's daughter's—Lev cannot articulate the word, cannot think it—but because a man so rude, so unrefined—*neotesanniy*—should never have taken his daughter's hand. No, no, no. Lev's heart shattered further when this occurred, when Zachariah took Rachel from him, its chambers breaking into smaller and smaller irregular shards, self-similar at the finest of scales. Fractal.

How long is the coast of Britain? How great is Lev's grief?

ELEVEN

The New Forest, Hampshire.

Rachel sits in a deck chair outside the cricket pavilion, feeling the presence of Aubry, padded-up, next man in, and wonders when it was that the French vintner's son, the Charterhouse and Cambridge boy, ichthyologist, became pugilist? Will the boxer return to ichthyology? Or to viticulture and France? Will he describe a circle? When does the boy with rod and wellies become ichthyologist and not countryman, a hunting, shooting and fishing man? A fish, Rachel decides, spoke to him.

"Boy," spoke the fish, "do not kill me. I beg of you throw me back into the blue waters. Someday I may be able to be of use to you."

Rachel looks up from her book at Zachariah, on 44 not out, as he strolls down the wicket to do a spot of ruminative gardening, prodding at declivities in the pitch, at rogue blades of grass and widening cracks and foot marks etched by fast bowlers for the spinner to exploit. He taps and prods at marks real and imaginary with the toe of his new bat, Gunn & Moore Purist Original. *Zachariah, Zachariah, my purist original.* He returns to the crease, takes a stance, eye on the bowler's arm.

Position, momentum. Particles.

—Rachel, what does it represent, the swing of a pendulum?

—A periodic cycle, Papa.

—Draw me a pendulum.

In a two-dimensional diagram with an axis x for vertical and y for horizontal, one can tell where the pendulum is at any one time, but not over time. If x shows its angle of displacement and y its velocity, the swing of a pendulum describes a circle. Phase space is an imaginary space. Strange attractors live in phase space. Phase space is a map of behaviour made up of available information, subject to variation.

Not all information is available.

Watch the ball. Be balanced. The manual of cricket coaching can never be complete. There are so many variables. The state of the ball, its release, flight, direction, where it pitches, how the seam is angled, how the ball might deceive, how Zach sees it coming. How Zach feels.

Rachel wants to get up from her chair. She wants to bowl at him. She used to bowl for him.

Zach the boy spends every last penny of his saved-up pocket money on a fine bat and a fine pair of gloves, drawing on ingenuity for the rest of his gear, bartering with the Games caretaker at school for a withered splintery set of stumps and bails and a mouldering net, and salvaging oddments of timber from a builders' skip, with which materials he mocks up a respectable practice net in the back garden. He paces out the twenty-two yards of wicket and mows it with the blades riding low, finishing up on his knees with gardening shears, shaving it close, before filling a wheelbarrow with bricks and recruiting Rachel to perch aloft them, whereupon he runs the barrow up and down the pitch until it is suitably hard and true.

Young Rachel faces her brother at the bowler's end and quotes cheerful instructions from memory, the Ribena-stained manual lying open to the sun for ready reference. On his orders, she wears his boxing headguard in case of injury, though they are playing cricket with tennis balls.

"Checklist," she calls out.

"Bowl, Rach. Line and length!"

"The STANCE," she persists. " '1. Side-on.' "

"I am bloody side-on."

"I think you need a haircut. How can you see the ball with all that flopping in your eyes. Sorry; *peepers, ogles, toplights, sparklers*—"

"Bloody hell, Rach!"

" '2. You are a boxer ready to move forward or back.' Ready?"

I am a boxer, Zach intones to himself, dancing forward and back. *I am a boxer.*

·   ·   ·

Rachel watches him now, Zach the man, on this fine day near Aubry's New Forest estate. She shields her eyes from the happy glare of a cloudless sky. He stands side-on, knees bent, back straight and head still, *gluteus medius* and *maximus* strained taut in his whites; he is statuesque. He slaps bat against ground behind his feet and stares over his leading shoulder straight ahead at the bowler, watching for the moment of release. Zach is in perfect readiness, a poise of manifest animal grace.

The regular swing of a pendulum represents a periodic cycle, as in the beat of ocean waves, or the vibrations of sound that make music, the migration of birds, the patterns of animal movement: behaviour repeating itself in equal spaces of time. This is also known as oscillation. Rachel watches Zachariah and often, quite regularly, her heart skips a beat. If you map the ECG of the heart in phase space, its strange attractor resembles a spider. When Lev tutors Rachel in the principles of complexity, he has a dream of determinism, immanence. Through chaos, he shapes her. Through it, he owns her.

—*Rachel? Strange attractor. What can it mean?*

—*The state of a dynamical system changes with time.*

—*Yes.*

—*To visualise the changes, one might map the variables in a graph, Papa, in which the system follows a path, homing in on certain regions to form a shape known as an attractor. An attractor is the geometry of behaviour, of behaviour over time.*

—*Otlichno! Well done.*

When he teaches her to love the principles of complexity and see patterns in everything, the strange attractor that is Rachel and Zachariah is not what he had in mind; it is not a phase space he ever imagined.

Thomas "All Souls" Aubry steps out of the pavilion. He stands by Rachel's steamer chair, leaning jauntily upon his bat, feet crossed at the ankles.

"Your brother was—sorry!" Aubry stutters. "Zach—"

"It's all right, Thomas," Rachel says. "Yes? Go on."

"He was a better boxer. Than I. Is a better cricketer."

"That's kind."

"Not at all. Straight up. Honest."

"Really, Thomas? I should say, *All Souls*. Zach calls you that, almost always."

"Embarrassing."

"I like it. A name full of old stones, don't you think? Nicknames are fun."

Aubry smiles and settles into a worn wicker chair that squeaks beneath his weight. He adjusts batting pads and plucks at the shirt that adheres to his chest and shoulder blades in the heat of late morning. He tosses his head from old habit, in a gesture effeminate in another man, and in spite of the fact he has recently shorn the flop of Viking blond hair that interfered with his vision. "I keep doing that. Ridiculous. Just cut my mop, you know."

"I do know."

Aubry smiles. "Had a *rug rethink,* as Zach calls it."

"Getting ready, aren't you?" asks Rachel. "For the big fight? Nearly time."

"Yes."

"Will you fight in the Europeans if you win the Nationals? *When* you do."

"We'll see," Aubry laughs. "We'll see."

"Zach never really had a nickname, did he? I mean, one that stuck."

"He was too good, I suppose. The greats don't always get them, cognomens. He was called Wolfman sometimes, of course. Or the Wolf."

"Yes. Oh dear," says Rachel.

"Well . . . the range of ideas in the boxing fraternity is not so very—vast."

"We play a name game," says Rachel. "Zach and I. Two types of name games. He'll quiz me, firing off names of boxers and I say the nicknames: Max Rosenbloom? Slapsie Maxie! Henry Armstrong? Homicide Hank! And then we play what I call 'strange attractors'—deterministic, you see? They have to be true, though. Actual, nothing made up. Mr. Rose the florist, Forrest the carpenter. And so on. You can't make it up. It's quite silly. But rather fun. Silly and fun."

"Pike the ghillie?" proffers Aubry.

"True?"

"Oh yes, absolutely. Fished with him in Caithness."

"Goodhand the philanthropist."

"Scott Speed was an F1 driver."

"I had a GP named Ward. And there's a book critic called Read!"

"Johnny Basham, welterweight."

"Yes, that's a favourite!" Rachel enthuses.

"Zach said you were a boximaniac! I'm very impressed. Right, then. Another one. There's a chap who writes in *Trout and Stream*. Catchpole."

"Teasing?"

"Not a bit of it."

"*Nom de plume*, surely."

"*Nom de* fly rod, I should say," quips All Souls; "*nom de canne*," he adds, displaying a smile of such abandon and appeal, Rachel averts her eyes in time to watch Zachariah race down the wicket, bat stretched ahead, taking the run in wolf bounds. *A wolf named Wolff*, she thinks. The bowler shakes his head in disgust at the run conceded and glares at Zach on the way back to his mark, a menace Zach shrugs off with a half smile, though Rachel can feel his hackles rising. Her own rise, too, in symbiosis.

"Thomas? The stare-down between—sorry, don't remember his name, the fast bowler—the stare-down between him and Zach seems a bit—fierce. Am I right?" Rachel asks.

"Not very jolly, is it?" remarks Aubry, telling her what a fine bowler Robert once was—as a schoolboy and then in the England Under-19 squad—until tearing a shoulder in a fall from a horse. He is now the youngest and keenest of directors at Aubry & Sons, if not the most cheerful.

"Zach's really *seeing* the ball today," adds All Souls. "And Robert's leaking runs. He's tried intimidation and it's getting him nowhere. Bowled a superb bouncer and Zach just leaned away, not one bit rattled. It's too bad, actually. A duel's good fun, but Robert's plain surly. A wicket might cheer him up. By the way, know his surname?"

"No," replies Rachel just as Robert clean-bowls Zach's partner.

"There you are! Good ball!" exclaims Aubry. "Right. That's me up," he adds, twirling his bat.

"Well?"

"Well? Ah yes. Cross," says Aubry, fitting his helmet. "Robert Cross."

"Very funny," smiles Rachel.

"Cross my heart," he says, setting off at a gentle trot to join Zach in what turns out to be a partnership of such infectious high spirits that at the umpire's call of lunch, even Robert forgets himself and smiles in appreciation as the two batsmen tap gloves and so all three players stride in together, faces aglow, chaffing happily in that enviable sporting manner Rachel so appreciates, sporting and male. A *pride* of cricketers, she muses. Stand up, Rachel. Stand up for them.

With his bat tucked under one arm, Zach carries his gloves in his upturned helmet and breaks away from his companions to greet her, a broad smile on his face, his hair set in damp curls at the nape and plastered in tendrils on his shining brow, noble warrior. He wraps his free arm around her and kisses her ear—*auricle, auricular*—and pearls of his sweat run into her neckline. As he takes her hand to bring her in to lunch, she catches a flicker of pain in Aubry's look and recalls, quite suddenly, that Zach told her Thomas Aubry's middle name is Love, he is Thomas Love. His mother, Zach explained, taught the Romantics and named her sons accordingly, extravagantly, tempting fate. She plays a terrible game of names. Thomas Love survives his beloved elder brother Percy Bysshe who died in a sailing accident. Percy Bysshe, buried at sea. The name and the man, a strange attractor. Everything is true.

In the pavilion, Thomas Love "All Souls" Aubry has had his own roses placed on the tables, *Eglantyne,* he says, *Fantin Latour, Muscosa.* There is white and red burgundy from the family vineyard in Volnay and there is champagne and poached and boiled comestibles, salmon and chicken and tiny potatoes, and eggs of all sizes on shredded nests of lettuce, eggs with pale blue and pale cream shells, and mottled quail eggs, plover, duck and gull, and boats of fresh mayonnaise and dishes of celery salt. There are summer things from the Aubry kitchen garden, strawberries, asparagus and cress, radish, dill and cucumber, and salad leaves sprinkled with scented geranium, viola and nasturtium. Thomas strolls amongst the tables, displacing the scents in the air as he goes, of sweat and warm lawn and rose and fish. Not a minute passes without Aubry searching Rachel's face for signs of pleasure in the luncheon he has laid on, though she cannot know this, largely for her.

What a feast, thinks Rachel, a merry party! She nods at Aubry across the room, so very busy, so very elegant in his ministrations, his hair flashing gold, a fevered sparkle in his eyes, a high glow to his zygomatics.

Rose-coloured. There are roses in his cheeks. How proud he is today! How sporting! How English! True-born, though he is half French. And though she too is true-born, she will never, can never be so English as he, so English as all this. In many ways, she decides, this has not ever been her native place.

Rachel turns to Zachariah, who is deep in exuberant chaff with Robert Cross the demon bowler, and she notes the runnels in Zach's face where perspiration has streaked the dust and dried in faint streams on his blazing physiognomy, exhilarated by sport. Illuminated by sport. There is a tiny daub of mayonnaise on his shadowy jaw, darkened already by midday beard. The beauty of the boy, she muses, the beauty of *this* boy! Watching Zachariah, she is so very instantly suffused with feeling, her heart begins to race and, discreetly gaping for air, she glances downwards and reaches for Zach's thigh, not so much in affection, but fear, fear of fainting. Fear of spontaneous combustion!

"Rach?" Zach queries.

"Nothing," she smiles, deftly wiping his chin, and kissing him there. "It's just—the roses and the wine. So many beautiful roses! English roses," she says.

Zach laughs.

She loves him so much. He is her native place.

Gloucestershire, England, 1716.

Jack Broughton takes the Bristol road, away from Cirencester and all the troubles there. He has heard much about Bristol and it is not very far. He extends a hand to his sister Rose and carries their necessities in the other and walks away from his native place. Jack is two years older than his sister. He is twelve years of age.

He cannot fathom how it befell them, how their cheerful home became a dangerous place so quickly, and noisome with shouting and gin and dirt. There would be no victuals were it not for Jack, who makes sure his sister is fed. It all happened so quickly.

When Jack and Rose's mother died, their father grieved and took to blue ruin and a new wife, a lushy, and then it was all change in Baunton, near Cirencester. Young Jack learned all the names for gin: *daffy, blue ruin, Old Tom, max, Geneva, white tape, stark naked, Fuller's earth, Jacky, flash of lightning, eye-water, blue tape, shove in the mouth.* He knows the words for drunk: *above par, castaway, shot in the neck, on the mop, foxed, dozzened.* He knows all the words and names, and he is leaving home and will never come back.

Jack's boyish forehead creases in an intimation of the future, of the broad brow and shaven bruiser's nut that will become so famous on the London scene and in paintings and engravings and other men's dreams. He will be famous also for moderation and cultivation and a fondness for flowers.

In Bristol, Jack the waterman catches the eye of James Figg, a shaven-headed master of cudgelling and pugilism whose business card is etched by Hogarth, who is likewise quite bald. When Figg comes to Bristol with his travelling booth and young Jack throws his hat in the ring, he displays such skill and natural ability, Figg takes him to London and employs him at the Academy in Adam and Eve Court and before long, Jack Broughton is justly renowned. The great master lends his name to the Championship of England, to the first rules of the Prize Ring, and to a blow of eminent effectiveness—a stomacher known henceforward as *Broughton's mark.*

The ageing Jack Broughton is finally beaten by Jack Slack, reputedly Figg's own grandson, an inferior pugilist, a brawling butcher from Norwich some seventeen years Broughton's junior who delivers such a blow between his famous opponent's eyes, Jack the elder is blinded and never fights again, ending his days in a state of fretfulness and dejection.

Jack Broughton was a fighter, the father of boxing. He had a fondness for flowers and for his sister named Rose. He knew many names of flowers and many varieties of rose.

There is no sweeter beauty, he believed, than an English Rose.

{ TWELVE }

RACHEL WONDERS how best to draw it, an expanse of six-cornered snowflakes. She thinks about frost and crystal symmetry. She unties the loosening ribbon in her hair, reties it tight. Now she can see.

Frost. A fairy tale.

In the Russian fairy tale, theories of extinction and speciation are somewhat fanciful, Rachel muses as she sketches an image of Father Frost. Though she gives him a furry Cossack hat and a beard of icicles, she models him on the distinguished cudgeller and pugilist James Figg, lending him the very same noble mien, folded arms and frown of displeasure as his likeness in *A Rake's Progress.* Hogarth was fond of Figg the man and Figg the model and, for a time, he was drawn to the fights. James Figg, Jack Broughton, Hogarth, Coram and Father Frost, they are all *bogatyrs*, decides Rachel. Men of power.

Bogatyrs and their horses of power, sororicidal axe-murderers, holy fools, palaces built of shipwrecks at the bottom of the sea, transparent apples through which one can see Petersburg, hair combs that become woods, and kerchiefs that become lakes and oceans containing talking fish, are all natural features of the Russian fairy tale. The Russian fairy tale is a chaotic system.

In *Frost,* poor little Martha's widowed father remarries and the lady is a harridan. This is a common situation. Look at little Jack and Rose Broughton, thinks Rachel. Lev would never fall for such a woman. Papa is well versed in Russian fairy tales. And Lev would never marry again; he loved Mama too much. If that is possible, to love too much.

Before long, Martha has two awful stepsisters, cynical and competitive, and Martha becomes a slave in her very household. Yet she is the prettiest girl in the village and kindness itself and a veritable songbird, chirping about the homestead with irrepressible cheer, outshining her half sisters. Time to get rid of her, decides Stepmother, who bundles her off in a sledge with all her belongings for betrothal to Frost, a rich and handsome chap, she says, and a *bogatyr*, a man of power. Papa deposits his sweet Martha in the snowy woods, and drives away weeping, tears *freezing on his cheeks,* as the story goes, *before they have time to reach his beard.*

Martha is so gentle and disarming, Frost is beguiled and begins to lavish her with gifts, and when her evil stepmother hears of it, she despatches her two natural daughters to benefit likewise. This is a mistake, not her first. Greed is an epic Russian quality, the flip-side of self-sacrifice, another epic Russian quality.

Frost has a trick question. He poses it over and over with variations.

Are you warm, little maid? Are you warm, little paws? Are you warm, little red cheeks?

Warm, dear Frost. Warm, little father, replies the kind sister, guilelessly choosing an epithet typically used to address the Tsar. Her sisters, however, are downright rude, borderline abusive, and earn nothing but death by exposure in the taiga. Martha endures the freezing climate, the temperature of exile, to wed her sweetheart Fedor Ivanovich, and on the occasion of the happy feast, Frost clothes her in marvellous furs.

Genuine courtesy, clearly, is paramount in the realm of Russian folklore. And kindness is a rarity. The good Russian respects the weather and weather systems. He respects winter above all, because ice and snow can kill. Exile can kill.

Rachel downs tools, consults her watch. She ponders on courtesy. Is it truly rewarded? Can kindness prevail? Is it recessive? What are the dynamics of kindness? She smiles. I am a woman of science after all, Papa! Yes, I am.

When young Rachel brought Lev a dead swallow one day, a poor swallow that had crashed to death against the windowpane, he told her how conservation biologists at Princeton University once examined the effects of competition on the extinction rate of bird species on an island in Trinidad and deduced that extinction is impartial. Fragility and resilience in a species have some bearing, yet largely it is a question of numbers. "Rarity," wrote the biologists, "proves to be the best index of vulnerability." The more populous species is more likely to prevail.

The rat species, thinks Rachel, scraping at a pastel with her Swann-Morton scalpel, is certainly very populous. Rampant indeed. In the Russian fairy tale, she decides, theories of extinction and speciation are indeed wishful, primarily moralistic. This is not the way of the world, she reflects as she inks in the outlines of the two cold-hearted sisters who are felled by hypothermia, realizing, quite suddenly, that she has drawn likenesses of Katya. I'm so sorry, Mama! I'm so sorry. Rachel sketches pine and larch and icicles with practised strokes. There is always forest in Russian fairy tales. Deep woods.

"FUCK your mother!"

"Fuck YOUR mother!"

Rachel's nerves jangle. Lord, she thinks, it's only twelve o'clock and the drunks are out in the Gardens. *Aliks.*

"No! Fuck YOUR mother!" screams a third.

Zachariah is working upstairs in the bedroom, on the park side of the house, propped against pillows with research scattered across the bed, writing on his knees, she knows, like Pushkin! She hears a cascade of books to floor and a rumble of sash window lifting.

Zach yells, "Oh, FUCK ALL YOUR MOTHERS!" before slamming the window shut again and stamping downstairs to Rachel perched high in her swivel chair, already turned to greet him, her expression amused.

"Hello," she says. "Having fun up there?"

"I counted. There are EIGHTEEN *aliks* on benches out there. It's not even lunch-time. Camden bloody Council installs any more nice wooden benches, they might as well roll out the barrel and serve drinks! Put up a dartboard on a tree, I don't know, offer daily tips on runners and riders, dish up door-stopping cheese and pickle rolls. Fucking twenty-four-hour open-air bloody boozer, that's what it is!"

"Why don't you stretch the legs?" she suggests, as he crouches by her, lays his head in her lap. "A walk will do you good."

"Think I'm getting a bit shirty?"

"I do . . . Anyway, I'm off to Chelsea soon, promised to see Papa. We can step out together."

"Why do you go? He hates us! How you can do it? It's beginning to—"

"Stop!"

"—fuck me off!"

"Zasha," murmurs Rachel. "Please. You could walk me to the bus."

"Fuck my father," he says softly. "Fuck my father."

"That's silly," Rachel scolds, stroking his head. "Stop it."

Rachel babbles in Chelsea. She tells Lev about the cricket match on the Aubry grounds in Hampshire and describes Aubry's mother, willowy, lofty, endearing, and recounts the death of Percy Bysshe, Thomas's brother. A sailing accident, Papa! Same as his namesake. She tells Lev that Thomas the ichthyologist, Thomas the corinthian, will retire from boxing and manage the vineyard in Burgundy as well as the estate in the New Forest by the Lymington he fished as a boy.

"Head in air and tail in sea," Lev begins.

"Fish, fish, listen to me," chants Rachel.

"You remember."

"Well of course, Papa. Of course I do. *The Golden Fish*. Tasha read them all, over and over. And I'm doing my own illustrations now, for a new edition. I've told you. How could I possibly forget?"

Rachel gushes on, telling the tale of the Hoxton rat, highlighting Zach's heroics. She chaffs and chirps, sings his praises, speaking his name repeatedly as if there were no awful conflict between father and son, hoping familiarity might breed consent, hoping there were no three-body problem, no chaotic motion between them. Hopes are so well constructed.

"A rat at Tasha's," Lev grumbles. "Whatever next?"

"Well?" she states amiably, slipping into her old seat at the dining table that Lev covers in papers and books from end to end, excepting at the place he persists in setting for Katya. "What shall we play? What shall we do? Go for a walk?"

"I am broken," he says suddenly, eyes glistening. "I have no shape. I have lost all shape."

Lev tells her he never eats at the table, but on the sofa off a tray on his lap, or standing up at the kitchen worktop, or at his desk. The whole house is now his desk, his office; there are no longer designations for times and places, no momentum; he has lost all shape.

"Oh Papa."

"I want you above all to hear how sad my living voice is," Lev recites before laughing at himself.

"What's that from?" asks Rachel. "I'm sure I know it."

"Oh, a Russian war song. *Zemlyanka.* Turgid stuff."

"Oh my goodness! I remember. Tasha played it once. When we were children. I remember now. Such a poignant song."

"Miserable. Russian songs are all misery, aren't they?" Lev scoffs.

"Do you mind that you never met your father, Papa?"

"What makes you ask that?" frowns Lev.

"I don't know," replies Rachel, searching. "The war song and how he died in the war. Yes. That was it. You don't have to answer, though. Sorry."

Lev examines his daughter. He smiles.

"Is it too early for a drink?" he asks.

"Hmm. Is that a scientific or philosophical query? Technically speaking," Rachel proposes in spoffish academic tones, "I'd say you are in a *critical* state. If we consider the drinking of vodka a *small external event,* is drunkenness a *bifurcation*? A catastrophe?"

"Not if we're careful," Lev replies, smiling.

"Then it's not too early."

"Good. Because I could drink vodka by the half-pail!"

"*Along Peterskaya Street!* Zach's so funny, he sings it all the time."

"Ah," says Lev distractedly.

"Wine for me, please!" pipes Rachel, humming to fill the sudden vacuum created by the utterance of Zach's name. "Aren't you impressed with me? How I can quote your lessons? Bifurcation! I thought that was rather good."

"Why shouldn't you remember?" Lev baulks. "You're exceedingly bright and I taught you well. Now," he declares, returning from the kitchen with glasses and cold wine and vodka. "*Vashe zdorov'ye!*"

"Yes. Cheers, Papa!"

"He was killed on the Belorussian Front, you know. My father. Your grandfather."

"Yes," says Rachel.

"The war was almost over. He was shelled. And froze to death. A study in crystallography, Rachel! The meteorologist freezes to death. How ridiculous. Well. Shall we drink right here?" asks Lev, glancing out of the dining room windows. "I think the garden is too . . . I think it's due to rain soon. Very soon. We could sit in the living room or . . ."

"Papa, this is a lovely room. We'll stay here."

"Yes," he says wearily, settling in a favourite chair by the sideboard, of stiff-backed Georgian mahogany upholstered in faded old rose. He fingers a threadbare split in the padding of one arm. "Wearing out," he says. "This old thing."

"Come closer, Papa. If we stay here, you'll have to sit at the table with me. You're so far away!"

Lev laughs. He rises and sits next to his daughter. "My papers. What a mess," he remarks. "I'll make some space."

"It doesn't matter," Rachel frowns, stopping Lev's hands. "What is it? I can tell you want to ask something. Speak!"

"Yes. I need to book the tickets and everything. Make arrangements. For the memorial. Katya's memorial. In Petersburg. You must decide if you're coming. Tasha won't. I know that. She will never return to Russia. But I want you to come. I need you with me. It will be two years soon. Two!"

"How can I go without Zach?"

"You must!" shouts Lev, smacking the table feebly.

"Papa! You can't stop him from coming," Rachel insists. "What if he travels separately?"

"No! And I can prevent him from attending the concert. I can have him barred. Easily."

Rachel hangs her head. "God! It's so awful, Papa," she murmurs. "So hurtful. Intransigent. I hate it."

"I need your answer," states Lev.

"Tomorrow," says Rachel. "I shall tell you tomorrow."

"You like the wine?"

"Thank you, Papa. It's lovely."

"No. It's just that I bought it especially. But in the shop I could not be sure whether it was a favourite of yours. Or hers. I did not want to make a mistake. I stood there in the wine department holding the bottle and the wine merchant came to me . . . It is possible—it may have looked as if—it was chilly outdoors and the change of temperature . . . thermodynamics, you see. An involuntary reaction. *Rhinorrhea*—what a horrible word! He thought I was crying. I was rude to him. I don't suppose he cared particularly. I think he did not want a scene in his shop. How English!"

"*Quelle cérémonie!*" exclaims Rachel.

Lev smiles. "Yes," he says. "*Quelle cérémonie* indeed."

"You might have been crying, Papa." Snow can sometimes fall from a cloudless sky, she wants to add. Isn't that correct, Papa?

Lev stares at his daughter. "Things I never told you," he begins, a rasp in his throat. "Katya. When she was dying. She said—she said I love you too much. That I *love* too much."

"No, Papa," whispers Rachel.

"She instructed me—told me—you must have a place of your own. As soon as possible after her—passing—you must have a house of your own. That was her wish. No matter what. That is what she instructed."

"No matter what?" Rachel repeats, expecting no answer. "I see," she adds, bowing her head. My palace of copper, she reflects. Rolled up in a hanky.

"Is Tasha still with you?" Lev asks more brightly, watching beads of melting frost run down his glass onto corduroy-trousered knee.

"No, she went home—but Pest Control have two more visits, it's all spaced out and quite scientific, the baiting. Zach took care of everything."

"Stop! I do—not—want—to hear his name. Do you understand?"

"Papa," says Rachel.

"It's hard enough to see *you*, do you understand that too? But I cannot do without you," Lev snaps, swallowing vodka.

"Please, Papa."

"As for that boy—man—it's not just that he grew up in my house! He's a peasant. A thug!"

"It's not true," Rachel gasps.

"I feel—horror. Revulsion! Can't you see? Do you remember Karlov, your teacher? Piano teacher?" Lev asks in an acid voice.

"Boris."

"What? Not Boris. What do you mean?"

"Nothing, Papa. Never mind. What about him? Of course I remember. In fact, I've seen him in Camden—in shops, or on his bicycle. He must have moved. From Chelsea."

"And I have seen him too. At Trojka."

"In Primrose Hill? Trojka closed ages ago. Some silly café there now."

"Yes. Primrose Hill. I never told you. I was there with an old friend, old colleague. Russian. Knew him in Paris. A head of research now at École Normale Sup. I had not seen him in years and that evening— Karlov was there. He came to our table. He remembered you well. And the *brother* who collected you after lessons. Then he said *pointedly* how he had spotted you in Regent's Park. And in the High Street. Touching and—"

"Papa!"

"And he pitied me, commiserated. Such a sensitive girl, he said. With such a ruffian. A boxer, no? He said, I thought he was her brother—am I wrong? He was *pitying* me. Pity! So I hit him. I have never hit anyone in my life. I knocked him to the floor. In a restaurant. Rachel! Violence breeds violence! Do you understand me?" shouts Lev, banging his glass on the table. "Can you?"

"Shall I go?" queries Rachel, very still.

"No, little paws. No," says Lev, dropping his chin, reaching across for his daughter's hand, waiting for quiet in his head, like the drop of a curtain, a kiss.

"We took Tasha to Trojka once," proffers Rachel, into the silence. "They said they might close. It's very likely they'll have to close, they told us. It was sad. End of an era."

"Natasha!" exclaims Lev. "Hoxton. Why doesn't she live with me? Three floors, a piano, no mortgage and she knows the house well, been coming here for years. Decades! We are a little closer to civilisation here!"

"I think," Rachel frowns, "she might feel—infantilised."

"Why?"

"Blindness, because of the blindness. People do, you know. Infantilise her. Or simply ignore the problem, as if that were more polite. Tasha hasn't changed, she's the same—"

"She's not the same! She is not! She's blind! And Nicky's gone, dead. Like Katya. Gone, dead! So I've changed," Lev says heatedly. "I'm not the same. We've all changed!"

"You're right, Papa. I'm sorry."

But I'm a little-bit-right, Rachel tells herself. Tasha still needs her place in the forest, she too needs a dacha all her own.

"Look, little pigeon! I've finished my drink. And, by the way, I'm not keen on Camden Town either. A dangerous place."

Rachel pours wine and vodka, thinking of the three adored princesses whose father the Tsar so fears for their safety, he builds them palaces underground from which he sets them free one day, ever so briefly, only to be captured and imprisoned in the underworld. Rescue comes, but not before lessons are learned. Here's one: though underground is not so bad as underworld, both are prisons of a kind.

"Papa," she begins. "If I lived here with you, and Tasha also, would you set all our places at table or just Mama's? Speaking of which," she adds, tracing a line in the white dust that shows black, of course, on her fingertip, "it could do with a wash!"

"Dust grains scatter the light," he says slowly. "Dust scatters the light."

"Yes," says Rachel. "You taught us that. Taught me that."

When Mama died, Rachel thinks, she left behind a three-body problem.

While she lived, she left and returned to a three-body problem. Again and again. Katya the peripatetic, conducting *across three times nine countries,* as the Russian fairy-tale saying goes, packs a bag and travels by train and plane and in her absence Lev tries to be father and mother. He cooks, wakes the children for school, and reads to them at bedtime, skimming the adventure stories and fairy tales, enjoying some Dickens, Lamb and Defoe, but revelling above all in science, pointing out the magical in the everyday, such as motes of dust spiralling in rays of light, or the span of time between lightning and thunder. The universe, he tells them, is predictable and predictability is not the same as determinism. He says that patterns are clues to nature and teaches them terminology and theory of a sophistication beyond their years.

"There are universal symmetries," he says, "but in mathematics symmetry is a transformation. Think of a mirror!" he exhorts. "Reflection is transformation . . . Morphology is determined not only by genes, you see, but the dynamics of growth," he explains, watching Rachel's rapt face, and young Zachariah's troubled one, ear cocked in an effort to comprehend. The boy listens the way an animal does, thinks Lev, disturbed.

"Reflection," repeats Rachel thoughtfully, "is transformation."

"Ears," Lev exclaims, "are older than speech! The vocal apparatus is unique to man! And look at you, now," he adds, noting their strained still bodies. "Galvanism, mesmerism!"

Franz Mesmer, he tells them, and Luigi Galvani explored the idea of hidden energy by passing an electrical current through the muscles of a dead animal to observe the ensuing contractions.

"It's like waking Zach for school," says Rachel, giggling.

"Very funny," goes Zach. "Did they kill the animal first?" he adds, a question Lev ignores.

One night Lev is inspired to impersonate the seemingly random drift in the paths of orbiting planets—chaotic motion—with each body exerting a force on the other two. He circulates Rachel as he speaks, and directs a startled Zachariah to orbit in a different arc at a different speed.

"What are the conditions of stability?" he asks excitably, whereupon Zach abandons ship and leaps onto his bed, trembling with rage and humiliation, clapping hands to his flaming ears before racing to the loo and slamming the door while Rachel stands stark-eyed, the pain of incipient tears in her throat. Leave him, Papa, she wants to say. Don't make him play this game, he can't play this game. Zach's ears, she thinks, his ears are so old, so much older than speech!

Zach shadowboxes in front of the bathroom mirror. He is relaxed and clear-sighted and moves very slowly, gaining power and muscle memory. This is the Sweet Science. This science is so sweet! As a right-handed fighter, he drifts ever so slightly left with a blow. If he could correct this natural drift, he would be harder to read, less predictable. An unpredictable fighter has the upper hand. An unpredictable fighter has his opponent on the back foot.

Zach does not see the science in this, he makes no connection whatsoever with periodic motions or symmetry, phase space or chaotic drift, determinism, galvanism, gait. He is so very happy, because now he is free. He's *gonna dance!* Oh, he's gonna dance!

Here at the dining table in Chelsea, nearly two years after Katya's death, Rachel fingers a path through a film of sparkling dust around Mama's plate and breakfast cup and linen napkin, orbiting twice. She speaks so softly, Lev is forced to lean inwards and closer to hear.

"Papa. Mama never ate breakfast. You lay a plate, but she drank tea only. Russian tea. Kusmi tea. From Paris. Every time she went to Paris, she brought some back. But if—"

"Sometimes . . ." he protests, faltering. "Sometimes she had fruit."

"Yes. But I was thinking that, if you laid out a soup plate at her place, if you were to make a fish STEW," persists Rachel, brightening. "A stew with PARSLEY, what THEN? Who knows what might transpire? Who might come calling!"

"Here comes my beloved," Lev sings.

"All alone in a troika," goes Rachel, rising from the table to dance across the room, shaking invisible reins. "Down the little side streets, hey!"

Come and kiss me, my darling.

When Rachel slips into her coat piping a promise of return, and hugs her father tightly, she observes a new slightness to his shape, an unfamiliar prominence of bones that causes her heart to lurch in its moorings. Rachel hurries away from Chelsea, which was once her home. She brooms for Zachariah and Camden by bus and on foot, noting the changes in boroughs as she goes, sometimes from street to street. There is change in weather and architecture, in physiognomy and habiliments, in accoutrements and voices, in air. All change! How vast is my London! How strange my native place!

London, Petersburg. The memorial. How will she tell him? Rachel feels a great sinking as she approaches her house, fearing Zach's anger, Zach's pain, and her heart speeds, her vision clouds briefly to black. She stops at the corner by the gates of the Gardens to take hold of a railing.

"Closing up now, love," says the keeper.

"Yes, I know," she says. "I was just . . ."

"You all right, love?"

"Thank you, yes," replies Rachel. "Goodnight!"

As she walks to her door, Rachel strides briskly, the sound of clanging in her ears. She could mark the hours and seasons by the sound of these gates: closing times, opening times, summer, winter, spring. She has come to search for it, the rattle of keys, the screech of hinges and scraping at locks, and the weight of chain and iron, clang, clang! Clarion as the tolling of bells. She summons St. Petersburg, a city she has so far seen but once, recalling the sound of water and of varying footfalls on bridges, and the odour of weather and sea. This is a stirring close to nostalgia. How can it be? Perhaps Russia too is her native place.

Motherland, fatherland, *Rus.*

FROST

January 1945.

The meteorologist attached to the 1st Belorussian Front is not altogether dead. Not yet. They are marching on Western Poland, crossing the frozen Vistula, but the meteorologist lies flat on his back near the banks of the Pilica, its longest tributary. He knows all about vectors and air pressure and fluid flow. His blood still flows within and without his anatomy and he knows also that before his blood freezes, the water content of his body will crystallize, turning to frost.

If only he could raise an arm, give a signal. I'm not altogether dead, hey! And where is his friend, the violinist? Shot? Is he shot too? Wave! Quick! Wave your arm. The brain commands the body, but the chain of command has broken. Some muscles, of course, are involuntary: the muscles of the eye, of course, and around the follicles, the muscles of the heart and stomach, of the uterus—*myometrium*—and penis—*intralacunar* . . . How does that song go? His best friend the violinist has filled him with song. *Steppe, endless steppe.* That song. *Give to my wife a word of farewell . . . tell her that I died here in the freezing steppe and that I have taken her love away with me.* And that other song . . . *Zemlyanka.* So many songs. O my wife. My love.

In his delirium, the meteorologist begins to panic: he will never see his child, he must get home, at least into the dugout, *zemlyanka.* If he were to raise an arm, give some signal . . . But then he might well be shot by his own side! The absurdity of this makes his blood flow hot, the absurdity of flying gunfire across the steppe, endless steppe, makes him chortle and weep. The next bullet might very well be Russian, he muses. And as he recalls the old soldier's wisdom regarding bullets and fate, how pointless evasion is when each shot has a man's name on it, he lurches upright, to the waist, a roaring sound in his ears.

"I am Russian!" he shouts, and into the meadow he goes.

In a snow-white field near Moscow, I want you above all to hear how sad my living voice is.

Lev turns his vodka glass round and round, round and round, so that shards of reflected light scatter across the mahogany surface of the table Rachel dusted and polished before leaving. He realigns Katya's place setting, a millimetre to the right, a millimetre to the left again. Just so.

I love you so much. Loved you so much.

THIRTEEN

London, June 1814.

Old Count Platov is issuing orders to his Cossacks bivouacked haphazardly in Hyde Park. What a spectacle they have provided for the populace! Tomorrow, the Russians are leaving. They will travel in ships to France and onwards and onwards, wherever the Tsar desires.

Aleksei starts. Who goes there? Is that my fox? Are you my fox?

Peering out into the gloom on his last night at the Pulteney Hotel in this city of stone, Aleksei rests his brow against the windowpane. Perhaps his fox will bring the English Katherine to him. Named like his sister! And the Tsar's favourite sister Ekaterina Pavlovna too! How fateful. Katherine, Ekaterina!

"Speak, Fox! Grant me a wish."

"Why are you so very drunk, young man?" queries Fox.

The Hussar is definitely drunk. He is drunk on longing and despair and blue ruin, a spirit brewed with beguiling botanicals, though still not so good as vodka, nor so vivacious as champagne. The English, for all their bruising, have a surprisingly sweet tooth. The Hussar is drunk again, *shot in the neck, above par, castaway, dozzened. Foxed!*

Well, if Fox won't help him, he must carry the message himself.

Aleksei hurries out of the Pulteney and into the streets.

He is luckless at Katherine's father's door in Soho Square where the butler waves him away in a dismissive manner, scowling with suspicion at the young officer with his small shabby parcel. Jumped-up fellow, the

Hussar decides. Nothing so imperious as a manservant! And he storms off for a cab to Holborn, to Tom Belcher's Castle, known only weeks ago as Bob's Chop House. How quickly things change! A new publican for new times. Yes, at the Castle, I will leave my parcel.

Where am I now? he wonders. How far is it from here to there? Everything is muddled in my head. The Castle! Everyone knows Bob's Chop House—the Castle Tavern, that is. In the cabriolet, Aleksei unwraps the parcel to assess its contents: drawings, a gambling token, a wild scrawl of a note with a promise of return written in French. Will it be enough to remember him by? Perhaps not, he reflects mournfully, removing his most treasured possession from round his neck, a medallion bearing the bust of Tsar Alexander I, a blessing upon him! No. Wait. Not the Castle. Not yet. First try her brother, she must be with her brother!

"Halt!" calls Aleksei.

The cabman is so put out with this lushy foreigner and the cheap ride to Holborn from Soho Square, he stops abruptly indeed and the Hussar pitches forward in an ignominious spill, righting himself quickly, however, and too hell-bent on delivering his parcel to express vexation. Stupid coachman! Never mind. There is no time to spare. *Voilà!* Well done, he tells himself, tugging at his habiliments, retrieving his hat. To the brother's rooms, he concludes. That's where she must be! At her brother Raphael's.

"To . . . to . . . where the violin makers live!" he orders. *'Allez, hop!* Walk on! Quickly, *vite, vite!"* the Hussar urges, mimicking the bowing of a violin, whereupon the cabman stretches out his huge open hand for payment and flips open the door of the cab to signify his journey's end. He will ferry this youth no further.

What a quiz is this nib sprig, thinks the coachman. Another cursed foreigner!

The Russian pays the fare, hops to ground.

A warren of streets, not far, I'll find it, swears Aleksei. A garden . . . Convent Garden. No. That's wrong. Never mind. Not far!

Aleksei walks, feeling through his uniform for the medallion he only just removed. This is an instinct of long standing. He has worn it round his neck for nearly thirteen years. Remember the day, Aleksei? How could he forget!

In September of 1801 the Tsar and Tsarina Alexander and Elizabeth travelled to Moscow, the old capital, for their coronation. They remained in the city for a month. The young Emperor hurtled here from St. Petersburg with the Imperial escort, his agitation mounting the closer he came to his destination. He reached Tver in six days, staying briefly to eat and nap, then sped on at 2 a.m. to cover the last dusty miles to the Petrovsky Palace on the outskirts of the city. These hundred miles he covered in sixteen hours, including a break for refreshments, leaving Alexander three days in which to rest before making his entrance proper.

Why the mad rush? his wife Elizabeth asked herself. Alexander is a boy racer. The road impels him. His country is so vast.

On one glorious morning of their visitation, the twenty-three-year-old Tsar dispensed gifts to the foundlings of Moscow. A brother and sister were presented to him, named for himself and his own sister Ekaterina. The Tsar was not surprised. How many namesakes are there in my tsardom? How many Aleksei-and-Ekaterinas?

"Look! Look!" the boy Aleksei exclaimed to his sister, opening and shutting his palm throughout the day to reprise the marvel of the gift his small hand could barely contain.

"Put it round your neck," said his sister Katerina who received one likewise from the Tsar and Tsarina, wed to each other eight years earlier when they were but fifteen and fourteen and close as siblings.

"Don't lose it," implored Katerina.

"I'll never lose it," he replied fervently.

Soon afterwards the boy is transferred from the Foundling Hospital to the military orphanage to be trained for the officer class. And soon, like his Tsar, he will cover many miles and cross the fatherland in all weathers, dreaming of home.

Where the devil does Raphael live?

What delirious and merry evenings Aleksei has spent there over music and talk and masculine jousting, amid bottles of wine and bread and cheese, and every phrase Aleksei uttered in Raphael's sister's presence sounding like bells, he could not help it, everything he said, a declaration of love! Aleksei stands in the darkened street, looking left, looking right, searching for clues to his whereabouts, heady with recollections, their three voices still ringing in his head, the fevered nights of argument and seduction mingling as one.

"Borodino," declares Raphael the violinist on one such night, "is a battle without a victor."

"All battles are won or lost!" shouts the Hussar, leaping to his Hessian boots.

"That is not true, sir!" asserts Raphael, who has never been to war. Raphael has only ever fought his own father, a battle of wills.

Aleksei slaps a berlin to the floor amongst the wood chips and cat gut and remains of the feast, yet even this is a blow without powder, ending in teases and mirth, and more wine. The three communicate in a felicitous blend of French and English with a smattering of German and occasional mime.

The Russian shows the brother and sister his unfinished poems and battlefield sketches and London impressions—the fox, a tree and boxers peeled to the waist at Lord Lowther's. And he shows Katherine his portrait of her, flushing deeply. He tells the story of his medallion of Alexander I then displays his London souvenir, a gambling token in the shape of a fish that he moves through the air as if through fast blue waters, his eyes shining as he speaks in Russian, in happy fluency at last, describing his home. He has a dream of the Caucasus and two Katherines at his table, his Russian sister and this English lady. Oh come with me. Oh please.

Later, the medallion becomes an atmospheric gauge and a thermometer, cold between the lovers until their bodies press so tightly, the temperature rises and Aleksei smiles to see the imprint on her left breast with fine chain-link indentations running away from it and disappearing. He peers closely at her fine skin and, for a moment, there it is, the bust of Alexander, bust on bust, beloved upon beloved. He takes it as a sign.

The Hussar has angel hair, Katherine thinks, and impossibly feminine curls, God's joke on him. On the 27th of June, the young soldier will sail away with Alexander, Tsar of All the Russias, who draped a medallion with his Imperial likeness upon it round Aleksei's neck nearly thirteen years ago. They will race to Ostend and on to St. Petersburg. Very soon. Life changes so quickly. She has only known Aleksei eighteen days.

Come and kiss me, my darling.

.　　　.　　　.

The Pulteney Hotel, Piccadilly.

Alexander, Tsar of All the Russias, maps his homecoming. First to Ostend and onwards to Ghent where he and his sister must part for now—Katerina, light of my eyes, adored of my heart, polestar of the age. Then for a race through the Rhineland to Bruchsal and Elizabeth, my wife, and on to Petersburg, home at last!

The Tsar loves to race, but he is not always timely. Had he not left Moscow on 31st July 1812, had he been present on the field at Borodino, might things have changed? Four mornings after the battle, he heard of the carnage. Could it be true?

Everything is true.

What Tsar Alexander could not possibly know is that not until the Somme one hundred and four years later had there been such a scything of souls as at Borodino. Estimates of Russian losses are still doubtful, falling either side of 50,000 and, in early 1813, when the battlefield clean-up began, it was recorded that 35,478 horses lay dead there, each, once upon a time, carefully groomed and rubbed with opodeldoc. Groomed and rubbed like Sam the Russian on the eve of his own battle with Young Dutch. With opodeldoc.

Neither is Alexander apprised of the occupation and fire of Moscow until six days after the fact. Oh the great fire, and enemy occupation! The shame and horror of it all. He ought to have a seer, if only he had a seer.

Little sister Katerina—light of his eyes, polestar of the age—had written to him in detail of his people's accusations, of discontent and recriminations. She berated him for his apparent betrayal of Moscow, his abandonment of the old capital. Alexander fell ill, suffering from recriminations and erysipelas of the leg, retiring to recuperate at Kammionyi Island where he stayed well into October while Bonaparte was holed up in the Kremlin, observing maps and mistaken weather forecasts and squatters' rights. The Tsar recalled the man stamping on his hat at Erfurt in a terrible huff, thwarted not only in negotiations but in a desire to divorce Josephine and marry Katerina, the curly-headed Tsar having offered up a less beloved sister in her place: Anna, who was just thirteen.

"Marry Anna, you may marry Anna."

"No, thank you!" replied Napoleon, in a very great huff.

Can this be only six years ago? Can it be that his sister Katerina, adored of his heart, has since been married and widowed? Yes, she is now eighteen months a widow. And it is seventeen months since Alexander last saw Petersburg.

In London, he knows, they do not like her. Political meddler, they coin her. Husband hunter. A Grand Duchess acting the Tsarina. She wears an oversized hat and hates music, demanding silence. Music, she declares, makes her ill. Society bristles and the Tsar is contemptuous of this city caught up in a dangerous whirl of blind frivolity. Napoleon is not beat, there is far more to come. Alexander feels it in his bones, his restless bones.

In spite of the summery revels, Grey the Whig says a local defence militia has formed and there is an abiding fear Bonaparte will invade England by way of a tunnel beneath the Channel. How ingenious! Why, had such a marvellous thing been in place, the Tsar might have sped to Dover in an open barouche instead of enduring the *mal de mer*! After the awful crossing, he raced from Dover through Kent in a landau, doing sixty-five miles in five hours to the outskirts of London and onwards, into the streets and through them, spurning the teeming crowds to pull up at the Pulteney where his sister awaited, waving from a first-floor window. The Tsar and his sister declined the invitation to lodge at St. James. The Regent is a more noisome fellow even than Louis the Bourbon king whom Alexander reluctantly restored to rule, only to suffer his appalling manners at table. No. We shall *not* lodge at St. James.

In London, Alexander knows, they like neither his sister nor himself. Society considers the Tsar silly and vain, a ballroom dancer with golden curls and a lorgnette up his sleeve, an aloof monarch who turns a deaf ear, as Napoleon said of him at Erfurt, to anything he does not want to hear. In effect, when the Tsar turns an ear, it is only to favour the right, as he is quite deaf in the left. Yes, Alexander loves to dance, he is myopic, he turns a deaf ear. What of it?

At the Winter Palace in 1812, on the eve of hotfooting it by troika and sledge to Vilna to join his hungry and typhus-ridden army and Platov's Cossacks relentlessly harrying the Grande Armée in their flight from Russia, Alexander saw blocks of ice flowing down the Neva a whole fortnight before the snows were due. *He felt it,* how winter would strike hard that year, how it would fight for him. The Tsarina felt it likewise, writing to her mama in Baden as early as September, *We shall see how Napoleon manages the winter there,* she wrote, mindful of the vastness of Russia. Oh yes. We shall see!

And what a winter!

Father Frost has a trick question.

Are you warm, little tsar? Are you warm, little paws? Are you warm, little red cheeks?

Alexander's visions are often meteorological. The weather interests him much. He has, for instance, a great fear of floods.

The Tsar of All the Russias stops at the window of his rooms in Piccadilly, London, in the summer of 1814 and fishes for his lorgnette. There is a fox in the street with an extravagant tail and unkempt coat and flashing eyes, ogling Alexander from below. Even the London fox is uncouth. Alexander cannot wait to be home again.

O Petersburg, O Jerusalem on the Neva! Alexander drops a tear and has a burgeoning dream of quiet isolation—*bezmolviye*—and an old dream of speed, both bound up in an ache for return.

A man should not stay too long from his native place.

Tsar Alexander I was prone to tears and he did weep over Borodino, but not *at* Borodino, as Tolstoy would have it. This is definitely poetic licence. Alexander was never on the field at Borodino. Later, he was certainly in London with his beloved sister Katerina who travelled there for the festive aftermath of the break-up of Napoleon's Continental System and Alexander's Liberation of Europe.

Tsar Alexander! Your Radiance! There is so much you did not see in your Liberation of Europe! You missed Borodino. And you missed the Fire of Moscow in September 1812.

Moscow is a city of magnificent wooden houses with plaster façades, a conflagration waiting to happen, and now it is blazing. The French have all marched out, except for the ailing and these are being killed by a rabble on the rampage, looting and murdering and setting siege, even to the Foundling Hospital where soldiers of both armies are battling wounds and infections.

Captain Thomas Aubry, Chasseur, has a terrible fever, but rallies to defend the Hospital with the help of three wounded Russian generals. They are fine fellows, he thinks, and speak French in beautiful accents. Aubry waves his sword in the air and issues the command to fire, holding off the mob until relief comes, until regular Russian troops can reoccupy the city. When news of the reoccupation reaches St. Petersburg on the 27th of October, there are gun salutes and ringing bells, though a very young Hussar, Borodino-worn, is stricken with fear for his sister, a Moscow Foundling Hospital nurse.

Ekaterina! I love you so much.

Captain Aubry has neither time nor the inclination to pause at the absurdity of his position. He has come through Borodino without knowing who won. He has run the gauntlet of Davydov's Hussars and ambush parties of Cossack regulars and irregulars, only to find himself here, waving a sword from his hospital bed. Aubry might complain, were he a less pragmatic man, at defending an orphanage in the burnt-out old capital, four-fifths destroyed, with but a tiny detachment of peg-legs, blind and maimed, at his behest, and enemy generals of singular charm. In his near-delirium, Captain Thomas Aubry takes command. He does not pause at the absurdity and helplessness of his position, but, for a moment, he does pause at the sight of an exceedingly pretty nurse. I could love you so much.

Ekaterina is a foundling and a nurse with tumbling hair, falling at the nape in rings. She wears a medallion of Tsar Alexander I just like her brother's, and fingers it now, stricken with fear for the Hussar her brother, Aleksei with his impossible curls so very like her own, yet less seemly, perhaps. Such hair is somewhat fairy-tale in a man. Poetic.

On the eve of departure from London, June 1814, Aleksei applies the finishing touches to his parting parcel, his curls damp with exertion and springy with the closeness of summer night and the excess of bub and blue tape, and fear of leaving. He rolls a note of farewell into a knot of the blue and yellow belcher, his gift from Tom Cribb—blue and yellow like Aleksei's uniform indeed! Within the kerchief are the bone-fish and medallion of Alexander. Remembrances. On the page facing the one he tore from his notebook, Borodino-worn, are his little pen-portraits of the Tsar and Davydov. Lt. Davydov was distinctly annoyed, Aleksei recalls, to be shot at by Russian locals with their hearty distaste for uniforms of any colour, and so Denis Davydov took to dressing down and let his beard grow out and wore a smock and an icon of St. Nicholas and, before long, attracted large numbers of *muzhiks* to his side, to wave salvaged and stolen enemy muskets at the old enemy in a brutal manner. Even in smock and beard, the portrait of Davydov has an air of Aleksei's sister Ekaterina about him, an effect due, not to artistic licence, Aleksei being no artist, but to fateful affinity. Ekaterina is in everything Aleksei draws.

Ekaterina! I love you so much. The most!

There. Finished.

Aleksei drips with effort and the long night of drink and roaming. He sits perched at a table at Tom Belcher's Castle, Holborn, to admire the fine package he has made of gambling token, medallion and sketches all tied up in the belcher Cribb gave him for remembrance. *Et voilà!* There! No. Wait. The note, perhaps, is inadequate. He tears it up. The Hussar calls for pen and ink and paper, for sealing wax and a length of string, and begins anew. Brushing the hair from his eyes, he folds the page in two and two again, before spreading it flat to write in each space, the four small squares forming shapes that put him in mind of window panes. *Je reviens,* he writes in each pane. *Je reviens, je reviens, je reviens, je reviens.* He draws a gull in the top right corner, for decoration. *Chayka.* He taught Katherine this word for seagull, and for the ancient Cossack skiff, the small reed-covered boat in which adventures were launched and taxes collected.

A drop of liquid falls onto the page and Aleksei shies away from his work, looking about sharply for a culprit, some Prussian, no doubt, slopping his hock. The Hussar is spoiling for a *barney,* as it is known, a *turn-up,* a duel. He has been too long on this island of punchy swells and millers, nearly three weeks. He raises a palm to the ceiling as if feeling for rain and realises his own perspiration is falling from brow and hair, the curls twisted with sweat, dripping like icicles. He has a boyhood vision of rain-splashed casements and watching at windows, waiting for spring.

Aleksei seals the note and rewraps the parcel, addressing it with an imperious flourish. *Raphael Solomon,* he writes. *Violin maker. Nr.* Near . . . In Convent Garden. Convent is not quite right. *Nr. Rose St.* Yes! He remembers this street named after a flower, because of the pub he was taken to there known as *The Bucket of Blood!* I have seen blood! muses the nineteen-year-old veteran of the War of Liberation. I have seen it run in streams. If he were not so drunk, if he had a feather left to fly with, Aleksei would hop into a cab and climb the steps of the patriarchal house and pound once again on Solomon the elder's door in Soho Square, but he is too drunk by now in the desperate early morning of his departure, too distressed for such endeavours. Instead, the Hussar seeks out the landlord Tom Belcher, into whose famed fists he commends the parcel, while babbling his dream of the two-Katherine dacha by the blue waters that border the Caucasian steppe.

Tom Belcher is the younger brother of the late and famous Jem the "Perfect Phenomenon," melancholy victim of pneumonia, blue ruin and dimming spirits. Tom, incumbent landlord—*boniface*—at the Castle, retired from the ring this very summer of 1814, a veteran of twelve prize fights with eight victories to his name, three matches lost and one drawn. Though forever overshadowed by his elder, yet is he universally acknowledged for the celerity of his blows and elegance of form. When Tom buried Jem three summers ago at Marylebone churchyard, the boxer Bill Wood leapt into Jem's long room straight onto the casket, his grief manifest, the tears dropping in torrents.

At the Castle, Holborn, Tom now lends an ear to the feeblish Russian with the angelic curls, clearly foxed on bub and red tape, and he cannot fathom a word. Nevertheless, he observes the fevered glint in the officer's eye and the crazy packet he cradles, as it were a precious infant, and reads the label once, twice, before bowing his fine head in acquiescence, at length construing the Hussar's desires. Tom murmurs reassurance, an expression of confidence and humanity marking his manly features as he clutches the warrior of Borodino by the epaulettes and rattles his slight bones. *Ne boysya,* he would say, if he knew Russian.

Don't worry, don't be afraid.

"Very good, old chap," states Tom, perusing the parcel with suitable gravity. "Leave it to me," he adds. "Set your anxiety at rest."

In Aleksei's fanciful dream of two Katherines by Caucasian blue waters, his sister and his English love, there is a child also, a fairy-tale girl, he fancies, with flyaway hair at the nape. She chirps gaily as a bird and is rosier than a red rose and whiter than white snow.

· · ·

The Hussar never does see his English Katherine again except in dreams and hopes and luxurious regret, and the child he dreams turns out to be a boy, not a girl, with flyaway hair. The boy kills Kath Solomon in the course of childbirth, which is a great pity, because even in exile from her family with her brother Raphael, violin maker and *Benthamite*—to their father's enduring horror—she would have made a fine mother and, to the last, was sought after for her skills in singing and teaching and gift for oratorio.

The Hussar never learns how Raphael's sister Katherine is buried in the spring of 1815 not three weeks into the life and strange surprizing adventures of his son, Samuel Alexander, Tsar of the Prize Ring. On the eve of Sam's novitiate in 1832, as he prepares to enter the lists in a match with Young Dutch under the aegis of Tom Spring, former Champion and present landlord of the Castle Tavern, Holborn—Spring having proudly assumed residency after the happy and successful fourteen-year reign of Tom Belcher—even now, in Sam's seventeenth year of age, Raphael Solomon, violin maker, weeps for his sister still.

Raphael Solomon has been weeping for seventeen years.

In the immediate aftermath of his sister's death in the early months of 1815, he simply cannot abide the sight of this boy with Hussar-blue eyes and head of dark Hussar curls, though he waits the eight days according to law for ceremonial circumcision before gathering all remnants of the Russian, remembrances that comprise a promise of return Katherine kept always on her person. *Je reviens, je reviens, je reviens, je reviens*, reads the note.

Ha! scoffs the violin maker.

Raph gathers it all up, after eight days, into Cribb's belcher: the hapless note, the fish made of bone, the Tsar's medallion; and he stuffs this inheritance into his greatcoat pocket. He lingers briefly in the doorway of his rooms and hurries away with the baby to Lamb's Conduit Fields and the gates of the Foundling Hospital there. Had the violin maker not been quite so blinded by grief and fury, he might well have noticed how during his race across Holborn to St. Pancras, the boy's eyes open wide and change colour from Hussar-blue to brown, tiger's-eye brown, warm as Katherine's own.

The boy sees the weeping man and the lowering sky above, weeping also, dropping a sharp rain that is turning to snow. He feels the firm hold around his child's anatomy, and this man is the first of his knowledge and is very marvellous.

You are my king! I love you so much!

The Life of Samuel Alexander, His Strange Surprizing Adventures, starts out like a song.

{ FOURTEEN }

The Castle Tavern, Holborn.

Sam the Russian, foundling boy, laid-in-the-streets, recites the articles in his head. He feels a thrill almost beyond endurance.

I, Samuel Alexander, that is known as Sam the Russian, hereby challenge Samuel Evans, born Elias, that is Young Dutch Sam, to meet me in three months for fifty pounds. The fight to take place near London and to be governed by the rules of the London Prize Ring.

"Sam?" asks Spring, following an application of farrier's oils and opodeldoc to the boy's anatomy. "Sam?" he says, between sweeps of the flesh brush. "How are you feeling?"

"Bobbish, sir! Feeling bobbish!"

"Good boy!" pipes Tom, gesturing for Sam to turn over, that he might work the hams and gluteals, the triceps and laterals. "Young Dutch will be surprised, the sarsy fellow! He is quick, but he lacks a punch and, furthermore, he's too much the young swanky for hard training, a forfeit that may well undo him! Conditioning is a superior acquirement!" he tells his apprentice in raised tones, mindful of the legacy of the Battle of Seven Dials and the boy's enduring deafness in one ear. Which auricular, however? Spring can never recall the which, dexter or sinister, meaning, as long as Sam lies upon his good ear, Tom does well to shout, yet with his hearing ear exposed, he is at some risk of causing general impairment.

"I wonder," shouts Tom, "do we require the three threes?"

Since his partial loss of hearing, Sam has a present fear of senseless-ness and, imparting this one evening to Dickens and Jonah, is subse-quently presented with a scientific tome describing *the Naturall language of the Head and the Naturall language of the Hand*, that is to say, of *chirologia* and *cephatologia* according to the theories of John Bulwer. Bulwer's dic-tionary of 1644 identifies sixty-four elements in his dialect of the hands with accompanying illustrations he calls *chirograms*. Sam makes a study of this *language of Humane Nature* in an effort to evade a fate of sense-lessness. He learns to search the face as he listens, the physiognomy that Bulwer likens to a clock and refers to as the *Dyall of the Affections,* all the features being capable of expression, he writes, even the ears, which, of course, interest him greatly. Sam learns to read a man's phiz and inter-pret the flutter of his fives though, to a fighter, the impulse to watch the hands and eyes to deduce intention or dissembling there is quite at one with nature. It is integral to the Art of Self-Defence. A fighter learns to read a blow and detect a feint, watching the eyes and hands for signs, and even the muscles of the chest. Chirologia and cephatologia come easily to Sam.

Three doses of salts, three sweats and three vomits a day for three weeks, ponders Tom Spring. No. The three threes are not required! What am I about? My boy is so spry, game, athletic! Why, a better bit of stuff might never be seen to peel in a ring! Spring knows that Dutch Sam, Young Dutch's father, trained on three threes of his own, three glasses of gin, that is, taken three times daily! The distinguished pugilist, famed for the uppercut and his dreadful punch and his three battles with Tom Belcher, lost his final bout in 1814 and died two years there-after. Dutch Sam, gone to roost, dead in the forty-second year of his age and Young Dutch, his son, but eight years in the world. Dutch Sam, they say, died from an excess of his favourite whet. At 5 feet 6 and ½ inches in height and little over nine stone in weight, Young Dutch's famous father was known to floor opponents one and even three stones greater in weight. Dutch Sam, they say, drank *for the headache.*

Spring slaps Samuel's lean hams and the boy lurches upright and to his feet, peepers bright, primed for instruction, scouring his master's dial and yet not reading the trouble there, Tom's nascent fear that his ward might not be so well matched against Young Dutch, over-matched indeed, in both poundage and experience. Walker! Nonsense! The boy is prime; he will contend in the field of glory.

"You are prime!" he remarks to Sam, who is momentarily distracted, sensing motion in the room, a shadowy flutter along the wainscoting.

Rattus norvegicus hulks in a corner, his grubbery churning, the spasms harsh and irregular. He has worked his way through all the courses on offer in Tom Spring's sporting apothecary of Dover's powders, blue salts, opodeldoc, farrier's oil and pickling liquids, feasting, for pudding, on a packet of Mrs. Spring's *Vandour's Nervous Pills for nervous disorders, lowness of spirits, tremblings, vain fears, wanderings of Mind, and Troublesome Sleep, etc.* Rat spewed like a statuary fountain thereafter, scoffing some clay and mortar to complete the purging of his stomach. He is nevertheless desperately shipwrecky. His ivories chatter, his eyes are shot with blood and swelled beyond recognition, but he endures, waiting and hoping for Jonah the Needle who comes every night. Jonah the Needle is much attached to Sam, and to animals.

"Help me, Jonah!" prays Rat. "Save me!"

Rachel draws a rat afflicted. *Rattus norvegicus* has violent abdominal pains and his head throbs. He weeps from the eyes and nose and gapes for air to fill his tiny bellows. Here he is, on the totter and like to die, praying for Jonah.

Rattus norvegicus
afflicted.

Contrary to general assumption, Rachel reminds herself, brain cells do not die to be lost forever, not in all cases. It has been noted that a rat engaged in the act of mothering is capable of self-regeneration in the brain, an abundance of new cells flooding the system to boost rat's capacity to learn and remember. For instance, *Keep away from Tom Spring's apothecary.* The obversant is noted in the infant rat or mouse starved of its mother's attentions for even as brief a time as twenty-four hours, his brain cells committing suicide at twice the speed of the consistently mothered infant. Did you not know this, Mama? Katya! Did you not think? How, because you were hardly ever home, our very brain cells were endangered? In the absence of Katya, Rachel recalls, she and Zach were quick to discover their aunt Natasha, her home full of cooking and music and Nikolai.

Nikolai is much missed.

Three weeks after Uncle Nicky died, Tasha's steady quiet weeping burst a dam in her eyes, resulting in compression of the blood vessels that supply the nerve joining eye to brain. This attack of glaucoma was followed hotly and cruelly by degeneration of the macula and so Volya the guide dog entered her days. Nicky would have approved. In Moscow, he adopted strays. The streets of Moscow and Petersburg, he once remarked, abound in strays, thousands of them. Some learn to ride the trains, stretching out on seats to rest their homeless bones. Such as the pair of you, Nikolai was wont to tease Rachel and Zach. A couple of strays! Riding the trains from Chelsea three times a week to sit on my doorstep! Don't you have a home?

"We hardly ever take the train!" protests Zach. "We walk or—"

"An analogy, Zachashka," laughs Tasha. "Silly boy!"

Mama is away again—*again*—in Moscow this time with her male choir, and Lev absorbs himself in the study of emergence and morphology, symmetries and attractors, resonance and reflection, while Rachel and Zachariah, no longer children, fly to Tasha and Nicky at weekends, and sometimes after school, typically racing to Battersea on their bikes. Tasha can still see, and Nicky is very much alive, busy in his ground floor osteopathic practice attending to displaced bones.

"*Dyadya?* Uncle?" says Rachel when Nicky enters the music room.

"Yes, little paws?"

"Papa says left-right symmetry—in man—is imperfect."

"Yes, well. In some it is more imperfect than in others. Keeping me in business, yes? What will your business be?"

"Zach is going to box!"

"Indeed," says Nicky, eyeing the boy. *He is growing so fast.* "Very good, very good. Tasha and I will need protection in our old age!" he adds, smiling at his wife and seeing his amusement reflected there. A reflection is a concept, a transformation. Nicky is transformed daily, it only takes one look, an act of entrancement, like the synchronous flashing of fireflies, a phenomenon, Lev once explained, caused by the coupling of oscillators by visual signals. I see it now, Nicky thinks. It is happening now between Rachel and Zachariah, no longer children at fifteen and fourteen years of age. Rachel and Zachariah, reflected and transformed. *Nothing we can do.*

"And you, little paws? What about you?"

"She'll draw and paint," states Zachariah, answering for her.

"I see, I see. Well. Downstairs with me!" Nicky announces, draining his glass of tea. "Into my den. My *zemlyanka*! Someone needs to do something useful around here. Pah! Boxing and painting and music-making. What nonsense!"

"Walk-er!" pipes Zach.

"Walk her?" says Nicky.

"No, *Dyadya*! *Walker* is an old word for 'nonsense,' nineteenth century. It means 'nonsense,'" explains Rachel. "But what was that?" she asks. "*Zemlyanka*? I've never heard that word."

"Ah," sighs Nicky, exchanging a smile with Tasha, and placing his near-empty glass on the piano.

"*Ne na pianino!*" Not on the piano! Tasha wails, snatching his glass away, a daily tussle.

"Not on the piano, not on the piano!" echo Rachel and Zach in Russian.

"*Zemlyanka*," begins Nicky, "is a dugout. A pit. And a famous song in the war. A song for the Battle of Moscow. Tasha? Will you play it? *Pozhaluysta, igrat'.*" Please. Play it.

Nicky sings.

> *The fire is flickering in the narrow stove*
> *Resin oozes from the log like a tear*

And the concertina in the bunker
Sings to me of your smile and eyes.
The bushes whispered to me about you
In a snow-white field near Moscow
I want you above all to hear
How sad my living voice is.
You are now very far away
Expanses of snow lie between us
It is so hard for me to come to you
And here there are four steps to death.

Tasha watches Nicky disappear downstairs. She watches from the corner of her eyes, right ear towards shoulder, two fingers pressed to lips. Zach grunts softly and retrieves his book from the floor and Rachel, budding cartographer and naturalist, applies herself to yet another map of St. Petersburg, Mama and Tasha and Lev's native place, Nikolai being the lone Muscovite in the family. Rachel has been promised a journey to celebrate her sixteenth birthday. She maps her cities with accompanying legends, cataloguing the flora and fauna to be observed there and, in the case of St. Petersburg, sketching in gradations of colour from dark to light to illustrate the emergence of city from swamp, marvelling in particular at the elaborate confinement of a tortuous river. The Neva courses manically through a flood-prone flatland, the broad waterway turning back on itself at the mouth as it veers north-west into the Gulf of Finland, branching fourfold with intersecting streams to create more than twelve islands. Upon one of these, Zayachiy Ostrov, or Hare Island, the last in the delta, Peter the Great built the St. Peter and St. Paul, an impregnable six-sided fortress erected on an island deemed too low and marshy for habitation, Peter's men shoring it up laboriously, ferrying dirt in their shirts, improvised sacks. Here it sits now, the Peter and Paul, bound by morass to north, east and west, and the fast-flowing Neva to the south. From an aerial perspective, Rachel muses, the Peter and Paul is the eye of a whale spouting water, running with scars and rivulets, lashed by the sea. *Neva* is Finnish for "swamp." The Neva is wild as anything, a flood in constant abeyance. Melting snow and ice shroud the river in springtime, threatening an untold rise in water levels, with the fierce southwesterlies off the Gulf of Finland able to stop the Neva in its tracks, causing a hasty retreat of waters and consequent burial of islands. The city is a place of turbulence and violent change. St. Petersburg, O Jerusalem on the Neva, is a folly Peter was fated to build. There is destiny in stones.

Some days, Rachel thinks, there is rapture. Everything connects, everything is right and good and there is nothing troubling, not even in paradox. For instance, the tissues in her body renew themselves every two years, yet she remains Rachel. She looks up from her map to see Tasha at the piano, working her symphony, and her brother on the great sofa they call the *troika* for its plush and ageing feather cushions and ornate curvaceous ends. All is right and good on days such as this, even Mama's absences.

Fate! Take the birth of the eye. Lev says the eye may originate in the chance mutations of a pigment cell in skin, a nerve cell sensitive to touch. I spy with my little eye something beginning with . . . touch! Lately, when Rachel spies her brother, her eye suffuses. *Optic, peeper, top-light, ogle, sparkler.* In such moments, she has an urge to speak or sing and if Zach catches her look, she startles further. He hears me. He feels me. Here's another perfect thing: how the words "symphony" and "fate," she learns, share the same ancient root signifying "to speak."

Symphony. Fate. Everything connects and it is very beautiful! Rachel has made a particular study of the senses.

Vocal apparatus, she learns, is a late development and a faculty unique to man, leaving the wolf and his dog descendant with the acuity to distinguish subtleties of pitch in one same vowel sound. A wolf cub knows his parent anywhere, the adult knows his mate.

Rachel draws the streets and bridges of St. Petersburg, a sensation of passing feet in her fingertips, of feet and hooves, carriage wheels and paws, causing an infinitesimal change in pressure as they go, marking the stones forever. She draws the streets and then she draws trains with cutaway interiors. She fills them with dogs.

Zach lays down *The Pickwick Papers,* a favourite. He closes the book on Sam Weller at the Blue Boar in Leadenhall Market struggling to write a valentine over brandy and water, fumbling with pen and ink and words. Zach puts down his book and takes up his cricket ball, flicking it from hand to hand, spinning it into the air with a roll of the fingers and wrist. He wonders aloud at the origins of valentining.

"You're right," Rachel says. "It is a verb. Can be. And birds valentine each other, make mating calls. And usually mate in mid-February. You see?"

"But why Valentine?" asks Zach. "Why valentining?"

"There were many Saint Valentines," offers Tasha. "I don't know what the link is between their martyrdom and love letters."

Zach is not very interested in the old tradition or the archaic verb. He is not bothered by the mating calls of passerines or the saints named Valentine and their associated symbols—he is merely fishing. Does Rachel think the tradition silly? If he were to send her a valentine, how strange would that be?

"*Tyotya?* Are we having supper here tonight?" asks Zach.

"If you like," replies Tasha, thinking, *The Valentine,* a piano sextet. Perhaps. She plays a few notes. Mendelssohn wrote a piano sextet, of course. Yes, yes. He was barely older than the children when he wrote it.

"We eat here a lot, don't we?" the boy continues. "With Mama away, Lev's not in the mood for cooking much, is he, Rach? And she's always bloody away."

"That's not true. And we can cook for ourselves now. He knows that."

"I've been thinking, though," adds Zach, flicking the cricket ball, "how it's not really a proper job, conducting. Who invented it? Who bloody needs it?"

"Look at it as captaincy," suggests Tasha.

"Captaincy," Zach repeats thoughtfully, weighing it up.

"And she's not always away," says Rachel. "And why do you say 'aunt' and 'mama,' but 'Lev' for Papa?"

"I don't want to talk about it," Zach snaps, sitting up sharply, dropping the ball, seeing red. "I often say 'Tasha,' anyway. '*Tyotya*' or 'Auntie' and 'Tasha.' I say all three!"

"I hate when you're in a huff, Zach!" says Rachel, rolling the ball back his way smartly.

"No! Leave it! You'll get ink on it. That's my best bloody ball!"

"For pity's sake, Zach. I'm careful. Don't be so rude!"

No! Leave it!

These are the same words Lev will snap at Zach, and they distress Rachel. *No! Leave it!* Lev snaps at the boy, lest he touch a book, a glass,

Zach's very presence in dirty sports clothes a seeming offence. Like a growing pup, such a boy might grow up believing his true name is *No!*

Tasha says, "If you are staying for supper, you need to ring your father."

"I'm not bloody calling!" Zach protests.

"I think it was a general suggestion," notes Rachel.

"I hate calling him! He always thinks I've done something wrong. Lev loves her the most," Zach blurts. "Rachel. They love her so much, the most. Better than anything."

"I'm ignoring you," Rachel exclaims. "If you say things like that, I'm just going to ignore you."

"Actually, I was talking to *Tyotya*."

"Same here, Zachashka," says Tasha. "I'm ignoring you also. Silly boy."

"Well, bloody forget it! I'm changing the subject. Valentine's Day tomorrow," he remarks, settling back into the sofa. "Now, *that's* what I call silly!"

"Why?" asks Rachel. "What's silly about it? Sillier than you, that is?"

Feint.

To lead towards one part of the body with the intention of striking another part if the opponent shifts his guard to protect against the original motion.

"Don't know," he answers, assuming indifference. "Anonymous bit, I suppose. Soppy cards, all that."

If your opponent cannot read you, if he cannot predict the next move, the next punch, then he is already on the defensive. On the back foot. Some fighters watch the eyes for signs, some the gloves, still others watch the chest muscles, ever seeking clues. Cassius Clay says, of fighting with Sonny Liston, "I just kept running, watching his eyes. Liston's eyes tip you when he is about to throw a heavy punch."

Rachel looks at her brother, her features still.

"It's not so silly," she says, unblinking.

"Really?" Zach says in the most absent tone he can muster, heart lurching in his chest, fit to burst. "Not if you're a bird, I suppose."

"Oh!" exclaims Rachel. "That reminds me. Tasha?"

The Valentine, the Valentine . . . a sextet for piano.

Tasha steadies the pages on the stand and touches one finger to her lips, then raises it in air. One moment, please. Quiet, please. She picks up her pen and makes a notation. She hears the sound in her head, glances again at the page. She is suddenly aware, sensing it with a flutter of inner turbulence, of the new way in which she examines the music—turning her head to right and left. She is aware, too, of how it is becoming second nature. It is happening. It cannot be denied. How will she work, how will she cook, dress, how will she love, with ever-dimming central vision? Perhaps it is merely a phase: fatigue, allergy, something passing. Like a bird, Tasha sees acutely on the periphery, and for a moment, before fear sets in, this feels somewhat prophetic. The periphery is always full of signs, of things to come, of things that once were, and of yearnings.

"Rachel," says Tasha. "Sorry. I am listening now. Speak."

"It's something I learned lately and wanted to tell you—about birds. When Zach said, 'if you're a bird,' I remembered. I can tell you later if you're busy, it's not important."

"Tell me now."

"Well. It's about how birds are an exception to the rule that says we are born with our complete share of brain cells. I mean, that rule is in question, I think—but, anyway, birds are definitely excepted from this—that we are born with our entire lot. And cells that die are lost forever, etc. Because they've discovered that as birds learn the songs of their family—their particular avian species—new cells bloom in the brain! And wrens, you know, pass on their vocalisations in so very precise a manner, their songs are especially valuable in distinguishing family ties. How about that? If a wren is lost, I daresay, he only has to sing. *Mama! I'm here!* Do you like that?"

"I do," says Tasha, thinking, the soul dwells outside the body, in some special place. The soul is in the song. "I do. I like it very much."

"Yes, I thought you would," states Rachel. "I told Mama. She liked it very much too."

"I like Nicky's mashed potatoes with cumin," pipes Zach, earning a smile from Rachel that flays him. He feels naked as a newborn, a slithering cub, deaf and blind and bleating, a mess of uncalcified bone and brain like a sponge. A dog's brain, unlike a bitch's, is sexed at birth, masculinized at birth.

What Zach meant to say all along, what he means to say when he speaks of potatoes with cumin, is, *You strip me clean. It hurts to be near you. I find it so hard to be near you. I love you so much. Rachel, Rachel. The most. Better than anything.*

[FIFTEEN]

St. Petersburg, late 1980s.

"Rachel?"

"Mm?" gurgles Rachel, mouth full of toothpaste.

"Don't rinse with the water. Here," says Katya, pouring vodka into a tooth-mug. "Now rinse."

Rachel spits and smiles broadly at her mother. "I drank sweet vodka, hey!" she sings. "I drank sweet vodka from a half-pail."

Katya's eyes flash.

When she is invited to Russia to perform a short series of concerts, Katya travels with Rachel, taking her out of school, as promised, to cel-ebrate her sixteenth birthday, leaving Lev and Zachariah to mind the palace. The males are skittish at first, wary of each other in the absence of women.

In the first week, Tasha and Nicky bustle round with casseroles and there is a brief flurry of merriment with shots of Moskovskaya slapped onto the table alongside side-dishes of rollmops and miniature potato pancakes, but when Lev and Zach are alone, the house is cavernous. Lev and the boy eat quietly, sweep their places clear and retire early with books, both men alert to the ticking of clocks, the timepieces out of kilter with one another, creating a mesmeric rhythm that is unsettling and arousing. Man and boy listen restlessly to the passage of cars and clatter of late-night heels and shimmy of brittle leaves in the wintry wind, and to the demonic wailing of cats and screeching of foxes, as if the very walls had thinned when Katya and Rachel left. On the day of departure, they sat momentarily on their luggage in the hallway after the age-old manner, laughing at themselves for their quaintness. Katya is an émigrée returning and exile is irreversible, it is a kind of immanence.

One evening of the second week, Lev announces to Zach he is making a fish stew with parsley and has bought bottles of ale, whereupon the boy appraises his father briefly before laying down his issue of *Boxing News* to follow him into the kitchen, where they chop and stir and sip with occasional shared glances and muttered exchanges on neutral subjects.

Later that week, Lev rings Tasha and Nicky to let them know he and the boy do not require their ready meals; he is teaching his son to cook. *"My son,"* he says, two or three times. Tasha and Nicky are bemused. By the weekend, Lev and Zachariah share the living room at night, the coffee table spread companionably with their reading materials, drinks and snacks. Lev buys smoked fish and cheeses from Fortnum's and, passing Hatchard's one day, forks out what he considers a ridiculous sum for the latest *Wisden Cricketers' Almanack*, presenting the latter to the boy in a spoffish manner, awkward and faintly ceremonial. They convince Magda, impoverished student of music theory, to save up her house-cleaning shifts for the eve of their womenfolk's return. And so the men are able to live in unembarrassed disarray until then, beds happily unmade and frying pans reserved respectively for eggs, potatoes and sausages kept to one side and merely dashed clean with a cloth between uses. Lev, more typically a fastidious housekeeper, revels in this throwback to student days of cheerful squalor. There are Lev-areas and Zach-areas for cups and glasses, one receptacle each for tea, beer, and water. Shot glasses they keep in the freezer. A team now, they are lofty in their scientific economy of unnecessary toil. They find communion in dust.

On their last Sunday, Lev takes his son to a refined gastro pub in Richmond, a place he knows well from afternoons of wandering South London, whiling away the hour or so until Katya has wrapped at the studio, finished rehearsals, closed a meeting. He waits here too when she sits her tests and examinations, as she coins it, at the Chelsea and Westminster Hospital, consultations she refuses to allow her husband to attend and that they keep secret from the children.

"What's the use in telling them?" she will say, ordering chablis. "No use at all. Nothing we can do."

"I need to sit with you there," Lev insists.

"You fuss," she replies. "It's unsettling. It is also unnecessary. I am such an excellent student of cancer! Top marks again today," she states proudly, reaching for Lev's hands across the table. "You have musician's hands," she adds in a voice barely above a whisper. "I've always thought so. Please don't be sad."

On this Sunday in Richmond, Lev and Zach grow red-faced and rosy-nosey'd by the Georgian fireplace over pints and guinea fowl and scalloped potatoes and Lev listens to Zach on the art of spin-bowling and the early days of pugilism and the history of retired fighters—*"bruisers"* and *"millers,"* he calls them—and their professions, the young man picking up speed as he discourses, racing like a train. Lev drifts at times, lost in the litany of sporting names and deeds, entranced and bewildered by Zach's enthusiasm. He thinks about other times spent here alone, scrawling notations on symmetry and the breaking of symmetry, the rhythms of bird calls and animal gaits, the independence of scale in a rock, a cloud, and on the laws of fluid flow and rippling of water, and on the beauty of it—how a pattern must exist in order to be broken. Lev revels in the dynamics of growth; he glories in numbers, counting the petals on Katya's posy: 3, 5, 8, 13, 21. Fibonnaci Sequence. He will look at his watch: 21, 13, 8, 5, 3 minutes until Katya comes! Attending to Zachariah again, he wonders at the strangeness of it, how the young man has come to resemble her in some ways and in certain familiar gestures, all the more startling to him in this rough-hewn boy, sculpted, powerful, so essentially unlike. In the morphology of living creatures, Lev recites to himself, genes are not the sole factor in the appearance of patterns or the causes of change.

Lord Byron, Zachariah tells Lev in an effort to shine, was an amateur of pugilism and coached by Gentleman Jackson.

"Gentleman Jackson?" Lev says. "Remind me."

"He beat Daniel Mendoza—you know Mendoza—to win the Championship in 1795. He was the stronger fighter on the day, but he cheated a bit. He held Mendoza by the hair, you see, and smacked the hell out of him," explains Zach.

"I see."

"It wasn't exactly illegal, but frowned upon, Papa. Not cool. He didn't like Mendoza."

"He was anti-Semitic?" asks Lev.

"Maybe. And Dan was a bit showy. Had long hair. Rach would know."

"Would know what?" says Lev, his tone sharper than intended.

"Why he didn't like Mendoza. It's more her thing. The personalities and everything."

Lev looks down, twists his glass round and round.

"She's read his memoirs. She says he never mentions it, the hair-pulling. But the fight was famous for it. The hair-pulling."

"I see," says Lev. "Rachel has a very . . . eclectic mind."

"Eclectic," Zach echoes. "I'll say!"

Rachel!

In the bathroom last night, after a late session at the gym, Zach splashed his sweat-smudged brows with soapy water and, reaching over to shut the door, pushing it too forcefully as per usual—slam, bang, sorry!—the nightgown Rachel left hanging there on a hook billowed like a sail, arousing him with a scent of such delicacy and precision, he raised his arms aloft and gathered the material in, for all the world like a wicket-keeper claiming a catch—*howzat?*—and was surprised by a stinging in his eyes and sudden rush of tears. Zach wept. Then he scrubbed the linen nightdress across his arms and chest in fierce brisk sweeps, willing the scent to enter his pores, so that he might dream of her in his sleep.

Zach prattles on about boxers—their day jobs, career records, deaths. He knows the names of graveyards, he knows the plots and stones. Here lies Gentleman Jackson, Jem Belcher, Young Dutch Sam. He talks of the fans—the *Fancy*—including poets and writers, Papa! Dickens, Thackeray, Clare and Hazlitt! Zach pipes the names, willing his sport to accrue in esteem by association, to wax in Lev's estimation.

He listens to the boy, observing the crimson in his cheeks, the light in his eyes. He never knew his son could burn so bright. He never knew his son. As he listens to Zach, voluble and effusive as never before, Lev bites his tongue for once and does not say it: *I will not let you box for a living. It is a revolting occupation.*

Katya, he thinks, would know how to respond. Not he. For a pioneer of complexity, Lev is a man of four-square morality. Conjuring her now, he is struck again by the uncommon resemblance between mother and adopted boy, uncommon, impossible, an *emergence*—like his affection for the boy, emerging also during this imposed isolation from Katya and Rachel, empathy displacing frustration with every passing day, a strong feeling for which, quite strangely, he is prematurely nostalgic, knowing it will dissipate upon the return of the girls, a special truce disturbed. Katya, for Lev, is a vortex, by turn alluring and animal, icy and disaffected, often in one same day. Katya is symmetry-breaking.

—*Katya? Katyenka?*

—*Darling?*

—*Where does symmetry go when it is broken?*

—*I haven't the least idea. I do not play this game.*

—*Into pattern-formation. It goes into pattern-formation.*

The two miscarriages of sons, her unflinching persistence, Katya's need for men, everything led to Zachariah, and when the boy came, Lev was filled with joy and anticipation and a creeping shame also, for the sense of exclusion he felt, as if his wife and daughter had been waiting only for this, the coming of Zach.

As a child, Lev recalls ruefully, Zach was everywhere, into everything, storm-tossed, electric and strange to Lev, his young skin soon a fretwork of scrapes and scars and contusions. He may never own him, Lev recalls thinking, but he might perhaps shape him, though this was an endeavour soon abandoned, an effort too great. The boy is so wayward! Yet see them now, in a pub, man listening to boy. The boy prates away, disgorging some excitable riff on boxing. The man leans in towards his son, listening hard, noting the flame-red ears he has an urge to cup in order to see if the heat of the boy will infuse his own hands, light him up like a torch.

I do not understand you, I bang my head against you, but today I love you so much.

As a side-effect of the tinnitus that is not yet diagnosed, a condition aggravated by knocks to the helmet from fast-bowled cricket balls and blows to the head in boxing club, Zach is wont to sit up in bed late at night because he hears a whispering in his ears, or a sound of someone calling. Rachel perhaps.

"Yes?"

Nothing. Not Rachel, you idiot! Rachel is in St. Petersburg.

Zachariah climbs out of bed and into the window seat, the recess where he and his sister would sit as children deep into the night, reading to each other, inventing, rambling. My thoughts, my learning for yours—tell me everything. Let me tell you everything.

"Picture this," says Rachel one night, laying aside the *Memoirs of the Life of Daniel Mendoza*. "Nowhere in the book does Daniel mention the hair-pulling in the fight with Gentleman Jackson. He lost the Championship of All England and he never mentions the foul. But he remembers it always. Sees it. Dan is old now. In his sixties. He is thinking about the great battle. Suddenly the ciliary muscle of his eye and the smooth tissue round his follicles, at the very roots of his hair, *tingle*. These are involuntary muscles. His eyes sting, his scalp prickles—he wants to cry! You know how if you remember something very horrid or something very lovely that happened, your heart jumps? Cardiac muscle is involuntary too, Zach! Remembrance is physical. Do you see?"

"I'm not surprised if Dan cried," offers Zach. "Fighters cry all the time. Even the hardest. Sonny Liston. He cried when he lost the Championship to Cassius Clay. The day he quit on the stool at the bell for round seven. He cried."

Now the recess he and Rachel sat in together as children barely contains him alone and he makes an accordion of his body, knees in air, back flat to one wall, soles of his bare feet against the other, Achilles tendons at full stretch. His brain is full of sleep. If I really push, he thinks, forwards and aft, the walls might shift. All this increasing growth, he thinks. Every year, new togs, new shoes—*understandings*—it is all somehow unseemly. None of Lev's garments can be handed down; the boy is already broader and taller. Nothing fits! How I no longer fit, Zach muses, cannot all be down to me. Perhaps the world shrinks also, just a little. This world cannot contain me, clothe me. The world no longer fits. Hand it down.

Zach's eyelids flutter and droop, his mind a pleasant jumble—things said tonight, last year, last month, things said in dreams. He sees Lev, Tasha, Rachel, and something he read earlier, what was it? In one of Rachel's books, circled in pen, a book of Natural History. "*Many birds and mammals, wolves in particular, have a—*" What? Oh yes. "*—a fateful preference for the ancestral nesting place.*" And Rachel wrote in the margin: "*Ha ha ha! It has a strange attraction!*"

I don't get it, thinks Zach. What's the joke?

He watches trees flex in the wind in the night, in the *darky*, watching through heavy lids, and there are no lights in any windows, not one. Though he has never seen it himself, Rachel says that fox cubs are born in March and can sometimes be seen in the low branches of trees. I don't know, Rachel. That's a bit bonkers. Can't be right. In the trees like birds? As he falls asleep sitting up, Zach imagines fox cubs in a nest, beginning life in trees and flying down to earth when grown, fledglings. Beginning in sky, in air, like St. Petersburg, Tasha's native place!

"Here," said Tasha over supper last week, quoting Peter the Great, "there shall be a city!"

"Why didn't you go too?" asked Zach that evening. "To Petersburg."

And by way of answer, Tasha told him that, in her opinion—not only hers—the beautiful town of St. Petersburg was built on bones. *Where wolves and bears were once the only residents.* Thousands died, she said, building the Peter and Paul Fortress alone, ten thousand at least, in four months. She told Zach how almost everything came from elsewhere, every kind of stone imported from other countries except for the limestone. She said how profoundly crazy an impulse it was, a fateful dream indeed, to erect a city in a bog, on sand, a flood-prone basin by the Baltic Sea where only wolves and bears made their home. The dream was so very crazy that a fairy tale was begotten in which Peter builds a city in the sky and lowers it to the ground upon completion. Here there shall be a city!

The stones are largely exotic, concluded Tasha, but the bones are local. St. Petersburg has a *graveyard odour.*

If Petersburg is Mama's native place and Rachel's ancestral place, maybe they're not coming back. Zach dreams of Rachel walking the stones and bridges of St. Petersburg, climbing its trees, nesting in the low branches of trees, chirping gaily as a bird. She feels a strange attraction and she's not coming back.

Chirped the bird gaily, All is QUI-et!

Zach's head nods sharply, rousing him from sleep. Someone called his name again. Definitely! He slips out of the high window seat and strides to the door, pulling it open.

"Papa?" he says.

Nothing.

The young man stares into the hallway, looking right, looking left, angling the ears, eyes bright. As an exposed and deserted Young Child, found abandoned fifteen years ago, oddly enough, in a plastic pet carrier in Mecklenburgh Square outside the doors of the Coram Community Campus, Zachariah's eyes were described as being of the deepest blue. Yet were a person to shine a light at him tonight, straight into his eyes, he would perceive them to be coloured amber, almost gold. He would perceive a wolfish glow.

SIXTEEN

St. Petersburg, late 1980s.

What a strange procession! So many faces, thinks Rachel, so many ages, can they all be related to Mama and Tasha, to Papa, to me? Even Katya, sitting so upright amongst them, seems strange to her, a stranger. *I know so little,* Rachel tells herself.

They come singly, or two by two, to the theatre, to the dressing room, and to Katya's grand rooms at the Pribaltiyskaya Hotel on Vasilievsky Island. Here, glasses of tea and vodka are consumed and visitors proffer fishy morsels with penetrating scents, or pickled things and greying cheerless chocolates. An aged gentleman with a threadbare silken scarf set in precise folds round his neck—*belcher!*—presents a packet of Sobranie Black Russians Katya will never smoke, and one lady brings golden brown lumps of burnished stones linked with nylon thread. *Ambre jaune,* explains Katya later. Amber. The Amber Room at Tsarskoe Selo, she says, was concealed by the Soviets behind wallpaper to prevent theft, but was nevertheless expertly dismantled and looted by the Germans and moved to Königsberg. Now, the Amber Room is proudly restored. The Amber Room came home again. It has taken nearly twenty-five years. Another ridiculous Russian tale, laughs Katya.

"Amber is fossilised resin, isn't it?" asks Rachel. "Washed up from the sea?"

Katya does not answer, but crosses the room to fetch the Richard Duke violin she was presented with after her opening concert in a hushed ceremony of gravity and artfulness, and obfuscation. *A gift of the state. This was your father's violin. A Duke, and a genuine. Genuine! Pozhaluysta primite. Please accept.* Katya accepted. She tried to smile without irony.

Katya takes the instrument now from the case, holds it up by the neck, lifts the bow from the lid. She indicates the frog on the bow.

"You see, Rachel? A piece of Baltic amber," she says. "Yes. I forgot amber was fossil. What strange things you know. But a fossil. How perfect. Do you see?"

Rachel watches the parade of faces, noting a commonality of hue, pallid, as if recovering from illness, long hidden from light. Even the younger ones are wan and, while the aged seem less diffident, less laconic, they are more ragged and febrile and lapse into French whilst making fluttery movements with their hands. They talk about food and cold and the price of things. Rachel imagines them sleeping under layers of heavy blankets after meagre suppers of colourless fish and pickled things eaten without pleasure. The pervasive air of misfortune induces a giddiness in her and an urge to race in tight mad puppyish circles and emit whooping sounds. The air in the room is one of subtle supplication and recrimination and, when the daily procession ends, Rachel is full of relief and queries.

"*Dyadya,*" murmurs Katya, gathering glasses and ashtrays.

"Mama! Was that man—is he—your uncle?"

"What man?" asks Katya, frowning, and Rachel makes fanciful tying gestures at her neck, denoting silken material and extravagant folds.

"Ah. Him," says her mother. "Yes, yes."

"Are you cross?"

"Why should I be cross? You always ask me that."

"When did you last see him? Here? Or—"

"Not here, not here. Paris. He came with us to Paris. I remember him from there. That time."

"But he came back, Mama. For good. To Petersburg."

"Yes, he came back. With the—openness. Restructuring. You know. *Glasnost* and—you know. All that."

"*Perestroika,*" intones Rachel. "And is he glad?"

"Is he glad? I don't know. He teaches, he has a flat. He teaches theory at the Conservatory. It's very good. He's fine, fine, yes. I suppose so."

"Like Tasha," remarks Rachel. "Like Tasha might have done."

"What do you mean?"

"Just that she teaches music."

"Tasha is a composer. She doesn't—"

"I know!"

"She doesn't need to teach. I can take care of her. Lev and I. So can Nicky. It's ridiculous. God!" exclaims Katya, dropping to the sofa. "Tasha! She'd be so much better at this. So much."

"At what?"

"Everything. Being here, seeing them. Explaining to them. Explaining *them* to you. At everything."

"Why didn't she come, Mama? She was invited too, wasn't she?"

"This country is . . . hard. She won't come. I've told you before. On principle, she won't. Principle! Who cares anymore?"

"When you say *hard*—"

"Difficult. Trying, demanding, hard. Full of . . . danger. Just danger. Does that sound overly dramatic? It does!" Katya laughs. "I'm infected! Three weeks here and I'm infected!"

"Danger of DEATH!" says Rachel.

"Well . . ."

"No, Mama! It's a joke. Something of Zach's and mine. You know that building—two streets away from the house, towards the river—a small factory or warehouse? There are two yellow signs and a cartoon-figure in black—figure of a man jumping and falling—and there's a black bolt of lightning, and it says DANGER OF DEATH. And we always think of Papa at work, as in a comic, you see—the frowning and then the inspiration, the bolt of lightning and the jumping in the air with revelation. Especially since Papa goes on about rhythms and electrical currents in the brain and heart. So whenever he scowls over a book, a pile of papers, we whisper 'Danger of death!' It's silly, never mind."

"What comics? What do you mean, in comics?"

"*Tintin,* for instance. Or—well, Zach likes *Battle*—but it's just a device in comics. The bolt of lightning. To denote surprise or a sudden idea. It doesn't matter, Mama. It's just a joke we have."

"Do *you* read comics? Still?" asks Katya, as if to a stranger. "I mean, what *do* you read? Both of you. You must miss him, I think you must.

DANGER OF DEATH . . . can't say I've noticed the sign. Two streets away? Frowns and inspiration . . . ah. Well, it is silly. Now we're both silly. We need supper. What do you say?"

Tired today, thinks Katya. Ready to go home. Home? And where might that be? Katya laughs.

"Mama? What's so funny? Is it me?"

"No, little paws. No, my dove," says Katya, startling Rachel not just because her mother is not prone to endearments, but because, in Mama's voice, they affect Rachel so much.

"Come," invites Katya. "Let's sit side by side and be quiet a while."

Rachel sits, thinking of the sofa at Tasha and Nicky's. *Troika.*

"There's snow, Mama. Look."

"Weather. Weather systems. Condensation and precipitation of water. How he loves it. Lev. Your papa."

"Papa's father, my—"

"*Dedushka.* Your grandfather."

"Mama!"

"What?"

"You don't—you always—you don't let me speak."

Katya looks intently at her daughter. "I'm so sorry," she says softly. "I'm sorry."

"I don't mind, really."

"When you were born," says Katya, "you were almost entirely bald."

"Oh."

And lovely, remembers Katya. And from the moment you opened your eyes, you never stopped watching me. Lev played and played with you and still you watched me, And I was not—prepared. For such—attachment. If I could give you a brother, I thought—

"It's sad. How he died, I mean. Papa's father. My—"

"He would have been killed sooner or later. Like mine. *Otets.* My father."

"Why?"

"Russia!"

"Danger of death!"

"Yes indeed. Lev's *otets* was a Jew, a scientist . . . an intellectual. There would have been so many reasons. So many black marks. Better he should die in the freezing—"

"And wasn't there nobility? Weren't they Whites?"

"Yes, Your Radiance! *Vashe siyatel'stvo.* A touch of nobility. A count or two, a petty prince. Nothing terribly grand. Merely souls in the end."

"In your family, too?"

"Oh yes, a plague of them in mine! Tasha's and mine. Titles and honours. So many questions, Rachel! Whatever is the matter?"

"We hardly see you, Mama. These days," Rachel states, rising to her feet, surprising herself. "You are always away. Now I'm away with you. I'm away with you," she repeats, her eyes prickling. *The ciliary muscle is involuntary.*

"That's the truth," says Katya, speaking low. "Sit. Please sit. 'Like a nightingale in flight, has my youth flown by,'" she sings in Russian. "Remember this one?"

"Yes."

"'Nowadays I feel overwhelmed by everything,'" she sings. "'I wander round the world: I shall part with misfortune—and meet with sorrow!' Did you understand all that?"

"Most of the words, yes."

"Lugubrious! Don't you think? I shall part with misfortune and meet with sorrow! The music is beautiful, though. *Do* you miss him, then? Zach? You do."

"If I hadn't come away with you, Mama," Rachel replies stoutly, "I would be missing *you.* May I ask you something? When I was born, after—"

"There were two. Two miscarriages. Both boys."

"I know, of course I know that. I wanted to ask—after Zachariah came, when they—I mean . . . I just want to ask about the—cancer. That's all. Because I know you are tested and everything's all right, but I never ask. You never actually—"

"It's interesting, isn't it? How, for so long, people assumed diseases were all air-borne, largely air-borne, when so many are water-borne. Lev often says that. Always saying things out of nowhere. Scientific things. Quite funny. Would you? Miss me? I mean now—if you weren't here. Would you really be missing me?" Katya asks with a flourish of gay hand gestures, in imitation of her extravagant uncle.

"Oh Mama!"

"It's not something you can feel, you see," says Katya. "Is it? You can miss a person, but a person cannot feel missed. You cannot feel . . . missing. Missed. So what is the point? What is the point?"

"What is the point? I don't understand," says Rachel.

"Quiet now," goes Katya, covering her daughter's hand with her own and staring straight ahead. They sit side by side in stillness, gazes attendant, as in a waiting room.

Katya notes the lights coming on in the street and in windows, some of the luminance milky, some a sickly yellow, sulphurous, none of it bright as snow. Stalin's eyes! It is said that in anger they flashed yellow. And that his underpants, however, were gleaming white. He liked to show off the whiteness of his underwear. Katya makes a puffing sound through her nose, amused and disgusted all at once, and inadvertently squeezes Rachel's hand.

Rachel thinks, What long fingers Mama has, like wands in fairy tales. All the better to conduct with, my dear! Ekaterina Wolff has conduits for fingers. Rachel muses on the conducting of music and the conducting of electricity, and of the yellow sign depicting a man falling, struck by a current. Danger of death! What fells the man? A powerful conduction of electricity? Of thought? Of sound? Which? Perhaps the man is felled by music. In the sign, he falls backwards.

Katya shuts her eyes, remembering all the lessons of her youth, the lessons and the milestones, how time is marked by her family, the survivors and émigrés of the motherland most had left behind. The Wolffs and the Byelovs fled to France. And nothing is forgotten. Nothing ever forgotten. Before the revolution, afterwards, the Terror, the Civil War, the world war, the invasion . . . Stalin said this, did that, threatened this, ordered that. Yezhov, Beria, shh! Don't repeat the names! As if anyone were still listening here in post-war Paris, Katya had thought. She was ten years old and even she knew they were all now dead. *All is QUI-et!*

All is quiet.

ONE STEP BACK, A MUSICAL INTERLUDE

On the 28th of July 1942, Stalin issues the infamous order Number 227, or *Not One Step Back,* as it is known, meaning it is considered inimical to the people, traitorous indeed, to retreat or surrender without orders. Lev's father and Katya's father survive Stalingrad. They leave the Volga behind and the Don, and advance towards the banks of the Dniepr and the liberation of the Ukraine. When the muddy season comes—

rasputitsa—it is hard to advance. It is hard to move in any direction in such mud.

In the spring of 1944 on the outskirts of Odessa, the meteorologist worries about his friend the violinist and curses this crazy concert-holding practice in prelude to battle. The little Red Army string orchestra plays sweet music out in the open, drawing opening fire. How very high-minded of High Command to expect a rise in fighting spirit and love for the motherland in the staging of maudlin plays, lectures on philosophy and string accompaniment to the singing of songs about the rivers, bells, woods and steppe of old *Rus*! Vanity and melodrama! A soldier might starve and freeze, rages the meteorologist, he may be shot on suspicion of malingering or used as a human minesweeper, no more prized than a Molotov dog, but he shall have music! Take not one step back, unless it be terpsichorean!

The meteorologist dies that spring, a minor noble, a petty prince, a young father, and, after he is buried, the violinist plays a maudlin tune over and over, "Little Blue Shawl." He never actually saw his friend fall, but in his mind he sees it, the meteorologist stumbling backwards to land softly on his shoulder blades and stare up at weather forever. Upon impact, before the fall, he took one step back, and a few years later, when the violinist writes a song about all this falling in *rasputitsa* and calls it, somewhat recklessly, "One Step Back," he is deemed an Enemy of the People. So one might say that music killed him, that he was felled by music. It's a theory.

String theory.

In the quiet of the Petersburg hotel and the falling snow without, Katya wonders what Lev is doing now, in Chelsea, what Zach is doing now. Sleeping? Not yet, she thinks, glancing at her watch. Not yet. Away from Lev, she craves his need for her. When with him, it enervates. Why is that? She cannot help it. Nothing to be done. Only with her sister is she unfettered. Tasha never makes her think about it, the terrible stature of love. Its shape, size, weight, the long shadows it casts. With Tasha she never goes cold as stones in a river, as Lev will accuse. You are suddenly so cold! Cold as stones in a river! What have I done wrong? he complains. *Nothing. Nothing, my darling.*

Some nights, when she is home late after a performance or dinner, Katya enters not her own bedroom, but Zachariah's and lies down in her coat next to his deeply sleeping body to watch his face centimetres from her own and she is amazed by the sweetness of his breath, pure sea breeze. She misses this, and other things, moments. Scenes and moments.

Katya strokes Rachel's hand quite idly and feels her daughter lean against her in response, the pressure light, tentative, the hesitation causing Katya pain. How cold she has been, how inadequate. She touches the top of her daughter's head, kisses her there. Who is this grave and pretty young woman? Not pretty. Beautiful. Yes, I think so. Who is she? I know so little. In the end, we know so little.

Katya shuts her eyes again. Scenes and moments, she thinks. And song. How often she and Tasha will break into song. The soul in all these things, the moments and songs. Memory, she decides, can be so urgent. Remember me! Katya remembers days and days.

Katya and Tasha have broken into song and Lev groans theatrically.

Tasha says, "You know, Lev, that the good mother in fairy tales is always beautiful, she always has a voice like sweet music."

"I am beautiful and good," proclaims Katya. "Do you hear that, everyone? And my voice is like sweet music!"

Lev says, "Music, at its lowest, is the rhythmic repetition of noises!"

"Indeed!" says Katya. "How poetic!"

> *The evening bell,*
> *How many thoughts it arouses in me,*
> *Of the days of my youth in my homeland,*
> *Where I knew love, where my father's house stands.*
> *And as I bade farewell for ever,*
> *I heard the sound of the bell for the last time.*
> *The evening bell,*
> *How many thoughts it arouses in me.*

To Katya and Tasha, singing together, Lev will quote his Gogol. "What's so good about this dreary singing? It only fills the soul with even greater melancholy."

"Your science, of course," quips Nicky, "is so terribly jolly!"

"Ah, but it is," Lev sighs.

"Black holes!" protests Nicky. "Dark matter, catastrophe?"

And Katya scoffs, "Let me tell you about *string theory,* my darling! The theory is that anyone can be taught to play the violin, the cello, viola. Which is rot, absolute rot! *Chush'!* Not only is this notion dangerous, it is also the cause of many headaches. Music is *not* a game of rugger! Or pin-the-tail-on-the-donkey. For pity's sake."

Tasha says, "The voice is the one true instrument."

"But, *Tyotya,*" says Rachel. "You write for piano and strings!"

"Little paws," purrs Tasha, while Zach leaps to his feet, raising his fists in the stance classical.

"The MUFFLER," he announces. "Mauley! Sledgehammer, flapper—FIST! This is the one true instrument."

"Hurrah," says Rachel distractedly, turning the pages of her book.

"What's the book?" he asks, crouching by her and flipping the cover to read the title, *Flora Britannica.*

"Did you know," asks Rachel, "there is such a thing as a Handkerchief Tree? Listen: '*introduced to Britain in 1901 by Ernest Wilson. Rare,*' it says. '*Davidia Involucrata.*' Handkerchief Tree."

"To be planted next to the WEEPING WILLOW!" Zach declares.

"You are all ridiculous," says Lev. "And I am moving to the Hebrides to get away. I am leaving you all!"

Nicky says, "It's time for a drink, I believe. Children too."

And they clink glasses, toasting each other one by one, calling out, "To the Hebrides! To the Hebrides!"

Where there are endless sea breezes, thinks Katya now, shivering a little in the Petersburg flat. Breath of Zachariah.

"So many people here today," she remarks to Rachel, breaking their silence. "Quite a procession."

"That's what I thought, Mama! A procession."

" 'Imagine,' " quotes Katya, " 'the triumphant procession!' "

"Peter AND the WOLF!" exclaims Rachel.

"In a way," begins her mother, "perhaps it was."

"What? Perhaps it was what?"

"I'm cold," states Katya. "Please bring me my coat. Do you think it is this cold in the Hebrides?"

Rachel laughs and heads for the door where their coats hang on stately brass hooks tipped in finely veined porcelain, and she removes Katya's overcoat, a luxurious length of black cashmere with two pockets at the hip. On occasion, Katya wears the coat in rehearsals, burying her hands deep in the pockets on breaks, collar turned up to the ears. The coat is much admired by Katya's assistant Liliya, who carries it over an arm in readiness, stroking the garment with bashful tenderness.

"Mama?" persists Rachel, draping the coat round her mother's shoulders. "Perhaps it was what?"

"Triumphant," she explains. "A triumphant procession. They could see, they could tell."

"Tell?"

"How one can never truly leave. And never quite return. Do you understand?"

"I think so."

"Rachel?" says Katya. "I would like a very *very* cold glass of vodka."

Rachel chooses the most sparkling crystal and pours a generous measure. She watches her mother drink, then sits by her again before the picture window to watch the snow fall, watching closely until she can hear it.

When a human hears a sound, he scans his library of sounds and assesses it for familiarity. This is the identification process. The wolf or dog, however, assesses for danger, and unless the wolf can rule it out entirely, then the possibility of danger becomes expectation, so a wolf is on perpetual high alert. A wolf can localise a sound to 8 degrees arc of separation compared to a human's 1 degree, and hear up to 65,000Hz to man's 20,000Hz at best.

It is no wonder, then, reflects Rachel, that his auscultatory faculties diminish so much more rapidly, surely no wonder at all. How long is it possible to hear at such a high pitch of awareness?

Rachel listens to snow, and beyond snow.

In bed later that night, Rachel wishes Zach were here, so she could do as she does in London, take her torch from the drawer and creep to his room to sit cross-legged at the foot of his bed and tell him whatever it is that cannot wait until morning. And tease him also, aiming the torch at his eyes and swearing they flash amber in the light, and not red, but yellow as a wolf's. The eye of the wolf acts like a mirror and glows yellow.

"Zachariah, you are a wolf!"

"So are you," he says, taking the torch and shining it at her. "You are a wolf."

If Zach were here, Rachel would tell him how she has acquired relations in St. Petersburg, not just in the procession of grey-skinned people in antiquated garments, but relations to the very *place,* how she feels the city, and those missing from the city, the violinist and the meteorologist who were killed, one at war and one in the aftermath of war. She hopes Mama is wrong. She hopes they feel missed. She feels the missing and the very streets of the city she will draw again tomorrow, mapping it from every perspective, from experience now, no childish imaginings. She will sketch insets of buildings and shoreline and twists of the Neva, and indigenous wildlife, such as White-Billed Divers and Arctic wolves, and fox cubs in low branches of trees. Are cubs born in late March here too?

The river can flow brown, Zach, she would tell him if he were here now. There is so much untreated waste. It used to be even worse. Will they ever clean it properly? Is it possible? She thinks of the Thames before Joseph Bazalgette. Could anything be as noxious? she wonders. When the stench was so appalling they had to paint the windows of the Houses of Parliament with lime? Oh the graveyard odours, the danger of death!

Zach, she would tell him, Mama and I rinse our teeth in vodka!

Rachel is too excited for sleep. She has never been so long from home and separation is so visceral. How strange.

I like it here. You'd like it here. Zachariah! Here is our ancestral place.

Mama said, an exile returns always. She said that one never truly leaves home. And that one can never quite return. Neither in dreams nor reality. One is, in a way, forever exiled. That's what she said. We talked and talked!

We'll be home, I'll be home, in three days.

Zachariah, Zachariah. I've never been so long away. I never felt so much special pain. I never knew I loved you so much.

·   ·   ·

At the airport, waiting for the Finnair flight to Helsinki, where Katya and Rachel Wolff will stay overnight before flying to London, Katya turns to Liliya before passing through the gates to the boarding lounge. Rachel watches her mother thank her assistant, something she does without smiling, almost drily, though she holds both of the young woman's hands in hers. And then, in a gesture so deft and natural it passes without remark, Katya removes her long black cashmere overcoat with two deep pockets at the hip and drapes it softly over Liliya's slim shoulders. Liliya opens her mouth, she gapes like a fish and her eyes flicker with feeling, but Katya is gone, her step brisk.

Rachel squeezes her mother's arm as they walk on, her face aglow.

"Rachel," scolds Katya. "Too tight."

"Sorry," says Rachel, releasing her hold.

I know so little, she tells herself again, searching her mother's face. *In the end, we know so little.*

SEVENTEEN

*F*ISH, FISH, *speak to me!*
    What do you want to know?
  I want to understand. Where does it all begin?
  Not all information is available, says fish with a flap of the tail, diving down beneath.

Lamb's Conduit Fields, Bloomsbury, March 1815.

Raphael the violin maker is at the gates of the Foundling Hospital and he swears that throughout his headlong rush from Covent Garden there have been eyes on him. He swears he saw the flashing eyes of fox cubs in the low branches of trees. He glances at the babe in his arms with the suddenly wide-open eyes, the look in them so very much like trust.

"Shhh," whispers Raph, though the child is quiet and still. "Shhh," he says. "I cannot keep you. I cannot be your mother and your father."

Here at the Hospital, the resolution has long since been passed to support the illegitimate as well as the children of soldiers and sailors killed at war in defence of the kingdom. The boy's father is a soldier, a Russian, good as dead!

Raphael Solomon paces without the walls of the Foundling Hospital in his shiny high-lows and curses the loss of Kath who died for this, and he curses the loss of other things, such as his gameness for living, his spirit and purpose. Shape. He has lost all shape. Shape of the day, of his days, the shape of her, of the wood in his hands—ebony, maple, spruce. And the bows, he has made one or two bows: each a construction of pernambuco wood and nearly two hundred hairs of a horsetail with a frog of silver, tortoise shell, ivory, even gold. Oh my sister!

"Kath, look what I have made! A violin. And a bow!"

"What a sound! It would surprise me if you ever make a finer instrument, Raph!" Kath says.

When she comes to his rooms from Lord Lowther's, where she is governess in musical instruction and performs at soirées, being much beloved by that household for her grace and talents, she brings always some pleasing comestible and scented blooms, peony or rose, and sprigs of blue-grey hydrangea. There will be cheese, claret or hock, a pie, oranges or apples. As she moves about his rooms one afternoon, tidying, chattering, singing airs, he catches the shape of her reflected in the body of the violin, and four times over in the pegs, and he finds the image of her, the vague outline, the dark hair, the glow of her dress, mesmeric. He turns the instrument this way and that and there she is, there she is! There!

Kath, my sister. You are a violin!

So what now, where to now? Now she is dead. To sea, should he go to sea?

Napoleon, as he understands, has re-entered Paris this very month. He shan't go to France, then. To the Hebrides? The Hebridean islands are exceeding remote, with much wildlife and weather and a negligible populace. This has some appeal. To the Hebrides? Oh where to now?

From the Hospital, Raphael will go to Bob's Chop House to begin with. There he will seek a pattern, a system; he might find a new shape in a bottle of claret. Meanwhile, he must ring the bell. He ought to ring the bell. Here at the Foundling Hospital in Lamb's Conduit Fields, there is certainly a system, so he is told. A system of kindness.

KINDNESS

Hogarth runs his hands through his no hair, leaving a smudge of ink at one temple and scatterings of minute copper filings across his bare pate. His friend

Coram teases that in some lights Hogarth shimmers like stars and like the elements—copper, silver, gold. Thomas Coram is bulldog-shaped and wears an oversized jemmy. He is renowned for his unguarded tongue, intrepid humanity and ready laughter, elemental indeed. And William Hogarth has seen him weep.

William works on Thomas's portrait throughout the Great Frost of 1739, the year George II grants the charter for the Hospital for the Maintenance and Education of exposed and deserted Young Children. In the Great Frost, Handel's opera cannot open for the cold in the house in Lincoln's Inn Fields, and Hogarth sees birds fall from the sky in frozen poses of flight and there are dreadful epidemics of influenza and pneumonia and innumerable cases of hypothermia. Trade, however, takes to the ice in a spirit of endeavour and resilience, the Thames becoming a makeshift marketplace and fairground despite the pall of death and disease. And Hogarth sees a boy beat a dog and it makes him sick at heart.

Snow can sometimes fall from a cloudless sky.

Good God, what have I done?

Thomas Coram sits on his bench in the courtyard of the Foundling Hospital in Lamb's Conduit Fields in the year 1750. His pockets are full of gingerbread and he takes his place with grace, though he is an exile in his own home, ousted from the board of governors in the very first year. He is an outcast, a castaway! Thomas sits on his bench and talks in his head. Eunice, his Prudent Wife, Quiet Spirit, has been dead these ten years.

Eunice, my wife, my dove, my dear! I am a castaway! Bah. He was never a man for committees. Nevertheless, he visits the children, is godfather to many. He stamps his feet, a little gouty now, not spry, no longer spry, and a buckle on one shoe flaps free—smack, smack—as he stamps to shake up the blood in his old sea-legs. His blood used to flow like a torrent. Thomas fiddles with the buckle on his shoe. He requires new shoes. Had he campaigned to defend the rights of cobblers as well as hatters, he might be kept in boots as well as hats until the end of days! Ha!

No. Thomas is not one for committees, but ever a man for campaigns. The English should not be mocked, undercut by cheap foreign hatters. Let them make fine hats to crown the English brow, in peace and fairness. Fairness is paramount, and usefulness likewise, and Thomas is not above going hat in hand, and on foot, walking ten or twelve miles daily as he once did to raise money and gather pledges for his Hospital. And look, Eunice, look! Here it is, my Foundling Hospital, with a Royal Charter, no less, for the protection of the Poor Miserable infant Children. My castaways.

Ah, Eunice, my dove, could you not have endured one year more, or eight months, indeed, if only to see the opening of my Hospital? How can I ask this of your spirit, when you were so long in bodily pain? And what a winter you would have seen, to begin! Colder than the Great Frost of '39! There was such ice on the Thames, floes of ice such as I have not seen since my ship-building days in Boston. Where we first met, my dearly beloved. Well, my dear! The people danced on the Thames and played at archery and cricket and there was a rough-hewn booth for exhibitions of boxing, with cudgelling also, and foil and backsword play—a tatterdemalion Figg's Academy! Birds dropped stiff from the sky that winter, Eunice, and many of the exposed and deserted perished in the streets and back slums.

And had you lived to see the mud and thawing ice that February of 1741, love, you would have heard from Hogarth about Broughton v. Stevenson! William is very enthusiastic for the Prize Ring. It appears that Jack Broughton felled George Stevenson—a Yorkshireman known as the Coachman—being a head-coachman, you see, by occupation. Hogarth recounted to me all the particulars.

George Stevenson suffers many blows to the nob, but fights on, delivering a rattler to Jack's proboscis and drawing the cork only moments before receiving a sledgehammer to the heart, the floorer, and when he is down, the claret splashes onto his phiz from Broughton's smeller as he bends low over the insensible Coachman, his great back forming an arc of concern, his famous shaven head pulsing with effort spent and shiny with sweat.

"Good God, what have I done?" Jack Broughton says. "I've killed him."

George Stevenson, the Coachman, retires to rooms above the Adam & Eve in Tottenham Court Road in that freezing February 1741 and he lingers one month, his victor attending him daily, the men forging a friendship in which is born a mind for change, a telling decision that will bring about a new system in the Prize Ring in the shape of Broughton's Rules of 1743. Jack reflects that it ought not to have taken the death of a man for the writing of rules to come about, but his thinking is hobbled by feeling. Truly, were it not for the Coachman's bottle and Broughton's blow to the heart, for their forged friendship and Broughton's kindness, for the death of this very man at the hands of that particular other, the Rules might not have come about. These are the dynamics of change.

As George lay dying in Broughton's corded arms, Jack thought of his twelve-year-old boy self and of his sister Rose, ten, yet he cannot tell why. Why? He recalls how he packed a small bag and took her hand in his and stumped it to Bristol not long after his grieving widowed father took to blue ruin and a new woman, leary and lushy. In Bristol, Jack worked as waterman and once his sister settled happily, he hurried for London and became Champion of England and Hogarth painted his likeness—as he did those of James Figg and Captain Thomas Coram. William Hogarth, plainly, felt a strange attraction for game fellows with bold bare pates and clear gazes akin to his own. Hogarth saw patterns everywhere.

Jack Broughton holds the dying Coachman in his arms and the reason he thinks of Rose, ten, and himself, twelve, is that the day he took her away with him is the first time he held a life in his hands and made a telling decision, and here he does so again. Every man has a part and a destiny, some stronger than others.

Dearly beloved wife, quiet shade, the Coachman died in Broughton's arms, as you died in mine. After forty years together. Eunice! Had you survived eight more months, until March of the year 1741, you would have seen the two first foundlings baptised in our names, Eunice and Thomas.

In sum, there has been much good and many advancements, but abuses likewise about which I have complained feelingly and angrily as will not surprise you. My manner cannot be helped and I have been expulsed from the committee, albeit with my complaints ringing in their ears, especially concerning certain nurses observed at Hatton Garden, our temporary premises, who are not fit for purpose, that is to say, regularly drunken—truly *castaway*, as the expression goes—on blue ruin, etc, etc. That is to say, gin. And so I am cast out, yet my portrait hangs there, as William did finish and donate it in March. It hangs eight feet by five feet, my dear, and it is very tremendous. It caused a stir, William having depicted me wig-less and in my old red jemmy, buttons undone on the waistcoat, and in my ageing buckled shoes with one foot dangling in a foolish posture, but they say it is very like! I am immensely pleased he has painted my hat to signify my endeavours on behalf of our fine hatters. This detail is most pleasing.

The kindness of Hogarth knows no bounds and he is still my neighbour in Leicester Fields, calling on me frequently. He has organised an annuity for myself, which is a godsend indeed.

Handel is also very good and very famous and raises copious funds for the Hospital and completion of the Chapel by way of performing concerts that prove uncommonly popular and which he conducts manfully in spite of suffering much weakness in the left eye. I am certain it is worsening steadily, though he perseveres without complaint and is unfailing vigorous and busy, even composing a song for the children of our—no—of *the* Hospital. This is the Foundling Hospital Anthem. The music is set to a psalm—"Blessed are they that considereth the poor and needy," so it begins. George is full of good works and William is very fine and ingenious, persuading his fellow artists to give paintings and designs for the benefit of our charity, by which token many are made Governors and take meetings regarding donations of art, etc., etc., whereupon great numbers come to see the works and attend performances and observe the children, inspiring polished society and other worthies to engage in charitable donations. All of which is of terrific consequence, and heartening. You see, my dove, the Hospital is, in sum, quite a hive of activity and good, despite certain obnoxious matters of administration with which I try to torture myself no longer.

It might perhaps be fair to remark, my dear, that much as in the making of a child—a blessing we never could count amongst our many—although one is responsible for its beginnings, one cannot quite command its every turn and eventuality. And so I view my—no, not mine own, *the*—Foundling Hospital, in this sanguine light, most especially when I am worn and vexed and out of sorts with living. I see things for the best and trust it to George and William and other like minds wherever they be, yes, I entrust it to Fate and Humanity.

I continue to witness baptisms and, do you know, Eunice? I am godfather to some twenty foundlings!

I am old and foolish now, and fond of sitting in the colonnade at Lamb's Conduit Fields—still unfinished, yet fine and plain and well-lit—within the large courtyard, an excellent situation for exercise and play with green spaces and fresh air beyond. I am able to observe the children and am very famous for the purveying of gingerbread! My old red coat is regularly stuffed with gingerbread and sweets and smelling so very much of pleasant things, I am very often followed home by stray dogs sniffing purposefully at my pockets and so, my dove, my dear, what with the children and the dogs, though I am profoundly bereft of thee and alone, I am very rarely unaccompanied.

I am exposed, not yet deserted.

Lamb's Conduit Fields, 1815.

Raphael is not troubled by weather until he stops at the gates of the Foundling Hospital. Now he feels the cold and rain like splinters, shards of freezing water stinging his neck and causing his ears and hands to ache, soaking his cuffs and collars and Kath's child in his arms. His arms are stiff with cradling the child and its few belongings: the brief note in effusive French written on a torn sheet of vellum, the drawings of fox, willow tree, bird and woman; and two other items, a gambling token in the shape of a fish carved from bone and a medallion bearing the head of Tsar Alexander I. These are the boy's sole belongings: along with the blanket and slip of calico round his body, punished by rain. Perhaps the child will die of cold and rain. Perhaps he will die before awareness comes of his origins and ensuing matters, namely Raphael's decision to forsake him.

Raph is certain that from the moment the child's eyes open they never stray from his physiognomy. He remembers them shut tight, two creases resembling cuts or the scars on his own digits, the chafing and striations of fingers well worn from the fashioning of violins.

It would surprise me if you ever make a finer instrument, Raphael! What a sound!

Raph feels a rush of heat in the vessels of his own eyes and a tightening of the nasal passages, and there is a terrible pain in his throat as if swallowing stone. He jabs wildly at the bell in Lamb's Conduit Fields and pulls at the child's sodden clothes in a sorry effort at grooming, but in the haste of ministrations, the bone-fish drops out of the swaddling to the slick paving beneath. Raphael scrabbles in the wet and darky to recover the item and there at his feet, still as any statuary, is *Rattus norvegicus*.

"Halloa, rat," he murmurs, but now the gates clang open and Raph gathers the fish, rising swiftly to thrust the baby at the greeting party of porter and servant and doctor. Take this boy from me. I cannot behold him any more.

"Come!" barks the doctor. "This way."

And still cradling the boy, Raphael hurries after them, their footsteps sharp, the procession military, into a small room where the Billet of Description is written, involving sparse remarks on health and aspect, age and sex.

"Ahh," notes the man of medicine, removing the child from the violin maker's arms. "A child of the Mosaic."

Against the description, a number is entered, and the tokens listed, all of these writings, observes Raphael, effected in a florid but tortured script, requiring untold dips of the pen and queries of infuriating pedantry and insignificance. Raphael hops from foot to foot and a lick of flame roars in his belly, rising to flush his neck and face. Lo! This must be it, he thinks, spontaneous combustion! I am to die of spontaneous combustion!

"A white fish," pens the assistant, holding the fish up to candlelight. "With a hole for an eye. Made of—"

"Bone," says Raphael. "What can it matter, indeed?"

"And a—medallion. Bearing a royal imprimatur."

"Tsar Alexander I," prompts Raphael, sighing deeply.

"I see. And a bundle of sketches. Do you mean us to keep these? A portrait of a woman . . ."

"My sister"—begins Raphael, snatching the paper away—"is dead!" he exclaims, pocketing the likeness. "Do keep the rest," he adds, waving the other pages at the spoffish scribe.

"And your name, sir?"

"I wish to remain anonymous!"

"And you are *not* the father, is this correct?"

"It is my sister's child! As I have explained! This is most vexing!"

"Ah," says the scribe, glancing at the doctor before returning to the weathered pages, clearly torn from a notebook. "One drawing of a fox," he recites in a tone of indifference, "and of a tree. Possibly willow."

"With thee," whispers Raphael.

"Sir?"

"Willow tree. Withy, willow stem. *With thee.* A willow . . ."

"Indeed," interjects the doctor. "Very good, very good!" he says, not unkindly, thinking, What a rum fellow!

When Raphael the violin maker is sent away with porter and servant, he murmurs apologies for his behaviour and exits in such intemperate haste, he forgets to glance back at the boy, his illegitimate nephew, and as he comes out of the gates and into the cold and rain, he utters an exclamation in a voice so strangled and full of hurt, neither porter nor servant can quite agree on the words.

"Good God," said Raphael. "What have I done? I've killed him!"

At Bob's Chop House, Holborn, Raphael sits in the open with his bottle of claret, there where he is most likely to be buffeted by the noise and shapes of men, of bruisers and bucks, scribes and the Fancy. He is in the vein for noise and buffeting. Here comes the landlord Bob Gregson, poet of the Prize Ring, a champion of Lancashire famed chiefly for his fortitude, a quality most conspicuous in his two losing contests against John Gully. Bob is prepossessing still, in appearance and mannerliness, yet failing presently at the business of tavern-keeping. He sails upon stormy waters.

Raph maps his own course for the future. He sails, in one instance, to the Hebrides, a tempestuous place with a negligible populace, which prospect appeals to him much, though there will unhappily be an insufficient call for violins. In the second instance, he repairs to his workshop to seek perfection, each instrument finer than the last, evidence of increasing skill and finesse. He has a mind to fashion frogs for his bows from Baltic amber. In the noise of Bob's Chop House, the violin maker's hopes are carefully wrought. He twitches, verily, with the impatience of great endeavour. More claret. Boy! Here! More claret.

Raphael will light out for home on this March night, stumping it first to Leicester Fields and his father's house, where he will weep in his mother's arms and Papa will offer it to him again, a career at the brewery and a seamless life of industry and prosperity and well-cut trousers and a change of high-lows according to the seasons, but young R. Solomon returns to Covent Garden instead, where he continues to fashion fine violins, some few very fine and beyond compare. He works until his eyes grow rheumy and oily so that he is perpetually blinking and his

digits ache and he breaks away from his tools to search the studio in a
dumb fever for something mislaid, though he cannot remember what.
He cannot tell what he is looking for. He is no longer quick, yet he is
not thirty years of age. It may be that he suffers from too many nightly
goes of scotch, of brandy, and pots of claret, or it may be merely the
mechanics of heartsickness that cause him to hold his fingers to his fluttering eyelids and behold the scarring and attenuation there, how he has
worked them to the bone, as the saying goes, to the bone from which
one might carve a fish, a gambling token with a hole for an eye.

Good God, what have I done?

Some fifteen years later, the twenty-year-old Felix Mendelssohn is in
London with a quartet and a head full of crashing waves and large
crying seabirds and other such images from a summer spent journey-
ing to Scotland, including the Inner and Outer Hebrides, separated by
the Minch. Felix walks. Pedestrianism is paramount for his health and
anatomy and his present condition of turbulence. He has never felt so
robust!

In New Row, Covent Garden, he enters R. Solomon's, where he
espies a remarkable instrument, desiring it keenly for his sister, but the
luthier will not sell, it being unfinished, he says, and quite imperfect
so far. The man has a high brow with long curling locks much like his
own, indeed, but his air is abstracted and his speech curious, the words
sparing and deliberate, signifying illness, perhaps, or deference to Mendelssohn's foreignness. He has noted it before in some persons here in
England, this manner of address in places of business, a heightened tone
of unusual courtesy and caution intermingled. This must be a quality
of Englishness, decides Felix. Everything is so interesting today! I am
robust in myself today!

Felix delights in the sight of a map on the wall, of Scotland with an
especial highlighting of the Hebrides, Inner and Outer, separated by
the Minch, and pinned to it, by means of a craftsman's nail, a fraying
pen-portrait of a pretty youth. No. A young lady. The sketch puts Felix
immediately in mind of his sister and how he must write to her directly
about this delightful coincidence of map on wall and map in head, and
the strange sensation of walking the streets of London and hearing the

calls of seabirds and the crashing of waves. He will tell her of the sad violin maker—*luthier*—and his not-for-sale violin, and of how robust he himself feels at present, in thew and sinew. He is immensely cheered and listens only vaguely to Raphael identify the portrait as being that of his own sister who lives, he explains, according to a fable of long standing, in the Hebrides with her son. He intends to join them, he adds, upon his retirement from the craft. She awaits him. They both await him.

"How curious!" exclaims Mendelssohn. "I have just come from there!"

"Oh," whispers Raphael.

"And I too have a sister!" Felix tells the violin maker, who turns away quite sharply, averting his fevered eyes.

Wait for me, Kath. Coming soon. I feel it in my bones.

Felix Mendelssohn is thirty-eight years of age when his sister Fanny dies aged forty-one, after which time Felix lingers barely five months in the world without her.

Fanny, wait! Wait for me.

{ EIGHTEEN }

Zach's hair grows very fast, thickening and curling as it lengthens, creating wave patterns in sleep or exertion, with crests and troughs. He has a fighter's hair, he goes twelve rounds in sleep. Rachel strokes it away from his temples and forehead.

"Byronic," she murmurs.

The closer I look, thinks Rachel, the more self-similar the view. Self-similar yet intricate, on the finest of scales. Imperfectly self-similar. Clouds, coastlines, waves, Zachariah's hair.

Rachel slips out of bed.

"Where are you going?" asks Zach. "Don't go."

"Back in a minute," she whispers, and crosses the hall to the studio.

Rachel parts the shutters at one window as soundlessly as possible and looks down at the street, glistening in the pools of lamplight from recent rain. It has been raining and Rachel cannot remember hearing it fall. She glances at the familiar swelling in the surface of the road at the end of the close, an irregularity she occasionally finds disturbing, as if an ogre slept beneath, causing the road to rise and fall with his breath. Why are things so ominous this night?

Rachel sits at her desk, shuffles papers, casts an eye in the early morning gloom over her unfinished sketch of Moscow, one of the endpapers for her book of Russian tales. A map is a pattern and full of clues.

Man builds a city. Take Peter the Great. He shaped a whole city and then it shaped him. Where does it end? The map of Moscow is a map of rings, as if the Kremlin and Red Square—*red* signifying "beautiful" in Old Russian—were a great stone cast into a pond creating concentric circles, rotational symmetry.

The brave war correspondent Kirill Simonov changed his name to Konstantin because his pronunciation of the letter "r" was aristocratic and suspect. He wrote a famous love poem inspired by the Battle of Moscow and it is later set to music and the song is much loved. It is called "Wait for Me." In that same terrible year of the Battle of Moscow, 1941, the poet Marina Tsvetaeva, sometime exile and a young widow, hanged herself, but not before cooking a fish in a pan for her son and leaving it on the hob. She was thoughtful. The frying pan is now a museum piece, which might have been interesting to Marina's late father, philologist and founder of the Moscow Museum of Fine Arts, a museum since renamed for Alexander Pushkin, another poet who died too young, knowingly ill-matched in a duel.

Rachel's approach to map-making is both scientific and chaotic. There will be seemingly random illustrations and insets, adding charm and curiosity to her work, though charm and intrigue are never her intention. In her map of Moscow, for instance, she draws a small boy with an aristocratic mien chasing a black dog on the outskirts of the city of enclosures and ever-widening circles. He shouts, "Wait for me!" And from a bridge on the Moscow River, a little girl with a name suggestive of boating and angling drops a long line with a wriggly worm on the end for the tempting of fish beneath. When Marina is grown and before she dies, she cooks a fish. Fish are partial to a diet of worms.

This is not a sweet skein of thought. Unthread it, Rachel.

Returning to bed, Rachel strokes Zachariah's black curls as he drifts into sleep and appreciates the shape and fractal geometry there, the self-similarity and infinity of scale. She breathes in at his scalp, then presses her ear to his, listening for the clamour of voices within, to the long line of fighting men who made him, his head a seashell. There is a template for the fighting man. Rachel listens across three times nine countries, as the fairy-tale saying goes, *across three times nine countries in the thirtieth tsardom . . .*

Distances to be travelled in Russian fairy tales are very tremendous and cannot be calculated in mere *verst*. In these tales, problems engender problems, eternal ones. Solutions to problems involve steps requiring skill and bottom to effect and, above all, the right set of precepts. There is a manual of instruction. Where there is, say, dismemberment of a lover, sister, brother or pet to resolve, rescue takes the shape of a quest. The rescuer will need water from two separate springs; the water-of-death spring and the water-of-life spring, and both springs are deeply hidden and very far away. How far? *Across three times nine countries.*

Once the springs are found, there are two distinct operations.

1. Sprinkle water of death over the pieces of body. Now it is whole.
2. Sprinkle water of life over the corpse. Now it is living.

Water is very important. And so are fish. Fish are very important. In Russian fairy tales, there is good and bad water to drink, and there is water of strength and water of transmogrification. Water of life and water of death. Vital items are regularly to be found at the bottom of the sea. And there are talking fish, of course, with special instructions to impart, wishes to heed and grant. There are clues everywhere in flora and fauna and the elements. Patterns are clues. Look and listen carefully! The pitfalls in fairy tales are various and prevalent, most typical being: kidnap, torture, starvation, beating, hideous death, transmogrification and cloning. Cloning is particularly nasty and often goes hand in hand with transmogrification. The three-body problem is rife in the Russian fairy tale. The lovers, the brother and sister, father and daughter, mother and son, all come up against something. Someone.

SISTER ALENUSHKA AND HER BROTHER IVANUSHKA

Alenushka and Ivanushka are orphans and set out on travels. Where shall we walk? Across the whole of the great wide world!

Ivan is young and a little impetuous and is suffering from thirst. Paying no mind to his sister Elena's words of warning, he drinks from the hoof-print of a sheep and, lo, turns into a little lamb. Luckily, the siblings meet a fine gentleman who loves Elena and her younger brother, even though he is now a lamb. He can tell they are inseparable and that is that. The fine gentleman marries Alenushka and adopts the lamb and the rapture of this household knows no bounds, inspiring the good-hearted, enraging the splenetic. One particularly bitter old trout pitches Elena into the river with a stone around her neck before assuming her victim's lovely shape, thanks to a spell. Now *she* is Alenushka, physically identical. She makes menu plans, beginning with lamb stew. The little lamb runs away and sings to the real Alenushka from the riverbank, his sister responding in song from beneath the waters.

> *Alenushka, little sister,*
> *They are going to slaughter me.*
> *They are bringing wood in faggots,*
> *They are heating up their saucepans,*
> *They are sharpening up their knives.*

> *Ivanushka, little brother,*
> *A heavy stone is round my throat.*
> *Silken weed clings round my fingers,*
> *Yellow sand lies on my breast.*

This plaintive song is overheard by a servant who apprises the fine gentleman of the terrible sad truth concerning his wife. The fine gentleman is not beat. He orders the river to be dragged with silken nets—no plain nets will do—and Alenushka resurfaces and is specially washed in fresh water, waking to fling her arms round the lamb who becomes boy once more, and grows into an upright fellow and a great hunter and marries the fine gentleman's own sister. When Alenushka is restored to even greater health and beauty than before her drowning, if that is even possible, her evil witch of a clone reverts to bitter old trout, uglier and nastier than before—if *that* is even possible. She runs screaming into the depths of the forest, which is, of course, a dangerous place.

Close the gate, Peter! If a wolf should come out of the forest, THEN what would you do?

Rachel hums into Zach's sleeping ear. She hums from *Peter and the Wolf.* She presses her own ear to Zachariah's, breathes in and out through the curls at the nape of his neck. She listens carefully, eyes shut, to his internal jugular vein playing a rhythmic sound against her cheek, like the skip of a rope, the tick of a metronome, the flap of great wings. There are patterns everywhere. Where does it all begin?

It all begins with the boy. Watch the boy.

Once there were two children. The girl was called Rose and the boy, Jack. When their mother dies, their father remarries and the woman is a witch, a hag, a bitter old trout. The man and the woman go *on the mop*, *foxed* the live-long day on beer and gin, and as Rose stands weeping, Jack takes her by the hand and heads out of the village on travels across the whole of the great wide world, calling at: Bristol. Destination: London. In London, Jack becomes Champion of All England, a man of power. *Bogatyr.* Along the road there, it rains and rains, and rain is melting ice, made up of crystals with sixfold symmetry.

Once there were two children. The girl was called Fanny and the boy, Felix. Felix writes music for his musical sister Fanny, for whom he feels a strange attraction. The boy sings to his sister, who responds in song.

Once there were two children. The girl was called Rachel and . . .

A wolf's sense of hearing is remarkably acute. A wolf can detect another's howl from as far as nineteen kilometres away.

When Rachel is taken to St. Petersburg before her first term at St. Martin's School of Art, she returns to note a change in Zach, how taciturn he is, elusive, indeed, no longer creeping into her room at night to chaff and chaunt. He trains late at the gym in the evenings and disappears for days on boxing club tournaments. At home, he buries his nose in *Wisden* at breakfast, or old copies of *The Ring*, his Manual of Carpentry and Joinery, or volumes of Dickens and Pierce Egan's *Boxiana*. When Rachel comes home early from a weekend away at a girlfriend's, she looks for her brother, finding him fast asleep on his bed, bare-chested, his ramshackle copy of *Robinson Crusoe, The Life and Strange Surprizing Adventures* on the floor beneath his dangling fives. She has missed him, she knows, and is disturbed by his beauty, increasingly Byronic, the curls lustrous, his epidermis taut and muscular, his eyes, whenever they do meet hers in this, his distant phase, an incandescent blue.

Sensing her presence, his eyes snap open and he watches her a moment without otherwise moving a muscle.

"I find it—hard—to be near you," he says slowly and softly. "I find it hard, very hard, to look at you. I can't—you have to—please—go away," he adds, burying his face in his book.

When he is on the eve of entering the novice championships, Lev, too, is disturbed by Zachariah, for other reasons. Lev is wracked by disapproval.

"It's primitive," he pronounces one night at table. "Educated boys do not box for a living. What are you thinking, what on earth will you do?"

He will have *Strange Surprizing Adventures*, thinks Rachel as Zachariah dips his head and mumbles something to do with the Gloves and the ABA—Amateur Boxing Association—and plucks a bone from his fish stew quite openly, as he would not do had Katya cooked the offending dish.

"*Shto vy skazali?*" asks Lev. What did you say? "The mammalian ear is many millions of years old, and though man may only have been speaking for one hundred thousand of those, one might expect my son to have caught on!"

"Papa!" says Rachel, stricken.

"Lev, don't," Katya demands coolly, knowing his unkindness to be aimed at her, bags packed again, this time for a short tour to Reykjavik and Oslo. Tomorrow she will perch briefly on her suitcase and watch Lev's sad still features.

"There are bones," Zach explains, rising. "Fish bones. In the stew. Do you hear me now?"

"I will not support you in a boxing career," states Lev. "I will not. And if you don't like the food here, you can fend for yourself. I don't know what has happened to you! Your manners are . . . And I will not let you box! Like a savage!"

"Let no one sneer—" Rachel intones ever so quietly once Zach departs, banging the dining room door, taking the stairs in bounds.

"—AT THE BRUISERS OF ENGLAND!" he yells from the stairwell, and Rachel smiles.

Later on that night of the fish stew with parsley, when Lev sneered at his son and Zach complained of bones, Katya goes about finishing her arrangements for Oslo and Reykjavik, and Rachel, poring over the pages of her souvenir book on Russian wildlife, its flora and fauna and extravagant places, hears the once very familiar scratching at her bedroom door and lets her brother in. His breathing is irregular, and colour high.

He enters the room halfway as she climbs back under the covers and he lays an overstuffed cricket kitbag on the floor without the typical clatter. He holds his favourite chukka boots by the ankle loops and is wearing his best coat, a camel-coloured Montgomery duffel, toggles undone, and pockets overstuffed.

"Have you just come home? Or are you going out? It's so late," she remarks warily, heart and head racing. Impulses of the brain, muscle fibres in the heart, she recites to herself. Periodic cycle, rhythm, oscillation, chaotic system.

—*What is an oscillator, Rachel? Why oscillate?*
—*When you need to move, but cannot escape.*
—*Example?*
—*A beating heart, a plucked violin string. Fighter in the ring, pacing wolf.*
—*Good.*

Zach places his boots by the kitbag, takes a step or two further into the room.

"Going, Rach. I'm going, I have to. Need to."

"Dance! You're gonna dance!"

"Rachel?"

"Ali. Like Muhammad Ali."

"Yeah, I know, but . . ."

"It's all right. I'm being silly. Where are you going? Where will you go?"

"Tasha and Nicky's first. I have keys. Then we'll see. I know some chaps in flats. Who could use a roomie, I mean. One in Harlesden, one in Holloway. And one in Battersea. It's all good. I have a sponsor, you know," he adds, kneeling by the bed. "For the Gloves. And there's a boxer I met. Always at the gym. He's had a few fights already, but works for a chippie. Said he can get me some work. He's done all sorts, restoration, sets for films and theatre and stuff. Not just crap work, joe jobs. Master carpenter, this bloke. And hey," Zach says with a small laugh, "I'm cool. Caught his eye. I'm advantaged, you know. I box, but speak in full sentences."

"Sometimes," she says.

"Sometimes, yeah," Zach chortles. "Anyway. Guy says I could be apprenticed no problem. I like him. He has a huge tattoo on his back. Raven in flight."

"Oh," whispers Rachel. "I see. You've thought about this a long time, haven't you? And never said."

"It doesn't matter. How long. Telling you now."

"Does," objects Rachel, "it does matter. And you've been so horrid lately. Ever since St. Petersburg."

"Rachel," he says, hanging his head.

"Well!" she adds merrily. "We'll have to put you in the beehive, won't we? Shan't we, I mean. In our Boxiana Bee Hive. Remember?"

"Course I bloody remember," says Zach very softly.

In their early teens, studying volumes of Pierce Egan's *Boxiana* and Vincent Dowling's *Fistiana,* John Ford's *Prizefighting,* J. C. Reid's *Bucks and Bruisers,* Mendoza's memoirs and other favourites, Zachariah and Rachel become amateurs of the times, noting all things from a boxer's beginnings to his classically early end. Zachariah logs the number of rounds in momentous battles, memorises Broughton's Rules and can rattle off even the previous occupations of boys turned bruisers, the number and variety of which astonish brother and sister, absorbed by the particularity of the professions, the abstruseness. *Skinman, oyster-seller, swan-tender.*

Rachel delights especially in the artwork of the era, in Hogarth, the Cruikshanks, Gillray and Rowlandson, so very animated, lusty, indeed, and when she and Zach come across *The British Bee Hive* by Cruikshank, George, she decides to draw one of her own, filling in each compartment of the honeycomb with a boxer at work in his previous occupation, making up for George's omissions, the necessarily narrow focus in his paean to Empire.

Cruikshank's hive of Empire is founded upon the "Bank of the richest Country in the World," flanked by Army and Navy, professional and mercantile. Above come three layers of workaday occupations, each character depicted in industrious postures under little archways separated by pillars. As the hive tapers towards the top, there is "Agriculture and Free Trade," with "Invention" and "Mechanics" and girl and boy apprentices. Next comes "Education," flanked by "Art" and the sciences, and aloft, the "Free Press," "Freedom to all Religious Denominations" and "Law & Equity," with "The British Constitution" as the penultimate layer of the honeycomb. At the apex, beneath the dome, are the "Queen" and "Royal Family by Lineal Descent." Behold Victoria, in the third year of her reign. Cruikshank designs the *Bee Hive* in 1840, altering it as late as 1867, fretting, Rachel fancies, about his omissions.

"Where are the sportsmen?" Zach protests. "No cricketer, no pedestrian, no jockey! I can understand the no boxer thing. Illegal and so on. But it would be truer, wouldn't it, Rach? Otherwise, it's just advertising."

"I think it *is* advertising," Rachel says. "At heart. Why else no graveyard charley? No peeler? No ratcatcher, tosher, night-soilman. Pawnbroker."

"*Tosher.* I always forget that one! What's the distinction?"

"Like bone-grubber and cinder-sifter, but a tosher searches for things in drains and sewers," explains Rachel. "Valuables."

"Damn! Yeah yeah, of course. And know what? There ought to be animals in the beehive," adds Zach. "A ratting dog, ratter. A bird-dog, foxhound, carriage horse, hawk. Plough horse, war horse, all that."

"True. And where are the women? There's only a dairymaid, and girls and women doing something anomalous at a table . . . seamstresses, probably."

"That's not surprising, Rach. For the times."

"I know. Still. It's not realistic. It really is advertising. Rah rah for Empire! Where are the workhouses, pawnshops, debtors' prison, hulks? Foundling home?"

"You'll have to do your own, then. Rachel's Bee Hive."

And so she does. It takes months.

For reasons of sentiment, Rachel sets Jem Belcher in the monarch's place at the apex, Jem with his dog Trusty. Rachel's Royal Family consists of as many favourites as she can draw in the space, the Toms Spring, Cribb, Belcher and Hickman, then Hen Pearce, John Gully, Daniel Mendoza and Young Dutch Sam.

Beneath are the professions, the job titles reading, says Zach, like a song. Butcher, baker, potboy, clown!

"Young Rumpsteak" Crawley—butcher! Jack "Master of the Rolls" Martin—baker! And street-porter, shoemaker, engine-worker, preacher, publican, jack. River-man, caulker, plumber, whip-maker, oilman, navigator, game-keeper, brick-maker, bricklayer, docker, coal-heaver, clown. Carpenter, bell-hanger, coppersmith, rose-gardener, sailor, waterman, skiver. Ostler, glass-blower, costermonger, swan-tender, button-, basket- and mattress-maker. Apprentice engraver, coachmaker, printer. Iron merchant, fiddler, potboy, oyster-seller, rope-spinner, barge-worker, cabman!

At the foundations, Rachel draws Newgate, the Marshalsea, a hulk, a pawnshop, and a little cart with cholera victims. In the centre, after Hogarth, she sketches the gates of Coram's Foundling Hospital for the Education and Maintenance of exposed and deserted Young Children. By the gates, she draws two small boys, one with uneven limbs and a leg brace, the other with dark curly hair. Lastly, she draws a rat at their feet, *Rattus norvegicus*. He is clearly benign.

This is Rachel's *Boxiana Bee Hive*.

"It was fun, the *Boxiana Bee Hive*, wasn't it?"

"Yeah," answers Zach. "It really was. You did most of it, though."

"Well," repeats Rachel. "You'll definitely have to go in the *Hive*. Apprentice carpenter, and boxer."

"Oh look!" Zach says suddenly. "Mustn't forget."

He forages in a pocket of his duffel, first extracting a scarf he loops quickly round his neck in a Chelsea knot. then the envelope stuffed deeper within, smoothing its creases against Rachel's mattress. "For Katya."

"You can say 'Mama.'"

"Come with me. Rachel. Live with me. Come."

"Mama will be so cross," she begins, sitting up against the bedstead and sliding over to make room for him, quite naturally, as she has done for years. Though not lately. Not since St. Petersburg. "With Tasha, I mean. If you go there to stay."

"She won't," he replies, slipping out of his duffel to settle by her, "She's never cross with Tasha. Not for more than half a minute. Mama with Tasha!" he exclaims. "She's always so—"

"You said 'Mama.'"

"She's always—"

"Soft?" Rachel suggests.

"Something. Yes, soft. Different. When she's with Tasha."

"She's soft with you," says Rachel.

"Sometimes. Not for a while. Not for ages."

"Mama's tired. More than usual. I've noticed. Haven't you?"

"You're always defending them," frowns Zach, removing Rachel's large hard book of Russian wildlife from between them and dropping it to the floor. "Fuck. Noisy. They'll know I'm in here."

"They always know when you're in here, Zach. And that you're always in here."

"Really?" he asks, somewhat astonished.

"Yes," states Rachel. "Really. Aren't you hot?" she adds, twisting at the hips to untie the scarf from Zach's neck coloured bird's-eye blue, Bristolian blue, a proper belcher to honour their idol, the dashing Jem, Champion of All England in 1800 and interred at Marylebone eleven years later, aged thirty. Jem Belcher died one-eyed, depressed and fretful, tubercular, ulcerated, reduced and revered, *universally regretted by all who knew him*. When his coffin was lowered to the ground, a fighter named Wood leapt in, his tears copious.

"Belcher," she says.

"James Belcher," Zach intones. "Of pugilistic celebrity! His sister boxed, you know. I love that."

"She had one prize fight lasting fifty minutes," says Rachel. "Did she win, though? I can't remember. I do remember the fifty minutes. Anyway. What I was thinking about before—was the magic handkerchief."

Zach takes the scarf from his sister. He flaps it three times to the right and asks, "Ready? Ride with me! I always loved that magic hanky tale! Do anything with a magic handkerchief. Raise a bridge, collapse a bridge, cross the River of Fire. Make your horse fly, anything. Which fairy tale was it?"

"*Marya Morevna.*"

"That's the one! Ride with me," repeats Zach, flapping his scarf.

"No, Zach. Not yet," she answers, grasping his fists. "Not yet. Let me finish school. Zachariah. I need to finish. I need to do that."

He rises off the bed and tries to speak, but cannot stop the pain in his throat, and cannot articulate a word, capable only of an animal sound, a strangulated wheeze that shocks him deeply, enraging him, this sudden loss of the faculty of speech that feels somehow bestial and low.

"It will be all right," says Rachel as he pulls on his Montgomery in such agitation the collar ends up in a twisted lump at the back of his neck. Taking his scarf from her, he begins to tie his belcher, hesitantly, not able to bear her scrutiny and, fearing his dexterity might desert him, he leans across the bed and wraps it swiftly round her bedpost. He ties his fogles to the ring.

Rachel slips off the bed and stands before him to rearrange his collar, aware that in this small gesture there is a quality acutely other than motherly, sisterly, companionable, and that, in this moment, everything ever intended for her, for them, has begun, that the beginning is in the rearrangement of his collar and not the first kiss they share now, Zach recovering his wind as quickly as he lost it, a Great Northern Diver resurfacing. Zach clasps his hands round her ears, steps into her body and breathes the very air from her lungs. His teeth scrape against hers and he rests his open mouth against her face, gasping for air, his eyes squeezed shut as in great pain. And Rachel and Zachariah are born. Now truly they are born.

"Zachariah, Zachariah," whispers Rachel. "My fighting man."

{ NINETEEN }

You are placed out Apprentice by the Governors of this Hospital. You were taken into it very young, quite helpless, forsaken and deserted by Parents and Friends. Out of charity have you been fed, clothed, and instructed; which many have wanted.

Sam the Russian has arisen from his brush with cholera and the Battle of Seven Dials an even gamer fellow than before, if that is even possible, albeit with loss of hearing in one auricular. He is changed. He knows that in his fevered sleep, he dreamed much of his beginnings and his dreams were filled with sights and sounds and smells from different times and places as if all the boys he has been, the infant, the child, the young man, played together at once in his head! Remembrance is so physical! The new pains in his ear recalled earlier pains and the winter of his tenth year, a year of prodigious frost in which Sam was apprenticed to an ostler in Kent. Jones the Apothecary says there have been many great freezes in the country and Frost Fairs in London upon the Thames itself. He says that ice is a transformation of snow and each snowflake has sixfold symmetry. Everything connects!

In the great freeze, Sam misses Jonah the Needle, apprenticed to a tailor in London. Jonah is still *within the stones.* Sam foresees a return to London where his father left him and might well seek him when he has finished with the great business of wars he is surely attending to. A man deposited me here, so I am told, and he shall return. My father will know me.

I smell the smell of a Russian soul.

In the prodigious frost, Sam suffers acute pain in his ears, especially when moving from the cold without to the warm within. He is amazed to hear a great humming and scraping in his auriculars and to undergo a sudden loss of physical balance, tears of discomfort and frustration springing to his eyes, shaming him. Lottie the ostler's wife applies wasp weed and administers infusions and, though these have no effect whatsoever, Lottie smells so much like firewood, bridle leather, ale and cheese and roast potatoes with goose fat and parsley, Sam forgets the pain and the strange sound only he can hear, a sound akin to the scraping of violins.

Samuel Alexander remembers violins from the Hospital, and singing, which they were all taught in the name of Handel whose living legacy to the Hospital is music and singing and funds raised by concerts for the building in Lamb's Conduit Fields with its two wings and chapel and arcaded walkways and courtyard facing south. Girls sleep in the east wing and boys in the west, two by two in a bed. Sam and Jonah slept side by side, one athletic in his limbs, the other uneven. This is the first place of Sam's recollections.

When the boys were given instruments according to the size and shape of their hands and length of their fingers, Jonah the Needle, despite his shortcomings, played the violin for the grace and nimbleness of his digits whereas Sam played the horn, due to his reach and wind. He played it manfully, yet poorly, and was removed from the orchestra.

Sam the Russian remembers music from his years in Lamb's Conduit Fields, but he does not remember Raphael the violin maker who carried him there. As he falls asleep with this new scraping and humming in his ears, he does, however, dream sometimes of strings, of saddle, tail piece, scroll and bridge, of sound post, purfling, neck and ribs. Sam dreams he is a violin.

Sam the Russian emerges from his brush with cholera and the Battle of Seven Dials as more than the confluence of the parts he has played in his short life, of all the boys he has been in different times and places. He has come back from the verge of nevermore and is changed forever, and not just for the new bumps and scars upon his young head, bumps with a story to tell. I am a boxer! Yes, Sam has a calling now and a destiny and, day by day, gains in fortitude and definition, further moved to emotion by his bosom friends and further restored to vigour in thew and sinew.

Tom Spring resumes Sam's training with greater purpose and resolution, because Young Dutch has proposed a bout of sparring in advance of Sam's formally entering the lists upon the occasion of their keenly anticipated encounter. Young Dutch is allowing, says he, for Sam Alexander's inexperience and inferior years, conceding some seven years, as he does, to Sam Evans, born Elias, seven years of age and thirteen pounds of weight. Young Dutch, furthermore, can boast seven years of boxing already behind him and not a single loss against his name.

"This is Sam's novitiate," declares Young Dutch. "I accept his challenge, but let us set to initially, unofficially, with the mufflers. I do not want to kill thee, Sam!" he adds, immensely satisfied with his own humanity.

Wherever Sam and Jonah go, observes Tom Spring, wherever they go since Sam's recovery, *Rattus norvegicus* follows. A rum situation. Jonah the Needle, apprentice tailor—one of the cutting-up tribe—follows Sam and Rat follows Jonah. Often in tow, also, is "A Miller," the young swell in the green fanteegs, one of the black-letter gentry presently making a study of Samuel and the noble art of self-defence. A Miller poses as a young gentleman and passes as such to the unobservant. This is very curious because there is not a mark or furrow on the scribe's gentle phiz, this corinthian being the finest-formed of persons, delicate as any angelic, which indeed she is. Miss Miller prefers disguise and her pretence is sustained in their midst as far as conscience will allow, though the most select seat in Tom's parlour at the Castle, Holborn, is reserved for her pleasing anatomy, and in spite of her vigorous protestations.

Sam the Russian is often attended by young Dickens, another scribe— a parliamentary reporter and amateur thespian. Dickens is always in a very great fever, though a splendid gill and bang up, in sum, what with his coloured waistcoats and florid belchers and spirited chaff.

"A glass of hock, if you please, Mr. Spring!" demands Dickens manfully, a high colour in his cheeks, recalling to himself, in the instant, how he strode into a tavern in Parliament Street at twelve years of age, nearly a lifetime hence, to order his first pint of bub, piping stoutly, *A glass of Genuine Stunning!*

And finally, there is Jones the Apothecary, a regular now at the Castle and increasing fond of Sam and so very much interested in his education, he is often seen examining not only the pages of learned medical tomes and periodicals, but the pages of *Bell's Life in London, and Sporting Chronicle*. Here he is this evening perusing last November's issue of the *Lancet* in which it is noted, quoth he, that in Vienna the Jewish community of Wiesnitz escaped decimation by cholera by way of a rub, a liniment containing wine, vinegar, camphor powder, mustard, pepper, garlic and ground beetles.

"Very interesting," he muses to no person in particular, raising his glass of port. "But are they drinking the *water*?' he queries with an expression of consternation. Jones has a terrible presentiment about water. The *graveyard odours* contained therein.

"Sam," Jones will remark, perched in Tom's parlour, "is of superior scientific fascination to me, Spring. Superior fascination! Why, he dealt death a hot one in eluding the cholera! A winder! A bodier, cross-buttock!"

"Jones," states Spring. "You have the true whiz of the Fancy. The vernacular. Very sporting, very stylish."

"I thank you, Tom."

As Spring spars with his apprentice, his adopted—*my son*, he thinks—he wonders at it, how this is only Sam's novitiate and look, see what a following already! And on the day he beats Young Dutch, of which Tom has no doubt he shall, only imagine the triumphant procession!

THE ADOPTION OF RAT

Rattus norvegicus is largely nocturnal. He has adjusted his biorhythmic clock in honour of Sam the Russian and Jonah the Needle, who are largely diurnal. Sam and Jonah exhibited infinite kindness and ingenuity in restoring him to health while he lay ailing, stomach to the skies and eyes rolling in his poor head, suffering terribly from that surfeit of farrier's oils, opodeldoc and Dover's powders, and dreaming fitfully in his fevers of his forebears swimming the Volga in hordes over a century ago, travelling by ship to Denmark and England. Jonah's rat is a true-born English rat, hardy and courageous, and very distinguished in the hunt.

Were it not for his fortuitous hunting skills, he may never have made the acquaintance of Jonah and Sam, with whom he is now a bosom friend.

When Spring and Jones were engaged in the nursing of Samuel, tending his wounds and calming the fevers, Jonah the Needle searched the pawnshops of St. Giles and environs for the medallion of Tsar Alexander I, convinced as he was that after the kyeboshing in Seven Dials, Sam's token will have gone up the spout, and wherever he roamed, he was keenly aware of being shadowed. Wherever he searched, a brown rat followed, stopping where he stopped, moving where he moved, until Jonah turned to face the creature, which stood its ground without flinching. Rat, he recalls, was very still, quite unlike any rat of Jonah's experience.

"Halloa, Rat!" said Jonah, and on he searched, very nimble and quick despite his irregular understandings.

Jonah examined every cobble of the battleground, the loosened paving stones, the drains and troughs, lest the medallion slipped from Sam's neck or the thief's grasp at the Battle of Seven Dials. It was an insalubrious task, and seeming fruitless, until one afternoon when Rat disappeared along a sewer to resurface gnawing happily on a shining disc, somewhat tarnished, and bearing the impression of Tsar Alexander I. Rat gnawed not in order to limit the growth of his incisors according to legend—a rat fallacy and one of many—but for the sheer delight of the champ.

Rattus norvegicus chewed away until the force of Jonah's gaze compelled him to let it fall. Rat let it fall and took one step back, out of respect and obeisance.

"Well done, Rat! Good hunting. You have covered yourself in glory. Hurrah hurrah! How tremendous!"

Sam the Russian was exceedingly pleased upon Jonah and Rat's return and fingered the medallion in his sickbed with especial intensity, the token he will not lose again, not ever. He pays no mind to the scratches and dents effected by the turn-up in Seven Dials and the irrepressible teething of Rat. These are battle scars, he reflected, such as his own father bears, no doubt, wounds of Russia's war against Napoleon, a Russian war and an English one also.

During Sam's convalescence, Rat made himself at home, racing round the boy's attic room by skirting the walls before circumnavigating the bed and settling at Sam's feet, not unlike a dog. *Rattus norvegicus* is *thigmophilic*—touch-loving. He has a feeling for place and he has muscle memory. Rat has a feeling for place, for where he has travelled and for where he finds himself presently, which is to say, he has a sense of history and this is how he recovered the medallion of Tsar Alexander I, monarch of his ancestral nest by the banks of the Volga. Rat is educated in history, but lacks discrimination when it comes to comestibles, and this is how he was nearly put to bed with a shovel due to a surfeit of farrier's oils, opodeldoc and Dover's powders from Tom Spring's medicine chest.

The Healing of Rat

Sam Alexander studies the *Account of Mr. Broad's Method of Attracting Rats and Mice, Taking Them Alive and Ensuring their Destruction,* finding it amongst the papers and pamphlets and penny sheets in Tom's parlour at the Castle, gleaning that embrocations for the attracting of rats *within* traps will surely attract them *without.*

"The materials for attracting rats," he reads aloud, "are, *First,* the oil of carraways; and, *Second,* good pale malt, ground for brewing, and not discoloured in the drying."

There follow many intricate instructions regarding the proper proportion of oil to malt ("about 1 to 9,000") and preparations involving half pints of malt liquor and the application of oil onto the palms with subsequent rubbing and massaging of malt, etc., etc. "Much accuracy is here necessary," warns Mr. Broad.

Sam and Jonah arrange a truss of straw and place in it a receptacle containing bread and ale, and hope for the best possible outcome. They consider a second recipe, with the intention, quite simply, of omitting the mortiferous ingredient:

"Take a quart of oatmeal, two ounces of pounded sugar, four drops of oil of rhodium (rhodia rosea. Lin.); four drops of oil of carraway (carum carria. Lin.); four drops of oil of anniseed; a quarter of a grain of musk; one ounce of fenegrate (fenugrec, or fœnum grecum). Mix these altogether, and put some of the mixture on a board, in a place where Rats resort; let them feed on this for four nights, and when they appear accustomed to it, take half an ounce of arsenic, finely powdered, and mix it with the other ingredients."

After close perusal of the above recipe, Samuel and Jonah decide instead to mix oatmeal and sugar and whatever restorative oils they find, courtesy of Jones the Apothecary, adding ale for good measure and blending purposes. They make sure no other person but themselves touches the truss of straw and receptacles, Mr. Broad having helpfully instructed that "animals of many kinds probably distinguish individuals of the human species, from each other, by their scent and smell: and that rats, after part of their number have disappeared, will sometimes take alarm at a stranger," meaning, as Jonah gathers, that if too many persons handle the instruments, in this case, of succour not murder, Rat's suspicions will be aroused. He will make the association between appealing mixtures and the strange and surprising decline in numbers of his rat family and acquaintance and refuse to partake of the mixture. Rat will sniff a rat. *Fee-fi-fo-fum, I smell the blood of an Englishman.*

Jonah reads that "animals have generally powers of conveying their apprehensions of danger to each other," though not in the particulars. Broad writes that they can in no wise communicate the shape of this danger nor the guise of the enemy.

So you assume, Mr. Broad, thinks Jonah, who has an unusually high opinion of the prescience and wisdom of animals and their powers of communication.

Sam the Russian and Jonah the Needle take pride in the restoration of *Rattus norvegicus,* most especially in the manner in which they adapt a method of *Attracting Rats and Ensuring their Destruction* into a method of Attracting Rats and Ensuring their Restoration. The foundling boys are blessed with ingenuity and enterprise where the fighting spirit is concerned. They remember their beginnings.

When Rat is hale again and vigorous in his limbs, he joins the party for the match of sparring at Finchley Common. Henceforward he will never willingly be parted from Jonah and Sam, his bosom friends. Not ever.

[TWENTY]

Finchley Common, Middlesex, 1832.

Tom Spring has the hire of a carriage on the day of the ride to Finchley Common, where he will find some wooded area of parkland and stage the session of sparring between Young Dutch Sam and Sam the Russian. He is filled with emotion on this day, recalling his own youthful introduction to the great sporting world in a sparring match at Mordiford in 1814 by the rivers Wye and Lugg in the far-off shadow of Hereford cathedral where he beat John "the Hammer" Hollands before the very eyes of the Champion of All England, Tom Cribb.

"Come to London," said Cribb, "and I will bring you up by hand. I will make you my heir."

And here, eighteen years later, is Sam, Spring's own heir, watering the horse after their journey and nosing the withers, smoothing the beast's flank and murmuring endearments for all the world as if he were a horse himself. Perhaps Sam is recalling his days as ostler's apprentice and then his days as waterboy at the White Horse Cellar where Tom Spring, ex-Champion of All England, discovered the boy one icy night battling two swells with sticks, and conducting himself most manfully, despite the odds.

"What a bunch of fives!" his friend Dickens is wont to comment with reference to that occasion, adopting a theatrical air. And Sam will smile at his fanciful friend, displaying a great fondness and indulgence beyond his years.

Spring is very full of emotion this morning, and agitated, but he takes a moment to wonder at it, how recollection connects to recollection, each to each, as links in a chain.

Spring was famous for endurance in the ring, possessing an uncommon ability to withstand pain and discomfort, fighting, in one instance, with broken hands. Spring was famous also for the weakness of his hands and their proneness to swelling and, in point of strength, he was famous also for lack of a punch. And yet, thinks Tom. And yet. *Lady's maid fighter,* they called him. *Light tapper, powder-puff.* And yet they still talk of it, his two final bouts he won to universal astonishment, the first great battle against Jack Langan in January 1824 and the return in June, both together amounting to some four hours and eighteen minutes of milling over 153 rounds, and both of them victories, epic in nature. Tom has always been a modest man, known for his humanity and even temper within and without the ring, but he recalls this with increasing pleasure, how the "Commander-in-Chief" himself, Gentleman John Jackson, cried out in admiration of his skills in only round three of the return, watching Spring move deftly on his merry, dancing feet.

"Beautiful!" he exclaimed.

Beautiful!

For this his last fight, Tom Cribb was chief second and tied Spring's fogles to the rail, and all the upper customers were in attendance, the Lords Lowther, Uxbridge, Fife and others, and Colonel Berkeley and the Dukes of Beaufort and Rutland and the boxers, the Toms Oliver and Shelton, and Jem Burn, and the Jacks Martin "Master of the Rolls," Randall "the Nonpareil" and Scroggins, oh, and Ned "Flatnose" Painter and Gully, yes, John Gully, ex-champion and once of queer street. And now, in 1832, Gully is M.P. for Pontrefact and winner of the Derby with his own horse named St. Giles! In 1824, Gully was at ringside for Tom's last fight when, notwithstanding his two broken fists, Spring floored Langan, the lion-hearted Jack.

At the close, Spring recalls, his backer swore he had never seen such hands.

"If you fight again, I will never speak to you," he declares.

"Sir," replied Spring, mindful not so much of his battered mauleys, but the knowledge he will not attain greater fistic perfection than on this day, "sir," said he, "I will never fight again."

Ah, Sam, sighs Tom Spring to himself. These are *your* beginnings. And in your beginnings, my end! Oh how the recollections connect, each to each, as links in a chain!

Spring marks out a ring. He is rope and stake man, allowing Jonah to assume his usual task of applying the rub to Sam's face and torso. He assumes the task with gravity and vigour, showing fierce pride in his friend. The boy has a singular candour of mind and, for a fellow with such unfortunate shortcomings of physique, possesses uncommon grace and power in those uneven limbs.

Rat sits up on his hindquarters, eyeing the proceedings. Rat is time-keeper.

Tom ponders a brief peroration for his man as he watches Jonah's industrious application of oils and camphor to Sam's body, of oils and camphor and other special ingredients according to the new recipe devised by Jones the Apothecary for the invigorating, says he, of muscles and sinews and the preventing of unnecessary bruising and slicing. Jones is bottle-holder and referee.

In truth, Tom is increasingly doubtful regarding the merits of this unofficial pugilistic encounter in advance of the official set-to. With mufflers on, this preliminary mill is little more than a mock-battle, and for the benefit and education of Sam the Russian, if Young Dutch is to be taken at his word. The benefits strike Tom as uncertain. Sam the Russian has issued a formal challenge to Young Dutch upon the latter's own urging, this battle to take place in the near future and to be governed by the Rules of the London Prize Ring. But today there will be no squaring of the magistrate required, no stake-holders, nor backers, and no hedging and placing of bets on first blood, first down, or victory. There is no contract, nor flash money. Spring cannot deduce the purpose of the contest.

Tom marvels at how different a son can be from the father!

Dutch Sam, Young Dutch's sire, was once tempted with a large sum of £1,000 to throw a fight. Yet this hero of the Mosaic, inventor of the uppercut, a cove who trained on three times three goes of gin a day, would not fight a cross and disclosed the affair. Tom Spring has instructed the Russian in the art of the uppercut, the blow being eminently effective in a clinch. Though Dutch Sam died dished and with-out a feather to fly with, his legacy is eminent. Dutch Sam invented the uppercut. He also bequeathed to the nation a son.

Young Dutch cuts a swell. He is not quite the trump his father was and neither does he possess his punch, but he has speed and superior boxing ability and, while his character is marked by high spirits and cheerfulness, he has an unfortunate disposition to engage in larks in the company of the more reckless and wanton sprigs of nobility, where-upon he is prone to occasional violence of temper. He is a tinder-box, in sum, and shrewd. A little *smoky*.

Young Dutch courts the well-breeched and is togged, at all times, like a buck. He will come rattling by in a flash drag, no doubt, with an upper customer or two to mix with, though he says he requires no seconds, emphasising that this is a mock-encounter, mere sparring practice with mufflers on and not a true fight!

Tom is doubtful.

Sparring with the mufflers makes the mill lawful, but a man may hit very hard with pillows on and aim most of the blows to the head for there is less fear of damage to his covered hands. If Young Dutch ham-mers my boy in the grubbery, he might drop his guard. And be floored by a facer. No, no. This may be Samuel Alexander's novitiate, but he is no flat, no easy mark, no Johnny Raw. He will not be beat! Sam is first-rate and spry! And behold his anatomy! The symmetry of his parts!

But consider Young Dutch . . . Seven years, *not one loss*.

Tom revives it in his mind, the scene at the Castle, Holborn: Evans tipping the whole nine in the company of swells and blades while there is Sam the Russian, presented to the Fancy in his youthful glory, a veri-table study for the sculptor. He invites the novice to issue a challenge. Young Dutch is in earnest and comes it strong, his manner reckless and very superior. Does Young Dutch see more than promise in Sam the Russian? A rival perhaps, a usurper? There would be shame in defeat against such a novice! Young Dutch is testing the waters, in sum. That is what Spring decides. What if he were to conceal stones in his muf-flers? A scaley fellow might well do so, a cheat. But this is idle spec, Tom Spring! Nonsense, *starch*!

Oh dear! Tom is not the same man who, only four years ago, as sec-ond to Jack Martin "Master of the Rolls," called for a lancet to slice at

Jack's swollen right sparkler to free the claret trapped there and, with no lancet to hand, gouged at the eye with a blunt pocket knife. He is not the same Tom Spring who gathered up his beaten man and tried to force him back to the scratch when he ought to throw in the sponge, yes, back into the sharp jabs and facers of none other than Young Dutch himself. And Martin was finished. He teetered on Tom's knee, flashing the hash, emptying the grubbery of meat, bread and bub, of gall and blood. Had Martin fought on, Young Dutch might have killed him.

"Sam!" says Spring, born Winter. "Young Dutch may not hit like a forge-hammer, but he is no powder-puff fighter, do you hear?"

"Yes, sir."

"He has bottom, skill and pace, and he will come at you with straight sharp hits and mill on the retreat, then dance in and peg away with jabs and fast clusters to the mark. He has a system. Though never a ruffian, no old-school bruiser, by no means, yet he may close on you, if distressed, and deliver a hot one to the short rib and follow with his nut. He might strike you on the upperworks—here!" says Tom, mimicking a head-butt to Sam's brows. "Or smash your scent-bottle!" he adds, mock-butting him now in the nose. "Or on the potato-trap," Tom says, straightening up and tapping the boy's chin, which, he notes fleetingly, is smooth as a girl's. "If Young Dutch should bear down low with his head, then what would you do?"

"Hit him under the ear!" shouts Jonah, effecting little rabbit punches in air.

"Sam!" Spring urges. "Answer me!"

"Do not counter with the right," Sam replies. "Lest our heads crack together!"

"Indeed."

"Throw the uppercut!"

"Yes, boy!" Floor Young Dutch with the muzzler, thinks Tom. His father's own specialty blow. "And if he should rush in fast as Stephenson's Rocket, what then?"

"Step aside, not back!"

Not one step back.

"Well done, Samuel. Good, good. How are you feeling?"

"Bobbish! Fairly bobbish."

And yet, Tom is doubtful.

My heart, he thinks, is in the boy's fives. He feels very crazy and, hearing the speedy rattle of a chaise drawing near—Young Dutch, so soon!—he remembers the Gas. Tom Hickman, the Gaslight Man, that prepossessing pugilist, met his early end in a drag-cart one night ten years ago, racing, it is said, to overtake a wagon right here on Finchley Common. The Gasman, blazing light of the Prize Ring, lost his head in all the hurry, spilling his very brains! We ought to have driven south, rues Tom, to Richmond. Too much crimson has flowed here on Finchley Common, he thinks, though he has never been a superstitious man.

"I hear a trap," says A Miller, resplendent in her green fanteegs and new braces fashioned by Jonah the Needle, in burgundy silk with a pattern of stars. "There!" she adds. "Here it comes!"

"So soon," murmurs Tom as Sam and Jonah, Jones and Rat all look to the sound of Young Dutch approaching, a clatter of wheels and hooves and laughter.

When Young Dutch alights from the carriage, he is all charity and good looks and very hearty and is on Sam in two bounds, to shake him by the hand and clap him on his glistening shoulders. Young Dutch has an entourage, his very own Fancy, a quartet of upper customers full of the sparks of nature. They descend in a cloud of perfume—a recipe of expensive unguents, cigar-smoke and claret—and drop to the earth quite soundlessly for all the high spirits, surprisingly light on their gams. Last of all comes a dog, a Staffordshire bull terrier with the skull of a boar and the waddling gait of a graveyard charley. The tyke is coloured white as curds, but for his speckled loins and ruddy sack of testicles, large as billiard balls, and that his bowed legs only just accommodate. He snuffles alongside the four blades and slightly to their rear, with an obsequious mien.

Following the preliminaries of introduction and some idle discourse on weather and the buzz in London, Sam "Young Dutch" Evans, born Elias, casts his topper into the ring according to official convention, as in a true fight, which he swears this is not. There is a glorious smile on his phiz. He strips, displaying his superior condition: lean and well proportioned in his musculature, tidy and vigorous. He presents himself, with a very gay countenance, in attitude, exhibiting biceps, triceps and pectorals that are a model for the lover of anatomy. He smiles at his opponent, flashing the ivories, benevolence in his eyes, as if to say, What a promising child you are, Samuel! But a *child* all the same, a child indeed.

"In an actual fight," declares Young Dutch, turning to one of his backers to beg a coin, "we would toss for ends. Shall we toss for ends, young Sam? Merely to honour the Rules? Spring? What do you say?"

"Yes, yes," says Tom. "Why not, why not?" he adds, prickling.

"What larks!" shouts the swell with spectacular sideburns.

Young Dutch wins the toss and elects to face the sun, ever magnanimous.

"I will not have it said I took advantage of thee, Samuel. Not in your novitiate! I do not mind the sun. Let me have the sun in my eyes," Young Dutch insists, shaking Sam again by the hand, clasping the boy's right flapper between his own with the most determined warmth.

"Boy?" sniffs one of the blades, addressing Jonah the Needle and prodding at Rat with his cane. "What oh what, pray, is *that*?"

I am not a what. I am Rat. My ancestors swam the Volga and travelled in ships.

"Boy?"

"This is Rat," says Jonah, glancing at the end of the fine lead he has fashioned from blue and yellow silk in a bird's-eye pattern, in homage to the original belcher named for the Perfect Phenomenon, Jem Belcher, and subsequently Spring's adopted colours and now Sam the Russian's own.

"*Rattus norvegicus*—a fine specimen, a most clever rat," begins Jones the Apothecary. "The cognomen *norvegicus*, however, is quite wrong, a misnomer; it being more accurate to refer—"

"Yes, yes, I'm sure!" interrupts the nib sprig, tapping the ground with impatience. "But what is the meaning of it? Of its presence here? What oh what!"

It would be more accurate to call me "Russian rat" is what Jones meant to say, thinks Rat. Norway is not my native place.

Rat squeaks, abseiling Jonah's leg to settle in the pocket of his jemmy from where he gazes warily at the tempestuous fellow with the busy cane, tapping and prodding away. The cane is topped with the head of a horse, as Rat can plainly see, a head carved in ebony.

"Rat is my pet," explains Jonah in a heedful way, "and I am Jonah, Samuel Alexander's second."

The swell ogles Jonah's shortcomings, the abbreviated leg and abbreviated arm, harrumphing. The human form has approximate left-right symmetry and in some humans it is more approximate than in others. The gentleman's sense of superior bilateral symmetry is a vanity, not his only conceit.

"Well," pipes the swell, "beware the whale, Jonah, ha ha! And Casanova here," he adds, poking the bull terrier in the withers with his stick. "An expert ratter, don't you know. Prize-winning!"

"Thank you, sir," replies Jonah the Needle, putting Rat in his box along with Sam's medallion of Tsar Alexander I. Spring forbids the boy to spar with it round his neck, for fear of injury, and so Rat sits upon it, as it were, a golden throne.

The sun, never strong on this autumn day on Finchley Common, except in Young Dutch's opinion, is weak and skittish now as the clouds billow and reshape and hurry across the sky, smothering and revealing the sun by turns, causing the light to pulse and putting Jones in mind, from his perch between the trees, of a scene in a zoetrope.

"Toe the line, gentlemen!" says Spring. "Stand to the mark, and may no man go down without a blow or I shall cry foul!"

"Stop, Tom!" says Young Dutch with his arms spread wide. "Seeing as we are alone here and well acquainted, that is to say, in agreement—if you judge your man ready and game, shall we not forgo the muffles after all? Call it sparring, if you will, that is to say, esteem it nevertheless an unofficial encounter, yet with fists bare. What do you say? Tom? Samuel?"

"Sam?" queries Tom, with a look at his man. Not a man. *A boy, still.* "What do you say? How are you feeling?"

Sam's heart lurches in its cavity, thudding against the walls of his chest. My heart goes like a train in a tunnel, thinks Sam. It goes like Stephenson's Rocket.

"Bobbish, sir. Pretty bobbish."

"Well then," says Tom. "Well then," he says, removing the pillows from Sam's hands. Never have knuckles appeared so naked, he reflects, though he has always been in doubt regarding the muffles.

"Gentlemen!" calls Jones the Apothecary in his best mimicry of Gentleman Jackson, the Commander-in-Chief. "You do not require instruction. You know the Rules. Commence! Set to!"

What have I done? Tom wonders. What are the odds upon my man? Good God. Let me not have killed him.

"Miss Miller! Miss Miller! What o'clock is it?" he asks of her urgently in hushed and private tones. "We must mark the time. Will you mark the time? And all the particulars!"

A Miller nods, her eyes burn bright. She marks the time and prepares to note all the particulars, the times and places and moments, connecting each to each as links in a chain. Mark them! A novitiate comes once only.

{ TWENTY-ONE }

ZACHARIAH WOLFF fought his first professional bout on the under-card of a name fight at the Sheffield Arena one October night on the cusp of Katya's perilous decline and shortly after Nicky's death and Tasha's degenerative blindness. Rachel was negotiating her final move out of the parental home and into Zach's flat above a framer's in Kentish Town and Lev was incandescent with rage, ravaged by loss and fear on all fronts. It was by no means a propitious time to attend a late-night professional fight debut, an affair distinguished largely, not by the conflict in the ring, but by that played out in its wake several hours south of Sheffield in a tall house in Chelsea where Lev Wolff forswore his adopted son forever.

Zach's opponent was a glorified carpark brawler, an Irish traveller turned boxer by an ambitious young promoter bent on filling the yawning space in the desert that was the middleweight roster, populated primarily by wiry, technically adept Asian boys and ponderous, failed light heavies of West Indian and African descent. The promoter gambled on pulling a crowd by virtue of the young man's white skin and education in quick unapologetic violence. Zach searched the Irishman's brows for clues and saw nothing there in that palest blue of impassive glares, seeing no tell in the eyes but a bald intention to wound. Zach was hurt in the match, suffering bad bruising to the ribs and a gash to the left cheek, yet he was faster on his feet, less mechanical in his returns and had the superior reach. And though the men were similar in build, both blessed with long lean muscle, Zachariah's own grace belied a surprisingly hard punch and he won in the third round by a knockout.

In London the following evening, Zach stepped past taped-up cardboard boxes in the hall to find Rachel in the bedroom staring into an opened suitcase filled with thoughtfully rolled garments and several tins of Kusmi tea, "St. Petersburg" blend.

"It was most curious," explained Rachel. "Mama packed them for me. It's her favourite blend, not quite mine. I had to take it. I had to."

"Are you here now, Rach? Are you here? With me?"

"Yes," she answered. "With you. *With thee*," she said, reaching over to touch the plaster across his cheekbone.

"I won. My *novitiate*! KO in the third. I won."

"Of course you did," murmured Rachel. "So did I. I won mine too," she added before losing her voice, overcome quite suddenly by elation as well as the grievous vision of her departure and of Katya, packing tins of Kusmi tea, her face attenuated and luminous, shocking in its beauty. Grave.

"Go now, little paws," she said, her voice pellucid.

And Rachel sees her father, his great head bowed in defeat.

Look what I have done! she thought. Let me not have killed him.

"Rachel?" asks Zach. "This is what you want, isn't it?"

Rachel nods slowly several times, with decision.

"You can see them any time, every day if you want to. And we'll find a bigger place. A house maybe. I can do it up. I know guys who found great places for cheap. Even round here. Repossessed ones, at auction. I'll find us a house."

"Everything is so hideous and so wonderful all at once!" cries Rachel, sitting on the end of his bed, still unmade from Zachariah's dash to Sheffield for his debut. She draws Zach in by the hands, then wraps her arms around his thighs, pressing her head against the tautness of his belly. She holds him very tight.

In every beginning, an end.

THE BATTLE OF FINCHLEY COMMON

A Miller writes:

The Battle of Finchley Common. Sam the Russian, or the Tsar of the Prize Ring. His First Contest, and bye-battles. The year 1832.

First round. The two Sams ogle each other across the line, having placed themselves in erect postures with the mauleys held high according to fashion—above the breadbox yet beneath the button—an eminently sensible position, as it seems to this reporter, ensuring an equal distance for the arms to travel to protect stomach or chin, and effective also in warding off blows and countering any assault. The younger Sam observes the elder with especial fixity, as if to measure the man and assess his purpose, and as he drops a shoulder to feint with the right, a lock of hair grown damp with sweat falls into his peeper and Young Dutch, quick as lightning, puts in a tremendous hit over Sam's guard, striking him in the neck and levelling the Russian in an instant. Man down.

Sam lies sprawled on his side like a trussed lamb before Spring drags the boy to his corner, the full respite being required for his breath to return, the first in-and-outs coming in great gasps and splutters as in rescue from drowning. Sam waves off the brandy, preferring to take only a tot of water from his seconds, which he swallows most gingerly. There is much yipping and hilarious theatricals of coughing and puffing, and ironic salutations of "laid-in-the-streets" and "Coram pug," etc., etc., from Young Dutch's lushy crew, accompanied by amused fingering of watches and tapping of gloved fingers upon breeches, to which mockery Sam the Russian is fittingly blind and superior. He steps gamely to the mark, this laid-in-the-streets, Coram pug, and frowns with intent.

Instructions to Apprentices.

Be not ashamed that you were bred in this Hospital. Own it; and say that it was thro' the good Providence of God that you were taken care of.

Second. Here follows a round of cautious sparring, with Young Dutch uncommonly circumspect and grave, as if himself suffering from the taunts of his backers, whereas Sam fights for wind and grows in strength. Neither man effects a lodgement of any severity, and both exhibit great skill and science in fibbing and rallying for the space of fully six minutes before Sam stops a terrible endeavour with his left arm, whereupon Evans seizes the advantage and, assuming the defending arm to be at least passingly useless, pins Alexander's right by the wrist and strikes him sharply under the left ear, felling him once more. Sam Alexander appears confused in his corner, yet rallies in time and with unusual gaiety, despite the claret seeping from his ear—Young Dutch having drawn the cork with his last blow of the second round, to raucous calls of "First blood! First blood!"

Sam the Russian thinks, Now I am entirely deaf.

Third. A curious round. Before Sam can raise his guard, Young Dutch closes and lets fly with both hammers, cutting Sam under the dexter ogle and slicing the cheek to the bone, so that Sam's phiz is a mess of crimson, exciting Young Dutch, full of spirit, to laughter and chattering, and an offer to wrestle Sam to the ground, thus allowing him respite.

"Let us fall together, Sam! And end the round!" Young Dutch declares, spreading his arms as if to embrace his opponent, whereupon Sam the Russian delivers such a hot one to the chin Evans pitches head foremost to the ground and shouts of "Foul, foul!" go up from the swells, who leap to their feet with such violence, the bull terrier sets to growling and barking, and bouncing on his front paws, straining at the lead and scratching the turf, its bellows swollen and the neck thick with the rush of blood and air.

"Never mind! Never mind!" says Young Dutch upon rising, still game, though evidently indisposed, and so ends the round.

What is half a minute to a man?

Perhaps three breaths in tranquillity, perhaps ten times three breaths in the ring. Between rounds, Sam murmurs in Spring's ear while his master swabs the claret from his face. He speaks in a voice so small, he makes almost no sound, because the boy can no longer judge the reach of his voice, neither in tone nor clarity. He cannot hear himself, but *feels* sound as never before, aware of the snarling and squawking of the Staffordshire bull terrier in a rumbling that passes through the soles of his stampers, a sensation keen as the gathering breeze he feels in the pricking of his fine hairs and the cooling of his sweating, bloody skin. There is a terrible grace in the loss of his hearing.

In a very small voice, on perhaps his twenty-seventh exhalation, Sam whispers in Spring's ear, "I am quite deaf, quite deaf," but there is so much competition for Tom's attention that all the ex-champion hears is Jones's call of "Time!"

"Hit him again, Sam!" Spring urges. "Hit him one for me!"

Instructions to Apprentices.

As you hope for Success in this World, and Happiness in the next, you are to be mindful of what has been taught you. You are to behave honestly, justly, soberly, and carefully in everything, to everybody, and especially towards your Master, Mistress and family; and to execute all lawful commands with Industry, Cheerfulness, and good Manners.

"Time!" calls Jones.

Fourth. Young Dutch closes and several blows are exchanged, with Sam the Russian very sprightly in his defence, displaying considerable science and dexterity. Some murmurs of appreciation from the spectators, and a smile from Young Dutch, followed by an expression of determined resolution and a blow to the Russian's kidneys of such violence, both men fall to the floor from the force of it and slide in the dreadful mixture there, of sweat, crimson, farrier's oil and Alexander's instant discharge of urine.

"Will you give it in?" asks S. Evans of S. Alexander, but no answer ensues and both men retire for a wipe.

Fifth. Sam's spirit is good and his style remarkable. He comes to the scratch, desperate and disfigured and bleeding profusely, yet showing the advantage of science all the while, boxing with hands low, his right drawn across the mark to stop the body blow, his left ready to fly at his opponent's nut. This is the longest round, and skill is manifest on both sides, with fibbing and rallying, and sparring for wind, then severe hits. Sam avails himself of his superior reach to effect a lodgement that lays open Young Dutch's nose. Great cries of surprise from his backers. Evans is thus excited to renewed vigour, working at Sam's wounds and attempting to amaze his opponent with fast clusters of blows and a rattler, evidently wishing to dispose of his man at last without further disgrace to himself, but Alexander observes his intent, evading the blow in a sidestepping movement of great elegance. Presently, Young Dutch closes again and infighting follows, with some wrestling and both men thrown, and Evans falling not upon his hands, according to honourable practice, but upon Sam, causing more hurt to the Russian and admonishments from Jones, though Evans swears it is accidental.

In his corner, Sam Alexander weeps. It cannot be helped. Great drops burst from his sparklers and steal down his phiz, thinning the crimson and jumping from button to chest to catch in the oil and unguents smeared there, and gather in pustules of moisture resembling blisters. His breath rushes in and out of his frame and the sinews and muscles flicker and twitch over the fine bones of his limbs, and the arteries pulse in his neck and wrists and temples much like the surface of the sea in a storm. Tom wipes tears from the Russian's eyes with a deft flick of the thumbs as the half minute is called so that Young Dutch may not draw strength from the sight of Sam's emotion, nor the Fancy mock.

Spring feels a bruising and swelling in his gullet, a prelude to tears of his own he dashes away with an angry swipe of the sponge.

"Time!"

Sixth and seventh. In these rounds, a paucity of science is prominent, with both combatants closing and infighting with little to observe of any note or consequence, except for the younger man being thrown with considerable violence at the end of the former, and Young Dutch, in ducking under a terrific jab, slipping to the floor to end the latter, exciting an indignant cry of "Foul, foul!" from Jones the Apothecary for going down without a blow. The cry goes unheeded and Alexander drops likewise in the confusion of limbs.

The ground is increasing perilous for milling, what with the new falling rain. Rain falls, mixing with the terrible recipe of human fluids beneath.

Hot air rises from the late-summer turf and the fiery bodies of the men gathered there, bringing moisture to cooler heights and rising without uniformity, symmetry-breaking. The movement of air is cloud-forming, creating clouds in which the atmosphere is dynamic, and with the warm air and breaking of symmetry, there is precipitation of moisture in the form of rain, which is a phase transition, a bifurcation or catastrophe. All outcomes are determined by sensitive dependence on initial conditions, even catastrophe.

—Rachel? Bifurcation, catastrophe. Explain!

—Dramatic change in a system, Papa. A system in a critical state. Small external changes can bring on dramatic internal change.

—Give me an example.

—Snow, Papa. Aggression in dogs—a dog excited by fear, frustration, anger, is in a critical state. Aggression is a bifurcation. A knockout is a bifurcation, a catastrophe.

Oh, Sam.

Sam the Russian thinks, Oh yes. Now I am wholly deaf. He watches Spring's face and reads the *Dyall of the Affections* and *Naturall language of the Head*. He reads Tom's inclination there, his desire to throw up the sponge.

"No," the boy whispers, uncertain of his voice. "Not yet!" he says, gripping Tom fiercely by the wrist.

Eighth. Spring visibly prepared to declare the fight over, yet Sam Alexander, his ogles bright, stands up, grasps his mentor by the wrist and steps to the mark with superior grace, though bleeding horribly and in a pitiable state. He gestures with his right mauley to his opponent in the gamest possible manner, clearly inviting further punishment, and this moment is prominent, the leading feature of a round marked by a sudden shyness in Young Dutch and much sparring for wind and several ineffectual hits. The two Sams close and Young Dutch has the younger Sam on the floor, throwing him easy.

In Sam the Russian's noiseless place, he has a dream of immanence in which everything he knows, and everything he has yet to learn, has shape and motion and is travelling fast. Robinson Crusoe, Tsar Alexander, *Rattus norvegicus*. Cholera is in the Thames, not the offshore winds. It is water-borne. Water of death. I will find my father, I shall sail in ships, I shall ride a train. I am the Tsar of the Prize Ring. Jones pointed to a diagram one day, an anatomical chart of a man stripped of flesh, peeled to his very loins, a delineation of arteries, veins and muscles, the figure raw as butcher's meat.

"To strike a man very violently," explained the apothecary, "here, on the button, is to force the jawbone up and into the base of the skull and sever the supply of air and blood to the brain, causing a tempo-rary loss of faculties. A boxer must protect his chin accordingly," Jones instructed. "According to science," he added apologetically, for he is ever mild in his manners and not a fighting man, merely an apothecary. He would never presume.

Ninth. Both combatants in good spirits, though the Russian showing signs of exhaustion and, unable to gain the distance, the boy falls short with a desperate facer, which Evans ducks very neatly, taking advantage thereupon to close immediately and give the younger man an excellent cross-buttock. The Russian thrown and, it is feared, one of his ribs is broken.

Tenth. Sam the Russian clearly on the totter, yet resolute, staring wildly at Young Dutch who, with utmost coolness, waits at the scratch until his brave opponent rallies and is enabled to resume. Which conduct draws feeling plaudits from Jones and Jonah in appreciation of Evans's surpris-ing humanity. Vexed cries from his partizans, however, of "Finish the fellow!" and "What odds on Evans to win in this round? What odds?" Mr. Hughes-Ball, well known as Young Dutch's chief backer and famous in society, says, "Why, I've not lost so much as a halfpenny on my man in seven years and will offer any odds, long as you like!" Hughes-Ball accepts four sovereigns against Young Dutch from the author of this account with an elegant display of amazement and ceremony and to general larks from the assemblage of swells. "Woe, woe, woe!" chaffs one, dabbing at his shutters with a belcher in mock pity of A Miller's rashness, while another makes a dumb show of tossing this scribe's money into the copse as if to say, "There it goes, your hard-earned blunt!" etc., etc., accompanied by other effusions such as "Another Johnny Raw, putting down the dust! Losing his rag!" and "Here lies Sam the Russian, Late of the Foundling Hospital, Coram's Fields, universally regretted, ha ha!" and "Ah me, my tears are dropping!" etc., etc.; after which interlude, the round begins with a dreadful nobber from Evans, a tremendous blow that fills the Russian's mouth with blood and sends him staggering, squirting the claret from the mouth like a stone cherub.

Water of life.

Young Dutch is no great hitter, indeed. His principal forte is in blows to astonish all spectators. The expression of Sam the Russian, however, is difficult to assess, what with his increasing shyness, his secret deafness and, foremost, the frightful bloodiness of his head, the right sparkler swollen large as an egg and his lips desperately inflamed, the effect being truly terrific. Loud shouts of applause from Evans's partizans, whereupon Alexander rises most gamely, appearing at the mark even before the half minute is piped.

"What a brave fellow!" exclaims Jonah the Needle, smoothing his fanteegs besmirched with Sam's crimson, red-black as any butcher's togs.

Quick, quick, thinks the Russian, sensing a change in the weather through the soles of his feet and the prickling of his scalp. And I swear I had a waking dream just now and heard the call of the diver—rain goose, loon. Quick, quick—let's finish, because a storm is coming.

Evans calls out to Alexander across the ring, laughing again, yet evidently indisposed. "I'll take no advantage of thee, Sam," he declares. "I'll not hit thee, no, lest I hurt thine other eye!" Plaudits from Young Dutch's crew and outrage from Spring, for these are famous words indeed, spoken, heretofore, as the Fancy well knows, in December 1805 by Hen Pearce, the "Game Chicken," to his friend Jem Belcher in the twelfth round of the Championship contest fought near Blythe in the days of Jem's decline, and two years since the loss of his peeper in a game of racquets at St. Martin's. Jem Belcher never wavered.

That battle went eighteen rounds before Jem admitted himself beaten and Hen Pearce, a bright spark albeit quite illiterate, renowned for his strength, agility and humanity, yet turned a summerset for joy in winning the title from his dearest friend, exciting raptures from the crowd and waving of his silken colours, bird's-eye blue. The Game Chicken suffered interment only four years later from consumption and surfeit of blue ruin. Hen was put to bed with a shovel, according to his request, next to his friend Bill Ward, his knee-man at Blythe, and once a distinguished pugilist. Never far from a friend in life, the Chicken lies by Ward's side in the churchyard of St. Giles, where tears were dropped to his memory. Companion planting.

And today on Finchley Common, Young Dutch mimics the call of the diver—rain goose, loon—and quotes the famous words of the Chicken, and the impression is so very like and singular as to astonish spectators and outrage Tom Spring, filled to an overflow now, with images of past milling heroes and anxiety for the health of his young charge, the of superior speed and accuracy and this, with his advantage in height, weight and experience, would seem to decide the fate of the battle from the very first round; in spite of which, and the terrible shape of Sam the Russian, fearfully disfigured and bleeding copiously, rarely has the author witnessed such a closely fought match, and uncommon manly, between two such beguiling purveyors of the fistic art!

Eleventh. A want of wind is conspicuous on both sides, but Alexander displays the greater composure, notwithstanding the heaving of his flanks and audible rasp in his throat. Young Dutch, bearing trifling scars of battle by comparison, also recruits for wind and appears much distressed, victim, at the last, of his famous impatience, dismayed by his seeming inability to summon the coup de grâce, the finisher. Sam is evidently a glutton and not likely to give it in and Young Dutch is so far unbeaten and will not surrender his laurels! What a contest of wills!

Several feints made and Sam on the look-out, very cautious, allowing Evans to put in a slight hit upon Sam's ear with considerable speed and agility, and Sam falls, causing much irritation in the older man who looms over the debutant, mauleys on hips, in mock disgust. "Stand and fight!" says he. "Get up, you pug!" Spring indignant at this play-making. Evans very sprightly, laughing and talking to the Fancy.

A MUSICAL INTERLUDE

When Dutch Sam died in 1816, young Sam Evans, born Elias, his son, was only eight years of his age. Young Elias worked at a baker's and a printer's and then as a runner in the offices of Pierce Egan's *Life in London,* where his prepossessing appearance and poise and high state of condition much impressed the editor, likewise his ability to perform the calls of songbirds with great musicality. Egan introduced Young Dutch to Gentleman Jackson, Commander-in-Chief, giving the office, so to speak, about his office boy. Young Dutch won his first battle by a knock-out. He was fifteen years old and is unbeaten since.

See Young Dutch now, perching upon his second's knee, Hughes-Ball having offered himself up for the purpose. Young Dutch perches on his second's knee and breaks into song, singing the call of the diver, the melodious complaint being so very true to life and singular in quality as teetering Tsar of the P.R. So very crazy is he, indeed, that he begins to chant himself, Tom's singing ability, typically heard on Friday evenings at the Castle, Holborn, being quite as well considered as his prepossessing appearance and civility as Host. Here on Finchley Common, where too much crimson has flowed—remember the Gas!—Tom Spring spills over with song, a piper at battle, and by this stratagem, innocent or fly, gains Alexander more than a minute and sufficient time to recover his wind. By way of this musical interlude, Spring enforces a long count.

> *Lavender's blue, Diddle, diddle,*
> *Lavender's green;*
> *When I am king, Diddle, diddle,*
> *You shall be queen.*
>
> *Call up your men, Diddle, diddle,*
> *Set them to work,*
> *Some to the plough, Diddle, diddle,*
> *Some to the cart.*
>
> *Some to make hay, Diddle, diddle,*
> *Some to the Corn,*
> *Whilst you and I, Diddle, diddle,*
> *Keep the bed warm.*
>
> *Let the birds sing, Diddle, diddle,*
> *And the Lambs play,*
> *We shall be safe, Diddle, diddle*
> *Out of harm's way.*

Twelfth. The Tsar of the Prize Ring very sprightly after this musical interlude and surprising entertainment, the half-minute respite having stretched to a minute and upwards. Close fighting ensues, with Alexander cutting Young Dutch under the right and then the left eye in furious succession, yet, in gaining his distance to aim a body blow, Evans rallies and, very indignant, puts in a tremendous hit to Alexander's neck, levelling him.

Alexander sits on Jonah's knee, that of his short leg, the brace and built-up sole of his high-low providing an excellent support for his ship-wrecky friend, and Jones the Apothecary is very busy, very spoffish in his dual role of bottle-holder and referee. Spring speaks advice while swiping at Sam's eyes, his words falling on deaf ears. Sam cannot hear any more, though voices ring in his head, voices of instruction, familiar and strange. He feels unusually free.

Instructions to Apprentices.

As you hope for Success in this world and Happiness in the next, you are to be mindful of what has been taught you.

Jones the Apothecary says, "It appears that the blows you miss are the ones that exhaust you. That is my conclusion. Precision is paramount. Hit the target."

"Listen, Sam!" implores Jonah the Needle. "Sam! Tom, he is gone deaf. I am sure of it. Tom!"

Jack Dempsey says, Kill the body and the mind will follow.

Cassius Clay says, Keep punching at a man's head, and it mixes his mind.

Muhammad Ali says, Get up and fight, sucker!

Dempsey says, Bob and weave. Crouch.

That's ugly! chides Ali. Rumble, son, rumble. Dance!

Sam empties his mind. He has a dream of immanence.

And now Miss Miller whispers into his ear, her face full of entreaty, and Sam's eye is caught by her new braces made by Jonah the Needle, lengths of blood-red silk with a pattern of dots like falling stars. He cannot hear her, but knows she has a voice like sweet music.

"Dance, Sam! You're gonna dance!"

Thirteenth. At the call of time, Alexander, one mass of blood, appears in a state of stupor and is slow to the scratch, whereupon his second, somewhat panic-struck, hoists his man upright and to the line with an uncommon shew of strength and dexterity for one so impaired. An ironic ecstasy of praise for Jonah from the partizans of Young Dutch and a smile of confidence on the dial of their favourite as he meets his adversary. Young Dutch's well-breeched supporters nod and smile at the sight of Sam's dismay and manifest affliction. His extraordinary new stance is greeted with loud cries of derision.

Shouts of "What is this, what have we here? What-what? Larks?" etc. as Alexander manoeuvres over the ring in a circular pattern, hands held low and at hip height, his exposed upper body swaying to and fro and from side to side in a truly astonishing manner and not unlike a yearling in a paddock. Young Dutch, full of spirit in pursuit of his opponent, strikes twice without consequence and closes, but Alexander puts in four quick sharp jabs to the stomach and breast of Young Dutch, the Russian's hands snaking out with such celerity as to cause a degree of concern among Evans's backers. Young Dutch on the totter and, much irritated, rallies, delivering a tremendous blow to Sam's head, which he parries, returning a hit to the cheekbone struck with such resolution, Evans is brought down. Alexander, smiling shyly, retreats for a wipe, but Young Dutch rises quickly and, in a circumstance never to be forgotten—the result of intemperance or debauchery, no one can tell—his countenance changes at a stroke from dismay to gaiety and he follows Alexander towards his corner and, throwing a left arm round his shoulders, catches his head in a hold to shouts of "Foul!" from Jones and Spring and trifling cries of confusion from his own backers, in spite of which Young Dutch merely talks and laughs at his prey, holding Alexander in chancery and dragging him about the ring. Young Dutch talks and laughs though the claret flies from the gash in his cheek and he begins to betray symptoms of exhaustion.

"Let us fight no more, Sam! We have had good sport! You have learned much, you are done in, I'll not kill thee!" he says, and more of the same, all the while pulling at Sam's hair in a playful manner and calling things out over the noise of thunder and thickening rain, such as "Remember Mendoza!" etc., etc., and "Surrender!" and such like, also laughing and prating, then gouging Sam's dexter ogle with his free thumb and burning his knuckles into the cut along the brow before the Russian neatly disengages and, in so doing, falls, his mouth a great O of surprise and hurt.

"Foul! Foul!" pipe the partizans of Young Dutch, full of spirit again. "Going down without a blow! Foul!" shout the swells, rising to their stampers and endeavouring to invade the scene of battle and interfere with the pugilists. In the unofficial circumstances of the mill, there are only a spoffish apothecary, a lame tailor, a rat and a foppish scribe to assist Spring in whipping out, but just as the ex-champion enters the ring, conciliatory and prepossessing, his apprentice, young Samuel Alexander, Tsar of the Prize Ring, rises to toe the line once more, himself calling "Time!" to universal amazement, most particularly from his antagonist, Young Dutch. Has Evans ever known such prodigies of valour in a combatant? Has a gamer fellow ever peeled in a ring?

Fourteenth. The spectators retreat, like the French in Russia, chastised by the determined courage on display and the irregularity of their hero, the hitherto invincible Young Dutch Evans, their Napoleon! All is quiet, excepting the noisome bull terrier, snapping at thunderclaps, his barks raw and punishing to the auriculars. Alexander leaps to the scratch, resuming his uncommon dance, mauleys low, head swaying to and fro, his feet merry, his sinister peeper unblinking, though he can scarcely see for blood, and the other eye quite useless. Notwithstanding his tender state, Samuel's grace and science shew very masterly, his tremendous pluck certain to live long in humanity's memory. The partizans of both combatants quite lost in astonishment as Evans follows his man over the ring once more and to the ropes, punishing him severely there, with Spring's concern conspicuous for, if magnanimity does not rise superior in Young Dutch, he will surely kill his adversary. Alexander protects his face, leaning this way and that as Evans plants excellent hits to the bread-box and ribs and, though in point of strength and experience the advantages are all on his side, he is not as patient as heretofore, and much exhausted, and as he gains distance in his desperation to deliver a knock-down blow, he fails in his judgement, so that the Russian eludes his grasp very neatly, slipping away like a fish.

Head in air and tail in sea, fish, fish, listen to me.

Young Dutch furious and bewildered. He receives several sharp but feeblish hits to the face, flapping blows such as an angelic might deliver, enraging him further. Evans closes, lowering his guard with the evident intent of throwing his man in exasperation, and there, from nowhere, comes the muzzler, the uppercut made famous by Dutch Sam, his own father, and put in by the Tsar of the Prize Ring with such terrific speed and violence, Young Dutch is knocked completely off his legs to land senseless upon the mud beneath.

Rasputitsa. Mud.

"Is he killed?" asks Sam the Russian.

Whereupon Jones, inspired by Sam's prowess, steps into the ring with rare agility and sets to palpating the vanquished in the most assertive and scientific manner, fingering the heart region and other pulses, at the throat, wrists and temples, much like a phrenologist, while the swells apply pressure behind, evading Spring's outstretched arms, an insufficient impediment to their advance, despite his famous reach. The upper customers push in to peer at their fallen man, shuffling in eagerness and pawing at the ground, losing their balance in the mud, with indignation manifest, their habiliments bespattered with dust and blood.

Jones pronounces Evans "Quite well. That is to say," he shouts to be heard in the busy scene, "alive and not ready for the long room!"

Spring, heart leaping, hoists his pupil in the air, carrying him over the ring to tumultuous applause, even from those partizans of Young Dutch not engaged in assisting their man to his feet, disregarding his furious protestations.

"I am not beat!" he complains, rejecting the ministrations of his friends. "That was a sickener—ha ha—but I am not beat! Another round! Another round!" he cries, yet in retreating for a wipe and a ball of fire, he falls from weakness, and Casanova, the Staffordshire bull terrier tethered at the corner stake and excited to a pitch, jumps onto Young Dutch's breast and licks the claret from his phiz.

Fee-fi-fo-fum, I smell the blood of an Englishman.

Evans, much irritated, on his high ropes indeed, aims a blow at the dog and, in shrinking from his aggressor, the bull terrier slips the lead.

The Bye-battle

First round. Rat, upon the alert, rushes from the roof hatch of his box towards the safety of Jonah the Needle, his cutman and second, his bosom friend, but Casanova, full of spirit, closes quickly and puts in a throttler, locking his ivories round Rat's neck and shaking him to and fro with tremendous ferocity so that the claret flies copiously from the jugular, describing patterns in the air, before the dog releases his hold on *Rattus norvegicus* whose ancestors once swam the Volga while the terrier's own were true-born English and bred to fight. Dog hurls Rat to the ground with sovereign contempt, thus ending the contest. Elated with the victory, the Staffordshire bull walks the enclosure several times to show his excellence, flanks proudly heaving and his breath coming in and out with great gusts of superiority, but as soon as the scream dies in Rat's throat, Jonah takes up the cry and leaps into the ring towards the dog's owner, hopping like a kangaroo to add force to the blow he delivers. In missing, Jonah falls, whereupon the enraged upper customer swings his stick and returns with terrific hits on the head and breast, which unsporting conduct excites the Fancy, rousing them to separate the combatants, just as Sam the Russian, though very much bruised and tender, rallies instantly in defence of his friend. Sam summons sufficient wind to dance in and effect so dreadful a lodgement to the swell's jaw, the fellow is hoisted off his legs to come down with uncommon violence upon the corner stake, his cork drawn, and only the thickness of his head saves him from giving it in.

A small number of vehicles and pedestrians having joined the assembly, attracted by the commotion, Mr. Spring and Mr. Hughes-Ball endeavour to restore harmony and make haste for home, fearing interruption from the magistrates when news of the riotous combat is noised further abroad. While the friends and pugilists come to their recollections and ready themselves to broom for London, words arise between the nib sprig, blood flowing from the crack in his nut, and Jonah the Needle. The swell mutters threats and insults in Jonah's ears while slipping the lead over the head of his Staffordshire bull and fondling him pridefully.

"You, boy, laid-in-the-streets, cripple! Even my dog, my Staffordshire bull terrier, is higher-born!"

And Jonah, never cool as a true fighting man should be, too sensitive to bear insults, Jonah the Needle, Coram's boy, apprentice to the cutting-up tribe, cutman on the day of Sam the Russian's maiden battle here on Finchley Common, plucks the lancet from his jemmy and buries it deep in the dog's body.

"NO!" screams the swell as if the knife were in his very breast and, pulling it from Casanova, swipes at Jonah who has dropped to his knees to unbosom his grief and weep for his misdeed, for the long day, for his uneven limbs, for Rat and now for the stinging blows to his frontispiece and cheek and cuts to the hands he raises to guard his eyes from the cruel blade.

And so matters precipitate headlong into chaos, the multitude manoeuvring in eager pursuit to observe the fracas and Mr. Hughes-

Ball and his friends thrashing at spectators with their switches and canes, amateur whippers-out. Young Dutch alights sharply from his barouche to assist Sam the Russian and though both boxers appear feeble from punishment and bloody in the extreme, yet they sport the famous colours in unison now, yellowman and bird's-eye blue, and rally to stop the mismatched contest between man and boy, Alexander disarming the swell and Evans falling upon Jonah to prevent further hurt, both pugilists displaying great skill and bottom in the name of the P.R., and the whole wide sporting world.

Loud cries and bold pressure from the immensity as the imbroglio ends, Spring taking the Needle in his arms and carrying him to the drag while the partizans of Young Dutch gather the dying bull terrier, his fallen owner issuing such a fearful scream it cannot be ascribed to grief or pain alone, and when the swell is lofted towards the barouche by his exhausted friends, no one can tell how it is he comes to bleed so terribly from the right ham and loins, nor can this member of the black-letter gentry, A Miller, swear with certainty to a fleeting vision of Young Dutch eking a bloody lancet from Sam the Russian's grip to toss it far afield in one graceful motion before hissing eagerly at the astonished Tsar of the Prize Ring.

"Be gone, young Sam! Quick!"

"Is he killed?" gasps Sam the Russian. "Did I . . ."

"Run, Sam! Fly from here!" begs Young Dutch, shaking him by the shoulders for emphasis.

And when Evans turns to the author, his countenance desperate, she is dazzled at once, despite the dirt and crimson, by his beauty, the bright ogles and elegant form, the dark curls so very dazzling and so strikingly akin to Sam Alexander's own, they might well be brothers.

"Miss Miller?" says Young Dutch. "Can you drive? Take the boys and broom for London. Go like a train! Spring and I will do the rest. Quick!"

"But not to the Castle!" adds Tom. "Take them to Jones's. We shall follow."

"Hurry!" pleads Young Dutch.

Sentimentalists, imagine not the fives of young Sam the Russian wrapped round the lancet that severs the femoral artery of the obnoxious swell, but the hand of Fate. And Moralists expatiate, as you will, on the manliness of pugilism versus those scalier modes of battle and revenge, and on the dangers, furthermore, of coming between a man and his dog, a boy and his rat, between any bosom friends. As for myself, for purposes of harmony; and respecting the surprising humanity of Young Dutch, I will not submit this account nor ever noise what I witnessed at the end. And so may it never be mooted that Young Dutch Sam suffered a blemish to his career, that he ever recorded a first defeat, and at the hands of a novice. No. No losses, still not, not yet. And may it only be surmised that as I pull gently on Alexander's bruised and bloodied right fist and urge him to mount the drag, I raise it briefly skywards in silent acknowledgement of his victory, destined to remain secret, aware as I am he will forever be uncrowned Tsar of the Prize Ring, and forever fugitive.

I hurry away with my bloody load, I go like a train, as Young Dutch urged, and broom for London.

A Miller

{ TWENTY-TWO }

MISS MILLER the scribe in the green fanteegs and burgundy braces speeds the horse on by voice alone. She will not use a whip. She has a great feeling for animals. The carriage hurtles from Finchley Common and Sam feels every twist, every declivity and bump in the road to Covent Garden, but he is numb to the pain now, he has become his pain. He cradles Jonah, insensible and shivering in Sam's weary arms, his friend the Needle cut and sliced like a fish filleted for market, and almost beyond recognition.

"Jonah! Jonah!" cries Sam the Russian, though he still cannot hear himself speak. He is almost wholly deaf. Sam watches the mud spin away from the carriage wheels, splashing shards of rain and dirt.

Sam remembers plunging the lancet into the swell, straight into the ham.

Good God, he thinks. What have I done? I killed him!

He recalls a sensation of digging at earth and coming upon roots, of severing roots. He has a fevered vision of Broad Street and Jones the Apothecary's rooms. He sees the anatomical charts there and the names of parts, of veins and capillaries and arteries, which Jones likens to the Thames and its tributaries, as if man were a river.

Sam searches Jonah's physiognomy for signs. He pinches his friend's anatomy with his own broken hands.

Jonah! Don't sleep. Don't go to sleep!

.   .   .

Wolves are extremely loving towards each other and demonstrative in their affections, being much prone to nestling and nuzzling.

"Wake up, wake up," goes Rachel's old refrain.

"Not yet."

"Wake up, Zach," she whispers, kissing his brows and the whitened scar along the occipital bone of his right eye. Cuts to this area, she knows, are so very critical in a match and result mostly from infighting, those dangerous and seemingly passive clinches wherein tops of heads hit chins and wayward elbows gash the eyes. *Sparklers, peepers, ogles. Shutters, toplights.*

"Make it a long count," mumbles Zach. "Rachel! Famous counts? Long, short."

"Mike Tyson v. Buster Douglas."

"Good. And more famous. Earlier."

Young Dutch Sam v. Sam the Russian . . .

"Easy-peasy," she replies. "Dempsey and Tunney, the return. Battle of the Long Count."

"Good," he says, mimicking Lev's quiz voice. "GOOD!"

"Stop it," she smiles. "And you're falling asleep again. Don't fall asleep!"

Jonah! Don't sleep! Don't go to sleep!

Rachel cups her hands round Zach's head, teasing him off the right cheek to face her and he resists, making himself heavy.

"Help!" he says. "I'm being smothered. Help, help, help!"

"I want your good ear. Please."

"Ah-ha," goes Zach, flopping onto his left masseter, eyes tightly shut. "Why? Do you feel a song coming on?"

"Indeed," she smiles, nosing him behind the pinna, breathing in, then touching her lips to the auricular, sending a gentle surf of sound down his auditory canal. "I love it, your ear smell."

"Hey! I feel that. Your voice, I mean. Down to my toes, Rachel. In my feet."

Rachel sings.

> *I love to dance, dilly, dilly,*
> *I love to sing,*
> *When I am queen, dilly, dilly,*
> *You'll be my king.*

Who told you so, dilly, dilly,
Who told you so?
'Twas mine own heart, dilly, dilly,
That told me so.

"Thought it was 'diddle, diddle,'" goes Zach, still full of sleep.

"In the earliest version. 'Diddle, Diddle; or, The Kind Country Lovers.' Very old nursery rhyme. 1680."

"Sing some more, Rach."

"Wake up then."

"Told you. I'm taking a long count."

Zach chuckles softly, a small implosion in the throat, a puff of air through the nose. He slips a sleepy right hand between her thighs, resting it just above the knee along the willowy muscle there, *gracilis*.

"He would have won it anyway, wouldn't he?" asks Rachel.

"Who? Won what?"

"Tunney. The return. Against Dempsey, even without the long count. Same as with Mendoza v. Gentleman Jackson. The hair-pulling match. Jackson was winning anyway, wasn't he?"

"Yes. GOOD, Rachel."

"Oh please. Stop doing Papa's voice. Stop it. And what I meant is, it's *how* a man wins, isn't it, Zach? That signifies. In boxing. Perhaps more than in any other sport? How a man wins. That's the touchstone, isn't it?"

"It is, Rach. It really is."

"And the fight game's a mess now, isn't it? How can you even tell? Who the good boxers are. Where they are."

"Talking about sanction fees and all that?"

"Yes," says Rachel.

"Yeah. Well, it's never been pretty . . . Boxing attracts—you know. Always has. But today? The worst. Promoters, sanctioning bodies, telly, advertising dosh, all the titles."

"The *alphabet soup!*" Rachel remarks.

"Yeah. That's what they call it. It's kind of hard to—to distinguish yourself nowadays. As a fighter."

"Perhaps how a man *loses*," suggests Rachel, "matters too."

"Maybe. You know, Rach? Fifty, sixty years ago there were eight weight divisions, right? Eight weights, eight champs. There's double that now.

Seventeen divisions. Plus four major organisations and any number of spurious lesser ones. Too many champs, not enough fighters!"

"So it's lucky you're out of the game, then. Isn't it, Zach?"

"I was pretty good," Zach murmurs.

"I know."

"And some days—"

"No!" says Rachel.

"Yeah. I think I could easily come back. Fight again. I do."

"Zachariah?"

"Mmm?" he replies, closing his eyes again.

"Hear me," she insists. "I shan't survive it, do you understand? If you get hurt. I shan't survive it."

A cloud moves into the morning blue across the sun, a merry billow of white, *cumulus,* and the light flashes hot through the gap in the curtains, illuminating Zach's face, causing a twitch of the eyelids and a fiery glow to suffuse the tip of his ear and cheekbone.

"*Vashe siyatel'stvo,*" whispers Rachel. *Your Radiance.* "Wake up now!"

"Not yet. Sing something else. A Russian one. Come on! And what's wrong with my doing the Lev thing, by the way? His quiz voice, what's wrong with that? It's not mean, it's just fun, for a lark."

"It hurts, though, doesn't it? That he never played the game with you. The testing, the science quiz. It irks you."

"It doesn't. I don't bloody care, Rach. Why should I?"

"And because you're very angry, really, that he hates us—the fact of us. And I don't like the contempt in your voice. It doesn't help."

"It's me he bloody hates, Rachel! And I don't care. Now sing. I'm still asleep. I don't fucking care. It's an old thing."

"He's my father!" exclaims Rachel. "I care! It's family. There's only us left—Lev, Tasha, you. Me. He's not the enemy. And you do. Care. I know you do," she adds, sitting up cross-legged and noting the light, how it fills the room in streams, etching out the shape of Zach recumbent, a bold coastline in a clarion sky. I drop anchor here, thinks Rachel. Anywhere here. You are my home, my horizon, my shore. *How long is the coast of Britain?*

"Lev thought—" Zach insists heatedly, "he *thinks*—I'm a numbskull. An animal. A peasant, *muzhik.* You know it, Rach. But it doesn't matter anymore."

"You didn't take to science, that's all. It disappoints him."

"Yes I did! I did bloody take to science."

"Indeed," Rachel concedes half-heartedly. "Zachariah Wolff, his science! Well . . . Mama always said you were musical, wanted you to pursue it. She never listened to me. No interest in me musically. And I was the one at piano lessons. So there."

"She conducted MALE choirs, Rachel!"

"And you made her laugh. I did not. She liked that very much, how you made her laugh."

"Where's my song, then? Sing to me."

Rachel touches his hair, parting the lustrous dark curls to follow her favourite path on his scalp, a thin seam of barren follicles and scar tissue tender as kid. *Tropa* means "path," it means "hope." "Soft," she murmurs. "And an old thing! Your wound."

"I'm an old bruiser."

"A bruiser of England."

"Let no one sneer . . ." Zach begins.

". . . at the bruisers of England," says Rachel, bending low to kiss him. "George Borrow. You smell a bit like damp dog, you know."

"Sing, Rachel."

"I'm no longer in the singing vein. I'm in the caressing vein."

"I see," he says. "Rachel. Don't let him take you from me. Lev— don't let him take you from me," Zach repeats as she runs her fingertips slowly down his flank, tracing the ribs, tapping each one softly, *piano*, to linger on the *ilium*, delighting in the graceful sweep to the pubis where she rests the back of her hand, marvelling at the delicate hollow there, where she presses her lips and wants to cry.

"Your hair is so long now," Zach says very quietly, with reverence. "When was it you cut it short? Only last year. So long now. My beauty, my dove."

Rachel sings.

> *O dear, what can the matter be*
> *Dear, dear, what can the matter be?*
> *O dear, what can the matter be?*
> *Johnny's so long at the fair.*

"Now you," she says. "Sing."

" 'He promised he'd buy me a'—what, Rach? I've lost the word."

"*Fairing.*"

"Right," Zach says, and resumes,

> *He promised he'd buy me a fairing should please me*
> *And then for a kiss, oh! He vowed he would tease me,*
> *He promised to buy me a bunch of blue ribbons*
> *To tie up my bonny brown hair.*

"Mama was right, you know. About your voice. How you can sing. Mama was right."

Zachariah sits up with a jolt. "Katya!" he calls. "Katya!"

"Mama!" echoes Rachel, squeezing Zach's hand. "Zach, I need to tell you something. About Katya. It's been nearly two years, you know and . . . Oh no, here they come!" Rachel complains suddenly, pressing one ear to Zach's chest and fumbling for his left hand to cover the other. "Stop my ears! Quick!" she says, and so he holds her tightly, lying back down to curl himself around her and make a cage of his body, an outer ring to keep her in.

My whipper-out, she thinks.

Turbulence.

Every morning at opening time in the Gardens, if still in bed, Rachel is assaulted by noise, a captive of her own poor timing. She takes the onrush of sound, irrationally, as an ill omen. The banshee yapping of four Yorkshire terriers on their excitable way to the Gardens behind the terraced close is an approach audible to Rachel a street away, a battle-cry. Havoc! They career through the gates with their pack-mate, an albino Staffordshire bull terrier, trailing their mistress, the five leads twitching in her grasp before the release whereupon she is heard screaming their names with music hall hysteria, and the worst sound is yet to come; the metronomic puff puff of the Staffie as he hurtles mindlessly after the ball on his bow legs. Doggedly.

Rachel recalls crossing the park one afternoon when the dogs were on their second outing of the day and the pack flew at her, apparently in greeting, the albino rocketing off the ground to head-butt her straight in the mouth. Kangaroo punch, uppercut, near KO.

"You OK, love?" the woman screamed at her, laughing as she clipped up the Staffie before peering into Rachel's face. "Let me see. Open wide. No blood. Yeah, you're all right, love. He was kissing you, that's all! Awww, he likes you!"

Rachel attempted a smile in response and fingered her chin and teeth surreptitiously for damage, glancing meanwhile at the Staffordshire bull, at his pink-black gums and bear-trap jaw and small red-rimmed eyes set too far apart. She listened to his ragged grunting, his squawk of a bark. The dog's name, the woman added with a cackle, is Tyson.

Rachel touched her tingling jaw and thought of Muhammad Ali replying to a question in an interview about just how it feels to get hit hard by George Foreman, say, or Joe Frazier—by a heavy hitter—and he likens the sensation to the kind of jarring you feel in your hand if you whack a stiff branch against the ground, but the jarring is of the whole body. He explains it can take up to twenty seconds for the mind to clear. This is one of the distinctions of great fighters, all of whom get hit, this ability to take a punch and hold on until the mind clears and, in Ali's case, allowing instinct to dictate his particular defence. Ali dances, ties up his opponent, holds his head down, does the rope-a-dope. His mind clears.

Later that day, Rachel watched her face in the mirror, the bruised chin, the fat upper lip. *Glasgow kiss*, Zach called it. She pictured the squat mistress of marauding dogs, ageless somehow, her hair shaped into an old-world beehive, dyed a lurid red. She heard the five-alarm voice in her head, saw the woman's name in bright gold filigree lettering round the neck. Dog-tag. Rachel tried to replicate her pattern of screaming and laughter, to shout and laugh in one go or, at least, in rapid fire, and could not. She smiled ruefully at her temporary disfigurement, her now more than normally imperfect bilateral symmetry.

—*Rachel, asks Lev, what is reflection?*

—*Reflection is a mathematical concept, not a shape or formula. It is a transformation.*

Especially when you are the recipient of a Glasgow kiss.

Rachel thinks of the pain she feels in her ears at the sound of the woman and her dogs, and remembers how very much older is the organ of hearing than speech. Hearing is so much older than speech.

.   .   .

"Has she gone yet?" asks Rachel, holding the pillow over her ears. The banshee.

"Not yet," Zach replies, stretching to flick at the curtains through the bars of their wrought-iron headboard. "And here comes Baba Yaga."

"Oh no!" says Rachel. "What a nightmare! We should never have slept in."

"Rach! You can hear it all over the house. Not just the bedroom."

"Not this loudly! It's right in our laps here. Like a curse."

Baba Yaga is a portly young woman in tall boots and a Cossack hat she exchanges for a turban in summer. She sports dark glasses in all weathers and is forever black-clad, and famous in the environs for her vodka-breath and whiplash mood changes, from flirt to harpy in tenths of a second. She is a dog walker of epic flair and incompetence, an amateur of miniature tykes with irascible temperaments, snarling and complaining at imperious pitches and regularly going walkabout on her watch, meaning few locals have escaped her urgent collaring, when she will demand in curiously airy tones, "Have you seen Darcy? Treacle? Princess?"

Baba Yaga is another strident presence in the Gardens, herself the owner of three delirious Pomeranians suffering from a gamut of infirmities; blindness, deafness, lameness, incontinence and neurosis, either trotting drunkenly in her wake or riding in a pram, all of them wild-eyed and churlish and yapping at shadows, or subdued as penitents, their little tongues peeping out foolishly to one side of their foreshortened jaws.

Coming upon Rachel reading in the Gardens one afternoon, Baba Yaga announces, without invitation, that when they go to the bridge, Rainbow Bridge, her dogs will on no account be fodder for worms; she intends to have them stuffed.

"There's a word for it . . . You must know, hon! You're an *author*, aren't you?"

"I'm more of a—I'm not sure I can help you," says Rachel, closing her book and rising purposefully from the bench.

"Yes, but you'd know," she adds, her voice cajoling. "With *your* education!"

"Taxidermy?" suggests Rachel with reluctance.

"Taxidermy! Bless!" exclaims Baba Yaga before bashing off with her brood, ostentatious and fly. "*So* clever!"

Not long afterwards, while working on the endpapers to her book on the peregrinations of Sam the Russian and Jonah the Needle and *Rattus norvegicus*, Rachel maps north-western Europe, marking in the cities of the Rhine—Karlsruhe, Hockenheim, Mannheim and Worms—and is troubled, as ever, by the name of this city port and of the historical meetings that took place there, the Diet of Worms. This time, Rachel pictures the Pomeranians on little plinths, not fodder for worms, no diet of worms, but frozen in a variety of manic postures like Furies situated about the rooms of Baba Yaga's flat.

"Zach, let's get up. Let the day begin! Quick, before anyone else comes. There's that awful couple, you know: with the waddling gait, booming voice, the fighting pit bull—"

"Pit bull *cross*. That's how they get away with it. Owning them, I mean. It's not *always* fighting."

"Yes, but that couple. They're so—*elemental*! Scary. Prehistoric. If I see them when I pass the park entrance, I have to look away. I rush home!"

Zach laughs.

Close the gate, Peter!

"Don't look at them, don't listen," says Zach, grasping her head gently and, with thumbs across her zygomatics, pressing lips to her brow and on to her eyes and mouth. "The old *aliks* in there call the Gardens the *boneyard*. Did you know that? I hear them on their mobiles. I'm in the boneyard, they say. How come they all have mobiles? Really expensive ones. Weird."

"I don't know," she whispers.

"Come on, Rach! Forget them. Stop listening."

"It's too late," she protests.

"Then play with me! Let's take a ride. Ride with me. To Lake Vostok!"

"Nearly four verst beneath?"

"Yes! And across three times nine countries to—"

"—the thirtieth tsardom," she says, completing the refrain distractedly.

"Why are you so sad?" asks Zachariah in full fairy-tale voice, casting his arms wide for emphasis, displaying his superior reach.

Rachel rallies, recovering at the sight of him arms akimbo, sitting high on his haunches. She marvels at his form, muscular and elegant: *trapezius, pectoralis, latissimus dorsi, serratus anterior, abdominal oblique*—loins! Rachel looks into his eyes where she sees herself reflected. Reflected and transformed.

A Miller writes:

Zachariah Wolff, his shape. One is struck with his excellence of frame, a high treat to the lover of anatomy, for his symmetry of figure cannot pass unnoticed and, when stripped, his athletic beauty defies competition. Wolff has experienced the good effects of cultivation and mannerliness, being a fair chanter and eminently fond of books, and withal the above pleasing traits he unites a prepossessing appearance, original style and peculiar science, exciting considerable attention amongst both the Fancy and, it is reported, our most elevated and beautiful countrywomen. Never has a finer fellow peeled in the ring!

Zachariah, Zachariah, my fighting man.

"Hey!" exclaims Zach. "Is that a smile I see before me? You're smiling."

"Do it, Zach," urges Rachel, plucking a tissue from the bedside box. "Do the wave. The magic handkerchief."

"Then you tell a story!" he says. "OK?"

"Yes," she agrees. "A story."

"Right then. Ready? I'm flapping the hanky. Let's fly."

Marya Morevna

This tale concerns disobedience. It's also about animality and humanity, and involves a talking horse and morphology. And a magic handkerchief.

When the young Tsarevich Alexis marries the warrior princess Marya Morevna, they live blissfully for a short while in her palace before she is called away, bashing off to defend some far-flung corner of her kingdom.

"Mind the palace," she tells her beloved, "but DO NOT DO NOT DO NOT open the locked closet in my inner chamber."

Mistake. She should not have said that. Proscriptions are so dangerous.

Alexis endures three days before giving in to curiosity and opening the door to the locked closet only to reveal the wizard Kashchey the Deathless within, constrained by twelve chains. The number of chains required to hold him ought to have been warning enough but the Tsarevich is duped into releasing him and the wizard flies off and captures Marya and takes her across three times nine tsardoms to his own country. After several abortive rescue attempts, Alexis learns from his wife that he requires:

1. Kashchey's magic hanky, which Marya has helpfully stolen for him.

2. A very fast horse with a white star.

And so the Tsarevich braces himself for adventure, suffering thirst, fatigue and hunger along the way. His empathy for animals is seriously tested as he passes up on potential meals of fledgling, honeycomb and crayfish en route to Baba Yaga. He travels across three times nine lands in the thirtieth tsardom, across the River of Fire to her hut on chicken legs which is surrounded by twelve stakes, eleven of which bear young men's heads. One stake is thus far headless.

"I smell Russian blood," sneers Baba Yaga upon the Tsarevich's approach.

Why has the Tsarevich come here to the crazy hut on chicken legs?

He has come for a fast horse with a white star, a rarity foaled every three years by a wonderful mare living far away by the sea. Monthly the mare gives birth to foals that are regularly devoured by a pack of twelve angry wolves. But every three years, Baba Yaga fights off the wolves for the white-starred foals, awarding one in wages to Kashchey the Deathless, Baba Yaga's stable-lad in his youth.

Thanks to help from the grateful fledgling, bees and crayfish, spared by Alexis in spite of extreme hunger, Alexis keeps his head on his young shoulders and secures a marvellous colt, youngest brother of the wizard's own steed, and he rides back across the River of Fire in three shakes of the magic handkerchief: three waves to the right raise a stone bridge, three to the left collapse it. Alexis rescues Marya with the wizard in hot pursuit, sword raised, driving on his white-starred horse, beating him on. Kashchey is an abusive master, merciless with a whip. He catches up.

"O brother, brother!" bemoans the younger horse, appealing to his elder in the name of blood and pedigree. "How can you be a slave to such an unclean monster? Throw him off!"

Brother horse is inspired. Enslavement is so mind-numbing, but now the horse awakens from subjugation and throws the wizard, that unclean monster, trampling him underfoot. And the Tsarevich, who has great empathy for animals, rides away with his love, but to his own palace, not hers. To his own native place from which a man must not stay too long, nor stray too far.

. . .

Zach raises the tissue at the end of Rachel's story. *Fogle, belcher.* He waves it three times to the right.

"Quick, quick!" he urges. "Ride with me!"

"I love how he stands up for himself and chooses his own kingdom in the end," laughs Rachel.

"Too right," says Zach. "She had a devil in the closet, that girl of his. Good thing they bloody moved out. Hey. What was it you wanted to tell me? About Katya. It being nearly two years. What about it, Rach?"

[TWENTY-THREE]

Before and in between times that a wolf's mate is pregnant, whelping, nurs-ing, weaning, a wolf will have a selection of dens to hand, as well as caches of food, so he is able to move house in case of danger, or overcrowding or uncleanliness. He is always ready to move his family. A wolf is a fatalist too.

Before Rachel is born and while they still have a lease on the flat in Paris, in case of a change of heart or circumstance, Lev and Katya buy a squat Georgian house in Chelsea near the Royal Hospital, hard by the river and the Chelsea Physic Garden, once known as the Apothecaries' Garden, and referred to by the child Rachel as the Chelsea *Psychic*. She parades the Thames as a girl, hand in hand with her father, walking the Embankment and crossing the bridges—Battersea, Albert, Chelsea, and Vauxhall, Lambeth, Westminster, and Hungerford—from The World's End to Waterloo, learning the blue waters and the old stones of her native place.

When Katya is in her twelfth week, she knows this child is a girl. She shall call her Rachel. Katya is fractious in pregnancy. She hopes her con-stitution and her mind can endure this kind of turbulence again, because she will have a boy. There must be a boy. Tasha, she muses, should not be childless. She would thrive in such a state. A baby on her lap, her hands at the piano: Katya sees it all so clearly. And how Tasha would revel in *this*, the flutter within, a beating of wings, the waking animal. Lev presses his ear to her abdomen, holding Katya's hips, enraptured.

"Baby has to move, but cannot escape. Not yet!" he exclaims. "Peri-odic cycle, oscillation."

Katya touches his head absently, hearing Russian music.

Above them flew birdy, chirping merrily.

"Oh what brave fellows we are, Peter and I! Look what we have caught!"

And if one listened carefully, one could hear the duck quacking inside the wolf, because the wolf, in his hurry, had swallowed her alive.

Katya Wolff laughs.

Baby, I have swallowed you alive.

Typically, for a few days before and following the birth of wolf pups, the mother keeps to herself, not even permitting the male to enter the den, although whelping is an occasion for heightened awareness amongst the wolf pack, with some members scratching at the entrance to the den and whining in excitement and, in one study, it is observed how the male kidnaps a pup not, the researcher writes, "to kill, but to care for. Wolves," she adds, "are crazy about puppies."

It takes ten to thirteen days for a pup's eyes to open and in three weeks they have milk teeth, explore the den, and can hear.

Within three weeks of Rachel's birth, Katya begins rehearsals for a recording of non-choral work for a change, a recording of Mendelssohn quartets and the exuberant octet, Katya fulfilling a long-standing promise to Lev, who is an amateur of Mendelssohn. It is a valentine recording. She baulks, however, at the Hebrides Overture, teasing Lev for his romanticism.

Every day she leaves for the studio, he holds Rachel up in the window, lest Katya should turn to wave, but she never does, and Rachel, in Lev's firm grasp, can feel the involuntary contractions of his heart through the thin skin and malleable bones of her back and, at the crown of her downy head and barely calcified skull, she also feels the pressure of his lower mandible and the heavy tap of his tears. She can hear him cry. Her sense of hearing is most acute.

"Rach? Are you listening to me? Asked you a question."

"I know," she murmurs. "In a minute."

Rachel glances towards the window, at the billowing muslin, and hears infernal yapping, coarse barks and rebarbative voices and other, less abrasive sounds. She hears the street cries of park keepers and cleaners, calls of fellowship, as are the early morning growls of local *aliks* well into their second tall tinnies of the day. The drunks make the most of the hours, passingly aware their best season is nearing its end, feeling it in the keener breeze now rustling the leaves of the London planes, causing some to fall through the air like handkerchiefs dropped from windowsills.

A handkerchief tree, Zach.

To be planted next to the weeping willow!

Companion planting.

The drunks feel the change in the falling of the leaves and might hear it in birdsong, were they to listen, the sound leaner and more urgent than the idle trills of deep summer. These are a drunk's dog-days.

Rachel wraps her arms around Zach, goes hip to hip with him, resting her head in the crook of his neck, her exposed ear open to the morning sounds of Alla pacing the boards of the house next door, her resentful tread surprisingly heavy given her attenuated frame. These old walls, the winds and sounds blow straight through. Hear the deep rumble of bedroom sash window on the sill of which Alla maintains a saucer filled with stones to hurl at loitering pigeons, bone-grubbing, mating or pecking at berries in the aged cotoneaster that sprawls across their neighbouring plots. She begrudges them even this. Alla watches the pigeons and the Gardens beyond, looking out for iniquity; she's a quisling. She casts a reproving eye at the world, blameworthy of all ills, pigeon shit, clang of playground gate, her own decay. Rachel thinks how un-Russian it is, Alla's angry soul, how rootless her coiled belligerence and disaffection, the self-similarity of her rage. Papa, her anger is strangely proportioned, similar on any scale, fractal as a rock, a fern, a cloud! Her old façade is stone over stone, also un-Russian. Alla is an émigrée with no dream of return.

"Why so sad?" Zach queries in fairy-tale tones. "Rachel?"

"O my brother Ivanushka," she recites. "A heavy stone is round my throat, silken grass grows through my fingers, yellow sand lies on my breast."

"That's perishing gloomy," Zach remarks.

"It ends happily though. Gracious! Everything sounds depressing this morning," adds Rachel. "There's a teacher at my school, she's very young, but she goes, Gracious! Just like a dowager. Makes me laugh.

Except this morning. I can't help it. I am too depressed. I hate those voices so much. In the Gardens."

"Stop listening," Zach scolds and puts his hands in her hair—*silken grass grows through his fingers.* "Rachel?" he asks. "Wear the green dress tomorrow."

"Tomorrow?"

"At All Souls's. At Aubry's. His party. The New Forest. I told you! You loved the last party! Summer one. This is just a few of us. I told you a hundred times!"

"Oh yes," she replies vaguely. "Thomas Love. His birthday party. Perhaps I can't make it."

"What do you mean? Of course you can. Why wouldn't you?" he insists, frowning and sitting up suddenly in consternation, legs crossed, elbows on knees, his welterweight abdominals in tight boyish creases across the *linea alba.* "He'll retire after the big fight, I reckon. It's an important party for him. Come on! You have to come. He'll retire soon and take over the vineyard."

"He told me his brother was destined for that," says Rachel.

"He told you?"

"That day at the cricket. That his brother was to take over the vine-yard. And he told me about the sailing accident. About Percy's drowning. How sad, it's all so terribly sad."

"Norfolk coast. All Souls was sixteen or so. And Percy—"

"Percy Bysshe."

"Hell, yes. Percy Bysshe. Mother was quite a—"

"Romantic," says Rachel. "So is Thomas not a keen wine-maker, then?"

"Don't know. It was definitely Percy's thing. He was hands-on every vintage as a lad. Mad about the place, the vines, phases-of-the-moon planting, the whole thing. But it does matter to All Souls. Definitely. I mean, he just sacked the cellar-master! What a chap, Rach! Read biology, specialist in—ichthyology—and now a fighter! Strange. Actually, I don't think he's a keen fighter either. Not a natural. You know? Fine cricketer, though. Elegant—fantastic eye, beautiful driver and puller. Can bowl a bit, too."

"He said that about you."

"He did? What? Said what?"

"That . . . Never mind. Why is he not a natural fighter, Zach? How can that be?" Rachel asks, resting her head in his lap, her locks tumbling across his loins. She traces the taut line of his inguinal ligament. "Wolff," she announces, "is considered one of the best-made men in the kingdom! His science is pre-eminent, his wind truly excellent, his bottom unrivalled and humanity resplendent! And his shape, oh his shape, uncommon prepossessing! To Nature, he is indebted!"

"That bloody tickles," says Zach.

"Tell me then, why is Thomas not a natural? Thomas Love."

"Well, he has technique. He can dance, cut off the ring, and he has that amazing back-pedalling hook ability—like Ali! And like Ali, he can do those tiny little head movements—confuses the other guy. Brilliant. And he has great balance, great hand speed. But there's no real—dominance. Domination. He fences, you know? It's like fencing. He has no—has little real violence. That's my view."

Rachel sits up, cocks her head to one side, bright unblinking eyes on Zachariah. "Did *you* have it?" she asks. "Violence?"

Zach answers slowly. "I could hurt a man. In the ring. I had—I don't know. Intent. I wanted to—could—hurt. Anyway. You'll come to Aubry's, yeah?"

"So much to do before I leave, Zach. And you can all be fellows together, if I don't go. It's fun for you. Boys' Own and all that."

"Don't want to be fellows together. I'm always a fellow, you don't stop me. And leave where? What do you mean, *before I leave?*"

"Petersburg, Zach. The memorial. I mentioned it once a long time ago. Months ago. And I've been trying to remind you. I keep trying and something always . . . Will he definitely beat Sandbags? Thomas?"

"Sandbag! Not Sandbags. You do it on purpose. Yes," snaps Zach. "He will," he asserts, explaining that Sandbag Shaw, all hard feelings aside, is strong, but still no match for All Souls, having trained poorly, sacrificing agility for power, increasingly burdened by tight weight-lifting muscles that diminish his range and speed. There is even a chance he may not make the weight. What Zach does not tell her is that Aubry, by turning his head so often in evasion, is vulnerable to hits to the back of the neck, and base of the skull. He is sparring, furthermore, with fighters of Sandbag's weight class and greater bulk, and this is dangerous too, because most injuries occur in the boxing gym, where mismatches are rife.

"How did he get that name? Sandbag."

"I've told you. Haven't I explained it before?"

"Tell me again," Rachel says.

"Always complaining," goes Zach. "He always lets fly some rumour, making sure it comes from a third party, right before a fight. You know. That he is ailing. He has flu, he has torn muscles in the back of his hand, he has a back spasm, something—anything—to lull the gullible into fighting loose, leaving openings, all that. Or just into wasting energy. You know. In wondering what Shaw's game is, what the truth is. That's sandbagging. And if Shaw loses, it's the same. He lost through injury—fought one-handed, he was blinded, etc. He wrong-foots a man. He's not straight. Part of that's normal—you shouldn't let a guy read you—but Shaw takes it to rude extremes. You know. Works hard at it."

"Sandbag Shaw. The name game! I played it with Thomas that day at the match. Summer party. Before he joined you at the wicket. We were discussing sporting nicknames. And his own epithet, *All Souls*."

"I have new ones! Tom Kitchen—chef! Wait! I wrote them down. Pass me—it's okay," he says, reaching for his jeans on the floor and finding a crumpled paper. "Here we go! I've been saving them up. Richard Pennycook—banker! Robert Grave—engraver! Seriously. And Coral the lifeguard. Howzat!"

"I have new ones too," Rachel proposes. "Lawes the prison warden. Hacker the journalist. Graves the undertaker!"

"Johnny Basham was a fighter," Zach adds, his voice strained suddenly, a troubling sensation in the pit of him, a pitching and roiling. "Truth."

"I know," Rachel says quietly. "I love that one. A favourite. And Gardiner the landscape designer. True also. And I just bought a book on trees by J. D. Vertrees," she says, cajoling, stroking the tumbled curl of hair from his lowered eyes, knowing she has transgressed, betrayed him. "Petal Wilson is a horticulturalist. Zach? Speak! What is it? Tell me."

"Hunter, Baker, Shepherd, Collier," he persists, sheepish. "Sorry. I'm stupid. It's *our* game, that's all."

"It's not an unusual game, Zach. Silly wolf. It's not Lake Vostok, is it? Or the thirtieth tsardom! Now *that's* private. Special."

"I know," he says. "I know. I'm silly, stupid. OK."

Zach draws her in sharply, close as he can, his right arm across her shoulders, the left round the hips, the abductors of his hands, hardened steel. He opens his mouth to taste the tender skin under the ear, and squeezes his eyes shut, the better to breathe her, even as she reminds him in a flurry of whispered words that she must go to Petersburg with Lev, for his conference at the State University and Mama's tribute at the Cathedral of Peter and Paul on the second anniversary of her death. Rachel addresses Zach in Russian, *Vashe siyatel'stvo,* she says with infinite tenderness—Your Radiance, she calls him—explaining she will be gone three times nine days and Zach will be so busy with Aubry and the fight he will barely notice her absence, the time will pass like a train. Like Stephenson's Rocket! In three shakes of the magic handkerchief! And all the while she speaks in his ear, her occipital membranes slip and shift and her eyelids flicker, the smooth and cardiac muscles of her body pulse wildly, as in a squall.

Anatomy lessons.

—How many muscles in the skeletal system?

—Nearly six hundred and twenty, Papa.

—And what is special about them?

—These are the muscles under our conscious control. Voluntary. The smooth and cardiac muscles are involuntary.

Nothing she can do.

"Ne boysya, Zachariah!" Rachel exclaims. *Don't worry, don't be afraid.* "Three times nine days," she says. "That is all!"

And Rachel does as Henry Cooper once did in consoling the loser of a junior bout, the English heavyweight clasping him manfully round the ears in commiseration, all the better to flick deftly at tears running from the boy's startled eyes so that no one might sneer at this weeping young bruiser of England. Rachel applies her hands to Zach's head. She flicks at tears with her thumbs.

"Be my wolf," she says.

"I am your wolf," he replies, fighting for wind.

Let the day begin.

[TWENTY-FOUR]

THE NATURAL HISTORY OF LONDON
or, Samuel Alexander, known to the Fancy as Sam the Russian,
uncrowned Tsar of the Prize Ring;
the Life and Strange Surprizing Adventures; Cont'd.

On the eve of the crossing to France arranged by Tom Spring and Nathaniel Jones the Apothecary, the somewhat enfeebled Sam the Russian is escorted to rooms in Bentinck Street by the journalist in the green fanteegs, known as A Miller.

In the misty dark interior of the hansom, she reviews each stage of the plan of escape in its each and every detail, as instructed by Spring and Jones, in order to imprint it upon Sam's fevered brain. Careful to address him in clear, distinct tones accompanied by gestures of the hands in deference to his damaged auscultatory faculties, Miss Miller arrives at the summation by describing Sam's prospective host as an uncommon fellow, very spry, and a member of the black-letter gentry with curious theatrical ambitions. She first encountered the nib sprig at the Fives Court and, latterly, in the library of the British Museum where they have both been toiling on sketches of London. Miss Miller's is an account of the Gentlemen v. Players match at Lord's, an event in the sporting calendar officially closed to the female of the species and which, therefore, she attended in disguise, togged in upper benjamin, breeches, tall tile and high-lows in the company of Pierce Egan, author of *Boxiana* and *Life in London,* "Glorious Pierce," "Pip" to his friends. Her fellow scribe in Bentinck Street, explains Miss Miller as the cab races towards Westminster, is presently a reporter with the *Mirror of Parliament.*

"Perhaps you have met him? The gloque," she articulates clearly and distinctly with movements of her fingers according to the *Virgin Philosophie of Gesture,* "is uncommonly well-togged for a man of humble beginnings and modest means. And very much in the bloom of vigour," she adds with a smile, whereupon she is arrested by an expression of tearful emotion and excited anticipation on young Sam's phiz.

"Why, I know him, Miss Miller! Is it Dickens?"

"Indeed, yes!" she replies, watching the young pugilist alight from the cab in a show of undaunted agility, notwithstanding his wounds. Presently, she directs him to the door of the reporter's crib, reminding Sam that she will come for him very early in the morning to meet Spring, Jones and Jonah and ready him for his journey to the continent.

"Thank you, Miss Miller!" exclaims Alexander. "I am profoundly obliged," he adds in shyness, noticing, perhaps for the first time, as she hands down his parcel of clothing, grub and bub, how, for athletic beauty, she is surely unrivalled. Sam notes how attractive are her voice and manners, how bright her sparklers.

"Until tomorrow, Samuel," she shouts, departing.

And so at the door to Dickens's chambers in Bentinck Street, the two young coves of old acquaintance greet each other lustily, Dickens shaking Sam by the hands with some spirit and, though he suffers still from the effects of his epic battle with Young Dutch (in spite of the studious ministrations of Jones the Apothecary), yet this brave heart prevents any display of weakness from discouraging his good friend's prolonged and gay effusions.

"Enter!" cries Dickens. "Sit, sit!"

What with the prodigies of valour he performed on Finchley Common and the trying conflicts ensuing, Sam is somewhat on the totter and readily accepts the proffered chair in Dickens's den, marvelling at his friend, who is in a fair state of animation and, having been apprised of Sam's difficulties, discourses in a mixture of loud cries, articulated whispers and extravagant motions of his digits in a vague effort at John Bulwer's *Chirologia, or, the Naturall language of the Hand.* Finally, and much to Alexander's relief, he resorts to mixing his speech with scrawled queries on paper, thus alleviating the dizzying assault upon Sam's poor senses and, by the by, revealing just how very fly young Dickens has become to all the subtleties of sporting lingo. Before Sam's startled eyes, Dickens loses himself in praises and curiosity surrounding the events on Finchley Common and so transforms himself in deportment and demeanour in the conjuring of the scene that he might well be mistaken for any young buck or member of the Fancy. A corinthian! Dickens comes it strong indeed, now stumping it across the boards of his crib, his ogles flashing and fists raised in attitude, now pouring stout—*heavy whet,* says he—from the bottles supplied by Spring, and all the while the lingo trips off his tongue until he falls, done-up, into a seat opposite Sam, as it were, a boxer floored.

"Man down!" says Sam in jest.

"Capital!" shouts Charles. "Goodness gracious me, what larks!"

"What a remarkable fellow you are," Sam offers feelingly as the two chums set about their supper of bread-and-cheese-and-beer.

"Gloque!" corrects Charles. "Gill, buck, blade!" he suggests.

"Cove," strikes in Sam.

"Kid!"

"A trump, sir, and a corinthian," pronounces the Russian, raising his peg of porter.

"Why, thank you, Sam. Lord bless you!"

"But do not enter the lists, I entreat you," Sam adds with a laugh. "Boxing, I daresay, is not your destiny. Your wind is, well, truly terrific, but—"

"*Pugilists cannot be too cool,*" quotes Dickens, exultant.

"Indeed," agrees Sam. "Indeed!"

"Pierce Egan, *Boxiana.* Glorious Pierce! Fancy's Child, Pip. Look!" says the excitable reporter, dashing to his library to extract his volumes of *Boxiana* and issues of *Life in London or The Day and Night Scenes of Jerry Hawthorn, Esq., and his elegant friend Corinthian Tom, accompanied by Bob Logic, the Oxonian, in their Rambles and Sprees through the Metropolis.* "Tremendous!" Dickens concludes, quite overcome. "Now tell me all the story," he demands, "of your battle with Young Dutch. In every particular. And rest assured, you have nothing to fear in my ken, from traps or beak, or scout. You'll not be quodded on my watch, Sam!" he shouts. "You may roost here in perfect happiness!"

"Not, perhaps," observes Sam with some hesitation, fretful he might give offence, "if we remain so, that is to say, LOUD, sir. What a noise!"

"True," says Dickens. "My dear Sam. Lord. What a queer lay! Speak, Sam, and I shall confine myself solely to nods of the conk—of the upper storey, that is—and to written remarks. Dear me!" he mutters, distressed, pulling on the tails of his yellow kerseymere waistcoat, lacking only the buttons engraved with the initials P.C. to distinguish him as a fully fledged member of the Pugilistic Club.

Surely, muses Sam the Russian, as he prepares to tell *all* his story, in every particular, a more fiery amateur of the fistic art was never seen in the kingdom. His friend Dickens shews an enquiring spirit almost beyond human nature to sustain.

"Begin, Sam!"

"Your waistcoat," Sam murmurs, drifting from fatigue and bodily pain.

Sam Alexander, Tsar of the Prize Ring, thinks on his early days in Tom Spring's backroom, following sessions of sparring and applications of rub, when the ex–Champion of All England would recount the history, rise and principles of boxing for Sam's education. In the course of this lesson, Spring related the particulars of the foundation of the Pugilistic Club, a society devoted to the celebration of pugilism and its advantages to the true Briton, his noble character and brave heart. The fistic arts, Spring expounded, as opposed to all manner of clandestine revenge and pugnacity, distinguish a man, checking corruption of the soul and unfortunate tendencies such as Frenchification, deceit, effeminacy and other deep behaviours. The society determines to prize courage, honesty and manliness, expose crosses in the ring and any other mode of unsporting conduct, and raise funds for boxers' purses by way of annual subscriptions. Members wear a blue jemmy, yellow waistcoat and engraved buttons bearing the initials P.C. Sam is lost in recollection and much distressed. He is appalled to know that he began by engaging in a noble battle on Finchley Common, according to the brave tenets of the noble art of self-defence, only to end in deep behaviours, namely in committing a vengeful act of the clandestine kind—a low transaction of knives.

Instructions to Apprentices.

As you hope for Success in this World, and Happiness in the next, you are to be mindful of what has been taught you. You are to behave honestly, justly, soberly, and carefully in everything, to everybody, and especially towards your Master, Mistress and family; and to execute all lawful commands with Industry, Cheerfulness and good Manners.

Sam Alexander drops a tear.

"What's the matter?" demands Charles.

"I was thinking on yellow and blue!" he starts. *Yellowman, belcher.* "And of waistcoats with P.C. engraved on the buttons. The Pugilistic Club!"

"P.C. on buttons," echoes Dickens, with an air of abstraction. "I see. P.C. . . . But now," he says, with renewed enthusiasm, "tell me *all* the story!"

And so Sam obliges. The two friends sit up late, late into the night and sleep only two hours before Miss Miller cries softly at the lock.

SAMUEL ALEXANDER, HIS PEREGRINATIONS
Part One

There is a small, tense leaving-party on the docks in the early hours of the following morning and, though Dickens cannot be there, he is not disappointed, enjoying the flourishes of his teeming young brain as he brooms for Parliament for another day of scribing minutiae in shorthand from the upper gallery. There he sits writing his reports, but seeing and hearing the morning mists and London cries of gulls and boatmen, the dark curling waters slapping against wood and stone, and the skiffs bobbing and rocking on the troubled surface of the Thames, with visions of grizzled convicts in chains appearing, and a boy in desperate flight to France, what larks! He sees and hears it all with much sensation, recalling, only briefly, the thwarted feelings and necessary grimness of his friend's harried departure this morning from his rooms and of their imminent separation, possibly forever. He vaguely recalls, furthermore, some words of Sam's concerning the P.C. and engravings on buttons, and the tale of Young Dutch and a Staffordshire bull terrier, and of a rat, a murder and a marvellous boxing match, and a lady of the black-letter gentry in green trousers and burgundy braces with a pattern of falling stars. And, even more vaguely, Charles remembers a keen monologue of Sam Alexander's regarding the Foundling Hospital and his mysterious beginnings. He recalls it in fragments—filling in the pieces for himself—this story of a father and the Battle of Borodino; of the Smolensk Road, New and Old, and of Jonah the Needle, a medallion of the Tsar, and a gambling token—a fish carved from bone with a hole for an eye.

A fish, thinks Charles when Parliament disperses for lunch. Fugitive Sam must be deep in the Channel by now, halfway to France. Charles hears the waters of the Thames in his auriculars as rain falls in Parliament Square. Sharp drops smack the pavement, leaving it slick and greasy. What a watery place is my city! The Thames is a river of watercourses, of feelers, brooks, creeks, sluices, ditches and sewers, open and flowing, spilling over; Stamford Brook, Beverley Brook, Counter's Creek. The Tyburn, Fleet and Wandle, Westbourne, Falcon, Effra and Peck. Black Ditch, Ravensbourne, Neckringer, Walbrook, Hackney Brook, Earl's Sluice, Lea River—yes, the Thames is a mighty artery carrying ships, fish, rats, night soil, cholera and now Sam the Russian, away and out to the sea, with fish beneath.

This is London. O my field.

Not for anything will Jonah the Needle entertain the suggestion he remain in bed instead of joining the leaving-party and attending upon his dearest friend up to the very last opportunity. Notwithstanding his dreadful injuries, therefore, the broken ribs and arm, the incisions about his hams, the left shutter swollen big as a heron's egg, and the loss of great quantities of claret, the boy is carried into the drag so thoroughly muffled in rugs, he comes nearest in likeness to a specimen of Egyptology or, as Spring ventures, he might more correctly be compared to the sleeping bat he once discovered in his cellar at the Castle. Jonah is also somewhat happily intoxicated by a recent concoction of Jones the Apothecary's designed to elevate the thinking processes whilst dulling the sensations of bodily pain.

"Bah! A ball of fire or two and the boy will soon be right, I daresay!" scoffs Spring, grasping a bottle of brandy.

"No, no," replies Jones in a spoffish manner. "This is much the finer option. *If* you'll allow me, Tom."

Jonah clutches a bundle to his person, wrapped in paper and tied with string and, in the folds of his blankets, a bird alights, the Needle, during his convalescence, having befriended a juvenile raven with astonishing purplish-green hues to his plumage, a creature much admired by young Jonah and repeatedly remarked upon in his fitful sleeps.

"Truly, the boy has an uncommon affinity," whispered Jones in the sick room and with such great consternation that Spring, busy about the rooms with ewers and linens and implements, stopped in his activity, much dismayed.

"Is it very bad, then, this affinity? Fatal perchance?"

"No, no, dear chap! By no means," replied Jones. "*Affinity*. With fauna. A good thing. Quite startling!"

"Ah," went Spring, none the wiser. "Well. We rise early tomorrow, Nathaniel. Very early."

Rattling across the cobbles, lurching at every turn, the drag hurtles towards the docks where Miss Miller is to meet them with young Sam, every jolt of the carriage causing Jonah to wince and groan inly, yet so ashamed is he to display any suffering, whenever Jones is moved to peer at him feelingly through the darkness, the young tailor asserts in tones of vexation that he is really "quite well" and, in fond mimicry of Sam his dearest friend, adds, "Feeling bobbish, indeed!"

The Beauty of the Benjamin

The first gift Sam ever received in life was a pouch Jonah fashioned from a pocket of his Coram foundling uniform and presented to his friend before they were placed out apprentice, and first set apart.

"For your things," had said Jonah, Sam's bosom friend he might never see again.

But on this day! Here on the docks in the early morning mists. What a party! And so many gifts!

"Hurry, Jones!" Spring pleads, well acquainted with his friend's spoff-ish ways. "The boat is here, already here."

"Certainly, certainly!" rejoins Jones, slightly wounded. "And so. Here find a *tonic*. For imbibing upon occasions of feebleness or exhaustion, do you understand? When you are dished, done up, etc. Is that correct? There we are. It is not perfect, however. Not yet perfect! But potent.

Though it lacks an ingredient. I have not had sufficient time to achieve perfection in the mixture and can only surmise, at present, what is lacking. That is to say—"

"Jones!" interposes Tom. "Time! I'm calling time!"

"When I am apprised of what is missing," Jones persists bravely, "and the tonic is perfect, why—I shall seek a patent and name it *Russian Elixir!*"

"I am overcome, sir," murmurs Sam. "Truly."

"It is stopped with a cork and wax. For the journey. Keep away from light and heat. Some elements are volatile. There is volatility. Do you hear me well enough?"

"Volatile," repeats Sam.

"And be wary of the French apothecary! His packages and bottles are most beguiling, but as for the contents, beware! There is much less within than meets the eye without. Remember it."

"I shall, sir. Thank you," says Sam as Jones steps aside to frown and polish his spectacles, his distress evident.

"Don't look at me, Samuel," commands the man of science sharply. "Pray don't look at me."

And without further parley, Tom Spring hands his apprentice and adopted son one parcel of bang-up bub and grub, ditto, spare shirt and undergarments, then holds up a roll of soft, a collection made for Sam through Tom's determined and judicious interference, having given the office uniquely to those of the Fancy whose approbation and high opinion of Alexander were equal to their superior humanity and discretion.

"One hundred guineas, Sam. But, stay!" says Spring, keeping hold of the purse and turning to Jonah the Needle. "Jonah? Are you ready?"

And so Jonah removes the bundle from beneath the folds of his rug and unwraps it carefully upon his lap from the bounds of paper and string to disclose a garment, which he holds up for Sam's inspection, an expression of proud humility upon the Needle's phiz.

Oh, what a beauteous vestment Jonah the Needle has wrought in his convalescence, compensating, in filigree and craftsmanship, most brilliantly for what it must by necessity lack in flash and fullness, lest Sam attract unwanted attention. But what style—what *twig*—in shape and detail! The silken stitching is elegant in the extreme, nigh invisible, the cut of the collar very particular, as are the narrow facings, rounding neatly at the buttonholes, with body tapering sensationally at the waist for the tails to drape over the buttocks and hams in the most becoming manner, yet wholly with the effect of emphasising his manliness, anatomical beauty and singular proportions, and never that effeminacy or excess of vanity that is often companion to personages blessed with such natural grace. Sam sports his new benjamin in utmost humility, admiring the plain worsted dyed darkest hunter green, and blushing before the assemblage at the surprising gaiety of the lining, of a silk coloured pale buff-yellow, much like the crown of the Northern Gannet.

"Tremendous," says Sam, in shyness.

"But mark the *lining,* young Sam!" exclaims Jones, bursting with revelations.

"I do, I do!" he replies, perplexed.

"No, no! You do *not* see," Jones protests, before Jonah intervenes, gesturing politely for silence as he fingers the interior of the benjamin, indicating tiny loops and closures that are a feature of every panel.

"Secret compartments," murmurs Jonah, signing the word "secret" according to Thomas Braidwood's combined system, made famous by Braidwood's Academy for the Deaf and Dumb and taught to young Jonah by Jones, fond of quoting the eminent Samuel Johnson who, after visiting Braidwood's, pronounced upon the system, *Whatever enlarges hope, will exalt courage*, and more teasingly, *After having seen the deaf taught arithmetick, who would be afraid to cultivate the Hebrides?*

"For your funds," Tom instructs. "For safekeeping."

"From rampers and prigs!" pipes Jones.

"Quite so, Nat," agrees Spring. "Be fly, Sam. Be fly."

Sam scrutinises the lining of his coat, much astonished at the fineness of detail, the disguised apertures and neat fastenings, the subtlety of the seams and pockets and impressive symmetry overall. He is startled moreover to discover a spare button sewn to the interior corner of the left tail, a button not at all in keeping with the rest and that he knows in an instant thereafter, recognising it as Jonah's own foundling token, a white porcelain bottle-ticket with two pin-holes where a chain once looped, and the word "ale" written upon it with fine cracks running into the ink, a flow of fine cracks that ever put Jonah in mind of the Thames and all its courses.

"Jonah!"

"For remembrance," the Needle strikes in. "I'll not need it!" he adds stoutly. "My hopes are extinguished. It is very plain. I am an orphan forever! Keep it in remembrance of our beginnings. Of Lamb's Conduit Fields and the Battle of Seven Dials. And in souvenir of Finchley Common. Of Young Dutch Evans and the death of Rat! Remember me!"

"Jonah the Needle," declares Sam the Russian with considerable firmness and piety, "Jonah, you are the uncrowned King of the Cutting-up Tribe. May you be covered in honour and pass your days without further harm until I may return to go alongside and defend thee."

"Thank you, Sam."

"Take my fish," Alexander says.

"No, Sam."

"I have the medallion. Take it," he commands, handing over his foundling token, the gambling marker made from bone in the shape of a fish.

"I thank you," whispers Jonah, clasping it tight.

And tears drop on the iron cheeks of bruisers, of the ex–Champion of All England and his apprentice, unrivalled for his age in bottom and science, yet thwarted in glory, his destiny, flight. Samuel Alexander, his sparklers shining in their suits of mourning, the colours faded from black and purple to blue and yellow, is a fugitive now, of his profession and native place. Tears drop likewise from the oculars of the apothecary and the tailor, the ex-laid-in-the-streets with a raven upon his shoulder and fish in his clenched fist and, while witnessing the general sympathy expressed by the party of males, the gentle scribe in the green fanteegs extracts a fine new fogle from the pocket of her jemmy, a belcher coloured bird's-eye blue and, before tying it feelingly about Sam Alexander's neck, she flaps it three times to the right.

"Fly, Sam," she urges quietly. "Be fly."

TWENTY-FIVE

ZACH WEPT. My fighting man!

It is so very difficult, thinks Rachel, flying in to Pulkova airport, to draw tears. To paint them, draw them, very hard. Depictions are maudlin, cartoonish. Rachel is sketching in the style of Hogarth's famous advertisement for his friend James Figg's London Academy for the Noble Science of Defence near Adam & Eve Court. By William Hogarth or attributed to William Hogarth. Hogarthian at any rate.

Hogarth downs tools and runs his hands through his no hair, leaving a smudge of ink and scatterings of minute copper filings across his bare pate. His friend Coram teases that in some lights Hogarth shimmers like stars and the elements—copper, silver, gold.

Rachel draws a ring, which is a square, of course, against a backdrop of St. Petersburg, the Peter and Paul Fortress, the Winter Palace, the Bronze Horseman, the Neva flowing. In the ring there is a violinist, a prize-fighter, a soldier and a single-stick player—or is it a conductor? And Rachel draws a wolf, tears springing from his eyes, tears of exertion, perspiration? Loss? In a cartoon sketch, the point is moot, though animals in reality do not weep or speak. Not yet. Not so far. Call it a question of scientific emergence. Anything is possible.

Hogarth is a walker, a watcher. One day he sees a boy beat a dog and it makes him sick at heart and his eyes fill with water, though he is not a tearful man. Snow can sometimes fall from a cloudless sky.

"Zachariah Wolff," writes Rachel beneath her drawing after Hogarth. "Master of the Noble Science of Defence."

Wolves do not weep. But bruisers do.

"Rachel!" Zach told her as a boy. "Fighters cry all the time!"

Cassius Clay became heavyweight champion of the world in 1964 when the man he coined "ugly bear," Sonny Liston, with his instinct for savagery, his surprising agility, tremendous left hook and epic two-fisted power, gave in at the bell for round seven in a manner not seen since Jess Willard lost the title to Jack Dempsey in 1919. Liston quit on his stool. After the fight, his cornerman helped him from the dressing room to a car and Sonny wept. In his hospital room later that night, Liston sat on his cot, swollen and dejected. The broken man resembled, said his manager, "a lump of clay." Which was apt. Sonny was a lump of Clay. Sonny lifted his useless bear paws and dropped them back in his lap. Liston admitted defeat and wept.

Animals speak, they weep.

"Rachel," says Lev, tapping her arm. "Tray, seatbelt. It's time."

Rachel downs tools, puts up her tray, fastens her seatbelt, eardrums imploding under pressure. The ossicles. She kisses her father's bearded jaw.

"Yes, Papa," she says.

"Zachariah, mind the palace," Rachel told her beloved before bashing off across three times nine countries. "But DO NOT DO NOT DO NOT enter the lists. No fighting! No barney, mill, contest, set-to, turn-up, battle, match!"

Zach laughed. He laughed and wept. Rachel stroked his head, his chest and forearms, his waist, thighs, loins and beautiful downy coat. Fur, pelt. The beauty of his coat.

Zach wept.

Exiting their gate at arrivals, Rachel and Lev are met by a broad-shouldered fellow with hooded eyes and a sensuous mouth. A comedy Russian, thinks Rachel, repressing a grin of delight as the man takes their baggage and leads them wordlessly to a long dark car. He opens a door to watch his two passengers settle upon seats of well-kept leather while a light snow falls in the evening air.

"A touch of weather," notes Lev, shivering slightly. "Memento mori!" he whispers, pulling his daughter close. "Whenever I'm here, snow makes me think of war. How ridiculous! Snow. People find it so beautiful and peaceful. Restful. And I think of death!"

"*Requiem*," Rachel teases, "does mean 'rest.'"

"I loathe requiems. Katya and those bloody requiems! The horror of them. Glacial! But an icy vodka! Now *this* I would find very restful."

"I daresay we are in the right place for it, Papa," remarks Rachel, exchanging a sweet smile for the blank stare of the driver meeting her open gaze in the rear-view mirror.

"*Credo in* vodka," he intones. "Hurry up, driver!" he adds under his breath.

"*Sanctus* and *benedictus* is he who comes to us with vodka," nods Rachel.

"*Miserere nobis!*" pleads Lev, eyes to the heavens.

"*Dona nobis* vodka," giggles his daughter.

"Or else!" Lev says, elbowing her.

Rachel peers into the snowy night from the car window. She watches snow fall on a St. Petersburg night. She has seen this before.

"Tasha, wait!" Zach exclaims to his auntie, who has come to stay while Rachel and Lev are in Russia. "Not warm enough, that's not warm enough. Is it the only coat you brought?"

"How many coats can a woman need, Zachashka?"

"Take my scarf, then. Or a jumper of Rachel's. Please. *Pozhaluysta*. And don't go into the park. Rough dogs there—Horror Dogs, Rach calls them. Out of control, aggressive. They'll go for Volya. And there are bones all over the joint. Foxes strew them around. Saw a whole carcass yesterday! Bones, broken glass . . . and a crazy bird lady spreads mouldy cake and buns in there. Man! It's a bloody wasteland!"

"Tell me. Will you fuss like this for as long as I stay? I'll go home."

"Live with us, Tasha! Then you don't have to go home. We'll sell. Find a bigger place. When Rachel is back. A proper garden. A piano. By the sea maybe!"

"The Hebrides? Shall we go to the Hebrides? With Lev?"

"Lev, Lev! You and Rachel, both. Would he be so . . . It will make no difference to him. Where you live. You want to die alone in the dusty flat with paintings of Cossacks and steppe and—and a useless maid who robs you—"

"Blind? Robs me blind?"

"*Tyotya!* Don't! But Lev—has he ever taken one step . . . one step back from his own self-something—I mean, what has he ever—well, why don't you live with *him*, then? Big old house, a piano. Housekeeper. One that actually cleans."

"Impossible. I remind him of Katya. And you would not visit."

"*Banished,* Tasha. Don't make it sound so polite. Not my bloody choice! My Siberian exile, Rachel calls it. And so what? If you want to live there, you can. If you want. Has he even asked? Or just left it vague? What has he ever, why can't he—has he said you can't live here? With us? Does he think I can't take care of you? Too stupid, am I?"

"'Ah, my God-given father and sovereign,'" quotes Tasha. "'Do you not *recognise me? You have always called me a simpleton.*'"

"Fairy tale?"

"Yes. A good one. 'Know Not.'"

"'Know Not.' Do I know it, ha ha?"

"Yes, you do. It's all about you, this one. The simpleton is a mighty hero in disguise. He goes unrecognised by his young wife and father-in-law the Tsar until—"

"Has Lev told you not to stay with us? Tasha! Tell me."

"*Zachashka, prikvatite,*" stop it, she says firmly, quietly. "It does not signify. I must do as I do. It can't be helped. How he behaves. And I am not under his command, but I will not cause him needless hurt."

Zach clasps his aunt tightly, a bruiser's hug. Bear hug. Then he holds her head, encompassing the ears and temples, and butts her gently, brow to brow.

"And," she adds teasingly, "I know what's for supper. You smell of the sea. To put it politely."

"Wait until I've finished cooking; we can walk together."

"No," she says. "We have plenty of time to walk together, play together. How long is Rachel away? Nearly a month."

Three times nine days, thinks Zachariah. Three times nine days.

"I'll be back in forty minutes," Tasha says. "I'll remind you of the story. 'Know Not.' Then fish stew?"

"With parsley!" Zach cries, escorting Tasha to the door.

"Can you do it?" she asks. "Sing the whole thing in Russian?"

"More or less," replies Zach.

"Katya was right, you know. How you can sing."

"Did she love me though? Hate me in the end?"

"Silly boy. *Glupiy.* Silly Zachashka," scoffs Tasha, pulling up her collar. "I shan't answer you. You know the answer to that. I'll be back in forty minutes. At the most. Have a shower, please."

"Not the Gardens! Don't go in," he calls out after her and Volya, watching her stride down the street, the willowy shape, shorter, perhaps, than in the boyish vision he harbours still, her steps a trifle tentative now. "And don't go to the Hebrides either!" he adds, flapping his hands under his nose. *Fishy indeed.*

With a toss of the head as she goes, aware his eyes are on her retreating form, Tasha waves her pointy white cane in the air, as it were, a conductor's baton.

Tasha hums from the Overture. *Die Hebriden.*

Wolves howling together sound different notes and pitches, producing an illusion, in this manner, of being more numerous.

Tasha remembers a sea holiday in Boulogne. When we were six. Now we are only four. And so divided. We were noisier then, as if numerous. She remembers a day at the beach and Lev teaching Rachel, forever full of instruction, always for her. The more distracted she was, Rachel his perpetual pupil, the more drawn to the boy, the harder Lev fought for her, his beautiful daughter. *The tsar's daughter was so pure and so beautiful one could see her marrow flowing from bone to bone . . .*

It was a spectacular day, as Natasha recalls, and she and Katya sat in deck chairs just beyond the surf while the children and men played in the sea.

Katya is working and Tasha has a book, a medical tome of Nikolai's. He wants her to understand the physiology of the eye, to know what is happening to her according to science, and what might ensue. He believes knowledge diminishes fear, but he is wrong. And she does not need to understand what is happening to her, knowing it will come quite suddenly, blindness, and there is nothing she can do. To please Nicky, she reads out the parts of the eye. She plays with language though it is not her native tongue.

"Sclera, cornea, pupil," she says. "Aqueous humour, retina, iris, eyebright."

"Eyebright?" shouts Nicky from the waves. "How's that?"

"Iris," she explains, "is a flower. So I thought of types of iris—Siberian flag, yellow flag. Eyebright!" Then Nicky tells her that eyebright is used as a remedy for weak eyes.

Nicky knew so many beautiful things.

"Iris, pupil, optic nerve," resumes Natasha.

"Pupil!" Lev says to Rachel, insistent. And he began to teach. Something to do with flowers and petals, a sequence, a system. Something. And Rachel needs to swim, to swim with the boy, to swim like a fish, thus enraging the man.

"Papa! Are you cross? I'm swimming! Don't be cross."

Nicky springs out of the sea, raising an invisible sword, body erect, fist under chin. *"Piqué!"* he exclaims.

"That's not the word. It's *touché!*" says Zach. "You don't say *piqué,* you—"

Before he can finish, Nicky has the boy underwater, whereupon Katya's glance strays from sheet music to middle distance.

"Piqué?" she says. "Yes, perhaps. Staccato. Just here."

Tasha laughs. "Nicky means Lev, Katyenka. Lev is having a fit of pique."

"Yes, I know, I know. It just made me see something. Look," she says, pointing to a page of notation, which Tasha brings close to her face, eliciting a frown from Katya.

"Must you do that?" she asks irritably. "Do you really need to? Maybe it's the glare, I'm sure in a different light . . ." she begins.

"Yes, of course. It's not serious. There *is* a strong glare. And I'm a little tired, that's all," Tasha replies, reaching out an arm for her husband on his way out of the water with Zach, who shakes his mop of hair, spraying mother and aunt.

Tasha remembers the seawater flying from Zachariah's head, how the drops caught the light of the sun and fell on her like stars.

"Isn't piquet also a card game?" Zach strikes in, hands on slim hips.

"Actually," says Nicky, "in French it can mean 'crazy.' *Fou.* Words, words, words! I believe it's time for a drink," he adds. "Did I ever tell you I was challenged to a duel once, when I was a student in Geneva?"

"No!" Zach exclaims. "Fantastic! I'd love to fight a duel!"

"So let me show you some moves, *Monsieur le boxeur,*" Nicky states, picking up the blackthorn stick he bought for Tasha, a stick she carries, she says pointedly, only to please him. "Engage!" he commands with a swagger of blackthorn. "Come on. Find a stick. Let's have a fit of pique. Fit of *piqué!*"

"I'll be your second!" Rachel calls to Zach as she rushes to and fro, hunting for driftwood, abandoning Lev to the waves. "I'm your second."

"I'm leaving the pack of you!" shouts Lev. "And going to the Hebrides!"

"Be careful," Tasha tells Volya. "This is Camden Town, there are bones everywhere. Beware the bones!"

A fine cold spray of rain patters against Tasha's face, the kind of autumn precipitation she identifies more with summertime and the brief delicate showers that glitter in sunlight and pass so quickly one cannot swear to it happening at all but for the welcome speckle of moisture on forehead and arms and the obscuring spume on eyeglass. She remembers all this. The light, how it falls.

Nicky always said she ought to compose a piece on weather.

"*A piece,* a piece? Why, my dove? And what kind of piece?"

"We met in weather. A quartet. I love a quartet! *Ya lyublyu tebya!*" he laughed. I love you!

Tasha thinks, Nicky! Nikolai Fedin was born laughing and jesting.

As a very young man at his first osteopathic practice in Geneva, a friend of a friend of the accompanist Natasha Byelova gives Nikolai Fedin a ticket for a recital of Russian songs; Tchaikovsky, Cui, Balakirev, etc. Nicky basks in nostalgia, but most of all in the shape of the accompanist, marvelling at the immaculate posture, the effortless motion of arms, the stillness of the head. Never has he seen such a superb alignment of bones! He waits in the tumbling snow at the stage door, practising his overture to her, an entrée granted him courtesy of his friend of a friend, and of nostalgia for home. For Rus. Nikolai is a joyful fatalist.

"We met in weather," Nicky said. "A snowstorm. That's why. And because you don't have the English affliction, you are not—a weather drone. Isn't it CLOSE today? Isn't it miserable? Isn't it bright? Doesn't it get dark early? Hot enough for you? Cold enough? Too wet, too dry! The day too long, too short! No. You never speak about it, you enjoy it all. Do you remember? That Geneva snowstorm?"

Of course I do.

And I remember your London funeral, Nicky, how the mud was so thick it soiled my stockings to the knees and caked my ankle boots, and when Katya undressed me sometime that night, the dirt splintered and crumbled to the floor and I would not have it swept, *not yet*, I said. Not yet. And Katya followed you so few years later and by then I had lost my sight, Nicky! Between your end and Katyenka's, I lost my sight. I have only what they call "peripheral vision." The periphery is my landscape, my field, not always so bad a place.

"'O my field,'" sings Tasha softly, "'*my open field. You are my wide expanse. In that field lies the fair body of a young man.*'"

Natasha laughs, recalling that line of Lev's from *Dead Souls*, one he would quote in a huff to taunt Katya to no effect whatsoever, as he well knew. "What's so good about this dreary singing?" he always said, quoting his Gogol, "It only fills the soul with even greater melancholy."

Yes, my darling Nicky. I should, I shall compose *a piece*. A love song and a requiem, because Lev and Rachel say war and weather are indivisibly connected, each to each. They say weather is chaotic and wars are won and lost in weather.

WAR AND WEATHER. A REQUIEM.

After Borodino, after Moscow and the Berezina Manoeuvre and before the successful Battle of Kulm, Alexander I watches his troops in a late wet August emerge from the narrow road into the Teplitz valley, a path attenuating to a width permitting but a single file of drenched and weary men between six-metre-high embankments with thick pine woods beyond. Some lose their boots in the mud and march barefoot and when Tsar Alexander observes them from an open field, he weeps. He is seen to retire for a wipe with a very clean white handkerchief.

During the retreat from Moscow, after the crossing of the Berezina, on the way to Vilna and back to the River Niemen, temperatures fall to −37.5° and many Frenchmen are struck snow-blind, the conjunctiva turning red and swollen, the eyelids puffing and the eyes shot through with such pain, they weep copious involuntary tears. Some walk hand in hand for guidance as, it is thought, do rats, which is a rat myth, one of many.

An officer of Chasseurs who is losing his feet to frostbite is hauled all the way to Vilna by a boy bugler who straps his own slight body to a sledge to pull like a sledge dog. Frozen flesh, it is noted, has a very particular stink. A Chevau-léger curls up to die by a hole in the ice that has swallowed his beloved mare. He will not endure without her. That's the end of his war. He calls it a day.

In early 1813, at Borodino, the clean-up begins. It is recorded that 35,478 horses lie dead there, each, once upon a time, carefully groomed and rubbed with opodeldoc and tender strokes of the brush.

Lev Wolff's father the meteorologist, whom he never knew, died in the mud, *rasputitsa*, on the outskirts of Odessa in the spring of 1944, and his friend Byelov the violinist wrote a song with an ironic title, "One Step Back," a mistake for which he paid in exile and premature death. The very young soldier musician was a father also, of two girls, Natasha and Ekaterina, and Katya he will never see because he withered fast in the frozen wastes of Siberian exile. He went for a song.

The rain falls with more intensity now, slanting across Tasha's face, rushing fast in cold straight lines and raising an odour of leaf-mould, crushed berry and detritus from the paving stones beneath.

"You'll have wet paws, Volya," she says. Must call for a towel, she thinks, upon return. Mustn't leave a muddy trail. "Shall we try the High Street? We need wine for supper."

Burgundy. Burgundy or a pleasing claret. And if there is nothing good enough, the fail-safe. From America or Australia. Oh dear. What is the name of it? Private Bin. Special Selection. No. Limited Edition, Special Reserve, Monopole? It's all very . . . Stalinist! If it's so terribly secret, so private and reserved, how can it be sold to me? Tasha giggles. The Gulag, she muses, was a Private Bin.

"Won't he be cross, Volya! If we go to the High Street! It's a dangerous place!" she adds, humming from *Peter and the Wolf.* "Dah-DAH, da-da-da-DAH, da-da-da-da da-da-da-da-da-DAH, da-da-dah, da-da-DAH-da-DAH! Volya?"

Volya has stopped in his tracks.

"Is it shit, Volya? You don't want me to step in shit?" Oh, the tell-tale squelch and slide, so very different from mud! Volya and Katya sniff the air. Brick-dust, wood shavings, grout, sweat, cigarettes. Beer.

"That's a fine dog, love," says Brick-dust from under an awning outside the Camden Head. "Let me help you. It's not a proper crossing here, as it were. And your dog wants you over the road, as it were. Clever lad! Couple of fight dogs ahead, you see," he adds in a low voice. "So I'll take you, love. Back in a tick, mate," he calls to a friend. "Hold my pint."

The builder grips Tasha by the crook of the elbow, his digits like pincers, a carpenter's vice. His skin is dry and rough and male as five o'clock shadow, as bear hugs and hands in pockets and rolled-up sleeves and perspiration, weather-induced, effort-induced, glistening on foreheads, showing dark between shoulder blades. Nicky! *Ya ochen' po tebe skuchayu!* I miss you so much!

"Where do you need to go, darling? It's pissing down! Sorry, love! I don't mean to be derogatory. Pardon my French, as it were! Going home, then?"

"Not yet. I need, I want to buy a bottle of wine for my nephew. He's cooking for me. I know what I want and where I'm going."

"Sorted, then! I'm taking you. Come on!"

Trust.

Hopes are so very well constructed.

When Katya was dying in hospital, Tasha recalls telling her of remarkable recoveries from cancer, expounding upon trust in medicine and in healers and other suddenly insignificant matters while Lev went in search of coffee and newspapers . . . Trust is important, she said. *Doveriye vazhno.*

How close these memories are tonight, marvels Tasha. How thick and fast they come!

Katya says, "Trust is for prospectors! Trust is a fund for debutantes and heiresses! Fool's gold!" she exclaims, before resurrecting the old story, how Papa wrote a song, *trusting* his audience to hear music, a simple elegy, only to die for it, in Kolyma. "Big sister! Natasha! Trust is for children," she laughs. And that is when she says it: "He went for a song! Papa went for a song."

The sisters sing.

> *The evening bell*
> *How many thoughts it arouses in me*
> *Of the days of my youth in my homeland,*
> *Where I knew love, where my father's house stands.*
> *And as I bade farewell for ever*
> *I heard the sound of the bell for the last time.*
> *The evening bell,*
> *How many thoughts it arouses in me.*

"My God!" goes Katya, a wry smile on her drawn face. "And what would Lev say?"

"What's so good about this dreary singing?" the sisters recite in unison. "It only fills the soul with greater melancholy!"

"Everyone in the corridor can hear you two," Lev declaims as he returns bearing cups of black coffee, broadsheets under one arm. "It's a good thing we're in a private hospital. How elitist of us! Marvellous! I found a French paper, Katyenka. I have *Le Monde.*"

When Katya reaches for him, Tasha takes the cups and Lev drops into a chair, checking the urge to fall into Katya's arms, rest his head on her breast. He holds her hand in both of his, presses his mouth to her fingers, her musical wands, downed tools. She can hardly bear to be touched in her long last days. She turns her head away from him.

Tasha also recalls a family supper, Byelova-Wolff and Byelova-Fedin, and a typical Rachel query, show-stopping. Rachel is not quite twenty.

"Papa? Who is more Russian, the Fatalist or the Romantic?"

Nicky stands up. "A toast to the old soldier," he cries. "Borodino, Stalingrad! Imagine this: an old soldier laughing, singing sentimental songs.

He teases his young comrade for crouching in gunfire, ducking and diving. The old soldier asks, '*What's the point of all this ducking and diving? Every shell, every shot has a man's name on it!*' Well? What is he? Fatalist or Romantic?"

Lev stretches across the table, takes his daughter's face in his hands. "Neither is the answer, little paws. To ask the question," he pronounces, "*that* is Russian!"

Fatherland, motherland, thinks Natasha. Russia, *Rus*. You are my father and my mother.

"Crossing Bayham Street now, love," Brick-dust informs Tasha.

Bayham Street! Rachel loves to tell Tasha how Charles Dickens lived in this very street as a boy, number 16 Bayham being his first London address and, though the actual house no longer stands, his footprints linger. Rachel tells her so every time they cross this road.

Dickens walks a path in Camden southwards to North Gower Street, his second address, from where he will stump the three miles to Warren's Blacking in Hungerford Stairs, and to the Marshalsea in Borough High Street to visit his father. To and fro, to and fro, on his young and dancing feet.

The builder accepts Tasha's banknotes and buys the wine, bringing her, she has no doubt, the change to the penny, pouring it into her purse. He escorts her to Zachariah's house and transfers the parcel, drawing her fingers through the handles of the bottle bag to make sure of her hold. He takes one step back.

"What is your name?" she asks quickly at the door, sensing his retreat.

"I'm Charley, missus. Madam. Call me Charley."

"Hello, Charley," she says.

"Lived in Camden all me life. Have my eye on you, now. As it were. You're all right. I'll be looking out for you. See?"

"Thank you, Charley. I do see."

"Snowstorms in Petersburg," Zach announces upon opening the door. "Who the hell's that?" he asks aggressively, watching Charley stroll down the street with a backwards glance and a hesitant wave.

"Who?"

"The chap waving! There's a guy out there waving at you!"

"Oh. That's Charley. We just met. What snowstorms?"

"Went online. BBC weather," he adds, by way of explanation. "What do you mean, you just met?"

"He helped me cross the road, Zachashka! Stop it now. Tell me about snow and pour some wine. And why wouldn't it be snowing in Peter?" Tasha adds. "It's almost November."

"Why didn't you go with them? For the memorial?"

"You know I can't. I don't go there."

"Not even for this, *Tyotya*? Two years."

"I remember her daily. Daily, nightly," states Natasha, her voice raw with feeling. "I don't need to sit in a concert hall half full of crocodiles."

"Tasha!"

"It's too sad a place. For me. Too dark. Katyenka would understand. She always understood. How is the wine? To your liking, sir?"

"I could drink it by the half-pail!"

"It's good, then, that I purchased two bottles."

After supper, Zach sits on the floor of the living room and rubs his hands across Volya's chest, eliciting a low dog hum of pleasure. He refills Tasha's glass.

"Tell me stories!" he demands.

"Don't spoil him," she warns. "He's a working dog."

"He works like a dog! Don't spoil him. As if you don't! Rach was going on about dog expressions the other day. Sick as a dog, dog-days. Die like a dog, not a dog's chance, doggerel. Hangdog."

"Why?"

"A Rachel thing—I don't know. Anyway, she explained 'hangdog' to me, the origin of it. There's a nursery rhyme. And there used to be trials and public hangings. Up to the eighteenth century, she said. For dogs. Can you believe it? For nipping a child's finger, attacking a priest. Things like that. Hanging offences. *Hangdog*. Bloody hell, *Tyotya*! I mean, how bad can a dog be?"

"Was there a defence lawyer? A learned barrister dog?"

"I don't think so!" laughs Zach.

"Volya stopped in the street," says Tasha. "Because there were bad dogs ahead. Well, Charley said they were."

"Why do you think I don't want you walking alone?" Zach protests.

"I'm not alone. I have Volya. You know Nicky had a dog? A long time ago. He brought him to Paris when he joined us there. From Geneva. He was so attached to Nicky, he leapt out of a first-floor window one summer because he saw Nicky below, leaving the house. He wanted to follow. Did Nicky ever tell you? I am sure I never saw him so very very sad."

"Why did you all leave Paris? And why to England?"

Tasha smiles. "Too many émigrés!" she exclaims, mimicking her sister. "And, of course, too many French."

"It makes no sense," Zach protests. "French—"

"Yes, I know. Nearly the mother tongue. But Zachashka, to speak French in the streets and drawing-rooms of Petersburg is one thing, to French people in Paris, amongst other Russian exiles, is quite, quite another! And Katya was especially unhappy."

Katyenka, thinks Tasha. I remember you daily. Daily, nightly.

O my field, my open field. You are my wide expanse.

"My God," Katya moans. "If we stay in Paris much longer, I'll end up conducting Ravel and Debussy to perfumed *muzhiks* in silken scarves! And the unctuous Monsieur le Comte de *ceci* et *cela*, his English tailoring, the tiny red thread in the lapel. So very discreet. *Légion d'honneur!* He was in *la Résistance.* Of course! They all were. Russians are so very charming, he'll say. Soulful. He'll want a quote from Pushkin. *Pouchkine!* Because we all quote Pouchkine! My God!"

"Katyusha," says Lev. "You are very silly today. The city is so beautiful, the University excellent. We are all in work, we can walk and walk and eat and drink our fill. There is so much—symmetry. Paris is so *sympathique! Séduisante.*"

But Katya mistrusts seduction. Except in Lev.

"If we linger here any longer," she threatens, leaning towards Lev at the table, speaking into his ear, "we'll become theatre Russians. You know. We'll sip from the samovar, install a great stove with shelves above. *You* will find a *banya.* We'll dream of cloudberries."

"*Moroshka!*" cries Nikolai. "*Moroshka!*"

"You see?" says Katya. "What about mud? Do you miss that? *Rasputitsa! Ça alors! La véritable nostalgie de la boue!*"

Very soon afterwards, the offers come in from London, a fellowship for Lev, a residency for Katya and then Nikolai and Natasha follow, and the Wolffs start a family, and Katya engages in a fever of rehearsals, recordings and travel, and in endless motion for which there is always sound reason, an imperative that goes unchallenged. The Mendelssohn series must be done *now*, there is no other time. She must conduct here, there. She becomes migratory, vagrant.

Before they leave Paris, Katya asserts, "This city is full of cats. Too many cats, not enough songbirds. And all those ghastly lapdogs—the protuberant eyes and ornate collars. Like ageing aristocrats. We must go. Please."

"You said Katya was especially unhappy. Why?" Zach asks.

"It's a dangerous place!" Tasha tells her nephew. "Dah-DAH da-da-da-DAH!"

"Tasha! Explain."

"She was bitten once. By a cat."

Zachariah ogles his aunt. He frowns, rests his head on her knees, an arm across her thighs. "*Tyotya*. Cats, lapdogs, cloudberries! I don't understand."

"*Moroshka!*" sighs Natasha, threading her fingers through Zach's curls, gently massaging the scalp, damp and radiant with heat from cooking, anxiety and drinking, and curiosity.

And so Tasha tries to explain it all, Katya's malaise, the unrest. She reminds him that in Russian fairy stories, folk tales, legends, tall tales, what you will, there is a belief that the soul, or heart, dwells outside the body, perhaps in something inanimate, seemingly inanimate, such as a tree, rendering this tree remarkable and sacred. The soul dwells outside, taking up residence in some special place. If you find it, it might speak, offer guidance. It might reside in a fish or in cloudberries. Find it.

"I know, *Tyotya*. I know all that."

"Of course you do. Now tell me. Rachel's nursery rhyme with 'hang-dog' in it," says Tasha. "How does it go?"

"Can't remember. No idea at all."

"Ah. Well. If you think of it, ask Rachel. I'd like to hear it. I keep having visions of a poor hanging dog."

"Sorry, *Tyotya*."

"No. It's fine. I just think if there is to be judgement at all, animals should judge animals. Perhaps."

"There'd be ganging up," warns Zach. "Hung juries. Think of it. A dozen squirrels condemn the whippet."

"It could be breed-specific," suggests Tasha.

"Rook parliament! Rachel drew one. Scary stuff."

"Quite Stalinist," says Tasha. "The rook parliament."

"Damn right, *Tyotya*! Bloody show trial. It's a great drawing! Two rooks surrounded by a circle of maybe forty other rooks. Well, I told her it looked like an old prize fight. Ringsiders at a prize fight! I'll show you—it's still on top of her desk, I think."

"No, no. Stay. We must ask her first. Maybe she is not ready for me to see," says Tasha. "Sit."

"I'm going to make a cheese plate," he says, walking to the kitchen. "Would that be good? Cheese, apples, bread, nuts. OK?"

"Yes," replies Tasha.

"Now tell me stories!" he demands upon his return.

"'Know Not.' I was going to remind you of that one."

"Right," says Zach, arranging portions of cheese. "The one about me."

"Why is he called Know Not, this youngest of three sons?" begins Tasha.

"Always the youngest, eh, *Tyotya*?"

"Actually, he is baptised Vaniushka and he is *neither clever nor wise, but sharp as a needle*. When he leaves home to sow his oats—"

"Wild oats, Tasha. They have to be wild. Unless he ran off to be a farmer."

"I see," she resumes. "Wild oats. Speaking of English errors, you'll enjoy this: I had a letter the other day from a festival in Germany. The music director is Italian. An admirer. The letter is in English. He wants to commission a piece—"

"Great!" Zach interjects.

"The letter is very charming, very Italian. Perhaps he is more Italian than in Italy, because he is living in Germany. He begins the letter, 'Dear *estimated* Natasha Byelova . . .'"

"'Estimated!'" laughs Zach.

"Yes. I laughed also. Then I asked myself, is it perhaps preferable to be estimated than esteemed? The esteemed are not free. The estimated are full of surprises. And we judge so quickly, yet know so little. We can only estimate. I think so, no?"

Zachariah searches his aunt's face and smiles. "I feel a moral coming on! Oh yes I do."

Natasha takes a deep storytelling breath and Zach has an instant recollection of music lessons at Coram's, and of the piano lady at her stool, the intake of breath before she played for the children, her tiny smile as she looked at them one by one, the powerful quiet she brought to the room. She spoke little and in accented English, she knew all their names, never mixed them up. And one day she brought her sister. And finally she brought a bearded man. Zach's memories come sharply, without warning, like gasps. He disregards his earliest days, telling Rachel they do not signify, yet he does remember getting into fights, and he remembers being moved around from family to family then back to the home, the Coram Family Institute. And he definitely remembers the piano lady. He definitely remembers Tasha.

Occasionally he will recall things with more precision: tiny incidents or sensations, things he was given to eat, the smell of tinned soup, of Spam, the feel of garters round his school socks, the scratchiness of sheets. He is not keen on remembrance. When Rachel asks him about days before his life as a Wolff, he will scowl and fidget and so she learns to wait for his recollections and, because it is so difficult for him, she will listen without speaking, collecting the pieces of his past painstakingly like a jigsaw maker, or a batsman accumulating runs, in awe of the impossible distance between a sliver of blue and a great sky, between three runs and a century, between a shard of memory and memory itself.

"Are you ready?" asks Natasha.

Zach nods.

"Well," resumes Tasha. "When Know Not leaves home and arrives in the capital, he spends his time carousing, squandering his modest inheritance in taverns and inns, and one day his name is asked by other young drunks. 'What's my name?' he echoes. 'What's my name? Truly, brothers, I know not.' Soon he is penniless. He hires himself out as a watchman in the gardens of the tsar and is typically drunk on duty. The tsar has three daughters and the youngest sits amongst the flowers in the garden all night and does not sleep. She watches the watchman Know Not uproot the apple trees and vines and shrubs and hurl them over the fence. The tsar's gardeners are irate. He explains to the tsar that he destroyed the gardens for good reason. The gardens were simply not in good order and he begs permission to replant. He does so to perfection and in a display of epic strength, lifting trees with one hand it would take twenty men to raise."

"Know Not!" exclaims Zach. "A George Foreman of a gardener, then. Foreman. Maybe the strongest boxer who ever lived."

"And what happens next?" asks Tasha. "It is time for the tsar to marry his daughters. All three are stately of form and agile of mind with eyes as bright as the falcon's and brows as black as a sable's. And one of them is very selective."

"The youngest?" asks Zach.

"Yes. The tsar presents the best and loftiest men of the kingdom yet none please her, so he casts his net wide in exasperation, inviting peasants and fools and drunks and dancers and singers and insisting she marry one of these, having refused all the knights and boyars. His court is suddenly filled with wastrels from amongst whom she chooses Know Not the Simpleton. He is taller and broader than the rest and has curls that fall over his shoulders like pure gold. The tsar is furious."

"Go Know Not!" cheers Zach, downing his glass of wine.

"And then the real trouble starts," continues Tasha. "Three Saracen warriors, brothers of course, had travelled to the tsardom for the youngest princess's hand. They have travelled a very great distance for nothing. They threaten to burn down the capital, slay all the people and murder the tsar."

"These guys mean business," notes Zach. "No messing around."

"Know Not tries to reason with his young wife. His brothers-in-law have fled the scene of battle and he cannot fight alone. He asks his wife to run away with him and she refuses. She will not leave her mother and father. Know Not dresses as a peasant and leaves the city to stand on top of a hill and shout a heroic shout and whistle a warlike cry and recruits himself a marvellous horse with magical girths and saddlery."

"The horse. Can he fly?"

"Higher than trees," answers Natasha. "Lower than clouds, never touching the ground."

"Tasha? That kid saves the tsardom, doesn't he? And beats all the warriors and their armies, yeah?"

"But nobody recognises him, Zachashka. He covers his face, even from his wife. And nobody expects the mighty hero to be him, so they cannot see. When he is in the palace, he wears his old clothes and lies on the stove, idle, aimless. His beloved wife is disdained by her father. He thinks Know Not a fool and a coward and berates her for not marrying a knight. Know Not slips out of the castle again and again to shout his heroic shout and whistle his warlike whistle, and only at the very end of the brutal war against the Saracens he wins almost single-handedly, does he lay his cards on the table. "Tell us, good knight, of what family are you?" the tsar asks the returning hero with the blood-streaked face. "Ah, my God-given father and sovereign, do you not recognise me? You have always called me a simpleton." And all pay him homage. And there is a great feast and he recovers from his wounds and upon the tsar's death, he ascends the throne and his life is long and happy."

"You know what, though, *Tyotya*? It doesn't say 'And the tsar changed. He never looked at a low-born fellow the same way again. Why, if he finds some guy lying on a stove in his palace, a bit the worse for wine and with uncombed hair and in the same jeans he has worn for three weeks, he treats him kindly because he knows the *muzhik* could be a mighty hero.' No, Tasha. It never says that. There's feasting and dancing and living happily ever after, that's it. And you know what else?" Zach adds, pouring wine. "I don't remember this tale at all. You made it up."

"I did not. You'll find it on Rachel's shelves. In the Afanasiev collection, *Russian Fairy Tales*."

"Best things are the magic hankies and the flying horses," adds Zach. "That's the moral for me. Get yourself a flying horse and a magic hanky!"

"You said the same thing as a little boy!"

"See? Nothing changes."

"When you first came," says Tasha, "you wore a yellow jumper and too-short blue jeans and you would not change. We bought you new clothes and you would not wear them, not for weeks and weeks."

"Thought I'd be moving on, *Tyotya*. I didn't want to get the new stuff dirty. And be in trouble."

"You stapled the jumper where the seams had split, Zasha. And Katya and Lev began to quarrel. He said you smelled. She said you needed more time. He said, Time is relative. And she said, It's all terribly simple; I shall take the jeans and jumper and throw them out."

"She did," laughs Zach. "Or Lev did."

"No. Rachel and I took your clothes away."

"Really?" Zach asks. "Rachel never told me that!"

"We deemed it," explains Tasha, "the most expedient way to end the dispute."

"I'm not him," says Zachariah in a quiet voice. "Know Not."

"Of course you are not. It's just a fairy tale, Zasha."

"Tell me another," he demands, worried he has hurt her.

"Let us pause a while," Tasha replies and, after a silence and cheese and drinking, she tells Zachariah how Peter the Great's father dictated an *ukaz*—an edict—against the telling of fairy tales, which he deemed an immoral and destructive practise. She tells him how he sometimes rounded up the *skomorokhi*—the tellers of tales—in order to excise their tongues.

"Then the soul would definitely be outside the body," Zach notes ruefully, opening more wine. "*Tyotya?* When you said 'cloudberries,' I thought about Pushkin. You know. You and Mama and Lev, you told us again and again—Pushkin dying in his study and . . ."

"Yes," says Tasha. "In the study of his flat on the Moika Embankment. He is dying and dreams he is scaling the bookshelves, like a mountain goat."

"And asked for stewed cloudberries. Right?"

'*Moroshka,*" says Tasha. "Yes."

"You're one of them, aren't you? *Skomorokhi.*"

Tasha feels for the cheese knife on the side table and hands it to Zach. "Here," she says. "Do your worst."

Tasha sticks out her tongue and Zach laughs.

"Live with us, Tasha!" he implores. "Live with us."

[TWENTY-SIX]

WEATHER. A REQUIEM.

When Tsar Alexander dies so very suddenly in December, the romantic and headstrong conspirators of 1825, latterly known as Decembrists, hastily advance the scheduled uprising in St. Petersburg to the 14th of the month and, in the freezing temperatures and revolutionary mayhem, soldiers fire on soldiers, some fleeing in distress, with many shot and wounded. In the hectic aftermath, the leaders are imprisoned in the Peter and Paul and amongst them is a vaguely disillusioned hero of 1812, the Hussar turned Cossack, Aleksei. Of the five hundred or so officers and young men placed under arrest and interrogation, he is also among the three hundred and seventy-nine who are released within weeks for giving evidence, in his case, for unwittingly betraying the identity of a ringleader, the young Major who has married his sister Ekaterina.

"Your sister," Aleksei is told imperiously by the investigating officer, "is the paid consort of the insurrectionist Major S."

"*Vashe blagorodiye!*" Your Honour! "Absolutely not!" trumpets an indignant Aleksei. "She *married* him." He smacks a glove to the ground, issuing a challenge that is coolly ignored.

What have I done? The poor Major. I've killed him!

The Hussar bemoans his idiotic mistake. He wallows in a drunken trudge through the wintry city, feeling through his coat, by instinct, for the medallion of Alexander I—a blessing upon him!—given to him as a boy by the Tsar himself in his coronation year when he distributed gifts to the foundlings of Moscow. Aleksei feels for the medallion, but it is long gone. He has been doing this for years, a nervous tic, as some might box with shadows.

"What have I done?" cries the Hussar into the sharp night snow. "I've killed him! And I have drunk vodka by the half-pail!"

Watching his sister prepare for Siberia, where she has chosen to follow her husband into exile, the Hussar is wild with dismay, pacing the rooms, head-butting the walls. Ekaterina says she *must* go, that she will start a school for villagers, for the less fortunate souls. *Muzhiks.*

"There are miserable souls right here!" Aleksei protests. "Souls everywhere! Less fortunate. There is me for a start! What shall I do?"

"Come with me," she says simply.

And the Hussar remembers Borodino, the fire of Moscow, the Smolensk Road and the Berezina. He thinks of Kulm and the War of Liberation and the fall of Paris, of Davydov and Platov and a uniform with sky-blue piping. He remembers the Pulteney Hotel, homesickness, the fox and Bob's Chop House that became Tom Belcher's Castle, and all the words for gin, and sparring lessons and Tom Cribb. He envisions the gracious Englishwoman, how he loved her! And her brother, the violin maker, forever cross with him. Why? What for? When he is such a pleasant fellow.

"I am such a pleasant fellow!" Aleksei tells himself.

Aleksei cannot remember the violin maker's name . . . He remembers the parcel and the note and the gambling token, and slips his fingers between the buttons of his vest, feeling again for the medallion that is no longer there. It is long gone. Gone the way of so many things.

"He should not have died, his blessed majesty, our Alexander I!"

"Aleksei, Aleksei, my darling foolish brother," chides Ekaterina. "He had changed. Everybody knows it. Even you."

The Hussar is torn. How can she do this to him? He so enjoys his Black Sea garrison, the company of men, the spa towns of the Caucasus, shooting, hunting, the baths! He might start a club, a boxing academy, why not? And he is a soldier, this is the fatherland, motherland, how can he forsake it?

Ekaterina drives away on Christmas Eve in a trap—*kibitka*—with flaking red paint and a tatterdemalion cab driver with extravagant moustaches. Aleksei, intolerably bereft, abandoned, is changed forever. He weeps bitterly while dusting off his cloak. He appraises himself in the glass. It is Christmas Eve, there are merry parties everywhere. He brushes his lustrous hair, highly prized amongst gentlewomen, the curls falling over his shoulders, like pure gold. Turning in profile, the Hussar notes the slight deviation in his otherwise fine nose, a relic of sparring at Bob's Chop House. It is dashing as any duelling scar, and much admired by ladies.

How vast my country is, he marvels. How brave my sister! What is to be done? Aleksei drains his glass and heads out of the apartments into the streets, where he decides to wait for a sign. He gambles on himself, recalling his fox in Piccadilly, a creature that, in the soldier's homesickness, spoke to him, offered guidance. If I see such a thing tonight, he decides, if such a creature should cross my path, then I am meant to follow my sister. I shall catch up with her in Moscow!

What a commotion this evening! Aleksei's ears are filled with sounds, the pad and squeak of boots in snow, the muffled flutter of wheels and the crazed whoops of revellers, notably a fellow Hussar in a speeding calèche who tosses a small parcel in his path, tied with ribbon. Some withered bouquet, assumes Aleksei, waving at the disappearing kolyaska full of officers, their happy voices fading fast.

What a night! Kicking the parcel into a drift, he strolls the embankment and down the little side streets, where he stumbles upon something solid and heavy, surely a sleeping alik. Stupid fellow! He is lucky to be wearing fur or he would surely freeze! Wait. What if it's a comrade, a drunken Hussar? Aleksei crouches to shake the snow-crusted shape and reels away in alarm. What is this? Not asleep. Cut, slashed, quite dead, the limbs and neck stretched in elegant repose but the eyes wide open with shock. Not asleep, and not an alik. Wolf! It's a grey wolf!

Aleksei, wine- and vodka-soaked, cannot fathom this apparition and peers into the dark, bending over to absorb the impossible sight of what is most definitely a grey wolf. He tries to make up his mind. Does it signify? If dead, ought I to consider this creature truly to have crossed my path? Just as he wonders, must I follow my sister? Aleksei is clubbed from behind, chopped with blows to the occiput, stripped of valuables, even his greatcoat, and tipped into the freezing Neva.

When the Hussar is fished out the next day, no soul can assert that he died of cold or concussion or both, the sharp blows to his dehydrated brain having caused it to oscillate wildly on its stem and sever the filigree óf blood vessels connecting organ to skull.

Aleksei, there was a sign and you missed it. Which is a very great pity.

The fateful sign came in the form of a small beribboned parcel thrown from a passing *kolyaska* and out of which wriggled a fluffy white fox cub, superbly formed, wondrous, a cub that even at so tender an age is blessed with finer night vision than Aleksei, and an infinitely finer nose. *Vulpes lagopus* pawed his way deep into the snowbank until the men with sticks had passed, the terrible area sneaks who would prey on Christmas revellers, using a murdered wolf for mousetrap. Fox concealed himself in a magic cloak of turbulent night air and crystallised precipitations of water vapour, each snowflake on his fur a template of perfect sixfold symmetry and branching fractal patterns, symmetric in overall shape, chaotic in detail. Chaos and symmetry are not mutually exclusive.

In Moscow, Aleksei's sister knows, they will try to dissuade her from self-imposed exile because, once beyond Irkutsk, she can only dream of return. Her journey to the taiga north of Mongolia, Manchuria, may take over eight weeks. Three times nine days plus three times nine days. How vast is my country!

Despite the swaddling and muffling, Ekaterina coughs in the back of the open carriage and the subsequent intake of air numbs the back of her throat and hurts her chest, as it were an empty room with freezing winds blowing through it. Aleksei! What have I done? He will be lost without me!

She coughs again, more cautiously this time and not without irritation. Why can't she shake this affliction? A whole year has passed since she contracted this cough in the aftermath of the flood, the awful inundation of November '24. So many dead, she thinks, recalling how the Neva climbed the embankments, making an island of the Winter Palace, with typhus ensuing and winter itself, its venomous cold trapping the city, locking in the damp and foetid air. This is her token of home, then, a rasp in the throat, a hollow feeling in the ear canals, a bruising of the lungs and persistent ache in the joints. How glad she remembers feeling, that her brother was billeted south, except for his missing the marvellous sight of the Tsar out in the streets with his people once more, supervising relief work, commiserating. Briefly, Alexander was restored to his youthful self, and seen strolling daily along the Palace Embankment and onto the Nevsky Prospekt in this city of carriages. Alexander walked, so his people took to pedestrianism. You cannot know the city until you feel the stones through your soles.

War changed Alexander I forever. He became a man who raced about in *calèches* on long feverish journeys and turned a truly deaf ear to his tsardom, and to talk of reform and emancipation. Instead, he listened to a prophetess and saw signs in Nature. He changed.

And Aleksei changed.

"When did it happen, dear brother? Where does it all begin?"

Ekaterina recalls her very young brother, sent with other foundling boys to the military academy, and how he flourished. How fetching he was in his Hussar uniform! Davydov took him under his wing and recruited him to ride with his Cossack partisans at Borodino though, unlike Davydov, he was unable to grow a *muzhik's* beard. He rode alongside Platov's 4th, attended to the hetman in London. Paris, London, Vienna. Perhaps he had seen too much, had stayed too long away from his native place.

Ekaterina coughs. There is a crackling in her chest, like icicles breaking. Frost and flood and fire, what calamities she has seen! The sound of ice cracking, the sound of embers sparking, how alike they are. She remembers another man who shone in a crisis, years ago, in a ward full of wounded soldiers, French and Russian, in a Moscow devastated by fire and siege. At the Foundling Home, while waiting for Russian troops to relieve the city, Captain Thomas Aubry, Chasseur, organised the defence of the Hospital with the aid of three Russian generals, and through a virulent fever. He had been wounded at Borodino.

"My brother was at Borodino!" piped Ekaterina, foundling girl turned Foundling Hospital nurse. "Perhaps you have seen him? *Vous le connaissez peut-être, Monsieur le Capitaine?*" asked Ekaterina, reddening furiously, acutely aware of her foolishness. How could they possibly have met? In such a place, at such a time, amongst so very many officers and men! *C'est à dire,* she resumed. "I mean . . . you might well remember because . . . we look so very much alike, you see."

"*Veuillez approcher, Mademoiselle,*" said the Captain. Come closer,

Aubry said, tearing a clean sheath from a roll of bandage and wiping her tears.

Moscow fire, Petersburg flood. Perhaps she, also, has seen too much. And she will soon be so very far from her native place. Three times nine days plus three times nine days. I feel the cold, dear brother. In the very marrow of my bones.

Ekaterina, you are so pure and beautiful one can see the marrow flowing from bone to bone.

At the end of the summer before the flood, Alexander I set out on another restless journey of exploration, deep into his tsardom, far and away to the western edge of Siberia beyond the Urals. He has travelled so far, he will surely not see home again until the end of October. His sight and the hearing in his good right ear have improved since his horrid long illness in January, the pain in his leg is less mortifying. He can always tell a fever coming on; he becomes almost wholly deaf.

Taiga.

From a distance, the tall thin birch trees appear as fine white plumes or Cossack lances held high, proud spears of light amongst larch, spruce and stone pine. The speckled Nutcrackers are already at work, mining pine cones, and the Two-Barred Crossbills wait for larch seeds. The *muzhik* belief is that this bird evolved with crossed mandibles from plucking at the nails in Christ's hands and feet. For its efforts at salvation, the crossbill earns the ability to nest in deep winter. The male's breast is stained blood-red in eternal remembrance. O my blessed Saviour.

In the Siberian taiga, in deepest winter, when the conifers are encrusted white and sparkle under the stars, the trees suffer from drought, as in a desert, because water is trapped in snow and ice.

Bury me here, prays Alexander, in the frozen forest, or on the steppe, the endless steppe, under the waving feathery grasses or by the blue Sea of Azov beneath the yellow flag and marigold or in my patron's monastery, the Alexander Nevsky. Do not do not do not inter me at the Peter and Paul. The Tsar makes a note of this for his brothers Constantine, Nicholas and Michael, along with a fervent entreaty to be noble and manly in all there is to come. Alexander knows he will not survive another illness.

O my dearest sister Ekaterina, the Tsar laments, how could you die so suddenly? *You* ought to be my successor. I am often lost without you. I miss even your ill temper. Do you remember London? How you shocked the English with your hatred of music and your politicking. Do you recall the curious display at Lord Lowther's, of pugilism? The Noble Art, they call it, of Self-Defence. Summer of 1814. Ten years ago. These are my dog-days.

A fortnight after the Tsar's return from Siberia, when the Neva floods, when bog, marsh and sea try to reclaim the city and the Winter Palace appears to float like an island, Tsar Alexander I looks upon the chaos and turbulence with a superstitious eye, folkloric, devout, native. There is retribution in this. The soul dwells outside, in some special place. It speaks to him, from the Black Sea rising.

O my field, my open field,
You are my wide expanse.

The foundling Ekaterina never reaches Nerchinsk, nor even Irkutsk, and she does not turn back for her brother in Petersburg or head for the Caucasus to meet him there, but dies of fever in Moscow surrounded by friends and shortly after news has come of the young Hussar Aleksei's senseless and unseemly end on Christmas Eve in a festive capital city.

"O my dearest brother! Foolish boy."

In her raging fever, though she is neither devout nor superstitious, Ekaterina sends up prayers to Aleksei and to her Tsar—not Nicholas, recently crowned, but Alexander I, whose bones, it is later discovered, are not within his tomb at the Peter and Paul Fortress, where he was buried according to custom and against his wishes. The bones are not contained therein, but lie elsewhere, outside, no one knows where. In some special place.

{ TWENTY-SEVEN }

W HEN LEV and Rachel arrive in St. Petersburg, the Neva is freezing over and night falls early with temperatures dropping at dramatic speed. In their hotel rooms, father and daughter huddle under the
duvets they pulled from their beds and wear silk glove liners and thick
walking socks and sit side by side on the ornate divan in their graceful
suite at the Astoria in Bolshaya Morskaya, where the heating has shut
down on their floor. Rescue, apparently, is imminent, though Lev and
Rachel are doubtful and increasingly high.

"A couple of *aliks* on a park bench, we are!" Lev declares.

"With iced Moskovskaya and curls of lemon zest and this HEAP of
beluga? I don't think so, Papa! It's like that film, isn't it?" says Rachel.
"The opening scene of *Anna Karenina,* the glistening mound of caviar
on ice, the laughing officers, smashing glasses, drunk under the table!
Hollywood Russians! And Garbo dropping in front of the train at the
end, onto the sleepers, falling stiff as a tree!"

Rachel pats the sofa in delight, reminded swiftly of Tasha and Nicky's
equally imposing divan. *Troika.* How many hours did we spend there,
Zach and I? Chaffing and chaunting. The troika, our beginnings.

"We require more toast," notes Lev.

"A walk to the kitchen might improve the circulation," Rachel suggests gamely.

"Move slowly," commands Lev.

"Lest we raise the wind chill?"

"Very good, Rachel!"

Returned to their scrummage over vodka and *ikra* on ice, father and daughter work as a team, Rachel pouring the shots, administering a sharp twist of zest despite her frozen fingers, enjoying the spray of lemon oil upon the surface of the liquid and in the air around, an anointing, their glasses, little censers. She watches Lev spoon the luscious caviar—*ikra*—onto slivers of rye bread, adding a most judicious squeeze of lemon, cold butter beneath for him, none for his daughter.

"Butter, Papa! Soon you'll need pickled cucumbers, garlic, onion, lard, the whole kit! *Zakuski,* yes? The starters?"

"Ahh, *salo*! Lard. Nicky loved it. You remember what *vodka* means?"

"Of course I do. 'Little water.' "

"We can move to another hotel, you know. With heating. We *can* escape this."

"Oh no, Papa! It's fun. They'll come, the men. They will."

"It's a bit like a siege, isn't it? Another siege of Leningrad! Oh that's an awful joke. I'm a terrible man. Anyway, what made you so—hopeful? Trusting. This does not come from your parents, I think. It can't have been us. You do realize I have to lecture at eleven in the morning. I can't wash in iced water."

"Now I know why there are so many beardies here. At least you can get away without a freezing shave."

Rachel summons an image of Father Frost, his beard of icicles.

"That's no laughing matter, little paws. The iced shave."

"Papa, you can always go to the *banya,* like a true-born Russian!"

"I am a true-born Russian."

"But now you're going native. Rustic. You used to call Zach *muzhik.* When you were cross, and superior. As if he were dirty, stupid. You hurt him so much, Papa. Sorry. We're having such fun. A lovely time."

"How can one—how can you know fun, unless you know the obverse," Lev says softly, stroking his daughter's neck under the duvet, chilling her skin, not unpleasantly. "Katya taught me that. How to know fun, how to seize it. Because of the obverse, her moods. She taught me this. Not . . . intentionally."

"The concert was fine, wasn't it?" Rachel interposes. "And the speeches—not that I understood every word—but a great deal of it, I did. The reactions—passionate. And the choir! Those terrific men, the voices and then the tears, the crying and laughter. Amazing! And all the people, the greetings, the effusions and bear hugs—do you know all these people? Remember them all?"

Lev frowns, absent suddenly.

"It was commendable. Fine," he agrees gravely. "As you say. So let's drink!" he adds, clinking Rachel's glass. "To Katya. Katyusha!"

"Yes. To Mama!" says Rachel. "Mama. I wish—I wish."

"What, little red cheeks?"

Rachel reaches for a sketch pad. She inks in an impression of the coastline of the Highlands and the Western Isles, at speed. She pens a Great Northern Diver, a grey wolf, a boat, and holds up the picture.

"You are so wonderful at that!" exclaims her father. "I used to believe—I hoped, I thought you would become a physicist. Evolutionary. A scientist of emergence. Like me."

"No. I was never going to be that, Papa," Rachel says quite simply, laying the sketch pad back onto her knees. "Are you—"

"Disappointed? No. No, honestly not. Strangely not."

"Well then," she resumes, indicating her drawing. "This coastline. What is it? Where is it?"

"The Hebrides," Lev replies, smiling broadly.

"Papa!" Rachel demands, mimicking her father's quiz voice. "How long is the coast of Britain?"

"Infinite. It is infinite."

"Explain!"

"The smaller the scale, the larger the answer. The coastline is fractal. The answer depends on where the observer is, how he measures. The Latin *fractus* means 'broken stone.' Irregular on every scale. Irregular, self-similar. We are looking at infinity. A fractal is the shape of infinity."

"*Good*, Papa. Good."

Rachel pours more shots, Lev watching intently, analytically. He watches her hands, her face. He looks for a sign. Lev takes the proffered glass, they clink. *Vashe zdorov'ye,* your health! He has not felt so young for years.

"Do you remember a holiday in Boulogne?" asks Rachel without waiting for an answer. "Zach a child still. All of us swimming, splashing and diving, riding the waves, except for Mama and *Tyotya*. Nicky must have been sick already, and we didn't know. Tasha, beginning to lose her vision. She and Mama on deck chairs like Russian nobility, laughing occasionally, surrounded by composition books, sheet music, newspapers, and the flask of tea in the sun—Kusmi, of course—and their *lunettes fumées*. Their *smoked* glasses, as Mama always called them. And *Tyotya* reading the medical book of Nicky's. He wanted her to understand the functions of the eye. None of us were truly aware of the scale of things. The difficulty. She called out the names of parts. The parts of the eye."

"I remember," Lev murmurs.

"And when she said 'pupil,' you called out: 'Pupil, listen to me!' And proceeded to explain it, plant—"

"Numerology," Lev interjects.

"Yes!" says Rachel, her voice heightening. "Plant numerology, the number of petals: three, five, eight, thirteen, twenty-one. Papa! Sometimes it was—you were—relentless. You couldn't see—in *Tyotya's* levity—why couldn't you see? I mean . . . Anyway. Never mind. Zach was pleading: Tasha! Swim with us! Swim with us, Tasha! And Tasha said—do you remember what she answered? *I'm not in the aqueous humour!* That's what she said. Remember now, Papa? And you railed at us all, for our silliness, the constant interruptions. I'm not in the aqueous humour. It was funny!"

"But I enjoyed it!" protests Lev.

"Not really. Not always. It was imperative, for instance, that you teach me the Fibonacci Sequence. At that moment! You required my full attention. You were visibly—clamorously—piqued!" cries Rachel, eyes brimming, nose running, the salt water rising. *Tear duct, lacrimal sac.*

"What's wrong, little paws? What have I done?"

"You do remember then?" asks Rachel, her tone insistent. "All of it? Do you? And how in the end you threatened us with the Hebrides, Papa? Again. How you would leave us all and go to the Hebrides?"

"A joke, my dove. Rachel!"

"Perhaps," she concedes, dropping chin to chest, "but it always ends with you, Papa. Begins and ends with you."

"I don't understand," says her father. "Please don't cry," he adds, snaking an arm around her warily.

"What is the answer," asks Rachel, shrugging him off, "to the three-body problem?"

"There . . . there is no formula," Lev answers hesitantly, distressed by emotion. "Each body exerts a force on the others—a non-linear force. There is no formula. It's—unpredictable. Chaotic. You know this, why are you asking? Rachel, what do you want, what can I do? What is to be done?"

"Forgive him!" she exclaims, the tears dropping, splattering her hands, the brine surprisingly hot.

"I brought you up—*we* brought you up—as daughter and son. Daughter and son, brother and sister!"

"Papa! You were brought up with Mama! For God's sake! Can't you see?"

"By circumstance, not design."

"I thought everything was design, Papa. Everything! I love him," Rachel insists, grappling her father by the shoulders, head-butting him in the chest, a lamb in a field exploring a gate, testing its resistance.

I love everything about him, she thinks as her brow contracts, her mouth trembles and tightens, and the tears drop again. Mouth! *Oration trap, kisser!* My tears! Fluid flow! Fluid flow is chaotic.

Lev holds her tightly and when she pictures Zachariah, clear as crystal, her breast heaves with longing and sharp puffs of air escape her nostrils, strangulated sobs sound in her throat.

> *Ivanushka, little brother,*
> *A heavy stone is round my throat.*
> *Silken weed clings round my fingers,*
> *Yellow sand lies on my breast.*

I love him, she thinks, his outbursts, his silence, his sleep, the obsessions, enthusiasms, the pugilism. Boxer! Boxer at rest! He was a boxer, is a boxer! A fighter on every scale! Fractal! I love him. Even his frustrations, his strange clumsiness with doors, opening and closing. I love the scuff on his boots, the uneven shirt tails, the hang of his trousers, his sweat, the way his coat pockets assume the shape of his hands. *Mufflers, muffles, mauleys, fiddlers, flappers, fives!* I love the clumsiness and his epic grace, epic and animal. His animal grace. I know everything, every nuance, every look in his eyes—*peepers, shutters, ogles, toplights, optics, sparklers!* I know his footfall, I can hear him streets away, I know his voice in the largest crowd, I know every movement, gesture. I know, I love, every hair and follicle, the lie of his fur, the single white hair on his pectoral, the stray one on the dexter eyebrow! I know the different scents of his body, scalp, arms, neck—*squeezer*! I know, love, every nick and scar, splinter, fold, freckle, mole. I know everything that came before him, made him, everyone who came before, made him. How he was meant to come to us, to me. We don't want—need—to find his parents, learn their particulars. DNA is nothing, nothing to me. I know the links in the chain and all the voices. *Zachariah Wolff, the Life and Strange Surprizing Adventures. Samuel Alexander* . . . He wants a child, I love that too. How he fights for a child. He was a boxer, is a boxer. Through and through. Zachariah, Zachariah, our foundling boy. Zachariah, Zachariah, my fighting man. Wolf, my wolf! Be my Wolff!

Rachel pushes away from her father, needing room to speak.

"I will never leave him," she states. "Never."

At the sound of the doorbell, Lev disengages very neatly and strides for the door, apologising softly as he goes.

"Ding-ding," whispers Rachel. "Half-minute time," she says, taking up her white napkin, drying her eyes. *Wolff retires for a wipe.*

Once the boiler is fixed, two hotel caretakers come in to tinker unnecessarily with light switches and radiators and bathroom taps, exchanging animated remarks on all operations and functions before pronouncing satisfaction in important tones. The men are sanguine, cheerful. They accept a shot of vodka, a spot of bread and *ikra,* and are soon on their way.

"*Vashe zdarov'ye!*" they chant in strong voices. Your health! "Your wife," they inform Lev in stealthy tones, "is very beautiful!" "*Za prekrasnykh zhenshchin!*" To lovely women! they call out from the stairwell above the sound of their clattering feet. "*Do svidaniya!*" Goodbye!

"Maybe I'll go with you," Rachel proposes when all is quiet, a half smile on her face.

"Where?" asks Lev, resuming his work with toast and caviar.

"To the Hebrides."

"Well," he says. "Very good, very good, but we have a bit of a three-body problem, little paws. Don't we?"

"It *does* end with you!" she laughs. "I'm right!"

"I am your mother AND your father," Lev replies intently, taking hold of her face quite suddenly, his hands surprisingly warm.

Are you still warm, little maid? Are you warm, little red cheeks?

"But what are you—what are we going to do, Papa? What is to be done?"

"I am your father and your mother," he repeats and Rachel thinks how she has said this to Zach before, several times, and in her muddled state, in the turbulence of the evening, she cannot for the life of her recall where the saying began, where she heard it first, whether it began, after all, with Lev. Tonight she cannot see where it all begins.

"*Ne boysya*, little red cheeks. *Ne boysya.*"

Don't be afraid.

{ TWENTY-EIGHT }

Every morning in St. Petersburg, before even opening her eyes, Rachel says it. In a whisper, she says it.

"Nearly home. One day closer. Don't be sad. Hangdog! Do you hear me?"

Zach walks.

"Nearly home, Tasha!"

He has so much to tell her. He found that nursery rhyme for one thing, the hangdog one. He found the heavily annotated and page-marked book by Rachel's bedside this morning in the course of his typically madcap preparations for work: Where's my watch? Can't find my wallet! Do you have my keys? Are they on your side? Rachel! Rachel is in Petersburg, man! She can't help you.

Zach hurries. It's been a six-bone, two-*alik*, no turn-up day. So far.

The bones, the bones! There was a whole leg of lamb in one street, picked clean as a specimen, anatomical, downright human! And the chicken bones, the endless trail. Zach remembers the *alik* he passed in the street one time, gnawing away heartily on a raw chicken wing, a whole supermarket packet of wings in his hands. Wild!

As Zach rounds Pratt Street and nears the entrance to the close—home now, *Tyotya*! I'm home!—he spies the slanting shadow on the white-washed corner wall of the Gardens where the park railings abut, the shadow of a street post that, in a certain light, takes the shape of a cross, simple and stark as a soldier's grave marker, soldier unknown, an evening shade so often a perturbation to Rachel.

Zach skids a step or two in a scatter of rubbish under a street lamp, noting, in the muck, an item that is most definitely the dorsal fin of a fish.

"Whoa there!" he exclaims, regaining his balance.

Odd's fish! Camden Town. Dirty as the *back slums,* the very *stews.* I'll have to change my tune for the day, my rhyme—*chaunt, crambonian!* Correction. It's been a six-bone, two-*alik,* no turn-up, ONE-FISH day! So far!

Zach laughs as he presses his own doorbell three or four times to alert Tasha, and plunges into a voluminous pocket, searching for keys nestling beneath the book Aubry made him a gift of today, a first edition of *Boxing, with a Section on Single-stick, A. J. Newton, 1910.* Zach is very pleased, can hardly wait to show Rachel. Before lighting out for home, he skimmed a page or two.

Walking.

No exercise is more beneficial to the boxer in training than pedestrianism. It is almost impossible to walk too much. In walking you use nearly every muscle you possess. While walking be very careful to finish each breath you take. You breathe in and you breathe out.

Rachel the walker will love that! But what, Zach wonders, is an unfinished breath? Finish every breath you take. Even a man's last breath, he reckons, is a finished one. A finisher! Zach smiles, pleased with his new book and with this likewise. And with his friend Aubry, who has great wind and is looking sharp in the gym, quick, intense, showing a rare new aggression. He is using up sparring partners, dispensing more and more with dancing and skipping, with bouncing on tyres, and jabbing with weights while flat on his back, and the one-foot hops and StairMaster. He is dispensing with the dance, conditioning himself for fighting, not fencing. Aubry is using every muscle he possesses, he is breathing in and out!

"Tasha!" Zach calls. "Home! Here I am."

Zach drops his bag in the hall and scouts the darkened ground floor, then sweeps up the stairs, taking two at a time, turning on lights as he goes: living room, stairwell, studio. He finds Tasha in her bedroom, sitting up quite erect, Volya at her feet.

"Tasha?" he says, flipping the switch. "Why the dark? Are you resting? Do your eyes hurt? I'm home now. Let's play! What's up?"

Tasha pats the bed and Zachariah sits.

"Aubry gave me a book. From 1910. A present. Listen. This bit is about training. For boxers. Exercises, diet and so on. Here, listen: *A very little champagne has sometimes a useful effect in freshening up an overtrained man . . .*"

"You're not in training, are you?"

"Exactly! So I can have a VERY LOT of champagne! Shall we buy some? Splash out? I can be there and back in twenty. Yes?"

"I want to come with you," replies Tasha, with unintended urgency.

"What's wrong, *Tyotya?*"

Tasha tells him it is nothing at all, that she is merely preoccupied and needs an outing in the fresh air and on the way to and from the off-licence, where she insists, at her most imperious, on paying for the wine, she is unusually quiet, reacting to Zach's chatter only with vague smiles and the changeable pressure of her hold on his arm. Volya baulks at a sudden vertical whirl of brittle leaves in the wind, leaves that clatter to the ground as the eddy dies and scratch across the road, tumbling in air. Volya walks on, glancing proudly at Tasha for shielding her from this onslaught of leaves. Walk on, Volya.

"The bottle's so cold!" exclaims Zach once they are home and he flies about the rooms, arranging a tray, ferreting for champagne flutes and comestibles. "There's smoked trout!"

"Yes, I know," says Tasha. "I shopped."

"Shall we have music?"

"Anything Russian, please. Just piano, though. I have a story to tell."

"Great! Oh. And I found that nursery rhyme. It's upstairs."

"Do you like it here, Zachashka?" asks Tasha, when they have settled. "Camden Town?"

"Yes. I think so, yeah. Very much. But Rachel—at times—finds it, ah . . ."

"Disquieting?"

"I like that, *disquieting*. Polite. You are so English, *Tyotya!* For a non-true-born."

"Not really," she says. "I know the old words. Not always suitable. Stuffy."

"But suitable for—what's the word? Storytellers. In Russian."

"*Skomorokhi*," his aunt replies.

Cut out my tongue, she muses. Cut out my tongue.

How many times, she asks herself, throughout how many years, has she told them, ever since they were old enough to listen, that in the realm of the Russian fairy tale vice is not always punished, virtue not always rewarded? Very many times. Vice not punished, virtue not rewarded, though there is judgement. Without fail, there is judgement. In the realm of the Russian fairy tale, she explains to Zachariah, yet again, as if for the first time, there is bargaining, betting and bargaining, and tests of endurance and skill, magic and pitfalls, extraordinary violence, chance, victory and loss. And justice. Some sort of justice.

"Bloody hell, *Tyotya*," Zach declares. "Call it a fairy tale? It's like a night at the fights! Isn't it? Let's get ready to rrrr-umm-ble!"

"I think," begins Tasha, "I met the woman you call Baba Yaga today. Baba Yaga and her daughters."

"Daughters?" says Zach.

"In the Gardens," she adds with a glance at the back wall of the flat, as if she could see through brick and stone and darkness, past the patio at rear and over the railings beyond. As if she could see at all, see it all, in infinite detail. Natasha's vision is, by nature, fractal. There are patterns everywhere.

Over his remonstrations—I told you: DO NOT DO NOT DO NOT go into the Gardens! It's a dangerous place—Tasha tells him how she stopped to perch on a bench on her way home from the shops, an increasingly exacting office but a trial she will not forsake, and wondered what possible harm could come to her on a park bench in the bright three o'clock light of an autumn afternoon with Volya at her side?

BABA YAGA AND HER DAUGHTERS

"Hello, love," says Jess, the woman with the banshee voice. "Everything all right, then?"

Middle-aged woman, odour of smoke, her tone lacerating. A big dog, the bellows heavy, breathing like a piston engine, an arrogant growl. And small dogs, terrier yaps, high-pitched, mindless. They snap at Volya, nip his neck, sniff Tasha's ankles, assessing. Secret police, hoodlum variety.

"They're all friendly!" asserts the woman, releasing a belly laugh. "OK?"

"Oh yes," says Tasha, pleasantly, reaching for Volya's withers.

Sit on my back, says Volya the Golden, and tell me where you want to go.

"Not from round here, love? Know everyone round here! Ain't a name I don't know. Try me! Speak English?"

Foreigner, stranger, exile, émigrée. Blind woman, aged, disabled, White Russian, Jew. *Fee-fi-fo-fum.*

"I'm visiting Rachel. Her brother. I mean, my niece and nephew," says Tasha, hesitant. "My sister's children. Oh dear. Rachel's away, I'm sure you don't know her. They've not been here long. They live just over there," she adds, vaguely indicating the terraced row that borders decayed wildflower enclosures and a dishevelment of Victorian gravestones, the etched names largely eroded to indistinctness now, a sorry blur of lettering and numerology. Zach pressed Tasha's fingertips tenderly to the carvings one day, so that she could feel the blurring of the names. *He's a graveyard charley*, said Rachel. *We love the old stones!*

"I don't know them? I might do. Niece and nephew?" asks the woman to Tasha's bewilderment just as Baba Yaga sweeps in on a cloud of vodka and perfume, a gaggle of nervous dogs in her wake, spluttering and snapping, barking peevishly.

"Love you, pinch you, squeeze you!" she says to the smoker in airy, vaudeville tones. "And who have we here?" she adds, addressing Tasha. "I know you! Staying with that artist, my darling. Saw you stepping out one morning! Love your boots! Love your coat! Old dear lives there, next door, am I right? Russian? Exotic! Name's Alla? Teency-weency bit *stroppy*? I've met the couple where you're staying. A whole house, they have! Very nice. Woman's an artist, *ar-TISTE*, very quiet. Very edu-ca-ted. Always with a book. Very lovely, I'm sure!"

"I do know her!" declares the smoker. "My Tyson smacked her right in the chops one day," she shrieks. "You know how he jumps? Should've seen her face! Bet she wipes her arse with the *Daily Telegraph*, that one! Bit of an Okay-yahh, know what I mean? Ha ha! Only having a laugh!" she quips, pressing Tasha's shoulder, cackling. "What goes around comes around!"

"I'm sorry?" says Tasha weakly. "What goes . . ."

"Boyfriend's a boxer, Alla says. *Was* a boxer," Baba Yaga resumes, ignoring Natasha. "Her PARTNER!" she exclaims, clutching her chest in mock lust. "So GOR-GEOUS! Oh my GOD! Might have to steal him! Only joking!"

"Brother and sister, Ange," says her friend. "That's what you said, love, no?" she asks, turning to Tasha again. "They ain't a *couple*, Ange!"

"*Alla*. What kind of name is that then? German?" demands Baba Yaga.

"Russian they are, love!"

"Ahh," trills Baba Yaga. "Mul-ti-cul-turalism! It's so exciting, don't you just love it? All the languages you hear now, right in the High Street! So colourful!" she adds archly, with a roll of the eyes.

"But they're not a couple, them two. Niece and nephew, she told me," insists the smoker, pointing at Tasha with a nod of her chin. "Or did you mean nephew-in-law, love? Brother and sister! Can't be partners. That'd be IN-cense!"

"Seen them smooching!! Yes indeedy! Tongues, my sweet, tongues! The full First Aid, oh yes! Mouth-to-mouth."

"Who's been smooching?" asks a third woman, her voice proprietorial, wry, her gait, a swagger. "All right, Angela, all right, Jess?" she says, before glancing at Tasha, tapping her arm. "Hello. All right? Something wrong?"

"No no. I'm perfectly fine," insists Tasha without being heard above the chaos of barks and scuffling that arises as the third woman's dogs enter the fray, her German shepherd growling dismissively, the two terriers snuffling and snapping.

Tasha blesses Volya for his peerless training and temperament, knowing that, despite his unease, he will not engage, but make himself invisible for her sake. Her safety is paramount and he will lead her home. He will not fight.

Volya, Golden Dog. Take me across three times nine countries to the thirtieth tsardom where Tsarevich Zachashka lives. Fly over the wall and through the dense forests and do not stop.

"This lady," explains Jess the smoker, "was just telling me about her family. Niece and nephew. You know. In the close. Have a whole house. Brother and sister."

"No. Not exactly," begins Tasha falteringly.

"But that's what you said, love!" squawks Jess as the women close in to peer at Natasha. "Never mind! It takes all sorts," she adds, elbowing her friend.

And in the ensuing silence, Tasha excuses herself, politely waving away the effusive offers of help and escort, and moving out of the centre of attention as gamely as possible through what now amounts to a crowd, several others having pressed in, halloing idly, heartily inquisitive. In the lowering light and her peripheral vision, Tasha's perception is of darkened figures with pointed noses, black-clad in woolly hats and gabardine, shiny parka and puffa coat, dispensing judgement, some sort of justice. A rook parliament.

And this evening, before Zachariah's return—*Tasha! Home! Here I am*—Tasha gathers the thin-skinned bags of dog shit that have been pushed through the letterbox, the clack and thud having alerted Volya and brought her to the vestibule. She wraps them tightly, first in brown paper and then into thick bin liner to bundle out of sight in a corner of the patio garden until she can think what to do. Then Tasha turns off the lights and retreats to her room with Volya to wait for Zach. She wants to sing, but is afraid to be heard, and the tears fall, spattering the backs of her hands.

Cut out my tongue.

The day after Tasha tells her story of Baba Yaga and Her Daughters over very cold champagne, Zach takes her to Izzy's gym, where she is fussed over mightily. Pounding music and swearing are kept to a gallant minimum, and Izzy the cutman and trainer brings her clear weak tea, to her polite specifications, and in the only unchipped mug in the joint. Aubry sits at her feet on breaks, holds her hand, strokes the dog, and Zach calls her *Tsarina*. They ride home in a cab to find the words "PERV" and "CUNT" in clumsy sprawls of spray paint between the ground floor windows and, bizarrely, a crude hammer and sickle on their front door followed by an equals sign and a Star of David, the hammer and sickle painted back to front. Alla's door has been tainted also, by association or merely in the broad sluice of vandalism, a gash of paint in the same fire alarm red marking it out above the handsome lion's head knocker as if for plague. Bestriding both properties is a strident command in more confident brushstrokes reading "GO HOME FUCKERS!"

"Forgot the fucking comma, you fucking idiots!" Zach seethes, calling the streets, another London cry, before sliding an arm round his aunt's shoulders to hurry her indoors.

A chicken carcass has been pitched onto the patio, Zach and Tasha discover, along with fish heads and used Tampax and condoms. This is not the handiwork of foxes. There are angry messages on the answerphone from Alla, who, it transpires, is not disturbed by mere words and offal, but by the possibility she might be liable for the cost of redecoration of her erroneously vandalised front door. Alla has seen this kind of thing before. She was in Leningrad when, three weeks ahead of the siege, her little brother was amongst the children evacuated from the city by train, the carriages bombed by low-flying Luftwaffe at Lychkovo. Flying low and close enough to see. Man shoots boy, knowingly. The siege of Leningrad lasted 872 days. Dog is one of the nicest things Alla was lucky enough to eat.

"Rude words! So what!" she snaps at Zach and Tasha when she accosts them across the garden wall to expound upon the present siege. "They are dogs!"

Once Alla has marched back indoors, Zachariah rages not so much about Alla's prating his affairs to the neighbourhood moot, but for her wilful oblivion, her refusal to acknowledge the betrayal.

"But I was the one who said 'niece and nephew,' Tasha protests. "Slip of the tongue."

"Innocent! That can mean anything, niece and nephew! Alla obviously gave them details. Don't you see? She already told them. Went out of her way! They were bloody primed for you."

"But Alla survived Leningrad."

"Yes, yes. Poor old witch, she ate glue and so on. Dog! And we're all still bloody paying for it! The whole world bloody owes her, Tasha!"

"The unimaginable horror, Zachashka."

"Tyotya! She wasn't the only one. Fuck's sake. And have you seen the gear she has up there? She's bloody mafia, bloody connected! Russkaya mafiya! But Leningrad's her own private horror, isn't it? Her bloody siege. It's not MY fault. And no reason for stirring up this whole bloody neighbourhood! Neighbourhood of know-nothings. They sit around with their guns cocked. Just waiting for a reason, anything will do. And along comes Alla to oblige. She's such a nasty guts, she can't see they're out to get her too."

"That's not fair, Zachariah."

"Fair? She put you in danger. These people fucking nearly scared you to death. Leningrad. There's no fucking excuse! Rachel always says, terrible things that happen, catastrophes, they just happen, nothing you can do; too many variables. It's what you do with it that shows you. That's where you get to choose."

"But Zasha, you say it too."

"When? Say what?"

"The other night. You played that film for me. Ali and Joe—"

"Frazier. Their third and final fight. Thrilla in Manila! What about it?"

"He was fighting blind for two rounds, you explained. And his men stopped the match, his cornermen, yes? Stopped him before the last round. Joe lost. And he was bitter all the rest of his life."

"He was such a great fighter. It was such a great fight. I just wanted him—Joe—to lose better."

"So you said it's *how* a man wins that counts. And *how* a man loses."

"Bah!" scoffs Zach. "Only repeating something Rachel said. She put it that way. I see winners who cheat or gloat, and losers who moan and I hate both!"

"'Know Not,'" quotes Tasha, "'was neither clever nor wise, but sharp as a needle.'"

"Yeah, yeah," smiles Zach. "And Alla, she nurses her pain, you know? What does she do in life? Fills her house with art and priceless furniture—Rach and I call it the Winter Palace, next door—and then goes out in the world shaking her stick at everyone. Hey, Tasha! They murdered your father. You lost Nicky and Katya, your eyes. And what do you do? I've never even fucking seen you in a bad mood. You make jokes. You make music! And tell stories."

"And get you into trouble."

"It wasn't you. It was Alla. And if ever again I have to hear what was on the fucking menu in Leningrad, I swear I'll punch her clock. Lights out once and for all! *I was sick as a dog! I had to eat dirt. I ate glue soup! I ate dog!*"

"Dog-eat-dog," says Tasha, giggling.

"Oh *Tyotya*! Live with us, Tasha!" Zach cries, flinging his long arms around her, kissing her temples. "Live with us!"

"Now that would *really* give them something to talk about!" she says.

.   .   .

On the Hermitage Bridge, by the Winter Palace, Rachel walks. She senses snow in the air. She breathes in and out.

Perhaps a storm is gathering in North London. If I puff gently into the Gulf of Finland from where I stand, wonders Rachel, here over the Winter Canal, might I blow it away, away and westwards, as far as Wales perhaps, and beyond? Far across the Irish Sea? Across three times nine countries? If I huff and I puff? And flap my wings?

Zach-a-ri-AH, I've been think-ing, WHAT a queer world this would be . . . What happy change I might effect with a breath alone!

Lev would dislike this, what he irritably describes as the *pilfering* of science, by which he means the application of scientific thought to the realms of fancy. Lev's disapproval is always a surprise to Rachel, who considers physicists very dreamy customers indeed.

When the meteorologist Edward Lorenz studies a simple model of atmospheric circulation, he discovers a volatility in the solutions to his equations. He discovers that they assume a peculiar geometry, later to be coined *strange attractor,* and, lastly, he notes how there is a divergence in chaotic dynamics over time, how weather systems display a sensitivity to slight variations in initial conditions within a limit of predictability. This he calls a *prediction horizon.* He delivers a paper entitled "Does the Flap of a Butterfly's Wings in Brazil Set Off a Tornado in Texas?"

Lev, whose father the young Red Army meteorologist was ten years Lorenz's junior when he fell backwards into the *rasputitsa* on the banks of the Pilic during the march on Western Poland, never *never* uses the expression "butterfly effect." His father was caught in gunfire he could not hear because he had been deafened by shell shot. Had he not been deafened, he might have been more circumspect in his anxious search for his friend the violinist and survived the war to meet his baby son and resume his career in meteorology and deliver famous scientific papers of his own. Given different initial conditions, things might have been so much happier. Lev thinks about this often, but he never *never* uses the expression "butterfly effect."

.   .   .

Here in St. Petersburg on the Winter Canal, Rachel calls out his name: "Zachariah!"

She looks out to sea, into the Gulf of Finland, to the horizon where sea meets sky. She has been here before, mapping Petersburg in her teens, missing him for the first time in this city of canals and bridges, of three hundred bridges and sixty-eight rivers and canals criss-crossing the city to form forty-two islands, a city of islands. She has been here before and will fly here again, with Zach next time; she will return and return. This is her prediction horizon. She has a dream of return and she has site persistence. The bird and the wolf have site persistence. Come home with me.

Zachashka! Nearly home!

Does the Puff of a Wolff's Breath in Russia Set Off a Cyclone in Camden?

Rachel walks. She walks and walks, breathing in the frosty air, careful to finish each breath she takes.

{ TWENTY-NINE }

In a fretful moment, Natasha wanders over to Rachel's desk spread with open boxing books and sporting magazines and picks up an old issue of *Sports Illuminated*. Illuminated? No. *Illustrated*. An article is indexed with a yellow sticker and she slips it into her Traveller, her portable reading machine, to struggle through an essay on the boxer Gerald McLellan, brain-damaged in a fight with Nigel Benn and now minded by his two sisters. After the fight, he endured a two-month-long coma, two strokes and a coronary and, though now able to walk, talk and hear, Gerald is not well. One of his sisters says, "The back of his brain is dead so it's not telling his eyes he can't see. He always thinks it's night time or he's in the dark."

Tasha frowns. She learns that McLellan takes tablets to ease his depressions, terrible lows involving a tendency to punch the air in frustration and weep in jags. He is hangdog. Rachel has attached a large sticky-backed note to the facing page and written:

Pre N. Benn / Boxing Monthly / 1995. G.M. "Let's put it like this: me in the ring with another fighter is just like a pit bull seeing another animal, you know, it's nothing personal, it's just something you have to do. Really, a dog is what you make of him. The one I have just hates other animals. When I'm in the ring with another fighter, I look across the ring and see this guy I have so much hate for, so much desire to knock this guy unconscious."

Tasha shudders suddenly, comically. Though she may just be feeling the cold. She reads on. Gerald's favourite colour is forest green. He still insists on dressing in green, though he cannot see. She switches off her machine, presses fingertips to her eyelids and rotates her chin to relieve the strain in head and neck. Enough.

"I missed the rugby today," says Zach that afternoon. "Going to watch the highlights, *Tyotya*, do you mind? You're OK for an hour?"

"I don't need entertaining, Zachashka."

"I know! Oh. And Aubry's coming round tonight. I told you, right? So I'll need to nip to the shops. Making fish stew with parsley. *Again*. Sorry. I promised him that stew. Said he wants the stew from that *blasted song*. He actually says 'blasted'! So I'll just watch this and I'm off."

"I can watch with you. As long as I don't block your view, I have to sit very close, as you know. Rugby is a good game. I am very sporting. I even read an article in *Sports Illuminated*."

"*Illustrated*."

"I prefer 'Illuminated.' And I enjoyed your gym the other day. I like Thomas very much. I am glad he is coming this evening. You've taken Rachel, of course? To the gym?"

"I have."

Oh yes, he recalls. Oh yes, I've taken Rachel. To the gym and to the fights! How exhilarated she was, how addicted she became.

"Sensational!" exclaimed Rachel. "The punches," she said, "are so noisy!"

Rachel sat up half the night the first time he took her to a proper fight, jabbing the air, marvelling at the experience, the sound of blows, the snap and crack, the weight and impact, the dance of feet. She talked of smells and lights and fluid flow, the flight of sweat in air, the blood and mucus, the intensity of breathing. She chaffed excitably, prancing the bedroom, throwing combinations, describing the scene as if Zach were the novice and not she.

"It's so . . . immediate," she said. "And it's so *loud*, Zach!"

Zach smiles at the memory, turns on the telly. England v. Samoa.

"Captains!" calls the referee, beckoning to the players. "That's the first little bit of indiscipline. Let's not see it escalate!"

Zach listens and thinks, Rach would love that, she loves rugby refereeing, how the ref is wired for sound and the viewer apprised of matters,
able to hear warnings and chastisements. Rachel revels in the words,
how clarion they can be, and articulate. She argues for Rugby Union
referees in daily life for the policing of street brawls, everything from
turn-ups to queue jumping, or mere random rudeness. Some sports, she
tells Zach, are so civil. And civilising! Moral.

"Even boxing?" he asked.

"Especially boxing," she replied, and they tapped imaginary gloves.

After the rugby, Zach pulls on his coat, wraps a scarf round his neck
and steps into his *understandings,* the beloved new pair of Alfred Sargent "Cambridge" boots Rachel gave him last birthday. *Tan rustic country
grain plain toe cap derby, Quality English Shoemaking since 1899.* I'm a rustic
and a gentleman, ha!

"Be right back," he tells Tasha with a kiss. "Don't answer the phone."

At Sainsbury's, Zachariah fills a basket with fish and yellow onions and
carrots and potatoes and herbs and lemons, then scans the wine and
spirits in the offers aisle, plucking out a bottle of Żubrówka. He heads
for the cashiers, stopping short at the display of reduced goods in the
seasonal range, amongst which he finds plastic spiders and bloodshot
eyeballs, cheap Halloween masks, three-pronged devil's pitchforks and
wind-up skulls with chattering teeth. *And witches' brooms.* Zachariah
laughs. He is illuminated by sport! He hurries home, staying only long
enough to deposit groceries and prepare Volya for a walk, calling out to
Tasha as he goes.

"Taking Volya for a quick spin, be right back!"

At Camden Garden Centre, Zach selects a besom broom from the
Yeoman range of gardening tools, one with the bushiest spray of gnarled
twigs for a brush and a smooth ash handle and strides off to the little
park behind their terraced row Rachel and he refer to as the Horror Gardens. At the main gates, he recognises the woman Rachel names Fun,
young, slight, sour and bespectacled, with a chestnut-coloured French
bulldog in tow, a creature with protuberant eyes and an expression of
immutable outrage. The young woman has a drudge's gait, listing from
side to side as she moves along, as if hauling a great and terrible load.

"Hello!" says Zach. "Ah—excuse me. I'm looking for someone—no—just tell me, please, the ladies with all the dogs, when do they come in here?"

"I don't get involved," replies the girl, an absent look in her eyes, canny, judgemental.

"In what?" asks Zach, watching her calculate the odds, tot up the risks and returns of engagement.

"OK?" she says, with dismissive obfuscation and strained civility.

Ah, he thinks, a *whisperer*. A sit-on-the-fence, Pike with the Long Teeth. Zach watches her back as she waddles off and he feels sure she was there, standing by, when shit plopped through his letterbox. Never mind, he thinks, I'll come back in the morning, he decides. And just as he turns to leave, he hears Baba Yaga stride in at the upper entrance where the young woman stops for a hushed exchange, glancing over her shoulder at Zachariah by the gate, marking him out.

"Love you, kiss you, squeeze you!" Baba Yaga calls airily to the gathering entourage.

"Oy!" shouts a woman built like a fight club bouncer. "Ace! Come 'ere! NOW!" she screams uselessly at her massive Staffordshire bull cross, who is squaring up to a passing Labrador, just for the hell of it. The Labrador owner loops a lead round her dog's neck and they sprint away for dear life.

"Ha, ha!" goes the large woman, without apology. "He's only playing! MY dog wouldn't hurt a fly! Too daft! Thick as two planks!" she adds, as if violence were the preserve of the quick-witted. She joins Baba Yaga and Jess, the smoker with the banshee voice, who lifts her thick jersey for her friends, exposing her flaccid middle even as Zach approaches at a leisurely pace.

"Look!" she screeches. "Day surgery! In and out in one day, I was! Had me tubes tied! Just look at that, love!" she says, indicating the ugly scar across her stomach. She roars with laughter and sticks the roll-up back between her lips, talking through the side of her mouth to address Zachariah.

"Is he friendly?" she asks, nodding at Volya.

Zach stares.

Baba Yaga smiles sweetly, repeating Jess's question in patronising tones.

"She asked you, is he friendly? We can set the dogs on you," she adds gaily. "We're in our rights. *Is he friendly?* Are you deaf? A few pennies short of a pound? Anyone home? Knock-knock."

Zach the Simpleton. *Fee-fi-fo-fum.* Zach's jaw drops at the absurdity of the remarks, the mindless provocation. *Is he friendly?* Could I floor you with a single right hook to the chin? Ha! Could I smack you in the chops so hard, you eat through a straw for the rest of your empty life? He takes in the view before him of yapping terriers, imperious bug-eyed French bulldog and ill-tempered Pomeranians, tongues protruding in permanent disgust. His own mouth curls at the sight of the trio of unsavoury dogs, the albino Staffie with pendulous mottled balls, a high-tailed Akita-Mastiff and the Pit Bull–Staffie with bear-trap mandibles and mackerel-striped coat. Zach takes in the view of Horror Dogs, coiled as springs. And Volya! O Volya, perched ever so neatly on his hindquarters at Zach's heels, eyes bright, ears flickering, neck long but relaxed, poised. Keeping cool.

Boxing, A. J. Newton, 1910.

Keeping Cool.

Steadiness and self-control are no less important than courage. Once you get flurried or a little out of temper, you give chances innumerable to your wiser and better controlled adversary. The man who keeps cool has half the battle in his hands.

"Well?" poses Baba Yaga. "Cat got your tongue? Speckenzie English?"

Zach controls his voice carefully. He speaks slowly, with deliberation.

"Yeah. I do. So here's the thing. Leave my aunt alone. My women. Leave us alone. And here," he adds, at his most casual, proffering the besom broom to Baba Yaga, tossing it to the ground at her feet. "A gift. In case yours is worn out. In case yours has too many miles on the clock. You know what to do. Just swing your leg over and FLY!"

Zachariah the Simpleton dodges the spume of saliva aimed at his face with the fine reflexes of the scientific boxer he once was, and the blood fizzes in his veins and the epithets and invectives flood his garret: Low-lifes! Know-nothings, straw-weights, bottom-feeders! Tiny little-brains! Like dried peas rattling! He jams both hands in pockets and flexes his fists there. He clamps his teeth tight shut and turns his back on them to walk on with Volya by his side. He keeps cool.

Baba Yaga calls out, "Come near me again and I'LL CUT YOUR FUCKING HEAD OFF!"

Close the gate, Peter!

.   .   .

Once home, Zachariah dances his aunt round the living room, a happy tsarevich, and they have a merry party, all three, when Aubry arrives to eat fish stew with parsley and drink by the half-pail.

"I'm in training!" protests Aubry feebly.

"Special party!" Zach scoffs, pouring more wine. "And next time, *Tyotya*," he exclaims, "at the garden centre, I'll buy her a PAIR OF LOP-PERS. So she can CUT MY FUCKING HEAD OFF!"

"Don't you dare!" she laughs. "But perhaps a mortar and pestle?"

"Mortar and pestle?" goes Thomas.

"A huge stone rolled away," recites Tasha. "And out came Baba Yaga, riding in a great iron mortar, driving it with a pestle, sweeping away her trail with a kitchen broom!"

"Mortar and pestle!" cries Zach. "Brilliant. Fan-bloody-tastic!"

"Wicked," japes Aubry.

"Baba Yaga BEATS the young man with her iron pestle," Tasha resumes, "flings him down, cuts a strip of skin from his back and drives away in her mortar!"

"*Tyotya!* Fab idea. Mortar and pestle! She'd never get it, though."

"But," argues Tasha, "it would certainly—"

"Flummox her?" suggests Aubry.

"I like that," she smiles. "Flummox. Now, I kiss you both on what Zachashka calls the *knowledge-box*—"

"He has a craze for fistiana. He is boximanic," notes Thomas. "I mean—a boximaniac. Or something."

"I'm a crazey crackd braind fellow!" Zach declaims. "Rachel calls me that. A John Clare thing. Poor sod. Poor bloody poet. Went mad. Loved boxing. Dreamt he was Tom Spring."

"John Clare!" Aubry says. "The Walking Poet. My mother loves him. Whenever she comes to London, I meet her at Waterloo and she says, *This is London. Oh Christ.* Every damned time. Clare said it, apparently. On his first visit to London. On the approach. *This is London. Oh Christ.* Floors me when Mother says it. Her voice! We should drink to him, I think," he adds.

"John Clare! And London. Oh Christ. Let's drink to bloody every-thing," suggests Zach.

"Excellent," agrees Thomas. "*Très chère Madame Natasha?*" he says, rising to pour her more wine.

"*Non non!* No more for me. *Je vous remercie, les enfants, et je vous embrasse tous les deux.* I kiss you both," she announces, smiling broadly, "and go to my bed."

"How does one say 'goodnight' in Russian?" asks Thomas, taking Tasha's hand in both of his. "I say. I rather like being an *enfant*. Don't you, Zach?"

"Tasha!" exclaims Zach. "Did you know? All Souls has a Russian connection. Well, Rachel has a theory he does."

"Oh yes!" All Souls smiles. "You've told me this."

"A theory," Zach continues, "that Aubry's great-great-great—how many greats?—grandfather was at Borodino! He was a Chasseur and really heroic. Half dead and laid up in the Foundling Home with wounded French and Russians and all the foundling kids and he organises the defence of the orphanage. An officer, a captain. Same name. Thomas Aubry. Howzat!"

"I have the same name as *le Capitaine*," adds Aubry. "That much is true."

"*Quelle histoire!*" says Natasha, delighted.

"Rachel bloody loves that story," states Zach.

"Do you know the poem?" she adds. "The Lermontov. *Borodino.* I wrote music to it when I was very young, I don't know why. Nostalgia, I suppose. I dislike war poems. They linger so. Here. I'll give you the first verse. In Russian, of course:

> *Come, old man, tell me: Was it all for naught*
> *That Moscow, burned to ash, was brought*
> *To bow before the French?*
> *Because there were great battles fought—*
> *They'll say it was a fierce, heroic fray!*
> *It's not for naught that Russia still*
> *Remembers Borodino's day!*

"It *sounds* beautiful," says All Souls.

"Ah, the sound of things!" smiles Tasha. "The sounds!"

"*Madame?*" asks Thomas once more. "How does one say 'goodnight' in Russian?"

"Goodnight in Russian," quips Zach.

"That's really not particularly witty, old chap."

"*Spokoynoy nochi,*" replies Tasha tenderly, planting a kiss on Aubry's head and leaving the men to drink and play, Volya the Golden by her side.

Lying at the edge of the bed the better to reach him, Tasha strokes Volya's neck and withers and she conjures it, Borodino's bloody field and the fire and pillage of Moscow, and Volya in the Horror Gardens with all the horror dogs and witches, and she thinks of Kashchey the Deathless, once Baba Yaga's stable-lad and apprentice. She pictures him in mad pursuit of the Tsarevich, sword raised, when he is thrown and trampled by his very own horse in the very nick of time. The *nick* of time.

"*O brother, brother!*" the Tsarevich's horse calls out. "*How can you be a slave to such an unclean monster? Throw him off!*"

"I know what you said, Volya the Golden," Tasha whispers. "I know what you said to your brother dogs. *How can you be slaves to such an unclean monster?*"

To quell the vision of Baba Yaga's hut on chicken legs with the twelve stakes round it, eleven with heads on them and one awaiting Zach's, Tasha now imagines the horror dogs fleeing back to the forest, some other forest many verst away, the brutalised to fight it out amongst their kind, the ailing to die in peace and the hale to find freedom, inspired by brother Volya. And *Volya* means "freedom," the Cossack variety, freedom of the steppe, endless steppe.

Yet the vision persists. Tasha tries to banish it, the sight of Baba Yaga's twelfth pole and Zachashka's head staked there, his *knowledge-box* with its curls of a poet, and of Izzy the cutman with all the tools he showed Tasha at the gym, the cotton wool swabs and adrenaline solution, the Endswell and ice pack, Izzy the tenacious cutman who can do nothing for Zach now, because there is nothing to be done.

Tasha shuts her eyes. She spies so many things with her blind eyes.

Tasha walks the forest, the dangerous place. She takes the shape of a crow, flaps skyward, glides down to earth.

"O Grey Wolf," she cries, because there is always a wolf in the forest. "Spare my child who has done no harm."

And the Grey Wolf says that across three times nine countries there are two springs so hidden only a bird can reach them, and that one is the water of death, the other, water of life. Crow flies away to return with two little bottles and, with a dash of water of death, Zach is made whole, and a dash of water of life, he is fighting fit, alive alive-oh. There. Finished. Crow's work is done.

Tasha listens to the cheerful rumble of male vocals down below, the infectious explosions of merriment, the inebriated rise and fall of pitch and tone, sweet music.

The feasting lasted until there was no one in the tsardom who was hungry or thirsty.

{ THIRTY }

THE FOLLOWING DAY, Zach rings St. Petersburg.
"Eight days," he says softly. "Eight days."

Rachel enjoys the tale of Baba Yaga and the Besom Broom, and though she knows he has been somewhat economical with the truth, Tasha having already provided the full particulars over the telephone without Zach's knowledge, she laughs along, encouraging the embellishments, applauding the jest and his eminent cool, indulging his omission of the more obnoxious truths, namely the sweeping away of shit, bones, semen and blood. He does tell her about spray-painted words and Alla's great huff, but that is the worst he imparts. Rachel agrees he should resettle *Tyotya* in her own flat, but she is not keen he should remain on his own, lone Wolff, to grow feral in isolation.

"Why don't you stay with Thomas? Until I get back."

"Matter of fact . . . He did invite me . . ."

"Go, then."

"Rachel! For now, this is our home. You're telling me to run?"

"Running," she says, "is not such a bad thing."

The young, fleet Muhammad Ali prances around the ring. No one can touch him. "I'm so pretty! I'm the greatest! There's not a mark on my face!"

"You want to throw in the towel, Rach?"

"It's a stupid fight," she replies. "Nasty and stupid. These women make me shudder, Zach. Their ignorance is frightening. Stay away. Normal rules of civility and rationale do not apply here. There is no reasoning with such people. And in the end, they're just tomato cans, aren't they? That's the expression, isn't it? Bums of the month! Not worth your while. Please."

"Marry me, Rachel!" he says, adding in almost a whisper, "Eight days. You're home in eight days."

The life span of wolves in the wild is less than ten years. In captivity life expectancy typically doubles.

Rachel hangs up the phone in St. Petersburg and shivers in the cold of the cavernous suite. *Those women make me shudder.* She hopes Zach will keep cool. She remembers her visit to Izzy's gym before flying to Russia with Lev. She arranged to see All Souls on a day she knew Zach was working from home.

Rachel watches Isaac wrap Aubry's hands.

"Eighteen feet of wrapping, eleven feet of zinc oxide tape. No more," explains Thomas.

"It's a rule?" she enquires.

"In a fight, yes. An official stamps the bandages before the gloves go on. Izzy? I need to talk to Rachel for a minute, OK?"

When Izzy leaves them alone, Rachel asks Thomas to look out for Zach while she is in Petersburg. She makes him swear not to let him fight.

"With or without headguard. No fighting. Not even in fun. No sparring, no lessons from Izzy, no heavy bag, no speed bag, promise me."

Thomas chuckles.

"Promise me," she urges. "Why are you smiling?"

Thomas Aubry promises. He stares at his feet.

"I love you, of course. You must know that," he says.

"Oh Thomas."

Aubry shrugs, a lopsided smile on his handsome face. He raises his taped hands in surrender, spreads the fingers in a show of apology and helplessness.

"Listen," he begins. "I'm really in trouble here. I do poetry too! I can make a right arse of myself. Listen. *And from my fingers flow, The powers of life, and like a sign, Seal thee from thine hour of woe; And brood on thee, but may not blend With thine.* I'm ridiculous, Rachel, a bruiser brought up on

Romantics and with a first in Natural Sciences, a specialisation in ichthyology and a future in viticulture. What the fuck! as Izzy would say. He likes gangster films," adds Thomas. "The lingo, you know. Of thugs. It's just—I don't know what to say. Zach, my new best friend. This. All this. One couldn't make it up! I love you."

"I see," says Rachel, bowing her head.

"*And brood on thee,*" Thomas repeats, "*but may not blend With thine.* How could I not know these lines? Shelley, Shelley, Shelley. Breakfast, lunch and dinner."

"Your brother."

"My mother never recovered. Never. And she should never have called him Percy Bysshe, for God's sake!"

"Or you, Thomas Love."

"Yes, yes. Risible. No. Ludicrous. And she loved him more, so much more. Always."

"Is that why you box?"

"Oh no, I don't think so. I'm good at it and I can afford it, but I'll do other things better. Suitable things. I fight for *insurance.* I'm already looking back. I'll never have what I want, so this is it, my summer, my English summer! I'm not a *boxer.* What I practise, as Zach will say sometimes to raise the fight in me, is fencing. I fence. I'm not a boxer. He is. He's a dog with two tails in the ring!"

"A dog with two tails!" exclaims Rachel.

"Happy as Larry. Who *is* Larry anyway? What I mean to say is . . ."

"I meantersay, old chap . . ."

"Sorry?"

"Nothing. Sorry. Just something Zach and I—never mind. I shouldn't have interrupted. It's very rude," she says, afflicted.

"You're not rude," says Thomas, leaning towards her. "You're beautiful."

"Rude and beautiful are hardly mutually—"

"I know," he interjects. "I know."

"So what did you mean then? About Zach. Happy as Larry in the ring, a dog with two tails. And you not a boxer," asks Rachel quietly.

"He's a boxer, Rachel. Through and through, I mean."

"Yes, I think so. *Matryoshka.*"

"Sorry?"

"Russian nesting doll," says Rachel. "Layer after layer . . ."

"Yes, exactly," Thomas agrees. "Boxer after boxer after . . . What's the smallest in the nest? Are they all identical?"

"They're made from a single block of wood, did you know that?"

"No," replies Aubry, feeling the flames in his cheeks as he watches her speak, adoring every shift of her features, every blink of her eyes. "No, I didn't know," he says, his fair skin burning red.

"Baby," smiles Rachel. "The last doll in the nest is a baby. A boxing baby in Zach's case. Self-similarity," she adds. "It's fractal."

"Fractal," repeats Aubry. "Ah."

"Promise me, though."

"Promise you?"

"Zach. Watch him for me. Watch out for him. Please, Thomas Love."

"Yes, of course," says Thomas, his eyes shining like glass. "I promise."

Rachel reaches for Aubry before rising. She kisses his taped hands, resting her head there ever so briefly. And then she is gone.

In Camden Town, the windows shiver slightly in strong wind, as if protesting. There is a kink in the Gulf Stream, Zach learns. A kink. Caused by El Niño. Meaning that Arctic air is blowing into England, rattling his panes.

Rachel? Are you puffing my way? Blowing Siberian air?

Last night's news revealed that Moscow suffered the coldest day in eighty years and, in the Scottish Highlands, a low is registered of −21°. Airports are closing and trains have stopped and people are calling for emergency services, including military intervention, which amuses Zach no end. Bright-eyed helpmeets and road safety types with a particular relish for crisis are interviewed on the Channel 4 News and babble a list of shortages and potential dangers and offer up rescue tips. Some admit spoffishly, modestly, to good deeds. People are snowed in, states one spokeswoman whose name is Susan Snowden. Fantastic! Rachel will love that. Zach races to his desk, writes it down. He rings Tasha. Whom he has safely resettled in Hoxton. DO NOT DO NOT DO NOT go out, Tyotya. Too slippery! It's a dangerous place! Perhaps the Thames will freeze over, Zach muses, and we'll have a Frost Fair with ice cricket and a boxing booth, an ox-roast, and dancing.

There is so much to do, he thinks, before Rachel comes home. He worries very much now, about airports and trains. They say the weather will not break for well over a week. Zach stuffs his coat pockets with keys, money, notebook, lists, travel card and other necessities and brooms for the gym.

The time is passing so fast now, fast as a train! Two days, she'll be home in two days.

By early afternoon, Aubry is ready to leave Izzy's for home. He needs to get ready for a night at the opera, collect the mater at Charing Cross Station, escort her to Sheekey's for oysters and fizz.

"Sure her train's running?" asks Zach.

"Yes, yes. Sup at Sheekey's with us, old chap. Oysters, fizz."

"No. Look at me!" Zach complains, indicating his habiliments.

"Come to Chelsea, I'll tog you out. We're more or less the same size. And you should see this opera, we'll find you a ticket. It's a Russian affair, old man. Your part of the woods! *A Dog's Heart*, Bulgakov. Strewth. It's going to be dire. I can't abide bloody opera."

"*A Dog's Heart?*" Zach says, thinking of Tasha, would she want to go, should he take her, are there tickets left? How much are they? His brain is sparking like an engine. He is very bobbish. "Another time, man. Thanks."

"Right," goes All Souls, eyeing Sandbag Shaw at the heavy bag. "Listen, ah. Why don't you step out with me, anyway? We'll hop a cab. Have a drink while I dress. Or I can drop you somewhere."

"Need to walk a bit," says Zach. "I'm keyed up!"

"Right. Well," frowns Thomas, shifting his stance. "Why stay on here, then? Going to work out or something?"

Promise me.

"No, no. Paperwork. Have to do a spot of admin for Izzy. Take me five or ten minutes. Then I'm bashing off. Lots on; Rachel's home in two days!" Zach replies, clapping All Souls round the shoulders. "Go on, don't be late! Opera calls. Brave fellow! England expects, etc. And best to your mater!"

"Right. Tomorrow, then," mutters Aubry. "You're in tomorrow?"

"Just the morning. Have to shop. Hey wait! That wine you said she'd fancy. Drank it at your party, summer party. Bloody loved it. Rachel, I mean. Write it here," Zach urges, handing Aubry a pen.

"On your arm?"

"Yeah, yeah. Can't lose it that way."

"No plans to scrub up at all, before she gets back?"

"Very funny."

Thomas smiles. "You'll have to go to St. James, you know. Berry Bros. Berry and Rudd, yes?" he adds, writing the name of the wine. "The wine is easy enough to find, but not that particular winemaker. Very limited distribution. Understand?"

"Not really! Just write it down."

"I should maybe give them a ring. I mean, most of it's on allocation and all that. That is, they may not have any in, sort of thing. Could be in Basingstoke. At the vaults, you know. Ah—"

"What the blue blazes are you talking about, Aubry? Just bloody write it down! Or the next best thing. Case they haven't got it."

"Hang on! If we hurry, I could run you there now," Thomas says with a great show of confidence. "On the way home for me. My manor, you know, as Izzy would say. Wait," he adds, checking his watch. "Ah. Bad luck. They'll be closed. Hmm."

"It's OK, man. Like to do it all myself anyway. I'll go tomorrow. I'm running in circles! Need to spend some of this energy!" says Zach, cuffing the air round his friend with a one-two to the knowledge-box, doing the Zach two-step on his merry dancing feet.

"Well, if you're sure," laughs Aubry. "Tomorrow, then."

"Tomorrow, man."

"Five, ten minutes and you're off, yes? You look a bit peaky, you know. Overdoing things, I daresay. Can't let Rachel see you like that, eh? I could wait five minutes, actually," adds Thomas, glancing at his watch.

"Get the hell out of here, Aubry!" smiles Zach, clapping arms round his friend. "Meet the mater! This is London. Oh Christ."

"Yes, of course," he shrugs. "See you tomorrow."

Zachariah finishes up in Izzy's office and grabs his coat from the cloakroom when Sandbag Shaw saunters his way. Zach notes his hollow look and flaking skin, dead giveaway signs of dehydration and hastened weight loss.

"What are you doing, Shaw? You take a hit to the head in that condition, you're for the near room."

"Sweet, Wolff. Really. Nice of you to care, mate."

"Not you I'm worried about, Sandbag. Just don't want you on Aubry's conscience when he knocks your lights out in ninety seconds of the first round."

"So you don't mind?" asks Shaw. "About All Souls, as you call him. Your best mate! Best china-plate! That he's shagging your sister, I mean?"

Zachariah hurries into his coat, crams his twitching hands into pockets, stares down at his *understandings*. *Quality English shoemaking since 1899.* It's not the lie that fucks him off, but the words *shagging, sister*. Fucking rude. Nobody *shags* Rachel. Not even him. Zach's sparklers burn, the eyelids flutter. Do not do not DO NOT FIGHT.

"Oh yeah," Sandbag continues. "Clocked them right here in the gym. Your sis left Aubry on a bench in the corner like Billy-no-mates. Kissed his ruddy hands! Like some poncey telly show, it was. BBC. Fucking joke. He sat there and snivelled, I saw him. Waterworks and everything. Crying like a girl, he was."

Zach shoves Shaw in the chest first, because he will not hit a man unawares, he is no street brawler, and he yells for Izzy in case of cuts and concussion. Zach wants to hurt this man, he really does. For all Shaw's weight loss, Zach still concedes in poundage and height, but he thinks, No problem; the bigger the man, the larger the target. Let's get it on, let's get ready to rumble.

Sandbag quickly blindsides the approaching Izzy and stands on Zach's right foot, pinning him to the ground while he throws a kidney punch, forcing Zach's head down, thus adding power to the violence of a terrific uppercut to the chin with head-butt to follow.

The blood flies in a fine jet from Zach's eye and literally pours from his mouth, dropping onto Shaw's shoulder as he closes to hold Zach in a clinch and throw a quick flurry of rabbit punches to his neck until Zach disengages, slipping away to gape for air, a wild smile on his face.

"You're an idiot, Shaw! Fucking low-life!" laughs Zach, dropping his guard, shaking his head. It's a taunt, a classic. *I'm not hurt. You can't hurt me. Come on, man. Hit me. Give me your best hit.*

Sandbag walks in with menace and without thinking, proving beyond doubt that natural intelligence is not his prominent feature by stepping straight into it, Zach's foppish teasing right followed by sharp left jabs to the head that rock Shaw back on his heels in a spray of sweat. Then Zach floors the man with a blow to the heart that fells him like a tree.

A much-irritated Izzy intervenes very smartly, examining Shaw on the ground to establish he is in full recovery of his senses, such as they are, and giving him the all clear before attending to Wolff. The cutman wipes Zach's face and stitches the gashes to chin and eye, muttering the whole while.

"This is a gym," he says sternly and with epic control. "*My* gym. For boxing. Leave your crap at the door. Or don't come back. Shaw, you're banned for a month. You're a small-hall fighter, a bully and a thug and I've never liked you. Fuck off out of here NOW."

Shaw slopes off without a word, hunched as a scolded youth.

"And Wolff?" adds Izzy, once Shaw has gone. "You ever heard of second-impact syndrome? Of course you bloody have. You've got it. Permanent-like. Which means it can get you any time. So *you're* the idiot. I can't even look at you. I'm so fucked off with you, I could spit. Go home."

"Golly, Izzy. I never heard you speak so many words all in one go. Must have knackered you, that speech."

"Fuck off," smiles Izzy, attending to Zach's face with swabs and plasters. "And look at you! Just look! Not pretty. Can't say it anymore, can you? *I don't have a mark on my face!* There fucking is now! And your right eye is blacking already."

A black eye, muses Zachariah. My *suit of mourning.*

"Sorry, Iz," he says, hurtling for the door. "Won't happen again. I really mean it. Last time. Sorry."

"Hey!" Izzy calls out. "Listen to me a minute! You took a butt to the head, son. A blow to the jaw!" states the cutman. "And rabbit punches. Shaw's dirty. A mean fighter. You go home and you rest, hear me? You go to Casualty if you're hurting! Give me a shout. I'll come round in the motor. Finchley to Camden that time of night, be there in a tick. It's a doddle. Got it? You fucking call me."

"I'm so pretty!" quotes Zach at the door. "I'm so pretty, I must be the greatest! I don't have a mark on my face! I'm the greatest!"

"Go home!" Izzy snaps.

Clean the flat, change the sheets, do some washes, Zach recites to himself, fiddling in pockets for keys and lists. I've run out of socks and pants! And tomorrow, the shopping—wine, flowers, quail eggs, he thinks. And? Smoked salmon, damn! Don't forget that. Some of those red eggs too, salmon eggs, which kind? So many kinds. Ask Aubry, he'll know. Make a note of that! Baguette, cheeses. No no no! Not baguette! Poilâne—the rye one, not the other type. Or the Hoxton rye. Flour Power City! She bloody loves those. And pomegranate, she's crazy for pomegranate. Can get that at the Turks in Pratt Street. Plus olives and those fresh dates and fresh figs they have and the syphilis, ha ha! *That's really not particularly witty, old chap.* Physalis! Now hurry, Zach. Step lively. Oh, you're gonna dance, man!

We're gonna dance.

{ THIRTY-ONE }

The Castle, Holborn. London, 1840.

When Young Dutch Sam acts as second to his friend Owen Swift in 1838, he is arrested because Swift's adversary, "Brighton" Bill Phelps, dies as a result of his injuries in that fight. "Brighton" Bill is killed by boxing.

Young Dutch and Swift flee to Paris where, on Tom Spring's request, they are entreated to seek Sam the Russian and tell him it is safe to come home. Before Young Dutch can comply with his wishes, he is arrested again, this time in Paris, for sparring with Swift in a city where pugilism is very strictly illegal. Upon receiving a thirteen-month sentence, he takes the high toby away from France straight back to his native place, where, for love of the sport, the illegality of pugilism is more of a moot point. At home, judge and constable are corruptible, turn a blind eye. Or, as Young Dutch puts it, at home the beak is a trump and a scout is easily squared.

Upon return, Sam Evans is held very briefly in Hereford jail for that queer lay between Swift and Phelps, yet found Not Guilty. What a bang-up jury, thinks Young Dutch, suffused anew with patriotic fervour. How great are these isles! This Empire, this England! How very fine to be home again. In my native place.

"I miss thee, Samuel," says Spring aloud over some heavy whet and a ball of fire when Young Dutch brings him no consolation from France.

"I sought him," bemoans Young Dutch. "High and low."

Spring watches the retreating shape of Young Dutch Sam as he exits the parlour, closing the door softly behind him. The Champion turned landlord swipes at invisible dust at his table with knotty, effeminate hands. *Powder puffs.* He recalls the last battle of his career, who could forget? At the end of that second of two bouts he won against Jack Langan, Tom's backer remarked feelingly, *I have never saw such bad hands in any battle. If you fight again I will never speak to you.*

"Sir," Tom famously replied, "I will never fight again."

Tom smiles ruefully, flexing his brave fists, recalling how in that second and last battle of his career, he broke both mauleys early in the fight and endured one hour and forty-nine minutes of milling over seventy-six rounds to emerge the victor. Yet, oh Christ, he thinks now in the parlour of the Castle, Holborn, while sorrowing so very deeply over Sam the Russian, oh Christ! I have never known such hurt as this! I am certain there can be no harder blow than this! I am very melancholy.

"Come home, Sam," Tom murmurs. "I should like it so vastly."

And the tears drop onto iron cheeks. Tom Spring, however, cannot know Young Dutch would never have found Sam in Paris, no matter how hard he sought, because Sam Alexander is in St. Petersburg. In Petersburg, Sam the Russian is tutor to sons of the gentry. He is giving instruction in the Art of Self-Defence.

St. Petersburg, 1840.

It is noised that the quiet young Englishman frequently to be seen tipping a glass with the cornet Lermontov of the Life Guards Hussars is expert in the fistic art and willing to give instruction for an honest reward. Sam the Russian is soon a great favourite with the nib sprigs of the Life Guards who cut a dash in their red and gold togs and, though they are undoubtedly game and bang-up fellows, they will tend to spar on an excess of champagne and copious slugs of a potent and colourless liquor they call *vodka*, and in spite of Sam's polite objections. Indeed, even when not lushy, the Russians display very little aptitude for the science and are, in truth, wholly undistinguished with the mufflers.

"Here's to milling success!" pipes Sam with heroic cheerfulness and yet, though never more attentive and full of gaiety, his pupils are so easily struck over the guard and so quickly levelled, Sam is puzzled to know how he should proceed with their instruction. The fellows typically retire after a knockdown for some horrible black tea and a game of cards, being partial in the extreme to gambling and fits of chaunting at which they excel tremendously. In sum, from his fellowship with the Life Guards Hussars, Sam acquires finer gambling, drinking and chaunting talents than the Hussars do milling talents.

Lermontov, only a year Samuel's senior, unites the manners of the swell and the artist, that is to say, he is intelligent upon all occasions and fond of fun yet his sensitivity renders him at times irritable and unruly. Mikhail is the author of stories and poems and has shown Sam his paintings of racehorses and landscapes of the Caucasus, including scenes of combat that strike the Tsar of the Prize Ring as being quite full of perfection.

It must be said that Misha's qualities are so numerous, his character so superior, Sam is quite desperate to hear of his intention to engage in that unmanly and clandestine practice much frowned upon in pugilistic circles, the *duel*. He is pledged to face the peevish son of the French ambassador, Ernest de Barante. Ernest's very pistols were borrowed by D'Anthès when the latter killed Pushkin in a duel three years earlier in St. Petersburg near the Black River. The very same pistols!

A Russian, explains Mikhail, believes that to recross a threshold moments after departure is to chance fate. It is said that when Pushkin stepped out of his Moika apartment before four in the morning in his light *bekesha*, he was seriously chilled by wind and frost and plummeting temperatures and quickly re-entered the flat to call for his bearskin coat. And when his seconds tamped the powder in the barrels on that dreadful day, Misha recounts, they used a wad made from torn lottery tickets, all of which particulars dazzle Lermontov, what with his anxious interest in the processes of fate and chance, etc., etc. Why, the marvellous knowledge that he will fight a duel not only with these very same pistols, but in the very same place Pushkin dropped and in the very same depths of snow, is astonishing in the utmost!

Happily, on the day of the duel, the Frenchy shoots and misses, whereupon Lermontov fires deliberately into the air and all the fellows shake hands, no harm done. Within weeks, however, Tsar Nicholas has Mikhail arrested, exiled to the Caucasus and transferred to the Tenginsky Regiment of infantry, albeit preserving his rank of lieutenant. The result is that Sam loses his new friend twice over, first to exile and then to eternity, because the following summer, Sam learns, Misha fights yet another duel and is shot, killed straight through the heart.

No, Sam protests. No! And Sam weeps.

In his own exile from home, Samuel Alexander, Lost Tsar of the Prize Ring, acquires a liking for the colourless liquor called vodka and he no longer searches the face of every man for the likeness of his father; he seeks instead the likeness of Jonah the Needle. My friend, my bosom friend.

Finding his father is no longer Sam's calling. He looks for Jonah instead, and for Spring, for Dickens and Jones the Apothecary, for Young Dutch Sam and Miss Miller of the Green Fanteegs. It is time to go home, to his native place. I am a foundling, laid-in-the-streets, but I do have a native place. And I am a fighting man, I am a boxer. Through and through.

Sam springs to his feet, takes up the stance classical.

A fighter fights.

INTERCONNECTEDNESS

Charles Dickens, novelist and magazine editor at *All the Year Round,* held a ticket in his hand for one of the most sensational fights ever witnessed, the battle between Tom Sayers of Camden Town and the American John C. Heenan contested at Farnborough, Hampshire, in April 1860 for the very first Championship of the World, but he was not there, no. Dickens assigned the task of reportage to another scribe, the author preferring his experience of sport and violence by proxy, most especially since the mournful day his friend Sam the Russian lit out for France, never to be seen again. He often remembers the foundling boy he first met in the yard of the White Horse Inn, Piccadilly, sharing dreams with a gentle, grizzled cabman named Old Abel, of speedy travel by rail and the driving of engines fantastic as Stephenson's Rocket. Sam Alexander had a great fancy, once upon a time, for trains.

Sam, where are you?

Sam the Russian saves up the fare for a first-class seat on the 2:38 from Folkestone to London after a ferry crossing from Boulogne. *What larks!* he thinks, with a boyish fervour despite his years. He is fifty years of age this summer of 1865, when, due to mistimed works on the line over the River Beult before Staplehurst involving the removal of two rails, all but one of seven first-class carriages career off the bridge and plunge to the waters beneath.

Dickens is travelling on this same train and escapes from the single surviving first-class carriage, which, though derailed and hanging over the side of the viaduct, is suspended by its couplings attached to the lower-class carriage to the fore. Saved by a coupling! *There is an interconnectedness to all things!*

At his most sanguine and composed, Charles fills his top hat with water and carries a flask of brandy down to the riverbed and attends to the wounded in the manner of a cutman, second and bottle-holder combined. He administers draughts of brandy and wipes the crimson from heads that are truly terrific, being terribly bloodied and blackened by dust, and stumbles upon a fellow in a hunter-green jemmy with flash yellow lining, a most enviable garment albeit somewhat faded. The man's form, Charles notes, is muscular and elegant without suggesting brutish power by any means, and his features, notwithstanding the desperate wound to the forehead, are prepossessing, and his eyes singularly bright. Round his neck is a medallion bearing the head of Alexander I, once Tsar of all the Russias.

Dickens drops to his well-breeched knees.

"Oh tell me this is but a shadow of the boy I once knew," whispers Charles, bending to the face to wash it clean, trembling as he goes. "Oh Sam. Oh Samuel. Is it you, really you? Oh no," he complains quietly, pulling a belcher from his upper benjamin to cover the unseemly gash in Sam's dear head. "Close your sparklers, Sam," says Dickens, brushing his fingers across the Russian's phiz. "Oh please close your eyes."

Charles rises to wave his arms and call for help that will come too late, he knows, no matter how soon, and so he walks the river with a faltering step as if he cannot quite feel the ground. He is a little crazy.

"I knew him," pipes Dickens to a railway guard. "He was a boxer," he adds, waxing epitaphical, though his hand trembles as he tugs the guard's sleeve and the tears spring freely from his eyes.

From this day onwards, Charles Dickens suffers terrors in travel, even by cab, yet he is an inveterate walker, with great faith in motion and dynamics, and the interconnectedness of things.

Walk on, Boz. He walks on and on.

. . .

The Castle Tavern, Holborn.

Notwithstanding his distress upon the embarkation of his dearest friend for France and places beyond, and in spite of his ailing condition following the Battle of Finchley Common, Jonah the Needle engages in a fever of industry, notably finishing a new waistcoat for Dickens in a remarkable fabric of the reporter's own choosing, a florid crimson velvet in keeping with his emerging dandyism of which notable features are comprised his increasing flow of hair and extravagant belcher knots. Dickens was lost in admiration for young Jonah's skills and, furthermore, for his pet raven, marvelling at his tameness and the creature's proprietary march to and fro upon the cutting-up table, envying the evident devotion to his master, the singular bond. Charles wondered that such affinity should exist between man and beast.

The tailor has fashioned a pair of garters for the bird of the very same worsted cloth coloured hunter green used in the making of Sam the Russian's exquisite benjamin with the secret compartments, Jonah's parting gift to his bosom friend. And so the raven puts the Needle in mind both of Sam and Miss A Miller, the reporter in the green fanteegs. The raven is in prime twig, stylish indeed! And quite as much the young swell as Charles Dickens!

A pet raven, mused the reporter, departing Jonah's rooms with his precious new coat. Tremendous! And in green gaiters. Capital!

Since Sam's flight to the continent, Jonah has been abiding in his friend's old attic rooms above the Castle along with a juvenile raven, or *Corvus corax*, as Jones the Apothecary will have it, a bird the Needle names Crusoe. He was so named on the day Jonah found Samuel's precious copy of *The Life and Strange Surprizing Adventures of Robinson Crusoe* under the pillow, the sight of which induced an immediate stab of pain in Jonah's heart for all his friend had left behind. Only when he began to turn the pages, quite slowly, did the Needle discover the inscription within: *For Jonah the Needle, my Brother, from Sam the Russian.*

"Oh Sam!" exclaimed Jonah upon this discovery.

Jonah sweats and shivers by night these days past, his oculars waxing large and somewhat crazy. He fancies himself a pugilist in training, dosed on Dover's powders and the blue pill, containing, as Jones expounded, both mercury and an infusion of senna, by far a superior method to previous regimens of sudorifics and emetics made up of tartar and ipecacuanha and other such salts ingested in the famous *three threes*, as the method is commonly known. *Three doses of salts, three sweats, three vomits for three weeks.*

The perspiration runs in a thin watercourse between Jonah's lean pectorals to gather in the hollow of his stomach and the creases of his loins, and his torso and irregular limbs adhere to the bedclothes, so that when he rises, aching in thew and sinew, the innards coiling and uncoiling, he observes the impression of himself left behind on the sheets.

"Behold my very shadow!" he reflects. "A tailor's pattern."

Crusoe, lately fledged, hops onto Jonah's short arm. The raven's *tarsometa tarsi*—his claws—flash green, and there is a quizzical mien to his dark shining eyes as Jonah the Needle rolls it over and over in his dextrous fingers, the gambling token wrought of bone, in the shape of a fish.

"Ah, Sam," whispers Jonah. "Sam. My bosom friend."

Jonah the Needle stumps it to the window, on the totter, and, pushing the casement open wide with the last of his wind, he stretches a hand into the cold evening air to watch flakes of snow melt upon his palm, a sensation both freezing and burning in the same instant. Snow sometimes falls from a cloudless sky.

"Snow, Crusoe! Look!" the boy exclaims, touching his blue choleric lips to the raven's crown.

"Crusoe, I am sick," he says. "Increasing sick and like to die. Find Sam. You must find him and watch over him. Give him this token and he shall know thee. Do not look at me, Crusoe! I cannot bear it. Pray, do not look. I have loved thee so much. Now take this fish, and fly. Be fly."

In the immediate aftermath of the disaster at Staplehurst, some thirty years since Crusoe's desolate flight from Jonah's attic window in Holborn, a raven with peculiar green *tarsi* is observed to haunt the scene, hopping about the riverbank as if in search of something, someone. He comes repeatedly; he has site persistence, like the wolf indeed, with which species ravens are well known to play. The raven with the green *tarsi*—fanteegs, one might say—builds a nest at Staplehurst where Sam the Russian fell, fabricating a dwelling of sticks and oddments, amongst them, a sliver of bone in the shape of a fish with a hole for an eye that he sets judiciously into the straw and mud, in pride of place. He builds this nest in the lee of the broken bridge and one day he is joined by a mate.

Ravens tend to mate for life.

{ THIRTY-TWO }

ON THE MORNING Rachel vomits copiously into the loo of their suite at the Astoria in Bolshaya Morskaya, a brackish and acidic spew of beluga caviar, rye bread and spirits, Lev knocks tentatively at the door of the bathroom and she calls out to him reassuringly in response.

"Papa! It's nothing. Too much *ikra* and vodka. We drank by the half-pail!" she pipes, gaily as possible.

Later she finds a new favourite bridge on the Neva and stands with her pale visage facing west, breathing in, blowing out. She looks into the icy waters and summons up the unfinished letter by Gilbert White, an addendum to the 1877 edition of *The Natural History and Antiquities of Selborne*, a book that, as a girl, she so loved reading to Zachariah.

"ON THE SENSE OF HEARING IN FISHES"

It has long been a question among naturalists whether Fishes hear or not. This subject I shall make no scruple to take in the negative; and without being biassed, or indeed without knowing what has been said before, shall proceed to give you my thoughts in my own way. When people advance that Fishes do hear, I would answer that after the strictest examination, the best modern Ichthyologists assure us they are destitute of any kind of organs for that purpose. But then if Fishes do not hear, some will say how do tame fishes in stews and canals come to be fed at the sound of a whistle?

Rachel can still hear his boy-laughter at the old word for fish-pond—

stew—and his singing from the song "Along Peterskaya Street." Fish stew with parsley is a Wolff family speciality. Song is a Wolff family speciality. Rachel looks into the icy waters of the Neva to the fish beneath.

"Head in air and tail in sea, Fish, fish, listen to me."

Well? says the fish. What now?

"Please take this message," Rachel asks, "and broom for London. A wolf cub is coming. Tell him our wolf cub is coming."

Go home, says the fish, and turns over, going down into the sea.

Zachariah walks.

He filches in pockets for the list of tasks and shopping, searching his jemmy and trousers—*inexpressibles*! The list, the list! He comes up only with coins and old betting slips. Oh yes, he recalls; the bets they placed, himself and All Souls, never Iz, he's not a betting man. First Test of the winter Ashes in Oz, and All Souls holds out for a five-for. Jimmy Anderson, he says, to take five wickets in the first innings! Zach opts more safely for a captain's century, but Strauss falls for a duck, third ball. Zach tears up betting slips, looks for a bin, stuffs them back in his coat pockets. Where the blue blazes is that list?

Dropped it, maybe. Left it in Izzy's office? Fuck. Don't want to go back in there. He's mad at me. Zach dashes back the few steps to the gym only to find his list and travel card on the floor of the hallway just across the threshold. You crazey crackd braind fellow, as Rachel would say! Idiot, he calls himself more bluntly. Gollumpus! Jingle brains!

Banging the street door again, Zach suddenly thinks up a retort he ought to have quipped at Shaw when Sandbag said Rachel left All Souls alone in a corner, "crying like a girl." He ought to have quipped, "Boxers cry all the time, man. Tyson, Liston, Belcher, Spring. Name a true-born bruiser who doesn't. Boxers cry all the time." Tears drop on iron cheeks.

Zach stops sharply, smacks his fives to forehead and leans up against a wall. He vomits. *Flashes the hash.* He has poo bags in a pocket from walking Volya and tries to clear up the worst, strangely ashamed of the mess he has made. I'm overexcited, he tells himself. Strewth! I look like some washed-up fighter. Take a squint at me. Stitches across the chin, spew on the pavement, no socks on my feet, and a shiner to boot. My suit of mourning! Lushy, *alik*, that's me all right!

Zach walks on. It's been a one turn-up, one-*alik*, no-bone, one-fish day! That fish fin he slipped on the other night was still there in the close this morning, so he noted, plastered to the ground near the pillar-box as if stuck with glue. The vision of decaying fish makes him queasy, and he breathes deeply, expelling acrid breath that condenses quickly in cold November air.

Hurry, Zach. You have food to buy! Comestibles! Walk on.

The wolf, according to the Russian proverb, is kept fed by its feet.

The lone wolf tends to cover large territory, is more injury-prone and suffers from a higher rate of mortality. He is particularly at risk when using man-made paths.

Zach is fleet, nearly running now, delighting in motion, his eyes light-filled. She's nearly home! From across three times nine countries.

At a stop in the traffic, several car lengths before the street corner, Zach begs permission to cross with a quizzical look to the driver, according to convention. The driver acquiesces with an imperious wave. But it's Baba Yaga! Zach notes, stepping into the road, and Alla! What the blue blazes is Alla doing in there? In the mortar and pestle, he laughs. Just as their eyes meet, the car shudders forward, half a wheel turn, a foot-fault, the bumper nudging Zachariah in the legs.

"SOR-ree!" trills Baba Yaga, rolling the window down halfway. "Oopsy-daisy! Hit the pedal by mistake, whoops!" she giggles while Zach thumps the bonnet in fury and Alla gazes stonily ahead, unseeing.

Zach stays in the road even as the lights change, watching Baba Yaga charge off with a grinding of gears, sweeping her trail with a broom. He turns back to the pavement and missteps. He falls hard.

"Get the fuck out of the road!" screams a cyclist. "Crazy bloody idiot!"

"*Muzhik*," Zach says very quietly. "Crazy bloody *muzhik*."

"What? What did he say?" asks a bystander.

"Don't know, mate. Foreigner," strikes in one of the small crowd, dispersing quickly, disinterested now there is no outright fatality, no tragic crimson lake. "Polish or something," the man adds. "Tons of them round here. And pissed, I think."

Zach blinks rapidly before blacking out. He enters the *Near Room*.

.   .   .

Dr. Flip Humansky, ringside physician, suggests that the KO is nature's way of protecting the brain. In a knockout, it is the brain stem, in charge of basic body functions, that blacks out and not the regions of intelligence above, i.e., the brain itself. A fighter taking such a hit will be suspended for sixty days, or forty-eight days in England, lest he expose himself to the risk of second-impact syndrome, wherein the possible eventuality of suffering a further hit before the cells have time to repair is wholesale cellular destruction, terrific swelling and demise.

Hispanic boxers call the knockout the "little death" and Ali, famously, coined it the "Near Room." Next stop, death. *Eternity box. Long room.*

In 1996, a new ruling is imposed in the United Kingdom that fighters submit to and pass an MRI once yearly, which is how Zachariah Wolff lost his licence to fight following his title defence against the Georgian Kubriashvili. He did not pass this MRI test.

In a concussion, the cells of the brain tear, they stretch, and chemicals flood the brain causing abnormal computation and reception of information. It's a kind of paralysis. A fighter who has once sustained this kind of injury is four times more likely, it is said, to endure it again and is more vulnerable, indeed, to a blow, and slower to recover from it, slower to heal at all.

University College Hospital, Euston Road, London.

Rachel perches on the edge of a green faux-leather-covered chair. Hunter green, she decides. Forest green. She sits huddled in Zachariah's overcoat, the collar high the better to scent him, her hands thrust deep in his pockets, her fingers flickering. She has already found the shopping and task list, the Pilot V ball 0.5 nib pen, packet of Swedish salted liquorice, Oyster travel card in its ripped plastic wallet, and torn betting slips. When he came into hospital, a nurse told her, he wore no socks. The nurse tells her so lest Rachel presume them mislaid from his pile of clothing. They are not lost, the nurse repeated. He wore no socks. Like Mike Tyson, Rachel thinks. Always sockless in the ring, the squared circle. She smiles because she knows Zach arrived here sock-less having run out of clean ones. She smiles even wider when she learns that the neurosurgeon's name is Mr. Tear. Tear or Tear. Tear the flesh, shed a tear. It's funny, Zach! It's a good 'un!

When Mr. Tear addresses Lev and Rachel and Tasha, he raises both hands in demonstration, the right clenched in a ball and the other held aloft, fingers spread wide in a vault shape.

"Here is the brain in its box," he states.

Mr. Tear smacks his clenched fist against the palm above and compares the action to the pranging of a vehicle and the helpless rattling of passengers within. He uses words such as *blood vessels, complex patterning, violent rotation,* and *bleeding,* to which litany of terms Rachel listens with increasing impatience. Before Zach entered the coma, the surgeon adds, his brain had been bleeding for hours and he is more than like to die, it will not be long now.

"Knowledge-box," says Rachel. "It's called knowledge-box."

Rachel hums very quietly to herself. A medley.

In *The Natural History of Selborne,* Gilbert White writes, "The titlark and yellowhammer breed late, the latter very late; and therefore it is no wonder that they protract their song; for I lay it down as a maxim in ornithology, that as long as there is any incubation going on there is music."

Incubation, Zach!

Lev and Tasha leave Rachel in Zachariah's curtained chamber, they leave her alone with him and retire to the corridor where they sit imbibing Russian tea from a flask leavened, now and again, by a vodka chaser. It is a scene from old *Rus.* Happily, Volya the Golden, Tasha's devoted guide dog, is permitted in the halls and waiting-rooms and makes himself small at Natasha's feet, as if chastened, alert to the tension and fear. From time to time Lev parts the curtains to peer in at his children. Lev's features are creased with concern and sleeplessness, the race home from Petersburg a day early with a stricken speechless Rachel will change him forever. Rachel glances vaguely at her father as she hears the scrape of curtain rings, and wonders at his gravity. His anxiety irks her. It is full of foreboding.

"He did it, you know, Papa," she whispers proudly. "Aubry told me, though he was not there. When Zach wakes up, he'll give us ALL the particulars! And then I shall write them down. For *Bell's Life in London, and Sporting Chronicle!*"

"Rachel?" says her father with a frown of concern. "Did what?"

"Miss Miller! Just call me *A Miller*, Papa! Miss Miller to you. Papa!" Rachel persists in a hush of wonder. "He beat Sandbags. Sandbag Shaw. KO. Once and for all. Zach's a *fighter*, you see. You don't understand!"

Lev Wolff shakes his head quite slowly, retreats from the cubicle.

"*Grandfather tossed his head discontentedly,*" recites Rachel. "*Well, he said, if Peter hadn't caught the wolf, WHAT THEN?*"

Rachel pulls her chair close to the bed.

"I brought caviar, Zach, *ikra*! Lots of it. We'll have such a feast, such a merry party! We brought vodka, too. Moskovskaya, your favourite. We can drink it by the half-pail. Let's swim in Lake Vostok! Beneath the ice four kilometres deep. We'll have to break the seal," she says. "It's a million years old, Zach. We'll dive in to meet the creatures there, treasures and creatures, we'll be Great Northern Divers. Loons! We'll fly across three times nine countries in the thirtieth tsardom! Ready? Let's do the magic handkerchief. Belcher! You'll never guess, but Papa's going to take us all to the Hebrides. What do you think? A holiday. So wake up now. Wake up!"

Rachel takes Zach's left hand and holds it to her still-taut belly and notes a smudge of ink on his wrist, several words written there. She bends low over the bed to try to make out the words, distinguishing one. *Meursault?* Does it say *meursault?* Yes. Her favourite. Zachashka! Your shopping list.

"Feel that!" she exclaims, covering his hand with hers. "I swear that was a right jab! Meaning he's a southpaw, perhaps. Or ambidextrous. Just like you. Zachariah, Zachariah, my fighting man. Zachariah, Zachariah, our foundling boy! My wolf. Wake up now. Be my Wolff! Live with us, Zachashka! Live with us."

She shuts her sparklers, presses lips to his auricular.

"All is QUI-et. All is quiet," chants Rachel softly into his good ear. "*Don't shoot! Birdy and I have already caught the wolf! Now help us to take him to the zoo. Imagine the triumphant procession!*"

Rachel sits up straight in her chair, replaces his hand, laying his fingers out with awful tenderness. She speaks with special clarity now, and decision, through a terrible pain in her throat, as if swallowing cold stone.

"You listen to me. I'm home now, Zach. You're safe. Not alone anymore. No lone wolf," she says, eyes burning. "'The life span of wolves in the wild,'" she quotes, "'is less than ten years. In captivity, life expectancy doubles. . . .' So there. I'm home now. And it's so very simple, you see. I can't live without you. I shall not survive this, Zachashka. *I will not survive this.* I won't count you out, ring the bell, throw in the towel, throw up the sponge, let you quit on the stool. No. I won't do it. Get up and fight! You are a fighter, through and through. Oh please. Please wake up now, please. Wake up now. Let the day begin."

When Zach dies, a small flurry of nurses and surgeons swoop into the cubicle with a brisk swish of curtains, whereupon dials are switched and buttons ping, notes are taken and hushed commands issued as appurtenances are removed, mask, canula, lengths of sticky tape. It is like the aftermath of a fight, decides Rachel. Remove the mouthpiece, cut off the gloves. Slip out of the box. Tenderloin plate. *Ms. Wolff! I have a lovely bit of tenderloin!* Rachel watches one doctor consult his watch and another address her, though she cannot seem to hear him all that well. So many doctors, Zach! Very spoffish. These saw-bones. With their graveyard odours.

When she is left alone and the curtains are drawn, Rachel circles the bed and sniffs Zach's body most methodically, breathing him in, scanning his body, unrivalled for symmetry of form, elegance and athletic beauty, his features prepossessing, the marks on his face, totemic. She breathes him in entirely, then sits in her chair and leans in close to rest her head on his loins, against the *linea alba*. She fits very neatly there, wrought for this place. Rachel and Zach assume a complex shape, symmetric overall, chaotic in detail. Fractal, Rachel thinks as her lungs swell with burgeoning sound. A fractal is the shape of infinity.

Wolves howl for joy, in play, in the hunt, in appeal, reunion, loneliness, stress and sorrow. A howl will last from half a second to eleven or more, and each wolf calls in a distinctive voice so one wolf can recognise the other over distance, howling with shifts in pitch and harmony, chord and discord, producing an uncommon song of epic immanence.

Wait for me.

HISTORICAL FIGURES

Tsar Alexander I (1777–1825, reign 1801–1825). M. Louise of Baden (**Elisabeth Alexeyevna**).

Ekaterina Pavlovna (1788–1819), **Tsar Alexander**'s favourite sister. M. George of Oldenburg (d. 1812) then William I of Württemberg.

Thomas-Joseph Aubry (1780–1865). Captain of the 12th Chasseurs, wounded at Borodino. Famous for defending the Foundling Hospital in Moscow during the riots and fire of 1812 with the help of wounded Russian officers while recovering from his wounds. He lived to a fine age and wrote his memoirs.

Pyotr Bagration (1765–1812). A Georgian prince and Russian general, he distinguished himself in many campaigns and was fatally wounded at Borodino.

Denis Davydov (1784–1839). Russian noble, guerilla leader, poet; Davydov was an iconic and romantic figure to the Decembrists.

Count Matvei Platov (1751–1818). Russian general, hetman of the Don Cossacks.

César Cui (1835–1918). Russian composer and music critic. He was one of "The Five," a grouping of composers led by Mily Balakirev and devoted to a specifically Russian style in musical composition.

Felix Mendelssohn (1809–1847). Composer, born in Hamburg. He made the first of many visits to England in 1829 when he also visited Scotland and the island of Staffa in the Hebrides, inspiring the composition of *Die Hebriden—The Hebrides* overture, Op. 26, also known as *Die Fingalshöhle* or "Fingal's Cave." He wrote the String Octet at the age of sixteen. He died in Leipzig aged thirty-eight, just six months after the death of his beloved sister **Fanny** (1805–1847), a fine, yet uncelebrated, composer in her own right. Her D major piano trio was not published until 1850.

Sergei Prokofiev (1891–1953). Russian composer. *Peter and the Wolf,* Op. 67, was written in 1936 for the recently rechristened "Central Childrens Theatre" in Moscow under the directorship of Natalya Sats, who was sent to Siberia a year later for "crimes" wholly unrelated to her commissioning of Prokofiev's Op. 67.

George Handel (1685–1759). Composer and philanthropist. Handel offered a benefit concert to the Foundling Hospital in 1749 and a performance of *Messiah* was held annually in the chapel until 1777, well after his death. He was appointed Governor, a position he initially refused out of modesty. He bequeathed a score and works to the Hospital in his will, which can be seen at the Foundling Museum in Brunswick Square, along with many other treasures in the Gerald Coke Handel Collection that is housed there.

Sergei Taneyev (1856–1915). Russian composer, master contrapuntalist.

William Hogarth (1697–1764). Artist and philanthropist. Hogarth was responsible for involving many of his famous artist contemporaries in donating and/or exhibiting their works for charity at the Hospital, creating perhaps the first public art gallery in London, in effect a precursor of the Royal Academy. He was made Governor of the Hospital, painted and donated his great portrait of **Thomas Coram** in 1740, and devoted many years to the cause, even designing the Foundling Hospital coat of arms and the children's uniforms. He was inspector for wet nurses in Chiswick.

George Cruikshank (1792–1878). Artist, satirical cartoonist and illustrator, this Londoner's most famous collaborations were with Pierce Egan on *Life in London* and, of course, with **Charles Dickens**, with whom he later fell out, on *Sketches by Boz* and *Oliver Twist*. In the 1840s his satirical brilliance was somewhat diminished by his new fanatical asceticism and obsession with temperance. He lived with his second wife **Eliza** in Hampstead Road, Camden Town. It transpires he fathered eleven children by his mistress and former servant Adelaide, who lived conveniently nearby. Fidelity and fatherhood were not his chief areas of temperance. Never mind. He originally drew *The British Bee Hive* in 1840 and reworked it in 1867.

Captain Thomas Coram (c. 1668–1751). Sailor, shipwright and philanthropist. A Dorset man, Coram spent much of his career serving in the American colonies and had a ship-building business in Massachusetts where he met his beloved wife **Eunice**. Upon his return to London, he was deeply moved by the sight of homeless and abandoned children and campaigned for seventeen years for the establishment of a Foundling Hospital. Compared to other European cities, in several of which there had been conservatories and orphanages since the thirteenth century, England came rather late to the field of child welfare. George II finally signed the charter for the Hospital in 1739. **William Hogarth**, a founding Governor, painted a marvellous portrait of Coram, which can be seen today at the Foundling Museum in Brunswick Square by Coram's Fields. Coram's Fields is the only park in London no adult can enter unless accompanied by a child.

Sir Joseph Bazalgette (1819–1891) A railway engineer who became Chief Engineer to London's Metropolitan Board of Works and had a great influence on the health of the inhabitants by designing a brilliant new sewage system, amongst other works, such as the grand embankments and bridges.

THE CHAMPIONS OF ENGLAND (mentioned in this story) IN ORDER OF CHAMPIONSHIPS

James Figg (1684–1734). The first bare-knuckle boxing Champion of All England, he held the championship between 1719 and his retirement in 1730. He opened Figg's Academy in Tottenham Court Road where he taught fencing, singlestick and boxing. There is a famous portrait of Figg by Hogarth and the card advertising the Academy is also often attributed to the artist.

John "Jack" Broughton (1704–1789). Jack Broughton held the Championship from 1736 to 1750, when he was blinded in a fight by the much younger and scrappy Norwich butcher-turned-pugilist **Jack Slack**, losing his famous patron the Duke of Cumberland some £10,000 as well as his patronage. When Broughton defeated **George Stevenson**, "The Coachman," in 1743, Stevenson died of his wounds and in Broughton's arms, a tragedy that inspired Broughton to codify the rules drawn up at the amphitheatre he opened in Oxford Street. These rules governed the Prize Ring until 1838. The famous punch to the short rib is known as "Broughton's mark."

Jack Slack (c. 1721–1768). Jack Slack, the "Norfolk Butcher" or "Knight of the Cleaver," was an unskilled fighter, but a hard-hitter. He is assumed to be **James Figg**'s grandson and beat the fading elder statesman **Jack Broughton** in 1750 to win the Championship and the patronage of the fickle Duke of Cumberland. He held the crown, fighting irregularly, until he was beaten in a half-hour match against Bill Stevens in 1760.

Benjamin Brain (1753–1794). "Big Ben" Brain won the title in 1791 when he defeated **Tom Johnson**, the well-liked Champion of 1787, a chivalrous man and adept counter-puncher who died six years after losing his title to Ben Brain. Brain died three years before Tom, of liver disease, and was buried at St. Sepulchre-without-Newgate. Somewhere.

Daniel Mendoza (1764–1836). Mendoza, the father of scientific boxing, was a Sephardic Jew born in Aldgate in the East End of London. He was a superb boxer and famous principally for his three epic bouts with Richard Humphries. In 1795 he lost his title in the famous hair-pulling match to the younger, larger and taller "Gentleman" **John Jackson**, whose abiding antipathy towards Daniel meant he denied him the use of the Fives Court in St. Martin's Lane for a much-needed benefit in 1821. Dan worked at many things upon retirement, yet was unable to hold on to his money. He wrote hugely entertaining memoirs and *The Art of Boxing*.

John Jackson (1769–1845). Gentleman Jackson fought three times only, defeating **Daniel Mendoza** for the Championship in 1795, after which he retired. This is a fight Jackson dominated, albeit more famous for an incident in which he held Daniel by the hair and pounded him with his free hand. He was not overfond of Daniel Mendoza, the "scientific Jew." He opened an academy at 13, Old Bond Street known as "Jackson's Rooms," where his most eminent if untalented pupil was Lord Byron. Jackson did a great deal of refereeing and earned a new epithet of "Commander-in-Chief." He was a page at King George IV's coronation along with **Tom Cribb** and other fighters of his choosing.

Jem Belcher (1781–1811). The "Perfect Phenomenon" or "Napoleon of the Ring." A Bristolian, son of a butcher married to **Jack Slack**'s daughter, Jem was a superb, graceful, brave and intelligent fighter who held the Championship from 1800 to 1803, when he retired for the first time after losing an eye in a game of rackets. He returned to the ring in 1805 to lose a poignant match to **Hen Pearce** and fought only twice more, in 1807 and 1809, losing on both occasions to **Tom Cribb**, after which Jem retired, depressed and dissipated. He gave his name to the belcher, a spotted scarf in a bird's-eye pattern he wore with particular flair. He died at twenty-nine.

Henry Pearce (1777–1809), "The Game Chicken." Another famous Bristolian, he was a fast and scrappy fighter and held the Championship between 1804 and 1807. He earned his moniker for signing his name "Hen." When he fought the elegant but fading and one-eyed **Jem Belcher** in 1805, he tried to force Belcher into retiring in the twelfth round, saying, "I'll take no advantage of thee, Jem. I'll not strike thee, lest I hurt thy other eye." Jem fought on until the eighteenth round.

John Gully (1783–1863). A failed Gloucestershire butcher, Gully became Champion of All England when his friend **Hen Pearce** retired due to ill health in 1807. Hen also rescued him from debtors' prison by fighting an unofficial match with him there and raising sufficient funds to cover his debts. He retired to become landlord at the Plough in Carey Street, won the Derby and the Two Thousand Guineas with his racehorses and was M.P. for Pontefract in Yorkshire. He owned the Wingate Estate and collieries in County Durham. He married twice and had a dozen children by each lady.

Tom Cribb (1781–1848). A Bristolian, famous more for his strength, size and courage than imagination, he was a ferocious counter-hitter and made a tactic out of "milling on the retreat." He claimed the Championship in 1808 upon **John Gully**'s retirement and after defeating **Bob Gregson**. He beat the great **Jem Belcher** in 1809, yet is probably most famous for his two bruising and contentious wins against the freed American slave Tom Molineaux in 1810 and 1811, after which Cribb retired, naming **Tom Spring** his heir. He was landlord of the Union Arms in Panton Street for many years.

Tom Spring (1795–1851). Born Thomas Winter in Herefordshire. Trained and patronised by the great champion **Tom Cribb,** Spring held the Championship between 1821 until his retirement in 1824, when he took over the Castle Tavern, Holborn, from **Tom Belcher.** A great defensive and scientific fighter, he possessed a long reach and a fine left hook in spite of his famously weak hands. He had two sons. His estranged wife died in a London workhouse, notwithstanding Tom's wealth and wide repute for kindness in and out of the ring.

Tom Sayers (1826–1865). Son of a Brighton shoemaker, Tom died in Camden Town. He was active between 1849 and 1860; he beat William Perry, the "Tipton Slasher," to win the Championship in 1857. He contested the first-ever international championship title match with the Irish New Yorker **John Heenan.**

OTHER ENGLISH PUGILISTS

Sam Elias / Dutch Sam (1775–1816). Born in Whitechapel, "The Man with the Iron Hand," inventor of the uppercut, often fought and won above his weight and size. Died in penury.

Sam Evans (born Elias) / Young Dutch Sam (1808–1843). Son of Dutch Sam. Brilliant, graceful and accurate, Sam was undefeated in his sixteen fights as welterweight fought between 1823 and 1834. He died aged thirty-five.

Bob Gregson (1778–1824). **Pierce Egan** referred to Gregson, the "Lancashire Giant," as the "poet-laureate to the Prize Ring" for his versifying. He retired from the ring to become landlord of the Castle, Holborn (when it was known as Bob's Chop House), but lost his tenancy in 1814, being a cheerful but ineffectual businessman.

Tom Belcher (1783–1854). Younger brother of **Jem Belcher**. A very fine boxer but could never overcome the hard-hitting **Dutch Sam**, his most eminent contemporary. Retired to become landlord of the Castle Tavern, Holborn between 1814 and 1828.

Jack Martin, born 1796, was a light- to middleweight fighter and known as "Master of the Rolls," being a baker by trade. He earns a mention in William Hazlitt's great essay "The Fight" (1822).

AMERICAN FIGHTERS

Tom Molineaux (1784–1818). Tom Molineaux followed Bill Richmond, another freed American slave, to England to fight in the Prize Ring. His most famous fights were the two he lost in 1810 and 1811 against **Tom Cribb** in circumstances that rather heavily favoured the Englishman. Neither man was a subtle fighter, but Cribb had quicker wits and more influential backers.

John C. Heenan (1834–1873). The American champion came to England to contest the first international championship fight with the Champion of England **Tom Sayers** in 1860 in Hampshire. The gruelling fight ended in a draw.

Jack Dempsey (1895–1983). The "Manassa Mauler" was an iconic figure in 1920s America and World Heavyweight Champion from 1919 to 1926, when he lost to **Gene Tunney** on points in ten rounds. He fought and lost to Tunney a second time a year later in what became known as the "Battle of the Long Count," in which Tunney was knocked down in the seventh and the referee did not start his count until Dempsey had retired to a neutral corner. Tunney was dominant in the match regardless. Dempsey retired thereafter for a life of business ventures.

Gene Tunney (1897–1978). Held the World Heavyweight Championship between 1926 and 1928. Shrewd in and out of the ring and somewhat pretentious, he married an heiress, flattered George Bernard Shaw, read books, and made a great deal of money.

Cassius Clay / Muhammad Ali (born Louisville, Kentucky, 1942; died Scottsdale, Arizona, 2016). Heavyweight Champion between 1964 and 1967, 1974 and 1978, and 1978 and 1979. The "Greatest" indeed, he won titles against the greatest out there, **Sonny Liston**, **George Foreman**, **Joe Frazier**. He lost three of his prime fighting years (1967–1970) due to his refusal of conscription. There is no question in my mind that Ali's habit of absorbing huge hits at the very least exacerbated the Parkinson's syndrome he suffered from and whose cause doctors have been so keen to attribute to anything but boxing.

Marvin Hagler (b. New Jersey, 1954). "Marvellous Marvin" fought at a golden time in modern middleweight boxing when Sugar Ray Leonard, Roberto Duran and Thomas Hearns were at their peak. He did indeed wear a perplexing T-shirt with his special saying emblazoned thereupon, reading "Destruction and Destroy."

Gerald McClellan (b. Illinois, 1967). Powerful but uninteresting middleweight forced into retirement due to brain damage when he moved up a weight in order to challenge the WBC super-middleweight champion, the Englishman **Nigel Benn**, in 1995. It was a brutal contest and McClellan suffered appalling injuries. Gerald was a keen amateur of dog fights, reputedly getting in the mood for a match by watching videos of his pit bull killing bait dogs with their muzzles taped up. Which is not to say one would wish brain damage upon him, of course.

THE SCRIBES

Alexander Pushkin (1799–1837). Author of *Eugene Onegin, Ruslan and Lyudmilla, The Prisoner of the Caucasus, The Gypsies, Boris Godunov, The Queen of Spades,* and *The History of Pugachev,* Pushkin was a great poet and writer rightly credited with enhancing and establishing Russian as a literary language. He attended the lycée at Tsarskoe Selo and occupied a loosely defined post in the civil service. He was exiled from St. Petersburg for his radicalism in 1820 and allowed to return to the capital in 1825, though he was under suspicion immediately for his association with the Decembrists. He was killed in a duel by the French officer **Georges d'Anthès** in 1837, dying from a stomach wound after several days of agony.

Nikolai Gogol (1809–1852). Extraordinary writer, author of short stories (among them, "The Overcoat"), plays (*The Government Inspector* is the most well-known) and the great novel *Dead Souls*. Very brilliant and a little mad, he died a protracted painful death, aged forty-two.

Mikhail Lermontov (1814–1841). Poet, novelist, painter and Hussar, Lermontov was the author of many poems and the wonderful short novel *A Hero of Our Time*. He was twice exiled to his beloved Caucasus, first for his contentious poem on the death of **Pushkin**, *Death of a Poet,* and later for fighting a duel with the son of the French ambassador, **Erneste de Barante**, in 1840. A year later he was challenged by **Nikolai Martynov**, once his fellow student at the School of Cavalry and a man Lermontov taunted for his pretensions. Martynov shot Lermontov straight through the heart in July 1841. Lermontov was twenty-six years old.

George Borrow (1803–1881). Born in Norfolk, Borrow was a travel writer and uncertain novelist, most famous for the novel *Lavengro* in which the lines "Let no one sneer at the bruisers of England" appear. I am the only person I know who has read *Lavengro,* though I have yet to join the George Borrow Society.

Charles Dickens (1812–1870). Writer, actor manqué . . .

Pierce Egan (1772–1849). Journalist and sportswriter, author of several volumes of *Boxiana; or Sketches of Ancient and Modern Pugilism* and *Life in London,* the monthly adventures of men-about-town Tom, Jerry and Logic, with illustrations by **George Cruikshank**. Pierce Egan coined the famous expression the "sweet science" for the art of boxing. He developed and popularised the extraordinary sporting lingo of the Regency era.

William Hazlitt (1778–1830). A radical all his life, Hazlitt was an epic and brilliant essayist, famous for his two volumes of *Table Talk* and also a piece of reportage called "The Fight," about the boxing match between **Tom Hickman** and Bill Neate, published in the *New Monthly Magazine* in 1822. I am not sure Hazlitt liked or knew very much about pugilism, but it is a terrific essay and perhaps the only contemporary account not written in extravagant boxing sporting vernacular.

Vincent George Dowling (1785–1852). Journalist and sportswriter, he became editor of *Bell's Life in London, and Sporting Chronicle* in 1824 and was the author of *Fistiana, or The Oracle of the Ring* in 1840, which later became an annual. His son Frank took over the editorship of both upon his father's death.

GLOSSARY

above par (castaway, shot in the neck, on the mop, foxed, dozzened) drunk

all round his hat reference to a popular Cockney ballad about a fellow mourning his love and wearing willow for grief in the brim of his hat

angelic young woman

apartments to let dim-witted

area sneak housebreaker

back slums low neighbourhood

ball of fire glass of brandy

bang up first class

barnacles eyeglasses

barney a fight

beak magistrate

belch beer

belcher neckerchief, typically in a bird's-eye pattern of dark blue with white or yellow spots, made famous by **Jem Belcher** and sometimes called a *yellowman*

bender sixpence

benjamin coat

berlins gloves knitted from Berlin wool, a fine darned yarn

black-letter gentry writers

blade a gallant

bluchers half boots named after **Marshal Blücher** (1742–1819), the Prussian commander at Waterloo

blue ruin (blue tape, daffy, eye-water, flash of lightning, Fuller's earth, Geneva, Jacky, max, Old Tom, shove in the mouth, stark naked, white tape) gin

blunt cash

bobbish cheerful, well

bodier blow to the body

bone-grubber scavenger

boneshaker jolting vehicle

boniface publican

bonnet, bonneting crushing hat down on wearer's head with a blow

bread-box, breadbasket stomach

broom hurry, run away

Broughton's mark hit to the short rib

bub drink

buck a blood or a dandy

bug hunter a robber of drunken men

button chin

castaway drunk

caudle a drink for invalids of warm gruel with spice, sugar and wine

chaff; chaffer ridicule, banter; to ridicule

chancery suit, to hold in chancery the head held fast under the opponent's arm

charley night watchman

chaunt a song, usually with a chorus

chimney pot a tall silk hat

cinder-sifter a tramp, scavenger

claret blood

come it as in come it strong, to impose upon

Commander-in-Chief **"Gentleman" John Jackson**

conk nose

continuations stockings worn with shorts or knee-breeches

corinthian man-about-town (early 19th c.); wealthy amateur of sport (late 19th c.)

cove a man

crambonian doggerel rhyme

crib a room

crimson blood

cross a thrown fight

cross-buttock a throw to the ground over and across the buttocks

Cyprian a prostitute

dabs light hits

daffy gin

darky night

deep sly

Diamond Squad rich and/or influential people

dished ruined, exhausted

done up ruined, exhausted

dozzened drunk

drabs dull light-brown clothing or breeches

drag coach

draw the cork draw blood

dry boots sly, humorous fellow

enter the lists join the ranks of professional fighters

eternity box coffin

eye-water gin

exquisite a dandy

facer blow in the face

fancy followers of boxing

fanteegs trousers

fib punch

fiddlers hands

file a pickpocket

fives fingers, fist

flappers hands

flash knowing, also relating to the underworld

flash the hash to vomit

flat greenhorn

flimsies banknotes

floorer a blow that knocks opponent to the floor

flue-faker chimney sweep

fly artful, aware

fogles handkerchief

frontispiece forehead

garret head

gill fellow

give the office give information about

gloque man

goes a measure of spirits

gollumpus a large, clumsy fellow

gone to roost died

gone up the spout pawned

grubbery stomach

half and half mild ale and bitter or ale and porter

ham thigh

heavy whet porter or stout

high-lows ankle boots

high ropes excitable, temperamental, to be in a passion

high toby highway

hop the twig run away

hook a pickpocket

hot one fierce blow

hulk large transport ship (or hull of) used as a prison

idea-pot head

indescribables (fanteegs, inexpressibles, unmentionables) trousers

inexpressibles trousers

ipecacuanha extract of the root of a Brazilian plant of the madder family used as an emetic

ivories teeth

jemmy short for *benjamin* or *upper benjamin*, i.e., greatcoat, overcoat

jingle brains a wild, rattling, thoughtless fellow

Johnny Raw bumpkin, novice

ken a room, short for *kennel*

knee-smalls breeches

kisser mouth

knowledge-box head

kye-bosked, kyebosh to finish off, destroy

lady's maid fighter lacking a punch

leary artful

light tapper lacking a punch

lodgement landing a blow

London particular fog

losing one's rag losing all one's money

lucifer match with a phosphorous tip, invented 1827

lushing crib tavern

lushy drunk

mace swindle, swindler

mark in boxing the stomach, as in "Broughton's mark"

mauley fist, hand

max gin

mill, miller, milling box; boxer; boxing

Mosaic of or pertaining to Moses, i.e., the Jews

mudlark scavengers in the Thames mud

muffle, muffler boxing glove (and, sometimes, hand, fist)

muzzler blow to the mouth

nib sprig gentlemanly type

nob, nobber blow to the head

November effect the cold, damp and fog

nut head

ogles eyes

on the mop drunk

opodeldoc liniment of soap, wine, rosemary and camphor

optics eyes

oration trap mouth

out-and-outer an extremely fine fellow

pedestals feet

peepers eyes

peg a drink, usually of brandy or whisky and water

peg away hit with thrusting blows

perpetual habitually worn garment

powder puff blow without force

phiz face (from *physiognomy*)

pillows boxing gloves

pot a quart

potato trap mouth

prig; prigged thief; robbed

prime twig very stylish; *in prime twig*: in a stylish, masterly manner

put to bed with a shovel buried

putting down the dust laying down the money

queer lay difficult business

quiz a strange-looking or ridiculous fellow; an odd or eccentric person

quodded imprisoned

ramper, rampsman a footpad, a thief who robs with jostling or violence

rattler coach

red tape brandy

roll of soft, mint sauce, pewter, rhino, gelt, flimsy, dibs, blunt money

roost sleep

rusty guts blunt, surly fellow

sad dog a wicked, debauched fellow

sarsy contrary, prickly, supercilious

scaley mean

scent-bottle nose

scout constable

scratch the line across the centre of the ring to which opponents are brought to face each other at the beginning of each round. They *toe the line* or *come to scratch*

sewer rat vagrant, tramp

sharp a cheat

shiver confuse, fox

shutters eyes

skiver person who pares leather

slap bang cheap diner

slum (or behaviour) deceit, deceitful

smeller nose

smoky shrewd, suspicious

sneezer nose

snuff-box nose

sparklers eyes

spoffish fussy, bustling, officious

square to bribe

squeezer neck

stampers feet

starch nonsense

stews lowest slums

stone-jug gaol

strum strumpet

stump it to walk

stunning (Genuine Stunning) best ale

suck-cribs taverns

suit of mourning black eye

surtout overcoat

swanky a smart fellow; swaggering

swell a gentleman

tall tile a tall hat

teazer a tricky opponent, a teaser

three-outs A dram glass is an *out*. Three-outs would be a glass holding a third of a quartern. A call for *"gin and three-outs"* would mean a quartern (a quarter of a pint) of gin.

thunder-and-lightning flashy, garish, startling

tip the whole nine drink one over the eight, one too many

toplights eyes

tosher sewer-hunter

trap a light carriage, usually two-wheeled

traps constables, thief-takers

trump a reliable fellow

turn-up a barney, a fight

twig style; see: in prime twig

tyke a dog

understandings shoes, boots; feet, legs

up the spout pawned

upper benjamin overcoat

upper customer upper-class person

upper storey head

upperworks head

walker! nonsense!

well up on apprised of, wise to

whet a morning's draught, typically white wine, to sharpen the appetite

whipper-out official responsible for clearing the boxing ring of invaders

whiz the buzz, the sporting trend, lingo

winder a blow that knocks the wind out of an opponent

without a feather to fly with penniless

yellowman see belcher

RUSSIAN

Accent marks on Russian words are a guide to pronunciation only.

álik slang: a drunk, alcoholic

alkásh drunk, alcoholic

bánya bathhouse

bekésha fur-trimmed overcoat

bezmólviye silence, isolation, quiet

bogatýr warrior, man of power; classic figure in Russian folk tales and epics

bózhe moy my god!

cháyka seagull

chúsh nonsense

dédushka grandfather

do svidániya goodbye; goodnight (when leaving)

dovériye vázhno Trust is important.

drániki potato pancakes

dyádya uncle

éto právda This is true.

glúpiy silly

ikrá caviar

khleb da sol' bread and salt

khoróshiy mál'chik good boy

kibítka a carriage, usually closed

kolyáska light carriage (also baby's pram)

krásniy red

matryóshka Russian nesting doll

moróshka Rubus chamaemorus, cloudberry

moyá my, mine (fem.); masc. version is *moy*

muzhik guy, lad, fellow, dude, man, peasant

ne bóysya Don't be afraid.

ne na pianíno not on the piano

neotésanniy coarse, rude

ostanovis' stop (imperative)

otéts father, Papa

otlíchno! Well done! Excellent!

pozhalsta / pozhaluysta, igrat' Play it, please.

pozháluysta please or you are welcome

prikratíte stop it, quit

prímite please accept

raspútitsa muddy roads or stretches, season of mud

sálo lard

saráfán traditional Russian dress—sleeveless, long, worn over a blouse

shto vy skazáli? What did you say?

shtráfnik member of a penal battalion (also one serving a penalty, as in hockey)

skomorókhi tellers of tales, dramatic chroniclers, performers and musicians

sládkiy mál'chik sweet boy

spokóynoy nóchi goodnight (when going to bed)

staréts elder, holy man

svobóda freedom

toská melancholy

tropá path

tsivilizóvannyi civilised

ty golovoréz i vandál You are a thug (literally, a cutthroat) and a vandal.

tyótya aunt

ubiráytes' go now, get out of here

ukáz proclamation of the tsar

váshe blagoródiye Your Honour (form of address in the Table of Ranks, applying to ranks 9 to 14)

vashe siyátel'stvo Your Radiance (form of address for princes and counts)

váshe zdoróv'ye Your health! Cheers!

verstá old Russian unit of length equivalent to just over one kilometre (plural: *verst*)

vólya freedom in the Cossack sense of the word, free will, liberty

ya lyublyú tebyá I love you.

ya óchen' po tebé skucháyu I miss you very much.

zakúski hot and cold hors d'oeuvres

za prekrásnykh zhénshchin To pretty women!

Záyachiy Óstrov Hare Island, island in the Neva in St. Petersburg on which Peter the Great built the Peter and Paul Fortress

zemlyánka dugout, earth house. Also the name of a popular war song written in 1941 with lyrics by A. Surkov and music by K. Listov.

ACKNOWLEDGEMENTS

Heartfelt thanks to my agent, Peter Straus, and my editor, Diana Tejerina Miller.

And to Louise Dennys and David Staines.

Tight hugs for my lovely sister Martha Richler, art mistress supreme.

And to Veronica Zolina, *ogromnoye spasibo*.

And to Deborah Rogers, in memoriam. How I wish you were here to see this.

Emma Richler was born in London in 1961 and lived in England until she moved with her family to Canada in the early 1970s. She is the daughter of Mordecai Richler. She studied French literature at the University of Toronto and the Université de Provence in the South of France. Trained as an actress at the Circle in the Square in New York City, she also worked in theatre, film, television and radio in Canada and, largely, in England. Her first book, *Sister Crazy*, was published in 2001. Her second novel, *Feed My Dear Dogs*, was published in the UK and Canada in 2005. She lives in London.

A NOTE ON THE TYPE

This book was set in Monotype Dante, a typeface designed by Giovanni Mardersteig (1892–1977). Conceived as a private type for the Officina Bodoni in Verona, Italy, Dante was originally cut only for hand composition by Charles Malin, the famous Parisian punch cutter, between 1946 and 1952. Its first use was in an edition of Boccaccio's *Trattatello in laude di Dante* that appeared in 1954. The Monotype Corporation's version of Dante followed in 1957. Although modeled on the Aldine type used for Pietro Cardinal Bembo's treatise *De Aetna* in 1495, Dante is a thoroughly modern interpretation of the venerable face.

Composed by North Market Street Graphics,
Lancaster, Pennsylvania

Printed and bound by Berryville Graphics,
Berryville, Virginia

Designed by Maggie Hinders